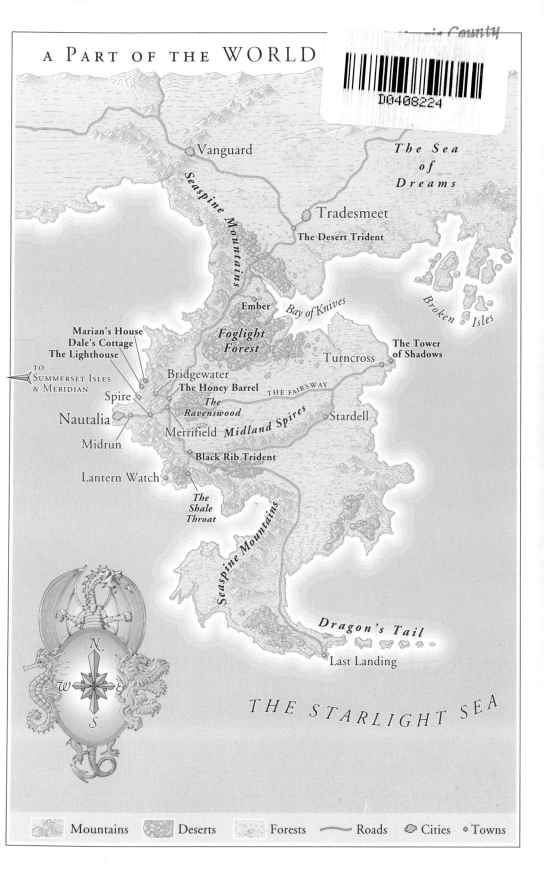

The
TOWER *of* SHADOWS

The
TOWER *of* SHADOWS

Drew C. Bowling

BALLANTINE BOOKS DEL REY *New York*

Copyright © 2006 by Drew C. Bowling

Published in the United States by Del Rey Books, an imprint of The Random House Publishing Group, a division of Random House, Inc., New York.

ISBN-10: 0-345-48670-6
ISBN-13: 978-0-345-48670-7

LIBRARY OF CONGRESS CATALOGING-IN-PUBLICATION DATA

Bowling, Drew C.
The tower of shadows / Drew C. Bowling.
p.   cm.
ISBN-13: 978-0-345-48670-7
ISBN-10: 0-345-48670-6
1. Fantasy fiction. I. Title.
PS3602.O898T69 2006
813'.6—dc22   2006047434

Printed in the United States of America on acid-free paper

www.delreybooks.com

2 4 6 8 9 7 5 3 1

First Edition

Text design by Laurie Jewell
Endpaper map by David Lindroth

To my father, Tim, who set me dreaming,
and my mother, Carol,
for blessing my dreams as they grew.

ACKNOWLEDGMENTS

First and foremost, special thanks to Chris Schluep, my editor and guiding light; Gina Centrello, a true champion of this novel; and Brian Davis, who turned a dream into a fairy tale come true.

A standing ovation for the Random House gang: production editors Nancy Delia and Laurie Kahn; John Harris, who graced the book with his fantastic art; Betsy Mitchell, editor-in-chief at Del Rey; my publicists, David Moench and Brandy Robinson; jacket illustrator David Stevenson; assistant editor Tim Mak; publisher Scott Shannon; managing editor Alix Krijgsman; production manager Erin Bekowies; and text designer Laurie Jewell.

I salute my agent, Robin Rue, because she's turned this project into something truly *"wonderful!"*

My family and friends were an enormous help, and I owe them all a great debt: James Schott, because we load our ideological guns together; Tim Gallant, for his unwavering loyalty; my sister, Mary, because her sweet smile has made this adventure much more fun; my grandmother, Phyllis Foster, for our Starbucks-fueled conversations; Bob Handler, a wizard of a teacher; Andrew Barden and Meghan Ryan, for their early reads; and Ilona McGuinness, who kept my sword flashing in the academic arena.

Last but not least, my heartfelt thanks to J. R. R. Tolkien and C. S. Lewis, two of the most magical writers our world has ever known.

The Sea of Faith
Was once, too, at the full, and round earth's shore
Lay like the folds of a bright girdle furled.
But now I only hear
Its melancholy, long, withdrawing roar,
Retreating, to the breath
Of the night wind, down the vast edges drear
And naked shingles of the world.

—MATTHEW ARNOLD

Remember upon the conduct of each
depends the fate of all.

—ALEXANDER THE GREAT

CONTENTS

PROLOGUE

A s THE SUN sank into the west, the forest canopy stood black against the burning sky. Few leaves still clung to branches, and a haunting wind wandered through the wood, whispering wild secrets among the trees. Ravens circled a clearing atop a rocky hill that rose from the forest. There, a dying oak thrust its bare limbs skyward, as if in prayer, and cast a twisted shadow on the earth.

A stone altar lay at the base of the oak, wrapped in crimson vines; more vines twined about the tree, curling up its trunk.

Figures drifted toward the altar, apparitions and chimeras, nightmares that breathed life from the twilight. Wings fluttered, beaks clacked, and faces peered from cowls, some nearly human, others ruined in their decay.

A rope-bound sack was dragged to the altar. A stooped hag followed, garbed in ragged robes. With a withered hand, she clutched something inside the folds of her clothing.

* * *

NOT FAR AWAY a man entered the forest. He trod a narrow dirt path as the lights of the village winked out behind him, vanishing into the dusk. Wind stirred his long black hair. His boots crunched on fallen leaves as his route wove upward, climbing the hill in sharp, sudden turns. Although the way would have confused another, the man did not hesitate. He held a staff before him—as if the blue jewel at its tip were a compass or guide.

Telltale objects dangled from the branches of the pines: primitive imitations of human forms, woven with twigs, then small skinned animals with nooses tied about their necks.

When he drew near the hillcrest, he left the path and plunged into the underbrush, tripping in his haste over protruding roots. Thorns snagged his tunic, and spiderwebs broke over his face and arms, glimmering between the trees like golden threads.

The man crept to the edge of the clearing and crouched behind a patch of brambles. He tightened his grip on his staff and peered out at the altar and the tree, where dozens of creatures stood waiting, wind stirring their cloaks and hooded robes.

The man did not move but only watched. He could afford to be patient now—he had hunted them for a long time.

Several figures, croaking in broken speech, hefted a sack onto the altar. Something inside it began to writhe. Flaming brands were thrust into the air, and dozens of throats howled as the hag stepped to the altar. She held up a hand, keeping the other within her robes, her voice rasping with the laughter of the damned.

The creatures swarmed around the altar, some beating flightless wings as they lashed the sack to the slab of stone.

Under the darkening heavens, the hag brought forth her concealed hand as a silence settled over the clearing. In the glow of the torches, a sapphire dagger sparkled. The man looked from the dagger to the blue jewel on his staff. He narrowed his eyes and tensed his muscles. Ravens alighted on the branches of the oak, their cries unnaturally loud in the sudden stillness.

The hag closed her milky eyes. "Now is the witching hour," she intoned, "and on this ring of blasted ground the light of this world will fade."

She reached again into her robes and took out a mottled gourd, then hurled it against the oak. It burst apart, splattering the tree with blood. "May the earth drink deeply and open its dark womb. When this blade pierces the flesh of my sister, the first of the Watchers will rise. We, the Coven, will sing in the realm of the undead."

As she lifted the dagger, the creatures began chanting. Irregular shadows spread over the grass of the clearing, and the vines on the altar and the oak pulsed like veins.

The man removed a thin chain from underneath his tunic. A circular medallion bearing the three gods glinted in the harsh light of the torches. Kissing the medallion, the man rose and sprang into the clearing, the jewel on his staff flaring with a pure blue radiance.

Several of the torches were snuffed out. The ravens burst noisily from the branches of the oak, their black wings stark against half-lit sky.

The creatures turned toward him as he swung his staff and charged toward the altar. Some retreated from the light, while others were enveloped in a magical flame.

Hissing at the interruption, the hag staggered against the tree, then hobbled back to the altar, raised her arm, and drove the dagger down toward her sister. Blue light flashed from the man's staff toward the descending weapon. The hag shrieked with pain and dropped the dagger. As quickly as it had come, the blue light vanished, leaving the clearing in darkness.

In an instant the man was fleeing toward the village, clutching the dagger to his chest, pursued by the enraged screams of the creatures.

* * *

DUSK HAD SETTLED over the village of Ember. Lanterns were lit in the few fishing boats dragging their nets through the deep, dark water of the lake. Lights shone in houses and taverns and twinkled in woodsmen's cottages at the edge of the village. Chimney smoke puffed into the evening sky.

A man and a woman rode toward Ember, guiding their mounts along a path that skirted the edge of the lake. The riders' cloaks matched the colors of their horses: The man wore black; his wife was wrapped in a cloak as gray as morning mist.

"I thought we'd never reach this place," the man said. He fixed his blue-gray eyes on the woman and ran a hand through his dark hair. "This forest is endless, Lori. We've been riding for days."

Lori's eyes were indigo stars. "I wouldn't have wanted this adventure to end any sooner."

"We still have one adventure left."

Lori glanced down toward the new promise in her body. "Wren, are you certain this is the right home for our child?"

"I'm not sure of anything," Wren said, touching the sword at his side. "The tides of fate wash over the world, and we are at their whim." He paused. "Why did you ever take up with a rogue like me?"

"It must have been madness," Lori admitted, smiling.

"Are you still mad, then?"

"I'm still in love, if that's what you mean."

Wren grinned. "You should have found another lover."

At the edge of the village, Wren brought his horse to a stop. He sat in the saddle, considering their next move, and then he led Lori down a series of narrow streets. Near the center of Ember they reached an inn, stabled their mounts, and entered a dimly lit tavern. Drinkers laughed, gamblers cast dice, jesting with ribald laughter, and everywhere men tossed scraps at the innkeeper's cats, streaks of calico fur that darted under their tables and chairs, mewing piteously. The innkeeper—tall, gangly, wearing a stained apron—lounged in a corner with a pipe clenched between his teeth.

Wren approached him about renting a room and some bedding. "We'll need lodging until we find a home," he said.

In their room, Lori kindled a blaze in the hearth as Wren stared out the window. Wharves lined Ember's shore; docks cantilevered over the lake. Boats bobbed beside jetties. Lanterns swung slowly above their decks like the spirits of drowned souls hovering above the tide.

Wren reached a hand to his face, tracing with one finger the scar that ran from his temple to his chin. He turned and regarded his wife. "What will we name our child if it's a boy?"

"That will be your decision," said Lori, blowing on the fire to make it burn brighter.

Wren snuck up behind her, grabbed her waist, and wrestled her onto the bed. "And if it's a girl?"

Lori giggled as he rubbed her stomach. "Kayla," she gasped. "If we have a girl, we'll name her Kayla."

It was then that the screaming began. They both heard it at the same instant, a faint protracted wail, then shouts and calls for help. A rumbling sound could be heard beneath the floorboards of their room; the men in the tavern had heard the cries, too.

Wren snatched up his sword, buckled it to his waist, and drew it from its sheath. The long blade of tempered iron shone in the firelight, its obsidian hilt as dark as deep night.

He grabbed Lori's arm and rushed with her out of the room, down a flight of steps, through the tavern, and out into the stable yard. Mounting quickly, they settled into their saddles and urged their horses forward.

Men shouted and brandished weapons. Women and children ran up and down the street. A burning scent hung in the air. Lori was the first to notice the flames. She pointed to the place where the smoke and fire had thickened, gathering above the roofs at the edge of the forest.

Then they saw the creatures: the ragged, scaly figures darting between the houses, chasing down the villagers, hurling torches through windows and onto thatched roofs.

"What do we do?" Lori asked, panicked.

Wren turned his mount toward the lake. "We run."

As they galloped away from the inn, a black-haired man on a white horse backed into the street directly in front of them, holding a staff that glowed with an orb of blue light. Creatures lurched after him from three sides, cornering him, their patchwork wings flapping in a mockery of flight.

Lori swerved her mount to avoid the fray as Wren leaned from his horse and swung his sword, catching one of the beasts in the arm. He jerked the sword free and severed its head. The black-haired man wheeled around and leveled his staff, blue light erupting from its tip. The other creatures reeled away, covering their hideous faces.

The man turned quickly toward Wren and Lori. "My name is Dale," he said, panting. "I owe you my life."

"What is this devilry, magician?" Wren asked.

"Ask later. If you want to live, stay with me and ride fast."

They broke into a gallop and charged through the swarming creatures. All about them were the cries of the dying, the crackling of flames, and snapping of timbers. At each new attack Dale wielded his staff, sending his assailants scurrying for cover. Wren guarded Lori with his sword.

Near the outskirts of Ember they found the street blocked by flaming wreckage. The three riders turned aside but were confronted by a burning house. A boy looked down from one of the windows. His parents stood on the ground below, his mother holding a baby, his father urging the boy to jump.

As the father pleaded with his son, monsters emerged from the shadows at either side of the house. Wren and Dale charged forward, yelling out a warning, and the parents turned to face their attackers.

The boy clutched the windowsill, crying, looking down at the street as fire licked up the house toward him.

His mother hugged the baby to her breast and tried to run, but one of the creatures leaped on her back and bore her to the ground. Its beak rose and fell, reddening with gore. The boy's father grappled with another; its claws slashed at the man's chest while—too late—Wren threw his sword. It slammed into the creature's back and stuck there, quivering. Dale cried out and swung his staff as the creatures fled screaming before him.

Lori rode to the mother, dismounted, and gathered the baby in her arms. "He's still alive," she said, tears sliding down her cheeks, "but I think his leg is broken." As she spoke, the baby's mother breathed a name and died.

Wren looked up at the window where the baby's brother had been, but the boy had disappeared. With a roar, a corner of the house collapsed.

"I'm going in after him," Wren shouted.

Dale grabbed his shoulder. "If any of us are to be saved, we must leave now. The boy is surely gone." He bowed his head and touched something at his breast that was concealed under his tunic. "So much death," he whispered. "By the three gods, I will do anything to keep the dagger safe."

Lori clutched the baby to her breast. They mounted quickly, and Dale's staff flared, guiding the way. Wren was grim and silent as they rode.

Far above the flames, the stars watched the three riders vanish into the night.

The
TOWER *of* SHADOWS

Assassins

A s the two horsemen peered across the moor, they sensed their curiosity darkening toward suspicion.

Barren and rocky, the blasted landscape stretched eastward for mile after mile until, with unexpected suddenness, it reared against the horizon in a line of serrated cliffs. Night was falling quickly. As shadows settled like carrion birds on their surroundings, pallid pricks of palest blue twinkled wanly in the sky. They gave off little light and less comfort.

"Even the stars are dead in this forsaken country," said one rider in a weathered voice. The iris of his good eye dilated with wary consideration; the crystal in the other glinted dully in the twilight.

His companion, dark of skin and cloak, turned a scarred face toward him. "We should never have come here. I've wandered some of the strangest lands in Ellynrie. But this place . . . I've never seen anything like it. There's malice on the wind. I can taste it in the air and sense it in the very bones of the earth." He stroked the hilt of his sword reassuringly and patted his whickering mount.

"Dragons and demons, Sarin," the one-eyed man muttered. "It's cursed, I say. For once the hearthside spinners of threads and tales were right." He paused. "Perhaps we should turn back."

"It's too late for that now," Sarin said. He frowned, stretching his cross-hatched scars. "Turncross is an hour behind us. Even if we were to ride at full gallop without resting the horses, the sorcerer would stop us long before we reached the town. His eyes are fixed on us now, One-Eye."

"How can you be sure?" One-Eye asked, shifting the twin rapiers bound crosswise to his back.

"I've spoken with him. I know what he is capable of."

"Damned if I ever take another job involving witchery. I should have stayed in that warm tavern, ordered another round of sweet cork ale, and then turned back on the road toward home."

Sarin's scarred brow rose in a mocking arch. "And what home might that be?"

The rider who had spoken first looked around slowly, his single iris constricting. He gazed across the immolated moor, up the cliffs, and into the sickly sky. "Anywhere but here," he said.

For the first time in years he shivered in fear.

*   *   *

FAR ABOVE THE cliffs in the gloom ahead, two sets of eyes peered from a dark tower window, watching the approach of the horsemen. Voices, deep and harsh, spoke to one another in the stagnant air.

"They are coming."

"I know."

"Shall I guide them?"

a pause, then

"Let them make their own way."

"How can you be sure they will find the entrance?"

"These two will know what to look for."

. . . a long silence . . .

"They may not like what they find."

"We didn't when we first arrived. But vengeance is a sharp spur, and we knew that if we paid the price, we would gain what was needed for our ends. These two who come now are driven by greed. It is the same."

then, after several seconds

"They will come."

* * *

AS THE TWO riders made their way reluctantly across the moor, their thoughts began to wander and grow sluggishly indistinct as if each northerly *clip-clop* of the horses' hooves brought them closer to their destination and farther from themselves. Earlier that morning, their eyes swollen and tired, their heads pounding out a painful farewell to the tavern's ale, they had left the Black Candle Inn on stolen mounts and started on the final leg of their journey. It had been easy going at first—the country was flat and free of obstacles—but now it felt as if they were struggling through thick webs of haze and mist.

"Something's wrong," said One-Eye. "I feel as disoriented as a sun-struck fly, only there's no sun to strike me. What direction are we going in?"

With one gloved hand tightly grasping his reins, Sarin withdrew a compass from a saddle pouch and held it steadily before him, his eyes bent intently on the thin sapphire needle. He looked more closely, eyes widening in surprise; the needle was swinging crazily from north to south with violent, aimless jerks.

"What in God's name . . ."

One-Eye leaned over, examined the compass, and chuckled grimly. "I was right—we should never have taken this job. You might as well toss that aside. There's only one direction left to us now."

* * *

THE EYES IN the tower stared, unblinking. The voices continued.

"Are they what you expected?"

"They should be adequate. You did well in finding them."

"Now that you have seen them, will you tell me why you brought them *here*?"

"Are you really that ignorant?"

. . . silence . . .

"Perhaps you are. After twelve damning years of preparation, I would sooner give up my knowledge of the dark arts than entrust this job to someone before personally *ensuring* their loyalty. The stakes are far too high to risk any missteps in securing my brother and the dagger."

* * *

THE HORSES, wild with fear, bolted long before they reached the cliffs. Ignoring their aching muscles, the two men struggled forward on foot, reaching the escarpment's rubble-strewn fringe, looking ragged as scarecrows. A thin, sand-laden wind scratched at the base of the cliffs like a stone rasping along the edge of a knife.

"What now?" One-Eye asked. "Don't tell me this is a dead end."

"The sorcerer told me to find him atop the bluffs," said Sarin, scratching the scars on his face.

"Burning blood, I'm beginning to feel uneasy about this spell weaver. If he plays us false, I'm going to hunt him down with my wands of iron and slit his sorcerer's throat."

"Bite your curses. This is no time to lose control. You're a hired man, and it would do you well to remember that. Assassins can't afford to let emotion interfere with business. The dance of our life is a dangerous one; we stay in step, or we falter and fall. It looks as though there's a hollow in the rock ahead. That might be our path."

One-Eye spit. "It had better be."

The hollow turned out to be a cave. Nearly hidden by boulders and thick clusters of a creeping blood-red vine, the awning gaped at the base of the cliffs like a hellish monster sprung to life from a child's darkest dream. The two men were not children, but they were deathly afraid. A stench drifted from the cave mouth like a diseased breath.

Sarin shuddered. "This is it."

"You first," said One-Eye, and hid his crystal orb in a slow, cruel wink.

Sarin reached under his cloak, unhitched a lamp from his belt, and used a flint to light its wick. An orange flame sizzled to life, filling the lamp with a flickering glow. He started into the cave, one hand holding the uncertain light, the other resting on the pommel of his sword.

* * *

THE TWO SETS of eyes narrowed, following the struggling men as they disappeared into the cliffs. The voices resumed.

"I was the one who arranged this meeting. They will be surprised to learn that I am not the master here."

"I trust they will be pleasantly surprised to discover their error. You have an . . . unsettling appearance. Remember, secrecy is our best weapon. The Aurian wizards, few as they are, cannot be allowed to learn of our actions. Not until the summoning of the demon is complete. Still, should more force be needed, I trust you have gathered more men in Nautalia and Merrifield."

"That should be the least of your worries. I have found the promise of riches to be most persuasive."

"Good. After today you must not meet again with either of these men until one has gained possession of the Exilon dagger and the other has found my brother. You will know him by his limp and the name I have told you. Now go down and greet them. They are almost here."

* * *

THE TWO MEN gritted their teeth and pressed upward through the cave. Cracks riddled the walls, dark clefts leading to darker secrets; mold covered the floor in a pulpy carpet that squished beneath their boots like overripe melons. Piles of cracked bones were heaped along the climb. Flies buzzed about them in a constant hum.

How any life at all could survive in such a wretched place was a mystery that neither of the men could fathom. They crowded together inside the tiny sphere of lamplight like boys huddling before a rattling bedroom closet.

Gradually they became aware that they were being tracked—although by beasts or phantoms, they could not tell. The creatures remained just beyond sight but advanced with a gnashing of teeth. Fear bore through the men like throbbing wounds until they finally abandoned all caution and broke into a wild run, the tunnel snaking by in a blur of sweat and pounding feet.

When at last they reached the exit, they propped themselves against a pair of rocks to steady their heaving chests. That they had come through with their sanity intact was a blessing. That they were still breathing seemed truly to be a miracle.

One-Eye grimaced. "If we're still in Ellynrie, then I've lost all faith in hell."

The sky was a dark kaleidoscope. Beneath them the cliffs plunged into the sea, which heaved and crashed in a lurid tide, void of any starlight.

"That must be his tower," Sarin said, pointing across the waste. "The Tower of Shadows."

A spike of black stone loomed above the ocean, twined with the same eerie vines that had hung over the cave's mouth. It reached into the sky like the gnarled claw of a buried giant.

"My trust in your judgment is wavering," One-Eye said. He eyed the tower skeptically.

"Don't take me for a fool. If it hadn't been for the size of the promised payment, I would never have entered into this bargain. But the sorcerer's offer was impossibly large. One would sell his soul for such a sum."

"Given the twisted state of your soul, that's a chilling claim."

"He's a chilling man. And there are devilish forces at work here. I don't like this any more than you, but it's too late for regrets."

One-Eye squinted. "Look to the east, near the tower. Someone's coming."

A robed man, back bent like a twisted limb, hobbled toward them. He moved with a shuffling step, negotiating boulders and bedrock cavities with the patience of a spider approaching a fly. A hood hid his face, but the two companions felt frigid eyes boring into them.

"Is that the man who hired us?"

"It must be."

The man vanished, leaving an eddy of dust. A whorl of air lifted Sarin's cloak from behind. He spun around as One-Eye drew his rapiers. The man stood just feet away, pale lips curled in a vulpine smile.

"The hired killers have arrived," he said, and the last word turned like a key in a rusted lock.

Sarin cautiously extended a hand. "Well met, Damon."

"Who are we to kill?" One-Eye asked quickly.

Damon ignored both the hand and the question. "Come with me. My master has been expecting you." He turned away and began hobbling back to the tower, hunched in a broken arch.

The companions exchanged an uneasy glance. *What master?*

As they started after him, they smelled the sea, though its scent was twisted, and heard the waves, though their sound was wrong. They crossed the expanse and reached the tower door. The door swung open. They followed the sorcerer inside.

* * *

HALF AN HOUR later, framed in the highest tower window, two pairs of eyes watched the assassins walk to the edge of the cliffs and descend back into the cave.

"Do you think they will succeed?"

"It's your job to make sure they do."

"Can they be trusted?"

"They know what will happen if they play us false. Now leave and do not forget to deal with Dale and the mercenary. Of the remaining Aurian spell weavers, Dale could prove to be the most troublesome. But he is a fool. Soon enough Dale will notice the sign of the demon's awakening, but by then it will be too late; my brother will be beyond their reach. Still, we cannot have them coming here, even after I've obtained my brother's blood. Better to kill them while they are still oblivious to our plans. My spells are working quickly, and the demon is growing restless. The time of our vengeance is near. Go, and do not fail me."

One set of eyes vanished from the window. Steps sounded on the stairs. They grew fainter and fainter until the sound ceased altogether.

The remaining pair continued staring from the tower into the night.

FARMER TWINE'S POOL

THE WIND THAT swirled around the Tower of Shadows on the far eastern coast had gathered water from the sea and was unleashing it upon the countryside many miles to the west.

Corin Starcross hurried along Woolthread Road, his mud-spattered cloak rippling in the wind. The wet road squelched under his boots, and his tunic, drenched and dirty, rubbed his chest like soggy sand. Pellets of driven water pummeled his face. He peered forward anxiously for any glimpse of shingle or brick. Once he reached Merrifield, he would take shelter in the homely inn called Rookery Rest, but neither town nor inn was anywhere in sight.

The surrounding hills, their outlines marred by rain, rose around him like earthbound clouds. Up ahead, the lonely road snaked through deserted pasturelands. Even the sheep and goats had enough sense to stay indoors on this dreary day. Corin imagined himself in a chair by a crackling fire under the eaves of Rookery Rest, a hunk of honeycomb melting in his mouth and a steaming mug of apple cider in his hands.

His friend Dusty would be at his side, embellishing the town gossip as usual, while rain spattered against the common room's windows.

It was an enjoyable fantasy, but Dapple ruined it with her braying. She plodded on the road behind him, hooves trampling puddles in *splish-splash* notes of irritated music. Corin reached back and stroked the donkey's neck. He felt a twinge of sympathy for her; she was getting too old for this sort of baggage work. Jyri should not have forced her out into this weather, but since the Honey Barrel's packhorse was lame with fever, alternatives had been few.

"Don't worry, old girl," he said, forcing a smile. "Things may be messy now, but you'll be in a stable soon enough." *And as for myself, I'll find a dry spot to wring out my clothes. Ariel take me, I feel worse than a river fish flopping on land.*

Underneath his cloak a leather pack scraped the skin between his shoulder blades. He hardly dared guess how much the sodden thing would weigh once he had finished shopping. Even with Dapple carrying three bushels of grain and several pounds of flour, iron hinges for the hives, the two new rolling pins, jars of wheat starch, and beeswax sealer for the kiln, he would be left with a heavy burden. In the end the downpour might spoil most of it before he got back to Jyri's inn.

So there *was* one advantage to this shower, after all: He would be forced to wait in town until the rain let up. Dusty probably would be around Rookery Rest. Corin hoped his friend had finished the day's chores: The two of them could sit through some laughs with the locals at the tavern, and Dusty's father could spare him some beer. Oswald was generous with food and drink, especially on dismal days.

And this day had been especially dismal.

Earlier that morning, shortly after waking, Corin had noticed the graying sky from his bedroom window. He had learned about the shopping trip from his uncle, Pyke Starcross, soon after and had begun using the threat of a storm as an excuse to delay his start, but beginnings could be put off only for so long in his house. Pyke, growing impatient with his nephew for lounging around the kitchen, had dismissed the cloudy skies as fickle and had sent him on his way with a shopping list of items.

"Oh, and Corin," his uncle had called after him. "Be sure to stop by the Honey Barrel. Jyri might be needing things in town."

Those had been damning words. Of course Jyri needed things; he *always* needed things. Corin had been handed a second—and much longer—piece of ink-scribbled parchment and then had been ushered onto Woolthread Road with a reluctant donkey in tow. The rain had started five minutes from the inn's front door.

Now it was coming down harder than ever.

Dapple snorted loudly and tossed her head. *She's probably dreaming of apples and hay,* Corin thought, scratching the hair between her ears. His head was beginning to ache, and it did not seem as if either the sky or his head would be clearing any time soon. If only the road had not melted into a quagmire, they could have been in Merrifield by now.

He was just starting to wonder if he had mistakenly turned down one of the flock paths that wound their way about the hill country when he saw a most welcome sight: an orange light glowing faintly through the rain. The light became two, and then buildings loomed through the mist.

Corin entered the town with a hastened step, passing through the Spinribbon Crossroads, named for the Spinribbon Fair that had made it famous. The Fairsway cut across his path, running from the capital port city of Nautalia and the Starlight Sea to the village of Turncross in the easternmost reaches of the kingdom.

Woolthread Road—the path Corin was treading—ran as most roads did, curling and shifting through the country, changing from packed dirt to pebble or flagstone when it neared towns and castles, veering to avoid unfortunate spots such as bogs and deserts, proceeding unhurriedly until it joined some larger way and vanished into strange and distant lands. Corin knew the road began in Bridgewater, a village known for its water mills and weavers of cloth that lay to the northeast of Merrifield on an aerie of stone in the Seaspine Mountains. On a clear day he could make out distant puffs of chimney smoke lifting into the air.

Now Merrifield rose before him on a palisade-wrapped hill. Houses and shops tumbled on top of one another like blocks stacked by a toddler's clumsy hand. Candles shone in windows. Their flames were the only sign of habitation. The streets were empty; most of the townsfolk were indoors, probably gathered around ovens and hearths, making the best of the weather by enjoying the company of family and friends.

Corin could see part of the Spinribbon Fair at the base of the hill. Thickets of pavilions—clustered around stages, game pens, and stalls—brooded dimly in the rain. The rain had darkened the brightly colored tents to more somber hues. Lanterns, lighted early because of the mist, twinkled bravely. Corin wished the sun were shining on a day free of chores, a day when the long hours of an idle afternoon stretched before him, a day he could roam the fair, browsing through trinkets, listening to the music of harpists or the words of wandering storytellers. Today there was little movement among the pavilions, but he could see livestock huddling together in their pens.

"There you are," he said, turning back once more to Dapple. "At least you won't have to stay out here like those poor animals for too much longer."

The donkey snorted, clearly losing patience with the dismal walk to town.

Corin did not blame her; he felt the same way. Rainwater was beginning to pain his left leg, which had been slightly lame for as long as he could remember. Pyke maintained it was a birth defect, but that had to be a lie. Corin would have welcomed an excuse for his limp, anything to help him explain its existence. But his limp had never bothered Dusty, and that was one of the reasons Corin had remained so close to his friend despite their dissimilar personalities. Dusty might be reckless, often witless, and loud to an annoying degree, but he was staunchly loyal.

Reluctantly turning away from the fair, Corin continued along a path of muddy stone until he reached the inn.

Rookery Rest was the largest link in a chain of buildings wrapping itself around a square at the crest of the town's hill. Twisty streets and alleys exited the square, flowing through rows of shops and homes like stone streams with wooden banks. The inn's tavern, resting below the guest rooms, was flanked on the left by the kitchen and on the right by the stable. A spire of timber and stone that in times long past had served as Merrifield's watchtower perched on the inn's roof. The structure was quiet now, but once the rain stopped, the rooks nesting inside would begin their piping pleas for food. Like the town's founders, they used the spire as a watchtower, but they were not on the lookout for enemies.

Corin first had heard about Oswald's Folly—a common Merrifield joke—from Dusty when the two boys still had been small children. Years ago, Oswald had discovered a family of rooks in his tower. He decided that they were rogue birds flown in from the Ravenswood, commiserated with them in their exile, and began feeding them with scraps from his kitchen. Birds, as most people know, are notorious gossips, and this family of rooks was no exception. Word spread quickly of free meals given by a foolish innkeeper, and within days an entire colony had taken up permanent residence in the watchtower. Oswald was too kind to shoo them off and the rooks were too smart to leave, so they sat there still, kings and queens watching over the town with beady eyes and sharp beaks, daring the innkeeper to forget their supper with commanding catcalls and cackles.

Corin's eye strayed from the watchtower to the ancient fountain in the middle of the square. For years it had not spouted anything other than dust. A trumpeting sea horse faced south in tribute to Ariel, the God of the Sea, while a lion roared northward, representing Lira, the God of the Land. The uppermost statue had eroded with age, but though elemental exposure had blunted its features, Corin still could recognize a winged dragon curling toward the heavens. Dragons were symbolic of the nameless God of the Air, but Corin knew of only one man who still held reverence for that being: his uncle.

Pyke had told him that most modern men—if they believed in anything celestial at all—had hearts only for the god who had the largest impact on their lives, the god on whose physical embodiment they could sail or walk, fish or farm. Corin thought the idea of an intangible God of the Air was hard to grasp, just as he knew it must seem for most other people. The fact that Pyke prayed to one was rather disturbing, but so was his idea of sending his nephew on a shopping trip under the imminent threat of a storm.

Corin knew that some people, including his uncle, maintained that Aurian wizards and enchantresses still roamed Ellynrie, but such views generally were disregarded. Pyke once had mentioned that the Aurians still revered the God of the Air. Corin remembered mentioning that he thought his uncle was insane.

In contrast, magicians were as real as the rain drumming on the hood of Corin's cloak, but there were not many of those, and only a few had visited the Spinribbon Fair during his lifetime. He had never seen one, but he hoped he would someday. Magic of any sort must be literally spellbinding to watch.

As he walked Dapple to Rookery Rest's stable, Corin noticed that the arched doors leading to the stalls had been shut against the rain. When he reached the doors, he pounded on one with his fist. The door swung back, and a young boy peeked out at him. It was Ricken, the stable boy, and it looked as though Corin had wakened him from a nap; his hair looked like a farmer's field after the autumn harvest, with twigs and bits of hay jutting in every direction.

"Are you going to stand and stare all day?" Corin asked. "Or can I come in and stable my donkey?"

Ricken scrambled aside and heaved the door open.

Corin stepped inside, bringing Dapple out from under the rain. He waited near a row of stalls, dripping on the straw bedding under the dim light of a lonely lamp while the stable boy hastily guided the donkey into an empty compartment.

"Sorry about that," Ricken said, shutting the gate to Dapple's stall. "This is horrible weather to be traveling in. I hadn't expected anyone else until the sky began clearing." He grabbed a pitchfork from the floor and began shoveling bunches of hay at the shivering donkey.

Corin shrugged off his pack and hung it on a wall peg. "I didn't choose to be out there. I'd rather be sleeping, too." He hung his cloak next to his pack. "Take care of her. She's walked a long way."

"Don't worry. I probably won't fall asleep for some time, at least not until Farmer Twine leaves the tavern. He's in there now, shouting and screaming about his pool in the Ravenswood. He says the water's possessed. I say he's crazy."

Corin thanked the stable boy and walked toward the common room door, ropes of curiosity tightening in his stomach. Possessed pools were about as credible as a God of the Air, but at least this story sounded entertaining.

Farmer Twine was a known recluse who lived alone near the Ravenswood just east of town. Rumors clung to him like fleas. Dusty maintained that the farmer ate crows and picked his teeth with their feathers, but Corin knew that was ridiculous. After all, feathers made horrible toothpicks.

When Corin limped into the tavern, he was greeted by sheer chaos.

Farmer Twine stood on a table in the midst of several dozen men. His bulky body shook, and his pudgy face contorted in a bright red mask of anger. Oswald, apron clinging to his willow-thin waist, edged toward the farmer with outstretched hands, evidently trying to calm the situation. He looked like a cricket approaching a bear. Most of the other men were laughing and jeering at the farmer. From the stable doorway, Corin spotted Dusty sitting on the bar, sipping from a pewter mug and looking rather amused, his short dark hair shining mischievously in the light of a nearby hearth fire.

Corin made his way along the wall toward the bar, warily skirting the knot of patrons; the commotion was creating a clangorous racket, and the air, already confused with smoke, was further muddled by their shouts and laughter. When Dusty caught sight of him, he flashed a grin and hoisted his mug, then took a long drink. Corin jumped up on the bar beside him.

Dusty was eighteen, a year older than Corin, as thin as his father and whippy like a pond reed. "The day keeps getting better and better," he said, and took another drink. He did not look much like Corin. His face was freckled, while Corin's was clear; his eyes were brown, while Corin's were green and flecked with gold; and Dusty had shaggy brown hair, while Corin had a mop of dirty-blond curls.

"It's good to see you, too," Corin said, catching a whiff of ale. "But what's so great about today? This rain's been miserable."

"I can tell—you're soaking wet." Dusty clapped him on the back. "Relax and enjoy the show. Just listen to the townsfolk; you'd think he was about to be drawn and quartered."

Corin pricked up his ears. The scene was growing more frenzied by the moment. Having heard what Ricken had told him in the stable, it was not difficult to predict where the confrontation was headed. Every time Twine began speaking, he was shouted down and ridiculed. Taunts came fast and hard.

Suddenly the farmer jumped from the tabletop. "Lira take you all!" he yelled. "What I say is true! Don't blame me if you wake one morning to find witches cutting your throats." He banged through the tavern door as the common room erupted in laughter.

"You think he made all that up?" Corin asked.

"He must have," Dusty said. "I've never seen—wait, what's this?"

Two men, purple and silver cloaks marking them as Nautalian knights, moved from the shadows to a spot near the bar. Corin had not noticed them before, though now they were standing just feet away from him. He exchanged a glance with Dusty.

The messengers began speaking with Oswald. One by one the men in the common room quieted, hoping in vain to overhear what was being said.

"Dark rumors have been circulating through the kingdom's eastern towns," the younger of the two said to Oswald in a hushed tone. Unkempt hair hung to his neck, and bristles hugged his chin. "They are the stuff of strange men who mutter stranger stories, but I say you'd have to be stranger still to believe them."

The older knight shook his head of white hair. "I wouldn't be too sure of that, Giles. We wouldn't have been sent galloping down the Fairsway if the stories had no credence. I won't believe we're reporting drivel to the High King in Coral Castle, and neither should you."

"It's drivel all the same," Giles replied, stroking his chin. "Some of the claims being whispered in the east are as preposterous as that farmer's devil-infested pool. *Think,* Aaron. We'll be laughed out of Nautalia."

"And mocked across the kingdom?" Aaron cocked an eyebrow and shot a furtive glance at the patrons of the inn. "I'm surprised to find Merrifield untroubled, Oswald. Hardly a day's ride up the Fairsway we spoke with people who knew of babies that had been stolen from their cribs and heard of a young woman whose husband, a woodsman, vanished into a grove one evening without a trace. The next day a search party found the woodsman's ax embedded in a tree. There was no sign of a struggle, and there was no sign of the woodsman."

Sir Giles dropped his hand from his chin. "The rumors began with the Turncross girl who wandered from her home. Ever since, the attention grabbers have been spinning yarns that even town gossips should balk at. Mind you," he said, turning to Oswald, "the child turned up on her doorstep several days later. Tired of running away, if you ask me."

Oswald nodded. "Yesterday I was told of a strange occurrence in Bridgewater. A bedraggled man stopped here for food and drink and hinted at a problem with the village's waterwheels. He said some of the other villagers had already left. But his words sounded like utter lunacy." He looked to Sir Aaron as several nearby taverngoers muttered their agreement, cursing the stories of fools and liars.

Immersed in the conversation, Corin reached for a drink that was not there, groped around the bar for a moment, and then rested his hand on a knee.

"I wouldn't dismiss his tale so easily," the older knight said. "The Turncross girl Sir Giles mentioned did return, but the way I heard it, her tongue had been cut from her mouth. Gossips aren't laughing off these stories, and neither are a great many other people. Throughout the east, doors are now being locked at sunset, and they are not opened until morning."

Save for the conversation between the two messengers, the common room had grown utterly silent. The crackling of hearth flames and the plinking of rain on windows were the only other sounds. All eyes were on the purple-and-silver-cloaked knights. Despite his initial inclination to laugh off Farmer Twine's story, Corin was beginning to feel uneasy. *Could any of this be true?*

Giles would not budge. "No doubt people are frightened, but there's not enough proof to trouble the High King."

"You speak of proof like a blind man."

"I speak of proof like a sane man. You're as spooked as that blasted farmer. Take that shepherd near Paliston, the one who raised a ruckus about his slaughtered sheep."

"What of him?" Aaron asked. "Men sent to his pasture found it empty, and the next day twenty-seven sheep carcasses—the exact number the shepherd had claimed slain—were being hawked around the town by a butcher. When questioned, the butcher admitted that the shepherd had killed the sheep and sold him their bodies, wanting to profit without paying the usual sales tax. The shepherd hoped to make a double profit of sympathy and coin from the fear in the east—"

"Then you admit that these rumors can be explained?"

"Have you forgotten the rest of the story? The shepherd was found dead in his pasture several days later."

"Suicide. The man was shamed and fined into poverty."

Aaron frowned. "He was clubbed to death. His hands had been crushed into pulp, and they were spread against his face as if he had been trying to ward off an attacker. The High King will listen to us, Giles. You can be sure of that."

Hushed whispers flew around the room like frightened moths, adding to Corin's disquiet. Dusty looked like a cat that had just seen a mouse race across the floor. If Corin knew anything about his friend,

Dusty was in the process of scheming up an idea, which was a dire sign. Dusty's sense of adventure was apt to yield disastrous results.

Just then Sir Aaron turned to the crowded room and announced in an officious if slightly drunken tone, "If anyone has word of strange oc-curences, let them speak now!" But his words were met with silence and downward glances.

"In any case it looks as though the rain has stopped," Giles said, shaking his head. He glanced at the windows. "If we leave soon, we should be able to reach Nautalia by tomorrow evening."

"I'll have another drink first," Sir Aaron said, and asked Oswald for more ale as the people around him broke into pockets of excited con-versation.

Dusty turned toward Corin. "I hope you aren't too tired to walk to the Ravenswood."

"What do you mean?"

"I have to find out if Twine was telling the truth!"

Corin tried to stall in the hope that his friend would change his mind. "I don't want to be stuck scrubbing Uncle Pyke's kiln or muck-ing Jyri's stable because I was late getting home."

Dusty downed the last of his ale and banged down his mug on the bar. "Then let's hurry."

Outside, the air was damp and chilly. An east wind blew over the hills, but the rain had ceased. Rooks in the watchtower screeched at Corin and Dusty as the two boys hurried down the street. On either side people began emerging from their homes. Shutters were thrown back; doors were thrust open. Activity could be seen behind shop win-dows and storefront facades. That was comforting; Corin knew his shopping would go quickly when he returned from the Ravenswood.

They left Merrifield by an eastern alley that changed into a muddy shepherd path upon its departure from town. Corin secretly thanked Dusty for keeping a slow place; his leg could not sustain a sprint. All around them extended a cloud-shrouded sea of slippery grass, yellow dandelions, and patches of wildflowers. In a few places, crumbling stone walls rose from meadows like spines of buried dragons. Mist lay like thickly folded blankets between the hills. Occasionally Corin glimpsed some wayward flock herder, staff in one hand and fife in the other, trailing after a group of goats or sheep. The whole scene was gray and vague, made for fantastic thoughts and mysterious investigations. Corin wondered whether this little expedition would end in a great discovery or a terrible disaster. If either Jyri or Pyke decided that he had been wasting time in town, he probably would find himself in the Honey Barrel's stable working Ricken's job for several days. *And that's the last thing I need,* he thought.

* * *

AFTER A SHORT time they came to the fringe of the Ravenswood.

"This is it," Dusty said.

Corin rubbed his arms. "Are you still up for this?"

His friend took an apple from a pocket. "Having second thoughts?"

"Not on your life."

"Glad to hear it." Dusty bit into the apple, swallowed, and then threw it aside. "Ready?"

Corin grinned. "Lead on."

Dusty continued forward on the cart track, walking under the tall, quiet trees.

The ground below their feet changed to a bedding of pine needles and soft soil. The trees—mostly ash, elm, and pine—were thick with leaves and needles. Roots laced their twisted way along the ground, and shrubs sprouted in pockets of low-lying green. Everything glistened from the rain. Drops of water fell on Corin's head from the canopy of boughs and branches.

The sounds of animals—cawing ravens, scurrying squirrels, foxes rustling in the undergrowth—faded as they journeyed deeper into the forest. The rooks and magpies that usually were found in abundance were nowhere to be seen. From every side, trees peered at the boys as if eyes were hidden under their leafy brows. As they plunged farther into the darkening wood, the tree limbs became more contorted and dense; the air was utterly still. Corin sensed something rotten at the core of the forest, an evil presence beating like a black heart. *I hope it's just my imagination.*

Then, without warning, Dusty stopped. They had reached a clearing, but not one they wished to cross, though Farmer Twine's pool lay on the other side. Corin drew level with his friend, staring.

The ground was all but covered in a sea of fog. Stone idols—monoliths of some ancient pagan religion—stood in varying states of decay, leering hideously with monstrous faces. A stone altar lay in the center of the clearing. Worn and broken, it was just the size of a man's body. The faces of the various idols were indistinct, as age and weather had blunted their features—much as they had done to the fountain in the town square—but those Corin could make out were terrifying, twisted shapes to which no name had been given.

Past the idols, the pool lay silent, a wretched splotch of dark red water. The farmer had been telling the truth. The waters, a swirling witch's brew of crimson and gray, were choked with scarlet vines, and tendrils of mist snaked across them like the ghostly claws of a demon's hand.

In a sudden burst of pain, Corin's left leg began to burn. He rubbed his knee and glanced at Dusty; the fear in his friend's eyes mirrored his own. *Burning blood, what's happening here?*

A moment longer they stood and stared, and then they fled back along the path for home.

SKETCHES OF HISTORY

KAYLA TIDENT LAY nestled in the crook of her bedroom window; the glass panes were wide open to welcome the evening's glow. Sounds drifted to her on the twilight air—wagons jostling, children shouting, merry bursts of laughter—like little bubbles floating on a noisy ocean, and in the distance she could hear the waves of the Starlight Sea lapping along Nautalia's stone-walled shore.

She was sketching a butterfly. The lithe creature had alighted by her feet only a moment earlier while she was watching the sunset, soaking up the summer air. A breeze blew in from the ocean, softly stirring the wave of her long blond hair. With the tip of her tongue poking from the side of her mouth, she glanced from the drawing to the butterfly, her thoughts wandering over the canopy of shingle rooftops crowning the city outside the window. She held a seagull-feather quill in her right hand. In a pattern of graceful strokes, a likeness of the butterfly unfolded on the parchment she kept spread across her legs.

Sketching was soothing. As far as she was concerned, time spent on beautiful pictures was never time wasted. Her father thought differ-

ently. If he could see her now, drawing a picture rather than memoriz-
ing the facts and figures *he* thought were so important, she would be in
serious trouble. Wren, for ridiculous reasons of his own, had always re-
jected the idea of sending her to school. He had placed himself in
charge of her education for as long as she could remember, though she
thought *torture* more aptly described the never-ending flow of text-
books, tests, and lessons with which he seemed determined to drown
her. The situation was hopeless. He had only stern replies for questions
about attending school with other kids her age.

"Your education is one of the most valuable tools you will have in life,"
he would say, lines creasing his forehead like iron bars. *"And at school
you would be thrust in with dozens of classmates who would only distract
you from your studying. While wasting time with them might seem enjoyable to you now, you'll end up with only regrets down the road."*

She wished she could convince him that classmates could also be
friends.

Wishing she had wings to carry her away from her room and her
work, Kayla looked up to study her subject, quill poised above paper.
Blue patches and white veins colored the insect's stained-glass wings,
which caught the setting sun in a translucent net of light. The butterfly
turned its head erratically, studying the room.

"Don't look in there," Kayla cautioned. "You'll only find a bed you
can't use, some clothing you can't wear, and an old textbook no one in
her right mind would ever decide to open."

But the butterfly did not seem to hear.

The latest book her father had given her to study, a thick, leather-
bound tome smelling of ink and dust, sat unwanted and neglected on
the floor. *The Pearl of the Starlight Sea: A History of Nautalia* was written across the cover in silver letters. The book's tassel—several frayed
threads tied to the tiny caricature of a trumpeting sea horse—was
jammed somewhere in the middle of the text as an illusory place holder
should her father drop by to check on her progress. She did not have
the slightest idea what was on the second page.

Kayla tried to push away the thought of unfinished work, but it was useless. She sighed and looked over the city as if she could somehow discern Nautalia's past in the winding streets that tumbled toward the sea.

Since she had been a small child, she had always followed the setting sun from her bedroom window. Red and purple ribbons would bleed from the sky like a fading dream, holding her spellbound. Now, as she watched, they danced like actors in a play, glimmering on the ocean, the city, and the butterfly. She was sorry to see their performance ending, but as the colors began bowing beneath the waves, excitement leaped like a spark in her chest.

Night's curtain was descending, but the labyrinth would soon take center stage.

If history was any judge, her father would shortly leave the house for Kendran's inn. There he would soon be drunk with his disreputable group of friends. Kayla had met them on occasion; they dropped by the house from time to time, looking for her father. They disgusted her, the whole lot of swarthy, hairy, overbearing, and foul-smelling sailors, petty merchants, and simple laborers with their crude manners and ignorant speech. She could not understand why Wren enjoyed their company; he seemed almost civilized compared with them. But none of that mattered. Once her father entered the Seasong Arms, he would stay there until the early hours of the morning, drinking and gambling. As far as she was concerned, this habit of his was just another of his many faults. But *this* fault did not bother her. He was welcome to his entertainment; she had plans of her own.

While he wasted his time with cards and coins and drank foul beer with fouler friends in the inn's tavern, she would be left alone in the house, free to take the secret passage leading from her father's wine cellar into the web of stone corridors that ran beneath the city. Being the daughter of a man like Wren had its fair share of drawbacks—her rather short supply of friends was a testament to that—but after discovering a false front on a barrel in her father's wine cellar, she had stopped wondering what adventures others her age were able to find.

Suddenly she heard the heavy tread of her father's footsteps marching up the stairs. The labyrinth winked out of her mind.

Kayla jumped up from the window, careful not to frighten the butterfly. She snatched up her father's history book, hurled herself onto the bed, and began flipping through the pages with feigned interest.

With a creaking of iron joints, the bedroom door swung open, and Wren stepped into the room.

Kayla stole a quick glance at her father. He was tall and sturdy, and his muscles looked as hard as his granite-gray hair. Crow's-feet in the corners of his eyes told tales of restless days and sleepless nights. A scar ran from his left temple to the center of his chin; his face, covered in prickly stubble, whispered a rumor of age; and his eyes were the blue-gray of a stormy sea.

That's what comes from your late-night drinking, Kayla thought. Suppressing a smile, she lowered her face to the book.

"Hello, Kayla." Wren's stern voice seemed to curl around the pages. "I'll be leaving for Kendran's in a few minutes."

"Have a good night," she replied, trying to seem absorbed in the text. She kept here eyes glued to the history's unread pages. *Left to right. Top to bottom.*

Wren cleared his throat. "I'm glad to see you reading."

"I can hardly put it down." Kayla hoped her heart's frantic beating wasn't as obvious as it felt. "Our city's royalty have led fascinating lives. My favorite is"—her eyes flicked to the top of the page—"King Lumin of the Thousand Statues."

"I'll agree with you there," Wren said. "Lumin was a great ruler and an even greater artist. He headed up some of our city's greatest feats of architecture. You can thank him for several public monuments, including those pearl sea horses along the Tidal Wall that you seem to enjoy so much."

That caught Kayla's interest. She loved those trumpeting statuettes, just as she loved the rest of Nautalia. The sights, sounds, and smells of the ancient seaside city were at once intoxicating and enchanting. And, of course, they were home.

Whenever her father gave her leave—which was seldom enough—she would wander from her house into the heart of the city and stroll up and down the colorful boulevards that were lined with shops and inns and swarming with people or spend her time walking the hundreds of alleys and crooked passages that spiraled and threaded needlelike in every direction, their patterns too complex for memorization and thus ever ripe for exploring.

One of her favorite haunts was the Tidal Wall that Wren, with his usual guile, had this moment woven into a lesson. Nautalia's first citizens had erected the turreted barrier along the harbor to ward off the winter storm waves that blew in from the ocean during the year's coldest months. Kayla knew next to nothing about Lumin's kingship, but if he had been the patron behind the sea horse statues, he was a capable ruler in *her* book. She had hidden several of her drawings of the Tidal Wall underneath her bed. Wren would never be able to confiscate those, thank Ariel; they were among her favorite creations.

The city's splendor overshadowed the ancient dark of the labyrinth, and the labyrinth provided a hidden door to the city. While wandering the streets, Kayla was just one girl in a vast maze. In the labyrinth she was royalty, a queen ruling over a forgotten realm where she made the rules.

Soon she would be there again.

"Tell me some of what you've learned this afternoon," Wren said, tearing her from her thoughts.

"There's so much here," she said, eyes darting crazily across the pages. "The Eastwatch Clock Tower, which stands near our home . . . the Merchant Quarter's bluestone streets . . . the Nautical Tower of Coral Castle."

"So you *have* studied some. Remember, even those venerable works are relatively new when placed on the city's time line. In the earlier chapters you've probably come across stories that have been difficult to believe." Wren stood next to her and plucked the book from her hands. He began turning pages. Kayla's heart beat faster with every flip. "Those accounts are not myths or legends. Most of them are based on records that have been handed down through the centuries so that young people like you can keep the past alive in memory."

Kayla had trouble seeing the benefit this book could have for any-one, but she thought her father could benefit her by leaving the room—and he could take his reading material with him. She peeked at the window to make sure the butterfly was still there. *My picture was turning out pretty well. I won't let him ruin it for me.*

It was still resting where she had left it, but her stomach was hit by a nauseating shock. She had left her quill and parchment on the sill. There they sat, rustling anxiously in the breeze.

Wren must have caught her glance, because the next moment he raised an eyebrow and frowned, tightening his scar.

"Reading, were we?"

"Father—"

He quieted her with a raised hand, anger flashing across his face.

"Drawing again, sketching pretty pictures; *that's* what you were doing?"

"Yes, but—"

"*That's enough, Kayla!* For once you will listen to me. Now is not the time to practice your hobbies. Burning *blood,* girl, why are you letting your time waste away when you should be studying?"

He dropped the book on her bed and stalked to the window.

She gulped.

"There will always be sunsets to watch," he said, gripping the sill while he looked out on the city and the sea. "But now you need to be working to make sure your sun will rise. How many times have I tried and failed to talk sense into that stubborn head of yours? I was blown about during my youth with my head in the clouds, a dream adrift, as it were. I never had anyone to guide me, and as a result, I never had anyplace to go. I looked at the world though yearning eyes, but since my mind was untrained, I could never truly see."

Oddly enough, Kayla saw an echo of that yearning flash across her father's face as he gazed at the ocean's darkling waters. Wren hesitated and grew quiet, almost as if he had sensed her thoughts. A silence set-tled on the room, and Kayla felt the richness and wonder of her father's past swirling through the window with the sea breeze. Framed in dusk's half-light, his hair shifting in the wind, Wren looked ready to dive from the window into an adventure. As she had many times before, Kayla found herself wondering what life he had lived and what lands he had seen before she had been born.

The butterfly regarded him quizzically.

Kayla did not know much about her father's past, only what she could gather from the brief stories he occasionally would tell her, little more than tattered segments, and the small patches of clues lying around the house. From those she had formed something of a picture quilt, but the collage of images was distorted and many of the images were frayed. There was the sword hanging above the fireplace and the maps, globes, and navigational instruments covering the walls of the study. In the attic there were several locked chests and an aging vest of chain mail that hung from the ceiling like a prisoner.

Wren did not know she could enter there, but then, he did not know she knew about the labyrinth, either. In fact, he did not know about most of the things she did. Between them, lack of knowledge went both ways. She had discovered where he kept the attic key long ago.

She was sure her father had been something of a professional explorer, but that was the only thing of which she could be sure. He had sailed west on the Starlight Sea to the Summerset Isles. He had ventured along the coast north and south of Nautalia, and he had even traveled into the Far East, where, at least for sheltered girls, charted maps ended and fantastic places gleamed like jewels on an imagined landscape. But Wren had never divulged any details concerning his travels, and so she was largely in the dark. She wished her father could be more open with her, but a small voice inside her warned that this wish would never be granted.

Wren glanced down at the sill, saw the butterfly and sighed, then brushed it outside. Shaking his head, he reached through the window and brought the panes together with a snap. Kayla's last glimpse of the butterfly—a colorful speck bobbing above Nautalia's rooftops—vanished behind a wall of bubbled glass. The room darkened considerably. Her swelling spirit was extinguished as quickly as it had come, and the draw of her father's past faded away. He was simply Wren again, a dull and predictable parent, one who drank too much and suffocated his daughter with reading and work.

Wren snatched up her picture and wheeled around, crushing it in his hand. "I'm disappointed in you. You're not to leave the house tonight or any other night for the next several days, and I want you to reach at *least* King Lumin's chapter by the end of this week. I'm going to head over to—"

"Kendran's, I know. Have a good time getting drunk, Father." If he was going to treat her like this, she was going to let him know just how highly she thought of *his* lifestyle.

Wren stiffened. "How I choose to spend my time is no concern of yours." Then, in a softer tone, he said, "I'm trying my best to raise you as your mother would have done. Please, Kayla, just read the book."

With a swirl of his cloak he left the room, closing the door behind him. *I guess closing doors is all you're good for,* Kayla thought bitterly.

She stared after him as his footsteps receded down the stairs, emotions overwhelming her like a tide of furious foam. When she was sure he had gone, she buried her head in the pillow, bitter tears gathering in her eyes.

THE SEASONG ARMS

L ONG AGO, before Kayla had been born, Wren Tident had been a jack-of-all-trades.

He had traveled far over earth and ocean, had climbed treacherous mountains and forded frozen rivers; he had robbed a thief and slain an assassin, ventured into the darkest caves, and sailed through the worst storms; he had slept in royal castles and eaten with beggars, begged himself, and readily killed. Once he had even glimpsed a dragon, and those creatures were thought to be myth.

All this and more Wren had done in his past as he wandered the world: a drifter, a lover, and a mercenary, moving ceaselessly across the face of Ellynrie, carried on the tides of fate.

For all that, in his time as an adventurer he had never encountered a job as difficult as fatherhood. If he had learned anything in the last sixteen years, it was that adventures were child's play compared to raising a daughter. But this role had lasted the longest of them all. Although Kayla was harder to deal with than any quest, Wren loved her more than anything he had encountered in any of his travels.

As he walked briskly from his house, he found himself counting the steps to Kendran's inn. He wished he could snap his fingers and forget the disaster that had just taken place in his daughter's bedroom, but he was no magician. Rows of houses loomed over him from either side of the street. The sky was darkening quickly, and there were few other people abroad. Nearby, Eastwatch Clock Tower rose from a square enclosed by serried lines of rooftops.

Looming no more than two stone's throws from his house, the ancient structure stood like a senescent angel, proud and wise despite obvious decay, her ivory clock face and brazen pinnacle ablaze with a golden light that filtered duskily down her sides to vanish, as if swallowed in a crowd of sinners, among the shadowed crevices of Nautalia's streets. Her hands were moving slowly, almost carefully, with a calculating precision that seemed far too unnatural for something created by the hands of men. As with the oldest constructs in the city, subtle ripples of otherworldly magic and long-forgotten mystery undulated from the tower.

The hairs on the back of Wren's neck prickled. For all the years he had lived there, he had never overcome the feeling that a mysterious presence pulsed its way through the bones of Nautalia.

Ever since he had abandoned his old life for a new start behind the city's walls, he had harbored a fascination for his home. Novel or history, fact or fiction, he had devoured them all in his quest to learn about the city that was known across Ellynrie as the Pearl of the Starlight Sea. Ruler after ruler, generation after generation, it had continued to grow in size and complexity as it developed into one of the largest and most powerful trading nexuses in the world.

Struggling to erase the memory of his argument with Kayla, Wren breathed in deeply.

Nautalia was full of summer scents: exotic odors of spices brought from the Summerset Isles; the foul stench of blood, fur, and fetid flesh wafting from the Rattlechain Pens—pits teeming with prize fighter beasts and heaped with newly slain carcasses—the thousand odors of the Seashell Square Market; the acrid wax that traders applied to their wagons in weatherproof coats before journeying inland. Then there were the smells that stayed with the city year-round: the staleness of aging stone, chimney smoke rising from tavern hearths and cooking fires, the briskness of waves.

Wren had hoped Kayla would enjoy the new book he had given her, what with their shared interest in Nautalia's architecture, but once again he had failed to ignite her imagination. Things had always been that way between them: strained and tense, full of misunderstanding and incomprehension. Their relationship was a struggle for supremacy.

She takes after me, he thought, frustrated. He had never been content with a book during his youth. He loved Kayla and wanted only the best for her, but he had never had the best himself, and without a worthy model on which to base his judgments, he feared he was failing her as a father.

Wren's childhood had been as chaotic as a whirlwind. His mother had died in childbirth, leaving him with his father in Lantern Watch, a cursed pirate town so far as he was concerned. Dirk Tident, heavy drinker and self-styled adventurer, left the coastal town shortly afterward, overwhelmed by his wife's death. He carried Wren north and south along the Seaspine Coast on a string of exciting, if rather lawless, business ventures.

It was no wonder he had turned out the way he had. Years later, one of Lantern Watch's pirate gangs carved Dirk up after a botched business deal, leaving Wren with only Dirk's sword and the clothes on his back. From that point on he had adopted his father's roving lifestyle. *But that's no reason why Kayla shouldn't have a better life than mine.* She was impulsive and careless—traits she undoubtedly had learned from him—but Wren was determined to give her the things he had gone without: an education, a family, and a place to call home.

If only he knew *how* to help her. If only her mother still lived and breathed. She would know exactly what to do.

Lori, if only I could have saved you . . .

As Wren passed the clock tower, eyes tracing the cracks between the cobblestones, his thoughts chained to memories of his wife, a new hour struck. The clock tower hailed its arrival. Six times it cried, each brazen note peeling forth like a pronouncement of judgment or doom. To Wren it seemed some heavenly judge was calling him accountable, but he did not flinch or shudder. Over the years he had hardened the armor of his expressions to the point where few things in the world could alter his steely appearance. Nonetheless, the familiar sting of sorrows, regrets, and rage struck his heart as his inner demons clawed to release themselves from his mind.

Just as suddenly, the tower fell into stillness. As he moved from the residence streets to the bluestone walkways of the Merchant Quarter, the air eddied around him in currents, tingling with the charged atmosphere that he always felt just before a storm. It carried the acidic taste of oncoming thunder.

Kayla will not turn out like me, he vowed one last time, quickening his pace as he hurried by dozens of shops and stalls closing for the night, each step bringing him closer to Kendran's inn. *My past will never harm her.*

Despite that promise, he felt the familiar pull of the medallion that hung from a chain about his neck as a galley slave felt the leaden tug of his own servitude. The wizard Dale had given it to him all those years ago, the small icon of the three gods through which the magic worker had told Wren he would be summoned should the life of the boy ever be imperiled. Wren had made another promise, a binding pledge . . . *But it has been silent for fourteen years. Ariel willing, it will remain that way until I die.* He shook his head savagely, bending his thoughts on the Seasong Arms.

At last he reached the inn. Kendran was a good friend of his, and the Seasong Arms, one of Nautalia's ancient establishments, was a good place to be, especially at a time like this. He had spent many an intoxicated night within the inn's sturdy walls. He felt better already.

Pondering which ale he would start the night with, Wren reached for the door, but his hand stopped short of the handle. By some ridiculously impossible chance, a butterfly had landed there, a very familiar butterfly. He could not be sure, but the blue and white wings looked almost identical to those he had seen in his daughter's bedroom.

"What the hell's wrong with me?" he muttered. *It's just a damn insect.*

He pushed his guilt aside, swatted it away, and jerked the door open, resisting the urge to watch the butterfly's retreat through the darkening air. A chorus of voices immediately engulfed him in a cacophony, drawing his senses into the boisterous atmosphere beyond the door's threshold. Sighing heavily, he entered, the muscles in his face relaxing.

He surveyed the room like the professional he was and located both the gamblers and the drinks in seconds. Never one to place a bet without wetting his whistle first, he walked to the bar.

Kendran, a limber, cheery man who looked and acted ten years younger than he should have, was vigorously running a stained cloth in ever-widening circles up and down the bar. The bar was not getting any cleaner and the rag he was using was hopelessly stained, but the innkeeper did not seem to notice that his efforts were wasted.

Stifling an impulse to laugh, Wren watched his friend for a moment. The moment turned into a minute; his thirst was not getting any lighter, and there was money to be made at the Jikari table. He cleared his throat, reached across the bar, and gave Kendran's shoulder a friendly punch.

The innkeeper looked up. "Blazes, Wren, you gave me a start. How's the evening treating you? You look like your gullet could use a beer."

"More than one, I think. I've been having some family problems."

Kendran knocked a fist against the side of his head. "There I go again, forgetting you have a daughter. How is she these days? Difficult as only a teenager can be, I'll wager."

"She takes after her father more than he wants her to."

"Does she, now? Why would anyone want to take after *him*?" Kendran grinned. "I've seen children who can drink more, and I've watched a half-wit cast luckier Jikari cubes."

Wren grinned back. "You're a liar and a bastard, Kendran."

"But I serve good beer."

"Most of the time."

"Tonight I have something you're sure to enjoy. Before I start you off with the usual, allow me to give you a taste of a new concoction I bought from a trader in the Seashell Square Market this morning." Kendran beckoned to a keg behind him with an exaggerated flourish. "One try and you'll buy the whole barrel."

Wren nodded uneasily. Kendran was always experimenting with new ales and wines, but the samples that made their way from his storeroom to his customers often came up much quicker than they went down.

The innkeeper whisked an empty mug from the top of a pile behind the bar, turned to a row of wall-mounted kegs, and filled it with an amber liquid until the syrupy stuff began foaming at the top and running down the sides. He placed the overflowing mug on the bar with a wink.

"Yellow-hornet ale, brought straight from the Ravenswood near Merrifield and the Spinribbon Fair. It packs a stinging punch."

Wren eyed the frothy container suspiciously, trying not to associate the drink in front of him with the mess on the bar. The two liquids looked too similar for comfort, though the latter smelled faintly like vomit. "Never heard of it."

"Drink up," Kendran pleaded. "It's on the house."

"I'm more concerned about what's on the bar." Wren raised the mug to his lips and took a skeptical sip.

It was strong. It was bitter. It was definitely not beer.

Wren spit it out and wiped his mouth, shooting Kendran an angry look. "I'd rather you didn't try to poison me every other time I came here. Do you honestly think this stuff tastes good?"

Kendran's smile fell. "You're right," he moaned. "I've made another poor purchase, one fit for a fool. Burning blood, you were my last hope. Most of the others"—he gestured vaguely about the room—"have already tried it, and none of them seemed to enjoy it at all."

"That's because it tastes like rat piss."

Kendran looked miserable. "It probably is. What in the Sea God's name am I going to do with it all?"

"Poison the rats."

Both men laughed.

"Damn you, Wren," Kendran said. "I'd better get you something decent to drink." He smiled wryly. "I can see you're itching to toss the Jikari dice around, and things seem to be heating up at the table."

Propping an elbow on the dry edge of the bar, Wren turned to the room while Kendran busied himself with a keg. The usual gamblers were seated at the Jikari table. He looked closely at the men who would soon be handing him their coins. Pulley, a sailor, sat with his massive arms spread on the table and his tiny legs propped up on an overturned beer barrel. Then there was Teran, the young owner of Caravan's Crook, a tavern and loading warehouse; Guzzler, an extremely obese hopeless alcoholic who looked the part; Flint, a red-bearded weapons merchant; and Hook, the oldest of them all, an accomplished boater with a sharp, angular nose and a face as wrinkled as a fishing net.

They were friends, but tonight they also would be victims.

Wren's eyes were drawn to a nearby table where two men, leaning conspiratorially toward each other, were engaged in a tense conversation. He had never seen them before, but their purple and silver cloaks marked them as royal knights. Intrigued, he tried listening to their conversation, but the noise in the common room was so loud that he could only hear snatches of jumbled phrases. Their talk seemed to reflect their grim expressions.

"Who are those men?" Wren asked as liquid bubbled into a mug behind him.

"Sir Aaron and Sir Giles, set out yesterday from Merrifield. Arrived about an hour ago. They've come down the Fairsway to report some troubling rumors that have been floating around the eastern half of the kingdom." Kendran switched off the keg. "They have an audience with the High King tomorrow morning, much good it will do them. Their stories sounded ridiculous to me." He set a drink next to Wren. "Still . . . Have you spent the day indoors?"

Wren nodded.

"Then you can't have heard. We have rumors of our own."

"What happened?"

"Sightings of a shadow flying south over the city, then east toward the Seaspine Mountains. Accounts agree on wings but not on the number. The caretaker of Eastwatch Clock Tower was up in the bell chamber oiling ropes and gears when the sun was momentarily blotted out. He rushed to a balcony to get a better view but only heard a distant thudding."

Wren narrowed his eyes. "That sounds like . . ."

"A dragon?" Kendran chuckled. "The stories are strange, no doubt . . . strange enough for a madman. But I'm not concerned: I've yet to see a legend take life. Nautalia's pearly light will shine eternal. Enjoy your beer and good luck with the gaming cubes."

For a moment Wren felt slightly uncomfortable, though he could not put his finger on the reason. He recalled the dragon he had glimpsed in the Summerset Isles long before, a mass of spikes and wings; he pictured the labyrinth under the city, a seemingly secret maze that he had discovered through the wine cellar under his home; he thought of the wizard Dale's magic. He knew things existed outside the sphere of rational thought, even if he was alone in his knowledge. Wren agreed with Kendran—rumors were usually the stuff of old wives and gossips—but the clock tower gonged in his mind, and a chill crept under his shirt.

Then, feeling silly, he acted as he had with the butterfly and brushed his feelings away.

"Thanks for the drink," he said, and took a swig. "By the way, I'd think twice before using that rag of yours anymore. It seems rather dirty." He walked to the Jikari table, Kendran's good-natured curses ringing behind him, and pulled up a chair, taking a seat with his gambling friends.

Teran and Pulley nodded at him. Guzzler belched, lifted his drink, and took a long draught. Hook smiled a wrinkled smile.

"How's it going?" Flint asked, shaking the two red cubes.

Wren took a gulp and swallowed. "Much better than before." He pointed to the table. "Throw them, Flint. It's my turn next."

Flint blew on his hands for luck and did as he was told. The dice clattered over the white and blue squares of the wooden playing surface. Their faces displayed the lion and dragon.

Pulley groaned.

Teran cursed; Hook cursed more loudly.

Guzzler took another drink, much longer than before.

"Looks like I win again," Flint said happily. He looked keenly at Wren as the others slid coins toward him. "You sure you want to cast in with this table tonight? I seem to be running things well at the moment."

"You know me better than that." Wren reached across the table and grabbed the playing cubes. "I'm never a man to miss a bet."

Suddenly a searing heat erupted against his chest.

Wren gasped, dropping the dice with tremulous fingers. The two crimson cubes rattled across the table and fell unnoticed to the floor. His eyes glazed over, his breathing grew heavy, and time slowed to a crawl. Under the cloth of his tunic a long-forgotten sensation began to spread.

The faces of the men around the table began to show concern, but Wren was blind to their expressions. His friends lowered their mugs and shifted their money aside. One or two leaned forward.

"Wren, are you all right?"

"Hey, now, what are you trying to pull? Tricky bastard, that's what you are."

"What's the matter with him?"

"How should I know?"

"He looks like he's seen a ghost."

Their voices drifted to him like hushed babbling in a great fog. With a reluctant dreamlike movement, Wren reached inside his shirt to withdraw the fate he wore from his neck. His hand closed on the medallion; its heat burned his skin. He brought it forth, uncurled his fingers, and stared into his palm.

His eyes widened.

The icon pulsed with a living light, each flare accompanied by a flaming pain, a pain that reached deeper and deeper into his consciousness, his heart, his mind . . .

With an intense blast, the inn's common room exploded in a swirl of color and furious sound. Images of the painted Jikari table, the row of kegs behind the bar, his friends jumping from their chairs, frantically knocking over drinks and scattering piles of coins to rush toward him, split at the seams as his world gave way to chaos.

Nightmare

A DRIEL WAS A wizard's apprentice, although in his opinion that title was a comical error of tragic proportions. He had no knack for magic or for anything even remotely magical. This was the first of the two reasons for his discomfort with his home by the Starlight Sea, a small sheltered world where he had grown up knowing that although the pursuit of a wizard's staff was to be his life's goal, he probably would never gain anything beyond a laughably dull twig.

The second reason was that Dale was not his father. Adriel had no memory of his parents, and that disturbed him endlessly. The full story of how he had come under Dale's wing had never been explained, but his parents had been murdered—the wizard had been clear about that horrid detail. As a result, Adriel's dreams were haunted by dark and disquieting questions.

But Adriel believed that everyone eventually finds answers if he knows where to look, and he was determined to discover the truth of his past someday.

Unfortunately, at the moment he was looking only for shellfish. He found this less interesting than an investigation into his past. It was clearly less rewarding; he had been beaten by the sun for nearly an hour.

Sweat soaked his tunic as he trudged down the beach. Whenever he came across a tidal pool, he would crouch down and sift his tanned fingers through the soggy sand but find nothing. The tide had left its generosity in the ocean. Adriel had brought a wicker basket from his master's house, but it held only a few mussels and clams, two crabs, and half a starfish, hardly more than a few mouthfuls and certainly not enough to prepare a decent evening meal.

Seagulls swung overhead in lazy circles, dipping and rising on the trade winds above the ocean's tumbling waves. Adriel heard them, but with little pleasure; the gulls were as much to blame as the ocean for the lack of shellfish along the beach. *If my luck doesn't change soon, Dale is going to be very upset when I return. Gods, he hates going hungry even more than I do.*

The beach curved along the ocean into the distance as if a serpent had rolled from the Starlight Sea and wriggled from its skin. As Adriel trudged along, his eyes were caught by a burst of movement near the dunes.

Two crabs scuttled across the beach, spidery legs leaving pinpricks in the sand. Adriel toyed with the idea of using magic—it would take only a small amount of energy to call the two crabs to him, and it would be much easier than scrounging along the shore—but Dale had forbidden him from working magic alone.

He doesn't trust me, Adriel reflected bitterly. *And why should he? I've been nothing but a failure so far.*

Although he looked the part—his spiky silver hair helped considerably—he had always been slow when it came to learning magic. Although Dale was patient, Adriel often criticized himself; he was constantly bungling even the simplest tricks. Sending a call to the crabs, though far from difficult, could end in disaster. *But if it works, I'll have something decent for the table tonight.*

Feeling guilty, Adriel dropped his basket and flung out his arms. An itching sensation tickled his mind and intensified, then shot down his back, along his arms, and into his fingers. He concentrated harder, squeezing his eyelids together, sweat pouring down his face.

Suddenly the two crabs shot into the air and sped toward him. But they were moving too fast to control.

Adriel jumped back as they swerved toward him, claws and legs flailing. One latched onto his ear, the other to his tunic, snapping pincers on his skin. He yelped and writhed until the crabs dropped to the sand and scuttled away. Groaning, Adriel picked up his basket and rubbed his ear. The pain faded, but his guilt returned. *Maybe I should just give up.*

Why did Dale continue to teach him? Adriel had not had much contact with the world beyond his home, but he guessed that Dale was surely one of the wisest men alive; he seldom did anything without a reason or a goal in mind. Perhaps the older man was simply lonely.

Just then he saw a twisted conch lying half-buried in the sand. Miniature turrets and towers spiraled across the seashell's length like the haphazard fortifications of a madman's castle, and its iridescent surface glowed faintly with a glossy inner light.

Adriel knelt and picked it up, pressing it against his ear to hear the ebb and flow of gushing echoes, but the shell was silent. He frowned and inspected it again. It was a beautiful specimen but as silent as a stone. *A bad omen,* he thought. *I won't catch anything else today, not after this.* He drew back his arm and hurled the shell into the dunes, then turned around for home.

He wished he had brought his coral flute; he had decided to sing a walking song to ward off his frustration, a song that Dale had taught him as a child, but he was better at playing than at singing. The thought of the flute brought a smile to his face—music, at least, was something he had talent for. He began to sing, spirits lifting with the song.

Several tunes later Adriel caught sight of his home, a weathered two-storied cottage poking above the dunes like a shell caked with wood and clay. A narrow brick-and-mortar chimney stood against the afternoon sky. Dale's glass observatory twinkled on the roof.

As he passed through the dunes toward the cottage, the sharp sea grass near the shore gave way to thorns and blackberry brambles. Adriel made his way around the prickly plants carefully; their stems were thorny, razorlike things that seemed to writhe under the glaring sun.

When he pushed the cottage door open, he heard a log snap. Dale must have lit a blaze in the study fireplace.

Adriel peered inside the study. An open book lay facedown on the reading table and a fire had indeed been lit, but the parchment-cluttered room was otherwise empty. His master's carving of the three gods—a dragon sheltering a sea horse and a lion with outstretched wings—hung from the wall above the fireplace. The figures glowed mysteriously in the firelight, almost as if they knew where Dale had gone. Adriel stared at them, but they did not reveal their secrets.

He turned from the study and called to Dale.

There was no reply.

The kitchen was as vacant as the rest of the house, but that was not surprising: Dale was practiced at making himself scarce when there was work to be done. Light filtered through a round seaward window, sending shadows sliding across the floor like wave reflections in a sea cave.

Adriel shook his basket onto a table, removed lumps of jellied meat from shells and diced them with a knife, then rummaged through the kitchen's pantries and shelves for spices but found nothing. *This is not my day,* he thought to himself.

As he hung a cauldron on a hook in the kitchen hearth, a fox trotted through the kitchen door, whining. It was Pearl, Dale's ridiculous idea of a pet. "What is it?" Adriel asked guardedly.

In return, he received more whining, followed by a whimper.

"I don't suppose you're hungry."

The fox nodded her head vigorously.

"And I don't suppose you'll leave me alone until you get something to eat."

The fox nodded again.

"There's hardly enough food here for Dale and me. You'll have to find something on your own."

Pearl grumbled and pricked up her ears, eyeing the shellfish on the table. Adriel started running, but he was too late. Pearl vaulted onto the table, snatched the starfish, and jumped back to the floor. She watched Adriel haughtily, munching her newfound prize.

Shaking his head, Adriel gathered the rest of the food, placed it in the cauldron, and went to gather water for the stew. Pearl gulped down the last of the starfish and followed him, tongue lolling.

Outside, the air had cooled considerably. A crisp breeze whistled in from the sea. It felt refreshing against Adriel's skin, but its playful touch suggested trouble; above the Seaspine Mountains clouds were brewing on the edge of an ashen sky. *Could be a storm tonight,* he thought uneasily. *What's taking Dale so long? He had better get back before the rain begins.*

He placed his hands on the well's lever and drew a breath, preparing to draw the water bucket. Pearl squatted nearby, grinning at him slyly, head on her paws, her tail swishing lazily.

"What are you looking at?" he asked.

The fox grinned harder and yawned. Her mouth, full of needlelike teeth, was still spotted with bits of starfish.

Adriel cursed but began turning the lever, muscles tightening as the pulley strained against the bucket, which clattered as it rose. When it wobbled above the rim of the well, he unhooked it and set it on the ground. Pearl darted forward, but Adriel snatched it up and glared at her. She shot him a pointed look and trotted into the house. Sighing, he looked out to sea.

The western sky was splotched with bruised purples and yellows like a rotten speckled egg, and every horizon was darkening. Clouds billowed westward, their shadows keeping the light from reaching the waves.

Adriel looked inland for Dale, but there was no trace of his master among the hills. In the near distance the Seaspine Mountains jutted like giant teeth.

Suddenly the shadow of a many-winged creature fell across the cottage, darker than the clouds. Adriel looked up just in time to see a sinuous shape overhead. He strained his eyes but could not make out what it was. Then, moments later, both the shape and its shadow were gone.

Blazes . . . what was that thing? Adriel wondered, heading for the cottage. *It must have been a cloud . . .*

When he entered the kitchen, he kicked Pearl away from the cauldron, filled it with water, and kindled a fire in the hearth. He stirred the stew and left it to simmer as he went about the house, checking every window and door to make sure each was sealed tight. Then he heard the distant drum of thunder, and a moment later the rain came hurtling down.

There was still no sign of Dale.

* * *

ADRIEL, WARMING HIMSELF by the hearth and stirring the stew, had just decided to begin eating alone when the front door banged open and the sounds of the storm whipped through the house.

The door slammed shut, and Dale strode into the kitchen, Pearl at his side. The wizard was drenched, his boots were muddy, and his hair—netted with twigs and leaves—sprouted everywhere in tufts.

"My hat blew off," he said, acknowledging Adriel with a curt nod. He hung his traveling cloak by the door and sat down in one of the two chairs at the kitchen table. "What is there to eat tonight?" His gray eyes turned to the rain-slicked window. "I'm famished."

Adriel stared at him. "Where have you been all this time? By the Sea God, Dale, it's like a hurricane out there."

Dale picked a twig from the long black locks that held it in place. "I'm quite all right. I just need something hot in my stomach."

Adriel was perplexed—who knew what Dale had been doing all day?—but these moods came upon his master every so often, and Adriel was used to them by now. He dished them each a bowl of the stew without any further questions, then sat down to eat with the wizard.

Silence separated them like a canyon, but Dale did not seem to notice. He ate from his bowl slowly, holding each spoonful of stew in his mouth for several seconds before swallowing.

"I'm sorry about the stew," Adriel offered, taking Dale's silence for disappointment in the meal. "There wasn't much on the beach today, and that fox of yours has already taken her dinner from what I brought back."

Pearl, who was curled up in a corner of the kitchen, jerked up her head and bared her teeth, but Dale did not reply.

"The shellfish stayed under the sea," Adriel went on, "and the gulls snapped up the few that crawled onto the beach."

"Yes," Dale said, "the gulls are beautiful . . ."

"What?"

"You're right about the gulls."

"I wasn't talking about . . ." Adriel paused, watching Dale stroke the side of his bowl and swirl his spoon through a wisp of steam. "Master, are you listening?"

Dale nodded.

Adriel sighed. "Where were you?"

Dale stared into his stew, eyes as distant as the morning. "I visited Marian."

"What did she say?"

"Her words were dark. She confirmed some unsettling . . . tidings . . . that I had gathered earlier."

"Tidings?"

"Riddles," Dale said, "riddles that need solving. A puzzle is wrapping itself about the earth . . . the vines are crawling into place . . ."

Dale was impossible when he spoke like that. Once his mind began wandering, there was nothing Adriel could do to bring it back to the present moment. He made a mental note to ask his master later about what had passed between him and the enchantress. Adriel met Marian occasionally, but Dale made the three-mile journey out to her cliffside home several times a week. *She certainly knows how to put him in a strange mood,* he thought.

Rain rattled the kitchen window, drowning out the ocean's storm-bloated waves. Flames danced in the hearth as shadows gathered in the corners of the room. Despite his master's odd behavior, Adriel felt safe and warm hunched over the table, sharing the food he had prepared.

At length Dale rose from his seat and placed a hand on Adriel's shoulder, smiling vaguely. "Sleep well," he said, and then drifted away, pausing to call "good supper" over his shoulder as he left.

Surprised by the compliment, Adriel looked down at Dale's bowl. It was nearly full of stew.

As the hearth fire faded into a pile of embers, he cleared the table and grudgingly placed Dale's bowl on the floor for the fox. Pearl slipped from the shadows and began lapping eagerly.

"That's more than you deserve," Adriel muttered.

Pearl swished her tail. Her stomach shook with a rumble that sounded suspiciously like laughter.

Adriel criticized the fox again for good measure and headed to his bedroom; his eyelids were growing heavy.

He glanced into the study on his way to the stairs. The fire had gone out. Above the fireplace the image of the three gods stared from its place on the wall in quiet speculation. Dale was not inside. *Probably in his observatory,* Adriel mused, *lost among his maps of the stars.*

When Adriel reached his room, he stripped off his clothing, dropping the garments haphazardly on the floor, and crawled into bed. He fluffed his pillow and pulled the covers up to his chin.

Sheets of rain drummed against the roof, and wind howled outside. From time to time muffled claps of thunder sounded through the storm. Adriel heard the distant crashing of breakers on the beach. *The sea is calling me to slumber,* he thought sleepily. *There's an enchantment in midnight waves . . .*

Seconds later he was fast asleep.

* * *

. . . violet and sapphire; silver and gold . . . a sea of flowers swaying gently like a field of stars . . . daylight cascading down to the music of a waterfall . . . and the birds are singing so sweetly . . .

. . . but something's wrong, a hint of crimson in the air and the taste of ashes on the breeze, reddening, darkening . . . a hellish glow burning on the eastern horizon, flaring in the night, for it is night now, and there is only darkness and dust without moon or star . . .

. . . the day has died and vanished, and the flowers are no longer what they were; they have been replaced by weeds and thorns on a moor with the bones of many beasts, and, oh, the ashes are falling faster and faster and the birds are cackling instead of singing; they are carrion birds swooping and diving and ripping . . .

. . . a man is coming for me from a tower by the sea where someone stares after him with burning eyes, and this man draws closer, dragging a staff like a knife and he reaches toward me, grinning darkly—

"Adriel, get up."

The voice was muffled by rain.

Adriel rose in a panic, wide-eyed, his breathing rough and shallow.

"Come to the observatory, and come quickly. There is something you must know."

The bedroom was empty, but the voice was unmistakably Dale's.

Blinking wonderingly, covered in chilly sweat, the young apprentice rose from his bed, walked from his room, and went to find his master, shivering as the images in his nightmare flashed before his eyes.

Pearl waited expectantly by the door to the observatory as if she also could tell that something was terribly wrong.

THE LABYRINTH

───────────

B ETWEEN SOBS KAYLA thought of her dead mother, the mother she had never known.

She hated Wren with every crystal tear that slid down her cheek and then hated him for making her cry even as her tears dried on the pillow. She hated the friends she had never made and the nights like tonight when she could not go out and would have had nowhere to go even if she could. She hated the studying she was forced to do. Most of all she hated her inability to simply *finish* the work and get it over with. And here she was with only a crumpled drawing to remind her of her butterfly.

Crying was not something she did often. Afterward she would feel clean and airy and lighter than before, but the receding tears always left behind a residue of shame. She dried her cheeks, rubbed her puffy eyes, and began to even her breathing.

Get a hold of yourself, Kayla.

She sat upright on the side of her bed and confronted her thoughts.

As far as she was concerned, *mother* was nothing more than a meaningless word. For as long as she could remember, Wren had been her only parent. She had no recollection of anyone else. Everything she knew had been fitted together from her father's vague allusions, accounts of a bright-eyed woman brimming with laughter, a woman who had been strong and courageous, too. But his descriptions never went far beyond that. Whenever the subject was brought up, Wren began to lose control of his rough, opaque composure. He had never broken down in front of Kayla, and she strongly doubted he ever would, but once long before, in the dead of night, her ear pressed against the door to his room, she had heard him sobbing and calling out to Lori in vain.

She wished more than anything else for stories of her mother, but Wren kept them locked deep within himself, too.

He seemed to enjoy imprisoning things, Kayla thought. She enjoyed spending time with teenagers when she explored the city during the day, but because of her home schooling and Wren's strict rules, truly close friends remained the stuff of legend.

Although his intentions were probably good, she knew intentions were harmful when misguided, and his were causing her constant hurt. Perhaps she would have been more interested in studying if he had allowed her to attend school with other children like a normal parent. The problem lay in the fact that Wren was far from normal. *Why is he so strange?*

But there was still the labyrinth, and she decided it was high time she got going.

As she left her melancholy behind on the rumpled sheets, her anger flared once again and Kayla left the bedroom. Since she had no friends to enjoy, she would make her own fun. *As for staying home, I'll listen to you when you can act like an authority figure, Father.*

She walked to the stairs, stuck out her tongue as she passed the door to Wren's room, grabbed a lantern sitting on the top of the balustrade—the labyrinth, ever unused and unlighted, was darker than the blackest inks—and descended down the steps in a sphere of wobbling light.

Down on the ground floor, she passed through her home's entryway.

Large leather chairs and overstuffed couches bulged from the floor. A small blaze crackled in the stone fireplace.

She stopped in spite of herself.

There, above the spitting logs and dancing flames, hung her father's sword. Despite her anger, she could not help staring at the weapon. It was magnificent. The obsidian cross-hilt locked into an ivory sheath that gleamed in the firelight like a portal to adventure. As far as she could remember, that sword had always been there. Where had it come from, and to what distant lands had it traveled while strapped to Wren's side?

Had it ever tasted blood?

Lost in conflicting thoughts of resentment and curiosity, she forced herself from the room.

She passed the study, resisting the urge to search for clues among Wren's maps and instruments, and walked into the kitchen. She opened a door by a pantry that led to a small room and a smaller set of steps.

Kayla crept down carefully, holding her lantern before her, flinching as the rotting wood creaked underfoot. Hair netted with cobwebs, she entered the wine cellar. Wine racks stood against the walls like wooden honeycombs stuffed with glass bottle bees. Flasks, herbs, and gourdlike jugs hung suspended by ropes and cords from the low timber ceiling. Five giant barrels were stacked horizontally on an iron brace by the far wall. Four were swimming with her father's red drink; the fifth led to the labyrinth. She had learned long ago which one to take.

Kayla stepped carefully though the dusty maze of glass and wood. Wren had a talent for observing anything out of place, and she did not intend to leave him any sign that she had been there. She was sure he knew about the secret path—he probably had found it on the day he had moved in with her, back when she was still a baby—but she doubted whether he had any use for it. One thing was certain: If he ever discovered these secret journeys, she would be punished severely— much more so than she had been for her neglected studies—and the passage would be permanently sealed.

She reached the center cask, placed her lamp on the floor, and rotated the false tap until she heard a click. Then, excitement mounting, she pulled on the barrel's face. It swung open. Lifting her light, she crawled into the barrel, pausing only to fit the circular cover back into place behind her. Holding the flame before her eyes, she pushed on the barrel's back end, revealing a narrow stone corridor that disappeared into darkness. She clambered out of the cask, took a moment to dust off her clothing, and walked into the labyrinth.

The smells of wine and wood faded. A stale odor of dusty decay hung in the air. Her light banished the gloom, but as always, there was little to be revealed. The walls and floor of the passage were lined with smooth gray stones. Iron torch holders jutted from the walls, but they were empty. Pale spiderwebs clung to the ceiling like tattered cotton lace.

She moved down the passage, avoiding the sticky spider-spun strands whenever possible. When she arrived at the path's first split, the tunnel to the left looped away at a gentle decline, heading for the sea. She seldom chose that route, as only a short walk would take her to a section of the maze that was riddled with hundreds of side entrances and exits that branched from the main passage with greater and greater frequency like limbs on a hollow tree. That area, she guessed, lay directly beneath the heart of Nautalia. Although she was practiced at remembering her movements, the horrifying prospect of losing her way always scratched at the back of her mind when she was in the labyrinth. It would be a terrible end: running through endless stone tunnels, wide-eyed, desperate, frantically trying to find the surface until her lamp went out and she was swallowed in darkness.

She shuddered and took the right-hand route.

The passages themselves were boring enough; she used them only as a means of traveling to places she wanted to visit. As far as she knew, the tomblike latticework of corridors spread beneath the whole of Nautalia. If it were not for her fear of losing her way, she would have the entire city at her fingertips. And Wren had no idea. She laughed and then considered where she might go tonight.

There was the Seashell Square Market, but it was late and the merchants would be closing their shops and leaving their trading stalls. The Rattlechain Pens could be exciting, especially if beasts had been brought from the Summerset Isles, but a rough crowd visited the pens—scores of drunks and gamblers—and Kayla knew her father might show up. He had been there many times before. *He's probably still at Kendran's, but it's not worth the risk.*

Then her thoughts turned to Coral Castle, and she realized she had not been there in weeks. *I could come up in the storeroom and sneak over toward the drawing room—not for the scribes and quills and stupid books but the paintings and maps . . .* It sounded like an excellent plan.

Nautalia's Royal Castle was a thirty-minute walk from her house by way of the streets. Running through the labyrinth, she made it there in ten.

* * *

THE TRAPDOOR SWUNG back grudgingly with a squeal of rusted joints, each of its metal clasps voicing its displeasure at being forced to move. A slender arm and a glass lamp slid through the opening. Light washed across a wooden floor. Blond hair bobbed into view. It was followed by a pair of large blue eyes that peered suspiciously over the edge of the trapdoor. The storeroom was empty.

Two thin eyebrows arched with relief.

Kayla scrambled the rest of the way out of the labyrinth, took a quick look around, and smiled a slightly guilty smile; she was inside the castle. She crouched between a desk and a barrel, making sure the room was empty.

She had never gone far beyond the drawing room. Guards patrolled the corridors, tower stairways, audience halls, and barracks, and just about every other chamber within the castle walls. She had been questioned when she had come here before—and had escaped trouble by feigning ignorance, pretending to be a serving girl—but she did not want to tempt fate by provoking the wrong soldier into a lengthy evaluation of her name and station.

Kayla had only to walk out the door before her and climb up a narrow set of steps. There would be scribes and teachers in the nearby library, perhaps even the High King's magician browsing through the thousands of books on the shelves, but they would be absorbed in their searches. No one would pay much attention to a single girl.

She eased her way along a floor littered with papers, quills, and books in varying states of disrepair. She reached the door to the drawing room, gathered her composure, pushed it open, and slipped inside.

Blue and red light streamed through a row of arching stained-glass windows on the western side of the room. The beams fell on the floor, illuminating a vast mosaic of Ellynrie. Maps of the Nautalian Kingdom stretched across the walls, interspersed with detailed sketches of Vanguard and Tradesmeet, painted cities shining in the colored light. Kayla moved from map to map, pausing at one of the Summerset Isles, then walking over a representation of the Sea of Dreams, that vast, barren desert bordering the northernmost reaches of the kingdom.

As she walked around the room, she began hearing unfamiliar noises coming through the library door: muffled shouts and screams. Immediately she thought of her father—of his sword above the mantel and then of him crumpling up her picture. Without another thought, Kayla crept to the door and cracked it open.

Her eyes widened in horror. She pressed a hand to her lips, barely stifling a scream.

Scholars and servants swarmed over the library's white carpet, which had been stained crimson. Bodies were strewn everywhere like rag dolls. Robed tutors, balding scribes, even a priest in temple finery—all lay sprawled in the grip of death, in pairs or alone, their limbs splayed in every direction, their faces contorted in masks of fear and pain.

Along the walls, statues of trumpeting sea horses seemed to blow blasts of warning at the carnage before them. Everywhere the shouts of the living fell on the ears of the dead.

Fighting down a wave of nausea, Kayla picked her way through the gore. New corpses came into view as she moved among the library shelves. Each step or turn of her head added to the disgusting nightmare, one from which she could not wake. *Ariel save me, what happened here?*

Still she moved farther into the room, driven by a strange curiosity, until she heard two voices, one a whisper and the other a weak groan.

"Is this the dagger?" said the whispering voice. "The one named Exilon? Tell me and I will spare your life."

"May the Sea God blast you from Ellynrie and drown your black heart beneath the Starlight Sea."

Kayla pressed herself against a bookshelf, listening. Something dripped on her shoulder, and she turned her head. A trickle of blood was running down the shelf of books, a tiny red brook flowing in a streambed of leather-bound rocks. She heard a blow and a moan.

"How does that feel, old man?" the whisperer taunted. "Shall I chop off any more fingers?"

"Enough . . . please . . ." There was a sob. "It is the dagger you seek."

There was a thud, then silence.

Suddenly a dark silhouette moved past Kayla. She held herself perfectly still against the bookshelf. The man's face was scarred, and his cloak was as dark as ink. A naked sword swung at his waist. As he swept past, he plunged something into the folds of his tunic and lifted a hood over his face, then disappeared into the drawing room, leaving the chaos of the library.

Barely aware of her own actions, Kayla followed and watched as he passed through beams of blue and red light, treading over the mosaic of the world. He strode into the storeroom. The trapdoor slammed shut over the labyrinth.

Kayla hesitated for only a moment and then began to follow him.

A Father's Fated Quest

ALL TRACE OF the Seasong Arms had utterly vanished.

Wren burst into an insane landscape where he was inexplicably blasted by wind and spray and engulfed in spouts of foam. Rain lashed him from every direction as he twisted and turned below a boiling mass of dark water, trying to get his bearings. As he oriented himself, he realized that the water was directly *beneath* him. He was skimming arrowlike across its surface. He was not turning at all; he had been confused by the swarming clouds and the ocean's churning waters. It *was* the ocean, he was sure, for the waves crashed and fell like thrashing beasts, and every horizon stretched onward into gray oblivion. The world, though still bewildering, began to take on meaning. He was *flying* through a storm at sea.

Then, as this impossible new discovery nearly overwhelmed his senses, the clouds began lightening, rolling away. The rain stopped, and the winds slowed. As he shot forward, he could see a beach. The waves grew calmer—if no less murky—and his clothing began drying at an astonishing rate. Land rushed up to meet him until he tumbled onto the beach like a washed-up sailor.

Wren picked himself up slowly. Down the beach to his right, a crystal observatory rose from the dunes. With a jolt he realized where he was. An instant later the wizard Dale appeared and stood before him. Wren knew his time had come.

"It's been too long," Dale said, and his gray eyes glittered.

"Hasn't been long enough," Wren said. "What in Ariel's name did you just put me through?"

Dale had aged since last Wren had seen him. His hair was still as black as jet, but wrinkles had begun to line his sharp, angular face. "I didn't want there to be any illusions. This time it will be much more difficult."

"Damn your illusions!" Wren shouted. "Come on, out with it. Tell me why I'm here!"

Far out to sea, thunder rumbled among the clouds. Dale did not respond at once, and both men fell silent. The air was lighter now and moving with a sea breeze. Tension lay between them like a quivering chord; if it broke, Wren sensed that a new storm would rise up on the beach around them.

"You know why you are here," the wizard replied. "I've summoned you to fulfill the debt you owe."

The clouds blanketed the heavens in a funereal cloth. In the half-light Dale stood like a creature of the sea, clothed in garments of pearl and blue, his long black hair snapping bannerlike in the wind.

He raised an arm and pointed at the ocean. "Look back the way you came. That is what I will be sending you into again. You will guard the boy until I can decide how to protect him from those who wish to use his power to end what has begun. Even now there are enemies searching for his home, drawing closer with each passing hour. I will not give you more details here. There are those about who listen and scheme. There are shadows within shadows. You must journey north along the Seaspine Coast to my home, this cottage by the ocean. You'll remember how to find me. Pack quickly, and don't forget your sword. I'll wait for you here."

"Why now?" Wren demanded. "Why, after all these years, when I've finally settled down and found some measure of peace? I have a daughter, Dale. You know that. What would you have me do? Leave the only child I had with Lori to go tromping around on some mad quest? I'm through with that life. The old Wren is dead; he died with his wife. I've seen firsthand what happens when adventure meets those I love. There's no way I'll ever forget. Have you?"

"Our pact is irrevocably sealed. Take some consolation from the fact that your actions here will have a lasting impact on the fortunes of our world. The fate of good and evil may hinge upon the success of your task, for I have seen a great darkness rising. If you should fail here and let the boy come to harm, I fear there shall be none who can prevent this world from falling into eternal shadow."

Wren listened quietly, feeling like a marionette whose limbs were under the control of a sinister puppeteer. Tears welled in his eyes as he thought of the daughter he would soon leave behind. He knew there was no way he could refuse the wizard. The bond between them had been sealed by word and blood, and Dale *had* helped him to avenge Lori's murder . . . even though it was their involvement that had first put her in jeopardy. *Kayla, I'm so sorry.*

He raised his head and looked Dale in the eye. "Although I am bound to do this, don't mistake me for some fool. Until I finish the job, you can dangle me from your strings all you want, but I'm doing this for my own sake, not some damned knight-errant illusion."

"Don't you remember what friends we once were?" asked Dale. "I cared for Lori, too."

Wren clenched his teeth and turned his back on the wizard. "That won't bring her back. We're finished here. The sooner I start, the sooner I can sever my connections with you forever."

The wind rose again, stirring the sand at his feet. Hundreds of pink and golden grains floated upward and swirled about him. His medallion began throbbing again as his surroundings bled into a meaningless haze.

Dale's voice came to him as if from across a chasm. "In the days ahead we all will need to make sacrifices . . . Good luck to you. May we meet again under sunnier skies . . ."

Then the wizard's voice was gone, and Wren began hearing whispers and murmurs, which were growing louder . . .

"By Ariel, I think he's dead."

"Not in my lifetime. Wren's tougher than that!"

"Then what the hell's wrong with him?"

"Fainted?"

"First the sightings of a dragon, then the tales brought by those blasted messengers, and now this."

"Wait, I just saw his eye twitch!"

Wren's head seemed to roar and crash with waves. He rose from the floor, gagging like a nearly drowned man coughing up seawater, and sucked in air. *The floor . . .* He blinked as his surroundings slowly came into focus. He was back in the Seasong Arms. His friends stood all around him, gripping and shaking him, their concern turning to relief.

Wren's head ached as his senses slowly sharpened. Blood pounded through his body, sweat gathered on his brow, and his damning conversation with the wizard replayed itself with horrifying clarity. Kayla had to be told, though he knew not how he would tell her. And he knew he had to get moving, though his heart pleaded with him to reject the wizard's call and stay with his daughter inside Nautalia's sheltering walls.

He staggered to his feet. *Why now, Dale? Why now?*

Kendran grasped his shoulders and peered intently into his eyes. "Wren, what the hell happened?"

"Much more than I could ever explain . . ." He trailed off hopelessly. His friends were down-to-earth and levelheaded. They held little belief in magic or wizards and knew next to nothing about his past. They would never understand.

Flint stepped up. "You can't just lose consciousness and then expect us to be content with *that* for an explanation."

"Yeah, what's going on, Wren?" Teran asked.

Pulley frowned. "I could have sworn you had a heart attack!"

"And here you are, moments later," said Hook, "acting as if nothing had happened."

"We just want to help," Guzzler said.

Kendran tightened his grip.

Wren wished he could tell them what could hardly be explained, much less believed. And what did he know about his task himself? It involved the boy again, of that much he was certain, but Dale had not revealed much else. *If only I could tell you. If only I had someone to share this with.* But Wren was isolated and had been sworn to secrecy. Only one thought took hold of him, and it burned with a fire far greater than that which the wizard's medallion had produced.

Kayla.

"This may sound mad," Wren said slowly, "but I've got to leave Nautalia as soon as possible. Can I trust you to look after my house and watch over my daughter until I return?"

Kendran looked perplexed but nodded.

"I'll be in your debt." Wren turned to the others. "Forgive me, friends, but I must leave. Goodbye."

Kendran dropped his hands from Wren's shoulders, and the other men stepped aside as he began heading for the door. A deep sense of loss followed Wren as he walked across the floor. His past finally had caught up with him. None of his friends would look at him the same way when he returned.

If I return, he thought grimly.

As he passed the Jikari table, he glanced at the two red dice lying discarded near his chair. Each face was turned to a hideous skull, the sign of death and a signal that the caster had lost his bet. Wren smiled to himself. *I've defeated death too many times to let it claim me now. The game has only begun.*

Trying to keep his chin raised under the heavy weight of his task, he swept through the inn's entryway into the night.

It seemed he was an adventurer once again.

Demonology

DALE STOOD WITH his back to the door, hands clasped behind him, feet spread shoulder width apart, staring at the stormy ocean through one of the observatory's rain-slicked windows.

Stargazing instruments, baubles, books, crystals, and other things not so easily named were strewn across the room in disorganized piles. Tallow candles burned here and there, their flames moving like actors in a shadow play. Adriel, still reeling from his nightmare, had not the slightest idea what to think.

Pearl scampered across the floor to sit by the wizard, back ridged, her eyes as dark as the stormy night. Dale turned, his face as grave as a tombstone. "The time has come for you to complete your apprenticeship," he said.

Adriel chuckled nervously, but there was no laughter in Dale's eyes. "Have you lost your mind?"

"Be quiet and listen," Dale commanded. "I have much to say and not much time."

Lightning streaked over the ocean, momentarily vanquishing the shadows in the observatory. Star maps shone on the walls; hanging globes revolved overhead, spheres of glittering evanescence.

Dale clasped his hands behind him. "The demons I used to tell you about as a boy are very real." As he spoke, the light faded and shadows crept back into the room. "Ages ago they scoured the earth, searching for souls to corrupt. They were once celestial spirits crafted by Lira, Ariel, and the nameless God of the Air, spirits who traveled the world's four quarters, in streams and oceans, in forests and caves, to help it flourish and grow. But Apollyon, their leader, grew vain in his power and sought to place himself among the gods that created him, coveting their rule. He gathered an army of spirits about him and brought forth his demands with flaming swords and spears. Thus was there war in heaven. It was a war of celestial Armageddon, but the three gods defeated Apollyon and cast him, along with all those who had flocked to his wicked banner, deep under the earth, away from all that was good in our world. The demons plummeted like falling stars. They still abide in Ellynrie, imprisoned underground, but they strive to rise again to wreak havoc throughout creation."

"You have told me some of this before," Adriel said, "but I had thought the demons long dead, specters of a time beyond memory, idle playthings to stir a child's blood at bedtime."

"I wish that were the case . . . I wish they were confined to the pages of a fairy tale. But they are not. With Marian's aid, I have discovered many things to which I was blind before, but even without her hints I had begun noticing unnatural changes in the landscape."

Adriel remembered the soundless shell he had discovered by the shore, the winged shadow that had flown overhead, and a chill sped down his spine.

"The causes of these changes are becoming clearer to me," Dale said, as another bolt of lightning burst across the sky. "As the demons beneath the earth struggle to rise, the ground above them begins to change: rotting, decaying, exhibiting unnatural characteristics."

"That can't be possible."

Dale ran a hand through his tangled black hair. "Man cannot imagine all the terrors of his world."

Adriel shivered. "What's happening?"

Dale crouched next to Pearl, mussing the fur between her ears. "Long ago, a demon escaped and moved across the land, leaving desolation in its wake. Knowing that the people of Ellynrie would need to defend themselves from this evil, the three gods crafted a dagger fused with divine magic and called it Exilon."

"What does it mean?"

Dale stood and began pacing. "The name comes from a long-dead language once spoken in the Summerset Isles; it's translated as 'demon bane.' The dagger was sent down to earth to be used in the event a demon was able to rise once more. It can be used to seal the demons' prison by reestablishing the barrier that keeps them under the earth. A man has found an occult secret, a way to reverse the magic of Exilon and use it to unseal the barriers. He wants to raise a certain demon, one he has particular cause to hate, so that he can destroy it."

Adriel's senses were reeling. "But where is the dagger?"

"Before I brought you under my roof, I took it from the Coven, a group of witches and creatures who have roamed this world since the fall of the demons; they are humans who have been twisted and ensnared by their dark masters. They had gained control of the dagger and were using it to summon one of the demons. Once I had the dagger, I left it with a friend in Nautalia, where it's now been kept for many years, locked somewhere deep inside the castle."

"Has this man found it?"

"I fear the worst."

"But who would do such a thing?"

Dale stopped pacing and turned back to the window. "The Coven sought to raise the demon near a forested village to the north. The demon, called up by a witch, began to rise. Only a very few managed to escape, and I was one of them. A mercenary named Wren fled with me and his wife, Lori, and a boy whose parents were killed by creatures of the Coven, Corin Starcross. I left Corin with his uncle Pyke in Merrifield, but he had an older brother named Cade, who I did not know had survived until recently.

"Cade has long studied the dark arts. It is he who is trying to raise Apollyon, the greatest demon of all, so he can destroy that which slew his parents. His goal is to vanquish a great evil, but he does not see—or does not care—that the task he has set for himself may claim many innocent lives. He has become so twisted by his hatred that he is willing to risk everything to slake his thirst for revenge. If he raises this demon, it will rage across the land, swallowing everything in its path.

"You, Adriel, must protect Corin at all costs. Cade is relentlessly searching for his brother so that he can use him to raise the demon. He needs Corin's blood to complete the summoning, as the black magic used to reverse the Exilon's magic and free a demon will work only when a sorcerer sacrifices the blood of a sibling. This sacrifice, smeared on the blade of the dagger, is what we must prevent. I believe that Cade has already obtained the dagger with the aid of his apprentice, Damon, and that a small army of hired assassins and thugs is even now searching for his brother."

Dale turned toward Adriel once more, his eyes harder than iron. "When people look for evil, it is never far away. Filled with a burning desire for revenge, Cade found it quickly. He discovered an Aurian wizard named Blaze and entered into a damning apprenticeship. Cade learned all he could and killed his master. Now he has an apprentice of his own. Together they've gathered a small army of servants that is searching for the boy even now. We must stop him; if we do not, our world will fall into darkness."

"But I'm not ready for this," Adriel said. "I know hardly anything of wizardry."

"I don't know if you're ready, but because of the impending danger, I need you to come into your own, become a wizard, and protect the boy. You must pass through the Seaspine Mountains by way of the village of Bridgewater. If you leave tonight, you should arrive on

Woolthread Road by midday tomorrow. Travel to Merrifield and the Spinribbon Fair. Corin lives there with his uncle Pyke. You should be able to identify Corin by his limp, a remnant of his childhood encounter with the Coven in the village and by his curly blond hair."

"You're not coming with me?"

Dale smiled sadly. "Cade wants me dead. He knows that I might interfere with his plans, and his apprentice is likely already on his way here to deal with me. I will wait for him and defeat him if I can, but should I fail, I'll at least have drawn him away from Corin. The protection of the boy is the highest priority. The time has come for you to learn the truth of a wizard's power.

"Men have forgotten the magic in the world. Most gain glimpses of it from time to time, as when a mountain traveler breathes in the crisp, chill air and chances to see a wilderness sunrise that dawns like a fiery lance on the horizon. Or when a village boy, filled with hopeful expectation, walks to the top of a hill that he has never climbed before and looks out on a wide world that he never dreamed lay beyond his mother's doorstep. But these people seldom retain any sense of wonder or enchantment. Such moments are lost like cloud-covered stars among the deep folds of their memories."

Adriel glanced at the ground. "I've not lost faith. I've seen you use magic. You've proved that it exists. But I know I can't wield it as you do."

"The belief in magic is only half the battle. To *use* magic, a wizard must feel its presence and act on that feeling. First one must feel the desire, then have the will to learn, and finally have the patience to acquire the knowledge itself. When the student finally reaches true understanding—as you must now—he has only one more hurdle to cross before he can be given his staff. This hurdle, Adriel, is the ability to draw magic and cast it by means of love or hate."

"Please, Dale, slow down. I *don't* understand, at least not in the way you think I do. How can love or hate conjure up magic?"

"Magic is the divine power that keeps the world in order. Humans are a central part of the gods' creation, gifted with the ability to wield this magic—and the freedom to choose between love and hate. With these gifts they have been trusted to be caretakers of the world."

"But why would anyone choose hate?"

"Think of your own parents. What would you feel toward those who murdered your mother and father if you ever chanced to meet them? What do all men feel who have been severely hurt? Anger at a universe absurd enough to wrong them."

Adriel nodded slowly.

"I've kept you from gaining your staff until I thought you ready to use magic wisely: for good rather than evil, for love rather than vengeance. The man from whom you must protect Corin is exacting his revenge. His intentions, though initially good, were tragically misguided, and his hatred has festered and grown until it has consumed him and cast him into darkness. He is heedless of the consequences his plan will inflict on the world. Unfortunately, my lack of foresight has left very little time for me to explain any of this to you now. The one who would bring destruction on us all for the sake of personal revenge is coming dangerously close to fulfilling his plan."

Dale turned to the shelf on his right and opened a long, narrow box. He withdrew a spearlike rod as white as freshly fallen snow and a thin chain necklace on which hung an interwoven symbol of the three gods. The staff ended in a gnarled tip inset with a sapphire. The medallion sparkled silver.

"Take these," Dale said, handing over the staff and the necklace. "I've been saving them for you. You're ready to use true magic now. Do not be frustrated if your first attempts meet with failure. Your ability will come soon enough. You have the knowledge. You have the staff. And I hope for the sake of the world that you have the strength to choose what's right."

Adriel ran his hands along the staff and touched the icon's carved figures. "I'm afraid, Dale. I'm afraid that I will be unable to use the power when I need it most." He lowered his voice. "I'm afraid of doing this alone."

"There will be plenty to be frightened of on the road ahead, but that last thing, at least, you need not fear." Dale crossed his arms. "I will be sending Wren Tident, the mercenary who escaped from the witches all those years ago; he's a skilled fighter and a good man. Don't let his harshness deter your trust; his life has been hard. He should be a day behind you. Look for him in an inn called Rookery Rest. You'll know him by his medallion; it's identical to the one around your neck."

Adriel felt like an actor caught up in a devastating tragedy, one he had not rehearsed for, one for which he had not prepared. He wished he had a script to follow.

Dale said, "Before you go, remember this. Men who understand the wonder in the world do not have to wield magic to be wizards in their own right. You have been a wizard from the moment you first believed and decided to use your belief to go and change the world. Guard the boy until you hear from me. Good luck. Farewell. Go in the grace of the gods."

Adriel embraced his master one last time, nearly numb with fear, then strode from the observatory, staff in hand, and went to his room to find his coral flute. *I'll need the music,* he thought. Pearl watched him go.

The home's front door stood like a final barrier guarding Adriel from all the dark things in the world. Gritting his teeth, he grabbed his cloak from a rack by the door, hoisted a pack of food on his back, and walked away from the only home he had ever known into the stormy night.

TOMBS IN THE TWILIGHT

THE CLOAKED MAN'S footsteps grew fainter.

Kayla knew that if she did not make her mind up quickly, his steps would soon stop reverberating off the walls of the labyrinth altogether. Then she would be left alone again and would never discover why those people in the castle had been murdered.

Although leaving that question unanswered would probably be the sanest decision I've ever made, she considered, but quickly wiped the thought from her mind.

She hesitated at the first juncture she came to. She knew she could take the left-hand passage, following the familiar twists and turns home, but a small voice in a corner of her mind told her this was a once-in-a lifetime event that she would be a fool to miss. Her pulse beat wildly. *Back to books, bed, and a drunken father? It's about time I had an adventure.*

There were also the corpses to consider, and she being their only witness. Their blood had stained her; their faces had been burned into her mind. If she did not get to the bottom of the thief's actions, she feared she would never sleep again.

Pushing aside her fears and ignoring her better judgment, Kayla hurried after the thief's swaying black cloak. Her steps were soft and quick, and she quieted the flame in her lamp until she was a wraith in the dimmest of lights. She walked briskly, concentrating on the harsh thudding of his boots for direction, and kept careful track of the turns she took. In this unfamiliar territory, she could easily get lost should she forget the way back.

The thief seemed to know where he was going. He navigated the labyrinth as if tugged by manacles.

After several minutes the stone corridor gave way to a narrow clay tunnel. The walls, glistening with moisture, smelled of damp, moldy earth. Kayla realized she was in a part of the labyrinth she had never been in before; it seemed much older than the rest. Hieroglyphics and colored symbols surrounded her. There was a mosaic of Eastwatch Clock Tower, strong, old, and proud, but a knotted red vine had pushed through the spongy floor of the labyrinth and crawled halfway up the tower. On another occasion Kayla would have stopped to examine the mosaic, but the pursuit of her quarry had taken precedence over everything else.

What could be so important about the dagger that the thief had been willing to murder those scribes to obtain it? She had to find out.

The thief halted in front of a narrow opening in the side of the tunnel and extinguished his lamp. A red beam of light spilled from the opening onto the tunnel floor, illuminating his face: it was black-skinned and scarred. He held up a compass and examined it with hooded eyes, then lowered it and went inside.

Kayla followed him to the entryway. A scratching sounded from within the chamber. There was a grunt, and the scratching stopped. Kayla peered nervously around the wall.

The beam of red light filtered down from a fissure in the labyrinth's ceiling, pooling on the floor like a puddle of blood. Steps were wedged like a ladder into the chamber's far wall, rising toward the fissure. Kayla smelled the sea. *You've come this far,* she thought, her blue eyes flashing. *You might as well go a little farther.* She set her lamp on the floor and walked to the steps, then scaled the wall like a lizard, her hands and feet nimble and lithe, her tongue between her lips as if to taste the salty air.

Wind blasted her body the instant she pulled herself from the labyrinth. Pushing hair from her eyes, Kayla clambered onto a steep, wild hillside. When she saw Nautalia's outer fortifications, she gasped. Banners emblazoned with a blue sea horse on a purple and silver field rippled atop the battlements of the city wall. The spires of Coral Castle flamed in the sunset, and at the castle's center, the Nautical Tower of the High King shone like a pearl spear.

"How did I get here?" Kayla whispered.

Cultivated hills rose around her, smaller and smoother than the one on which she stood. Her hill was barren, but the others were lush with growing things, home to orchards of orange trees and olive groves, sweeping arbors of grapes, and terraced rows of pomegranates. A sprawling home or winery topped each hill, and a latticework of pasture walls crisscrossed the dips between them. The scene was bathed in a swath of dying light.

Kayla quickly gathered herself and searched for the thief. The remains of what must once have been a wealthy man's house rested at the top of her hill. Dozens of half-buried stones studded the ground near the building. Kayla could just see the thief—hardly more than a swirl of cloth and shadow—as he picked through the bulky rocks, passing from her sight into the ruins.

She began following him once again, keeping low in the grass. Her spine tingled apprehensively. She knew what would happen if she was discovered; that fate did not require much imagination. An image of the slaughtered scribes in the castle library—silk robes stained red, faces contorted in fear and pain, bodies slumped on top of one another, lying in heaps on the blood-soaked carpet—emerged before her eyes. She pushed it away with a shudder.

It was not until she was among the stones that she realized they were tombs. Many were covered in withered flowers, wreaths and garlands, or faded bows. On each one was written an inscription: a name, a message, and a date of death. Glancing at the stone-wrought words, Kayla gathered that a disease, taking them one by one, had sent every member of this once noble house to rest beneath these still and silent markers. The house had died with the family; its corpse was in a state of decay.

She drew near a crumbling wall and paused by a broken arch to listen for the thief. After several seconds she heard a voice. "Do you have the dagger?" The icy words carried an accent Kayla had never heard before, and that was unsettling. Nautalia hosted people from every land in the world of Ellynrie, but Kayla had never heard someone speak as this man did.

"Is this the blade?" It was the thief.

There was a pause.

"Excellent work," said the icy voice. "You did your job well. How many did you have to kill?"

"I didn't count."

"I thought assassins kept track of that sort of thing."

"This was thievery. The only killings that took place were carried out against helpless scribes. I take no pride in that."

"A hired killer with pride?" the icy voice asked.

"I'm skilled at what I do."

"I hope you're ready to use your skills again. There's someone in the city I need you to kill."

Silence settled between the speakers, punctured only by breathing. Kayla could hear her heart beating. *What am I getting myself into?*

"I did my job, Damon." The assassin's voice was harsh. "Pay me and I'll be on my way."

"My master will not be pleased to hear of your uncooperative attitude."

"But our agreement—"

"And you can be sure I will tell him."

"Bastard."

"Careful with your curses," said the man named Damon. "They may come back to curse *you.*"

Kayla shifted forward, pricking her ears.

"What must I do?"

"Go to the house marked on your map. Lackey and Scratch, the two men I introduced to you earlier, should have dispatched their target by now, but I want you to visit the place nonetheless. The man living there might prove difficult to deal with. Lackey and Scratch aren't exactly professionals. Nothing of *your* caliber."

"You can be sure of that," said the assassin. "Who else could have stolen the Exilon straight from Coral Castle? Not you. If you had the means, you would have done it yourself."

"A tone like that can be a dangerous thing when used with the wrong person," Damon said darkly. "As I've said before, my magic will not work inside the city. Enchantments older than any living memory rest within those walls, and I'm not eager to encounter them."

"Yes, cast millennia ago."

"The Aurians have all but died out, and the gods are *nothing.* They have never smiled on either of us. They do not care for mortals. Finish this last assignment. I am losing patience. My magic may be useless inside Nautalia, but we are not standing in Nautalia now." The man named Damon chuckled grimly.

"My partner and I are the best. We won't fail."

Silence replaced the voices. Kayla scurried behind a tombstone and pushed herself tight to the ground. Footsteps sounded nearby. They halted for a moment as if in wary investigation, then began again, quicker than before. Kayla peeked around the grave marker.

The assassin was striding toward the city. His cloak billowed out behind him, and his hood was pulled over his head. It looked as though he would not be using the labyrinth again. *He must only know the passage from the castle to these ruins,* she thought.

She did not know where Damon had gone, the man with the strange accent who had spoken of demons and enchantments. No one else emerged from the house, and after a few moments Kayla left the tombstone and made her way swiftly down the hill. There was no chance of following the assassin undetected, for the path he walked offered no concealment.

She returned to the fissure at the base of the hill, swung her feet over the edge, and climbed into the labyrinth. Once safely inside, she picked up her lamp and ran as fast as she could. *I've seen and heard enough to last me a lifetime,* she told herself, her light swinging wildly. *What was I thinking? I could have been killed, murdered like the castle scribes and those poor people the assassin is going to find . . .*

Driven by fear, miraculously remembering the turns she had taken, she raced toward home.

* * *

AFTER WHAT SEEMED like an eternity, Kayla found herself back in the empty wine barrel, shoving her shoulder against its false front. It swung open with a recalcitrant squeal, welcoming her with the familiar smells of fermenting wine and decayed wood. She crawled through, dropped to the cellar floor, and quickly lifted her light high above her head. Her nerves jumped as she surveyed the room.

Contorted shadows swayed away from the barrels on the floor and slanted from ceiling flasks in odd hourglass curves. They twisted, wobbling like pagan dancers around a midnight bonfire. Or like hooded assassins, dancing the dance of death, knives held high above a hapless victim.

Kayla started to shiver, but she shrugged it off in annoyance. "You're only a trick of the light," she told them, her words echoing off the quiet walls. "I've seen worse than you tonight."

Shadows could not hurt her—she was finally home. She was safe.

Even so, she would feel better resting under her thick, warm covers. Once Wren returned from the Seasong Arms, she would know he was watching over her from his room across the hall.

She hung the lamp on a rafter and shook the dust from her clothes.

Almost impercebtibly, the sound of rustling cloth invaded the room's stillness. Kayla righted herself, suddenly feeling alone and afraid. The silence pressed in around her, thick and heavy, but the shadows had not moved.

Something else had.

An instant later she felt a sharp pain on the back of her head, and then she felt no more.

INTRUDERS

THE SEASONG ARMS lay far behind; Wren was drawing near his home.

Lamps and candles had been lit in many of the windows along the street. The lights flickered in the forest of towers, homes, shops, and inns like a mocking swarm of fireflies. Rising before a hidden ocean, Coral Castle spiraled above the wall of roofs and chimneys to his right. Ordinarily Wren would have thought the sight majestic, but now, before his sorrowful gaze, it was reduced to little more than a hollow husk of stone. A pallid moon was cradled between a twin pair of the castle's towers. Covered in star shadow, ending in conical points, the towers looked as blue and sharp as icicles. For a moment Wren wondered how they refrained from melting among the buildings and alleys clustered about their base. He wished they could. Perhaps the flood would wash away his pain.

While he walked from the Merchant Quarter to his house, a string of memories tightened about him like gallows rope.

There was a memory from his childhood, an excruciating image of

Dirk dying in Lantern Watch, unloved by anyone but his young son, on a hard wooden bed in the attic of a ramshackle inn. His father's face had been beaten to a bloody pulp, and his body had been slashed by jagged knives. Wren remembered holding his hands against his father's wounds, trying to stop the bleeding, weeping as his father drifted toward death.

Then came a memory of Lori, his wife. She sat on a sill, watching the ocean through one of the seaward windows of their cottage. Sunlight dappled her lashes and gathered in eyes as green as the sea. Until he had met her, he had drifted along like a weather vane, allowing fate to blow him where it would, accepting changes in life's direction with reckless abandon, much as Dirk had. He had lived an existence without purpose in which north, south, east, and west were each and all the same.

But Lori had given him a valuable gift: someone else to live for.

The memory changed. Lori lay in a pool of blood among the trampled sunflowers and splintered lemon trees of their garden. He had just sat for a moment atop his horse, baby Kayla on the saddle in front of him, his hands pressed over her eyes, as he tried to make sense of the scene before him. The burning cottage looked strange: Fire and water never mix. His tears had distorted the flames.

Then he thought of Kayla, the light of his life. She looked so much like her mother with her golden hair, her deep blue eyes, her slender figure, and her sun-browned skin. But she acted so much like him: strong-willed, with a heart of fire and a desire for adventure.

Adventure! He spit on the word. What would happen to her if he were not around to protect her? What would happen to him if *she*—

"No," he said, speaking aloud to the street. "She will remain safe while I still have life and breath."

But the firefly window lights twinkled back in taunting laughter.

He rounded the street corner and caught sight of his home.

A lantern lay on the ground below a shattered window. The lantern had burst; shards of glass surrounded its twisted iron frame. The front door creaked back and forth on broken hinges. Time slowed to a deadly crawl, and someone began to yell.

A girl was shouting—shouting *his* name.

Not *a* girl, *his* girl.

It was Kayla.

He reached the door in a matter of seconds, bounded up the steps, and hurled himself inside.

Kayla's cries stopped the moment he entered the house.

The hearth fire had been extinguished; the entranceway was dark, and all the furniture was draped in shadow. In the dim light he could see that the couches and chairs were ripped. The floor was strewn with shreds of cloth and clumps of cotton. It looked as if someone had sliced at them with a butcher knife.

Wren's senses instantly sharpened. His fighting instinct took over, and his body became poised, his eyes alert. His hands curled tightly into fists.

A shape detached itself from the hallway and moved into the room. It was cloaked and hooded, and it was holding a sword. *His* sword. Wren's eyes flicked above the fireplace, confirming what he already knew; his blade was in the other's hands.

The darkly clad figure spoke. "So this is the deadly mercenary, the one called Wren. We knew you would—"

Before the intruder could finish the sentence, Wren bolted toward him. A black-gloved hand raised the sword and brought it down in a sweeping arc, but Wren spun away within a hairbreadth of the whistling metal and drove his fist hard against the other man's stomach, causing him to gasp and double up. The man tried to move back, but Wren darted forward, jerked the sword from his hands, whirled the blade around, and drove it through the intruder's chest in a single motion. The man struggled to scream, but his voice was lost in a gurgling fountain of blood.

He died quickly.

The body slid from his sword with sickening ease, but Wren paid it little attention. He stepped lightly over the dead man and moved deeper into the house, his eyes riveted on the blackness before him, the tip of his sword making small circles in the air before his face.

The study, the kitchen, the wine cellar, and the remainder of the first floor were all empty, but the rooms had been ransacked. Wren started up the stairs, each step creaking under his boots, his mind possessed by a cold clear rage, his heart stricken with fear for his daughter. He caught sight of a shadow moving swiftly across the top of the steps.

"Wait!" he called. "Come back!"

His cries went unheeded. The figure blended into the darkness of the bedroom corridor and vanished from his view.

Wren crept to the second floor and looked around warily. The doors to the two bedrooms were shut. He crept to the first—leading to his room—and tried the handle. It turned, clicking faintly.

The door creaked inward, a thin frame of wood passing from darkness into darkness. Wren peered inside, his sword held at the ready. An overturned dresser lay on the floor. His shredded mattress looked like a corpse buried under a pile of sheets and pillows. The room was empty.

Then a floorboard creaked behind him.

Wren threw himself to the ground as something sliced through the air where his head had been half a second earlier. Acting on battle-honed instinct gained from conflicts long past, he rolled at his attacker's feet, but the other man jumped aside and slashed down with his blade. Wren slammed his sword upward, barely countering the stroke. The two blades locked together with a harsh sound. Wren shifted his weight from his shoulders to his legs and kicked out at his attacker, this time catching him off guard. The man toppled to the ground with a thud. Wren was on him in an instant, his boot crushing down on his sword arm.

"Who are you?" he roared, pressing his sword against the man's quivering throat. "Where's my daughter?"

"The name's Scratch," the pinned man stammered. "I don't know anything."

Wren stepped down harder on the man's arm. "Who else is in this house? Answer me, or when I throw you out on the street, it will be headfirst."

"The sorcerer isn't here. Besides Lackey, it's just me, you, and the girl."

"Your friend's dead in one of the rooms downstairs. Unless you want to join him, I suggest you answer my questions."

"The girl's in the other bedroom. I swear she's alive. Please, I'll leave. Just let me go."

Wren grabbed the scruff of the man's tunic and hauled him to his feet, then hurled him hard against a wall and whipped up his sword, setting the icy point of his blade on the small of the man's neck. "If I ever see you again, it will be the last time you have sight. Tell your paymaster to come and try his hand in person."

Wren slammed the flat of his blade into the man's back to send him running and went to find his daughter.

*   *   *

KAYLA WAS IN her bedroom.

She was propped against the bed, her ankles and wrists bound with a thick rope, her mouth stuffed with a dirty cloth. Wren rushed to her side, hastily removed the gag, and unfastened her bonds. He threw his arms around her, and she burst into tears.

"Oh, Kayla," he murmured, holding her tight.

"Those men broke into the house. They clubbed me in the wine cellar. One of them had a sword, and they tied me up. I screamed for you, but they gagged me. I thought we both were going to die."

Wren rocked her gently back and forth. The touch of his hands was soft, but his thoughts seethed like an angry tide.

I swore by the gods to never let my past hurt my daughter. To hell with Dale . . .

Then Wren decided to do two things: First, he would leave the house and hide with Kayla in Eastwatch Clock Tower until morning; second, at first light he would leave the city for Dale's cottage to wring some answers from the wizard. Kayla would be coming with him. Scratch or someone like him probably would be back soon, and he would not be alone. *I'd sooner throw myself into the sea than leave her here as sport for hired killers.*

Kayla pulled her cheek from his shoulder and turned toward him. "I love you," she whispered. "I'm sorry for all those times I—"

"You have nothing to be sorry for," he said, shushing her with a finger.

He gave her another squeeze, stood up and looked around the floor, then bent down and grabbed something. He returned to his daughter, holding a crumpled piece of parchment. He smoothed it carefully and placed it in her hands.

"It's beautiful," he said, and that was enough.

Kayla took one look at her father's gift and flashed a beaming smile. It was her drawing of the butterfly.

THE WATCHERS

WITH RAIN SOAKING through his clothes and mud plastered to his boots, Adriel moved closer, peering hopefully under the dripping overhang. Someone lived in the cave; that much was obvious. Orange light flickered like a pulse against the root-webbed walls. The scent of meat browning over a wood fire drifted from the tunnel, beckoning him inside, a promise of sanctuary from the storm.

Adriel would have hurried in at once, but something about the cave felt wrong.

For all his physical discomfort, he was slow to ignore these premonitions, for he now inhabited a world alongside diabolical spirits, ancient evils working to bring about a ruinous realm. Their plotting stemmed from beyond the count of years. Since the staff Dale had given him seemed little more than driftwood, he was in no hurry to meet them.

"It's already been a wonderful night," Adriel muttered sarcastically to himself, glancing up at the hill's steep slope before looking doubtfully again at the dim entrance. "But *this* . . . this could be just splendid."

Hours earlier he had been a humble wizard's apprentice, sleeping soundly—despite a somewhat unsettling dream—in a warm, safe cottage by the shore. The cottage had been left behind, but the dream still clung to him. Dale's revelations concerning demons had changed the terrors of his nightmare into a grim new reality.

Now, staff in hand and a mysterious medallion hanging from his neck, he stood before the first sign of civilization he had come across since his master had ushered him out the door. Adriel was supposed to find a boy and protect him against a sorcerer's plot to summon and slay a demon, yet he could not decide whether to explore a simple hole in a hill. Dale had named him a wizard, but wizards were supposed to be wise, not indecisive.

Adriel planted the staff in the ground, wondering if it could somehow divine what lay deeper beyond the opening. He stared at the staff, shook it, rubbed the sapphire at its tip—nothing happened. He sighed. Wet and weary, he was as helpless as a jester without jokes, and he was not sure he could even use his magic. He wiped water from his eyes, cursing the world's unfairness.

Then, casting caution to the wind, he decided to go inside.

The cave looked strange, almost hostile, but he had been treading under lightning-laced skies for several hours and was in no position to turn up his nose at a roof of any sort. If there were flames inside to warm him and good food to fill him, then despite its spooky appearance, he would risk a quick look around. He hoped the hospitality of the inhabitants would be as welcoming as the aroma of their cooking.

He shrugged his traveling pack higher up his shoulders, pulled the hood of the cloak from his head, and crossed the threshold, leaving behind the swirling morass of wind and rain. The overhead earth provided him instant relief. He wrung water from his sopping curls and started down the tunnel.

Sloping slightly downward, the passage curved and bent at odd, sharp angles, changing direction continually: a corkscrew winding into a giant earthen cork. The fireglow brightened as he continued forward, but its pulsing light seemed increasingly unpleasant. Beyond the odor of the cooking meat lingered something subtly foul, whispering in his mind like his memory of the nightmare from the night before.

After several turns, cloth hangings appeared.

They draped from the ceiling in gradually thickening rows. Each varied in size, length, and thickness; all were tattered and ripped. Gusts of wind blew in from behind Adriel, rustling the hangings before him. His boots thumped on the tunnel floor. His staff *tip-tapped* like a warning call, but he pressed on, pushing through the murky sea of cloth.

Wondering how deeply the tunnel extended and how the light of one fire could illuminate the entire length of the passage, he ducked under a particularly frayed hanging and abruptly reached the end of the cave.

The smoke hit him first. It stung his eyes and infused his nostrils with a harsh, bitter odor. The tunnel widened into a cramped hollow chamber. It seemed as though he had stepped into a withered stomach. Clay walls, thickly woven with still more roots, slanted together to form a ceiling so low that Adriel, careful to keep his hair from snagging on the clawlike roots above, had to duck as he entered the room. He coughed and looked through the vapors.

A short, wildly garbed man, his back to Adriel, was busying himself at a wooden trestle on the far wall. With his ragged clothes and unkempt hair, he resembled some sort of hermit. His arms rose and fell in brief, hard chops. Sounds of scraping and cutting filled the smoky air.

Adriel cleared his throat, but the man did not turn.

Waiting for him to finish his work, Adriel glanced around. It was easy to believe the man made his home there; the chamber looked like a grotesque mockery of a hermitage. Rough-hewn shelves lined the walls, filled with an odd assortment of items: pieces of rope, clothing, bits of cloth, oddly shaped stones and rocks, dusty jars, and broken fragments of crockery. There were weirdly shaped bottles full of colored powders and liquids. Gutted animals hung from the ceiling: several pheasants, a boar's head, and the upper half of a deer. The fire burned from a ring of stones in the center of the floor. Flames scattered shadows about the room, moving across the walls and ceiling in a doppel-gänger dance of light and dark.

Adriel turned back to the hermit, watching him work for a moment longer, and then cleared his throat, more loudly than before. The hermit did not respond. Was the man deaf, or was he choosing to ignore him?

"Hello," called Adriel. The hermit's hands paused. He straightened but continued to face the far wall. "Sorry to bother you, but I was on the road to Bridgewater when this blasted storm set in. I'm hoping to wait out the wind and rain in this cave. Would you mind my company?"

"I hear you," the hermit said. "I hear you now as I heard you tread-ing under earth and stone. Come. Come farther in." His voice whistled like a cracked flute. "Come sit down, there by the fire. The flames are eager for company. Take off your cloak and make yourself warm. Food is almost ready."

Adriel hesitated, unnerved by the man's strange speech.

The cave, for all the shelter it provided, was not exactly a homey place, and the hermit did not look pleasant, either. In fact, he seemed rather mad. A metal cage had been set over the ring of firestones, and a rabbit, still wearing its skin, dangled from its top into the flames. Bones poked through its charred flesh.

As Adriel's appetite vanished into the smoke, the hermit slowly turned. He was holding two knives—one short and hooked, one long and straight—and clicking them together, cleaning them of blood and gore. Mismatched pupils, yellow and black, stared out at nothing. "Stand there," he whispered, "and scrutinize your host. The walls open and close, and nobody knows. You can hear them rumbling. Come in, friend. Come to the fireside."

"Really . . . I don't want to be any trouble."

"There's no trouble here . . . only hunger."

Adriel shrugged off his cloak and sat by the fire, disturbed but un-daunted. He began warming his hands by the blaze, warily eyeing the rabbit.

The hermit smiled vaguely. "It is my pleasure to serve, and so shall I serve—until I am no longer able. Then the Watchers will have me. They will nurture me . . . nurture me in their eternal embrace." He reached behind himself and brought forth another rabbit, this one skinned and dripping blood. "Your cloak . . . I'll take it from you after the meal. I'll hang it, and then let it hang."

Adriel wondered who these Watchers were and whether his host was as crazy as he sounded. At a loss for any other response, he asked, "Do you have a name?"

The hermit tied the second rabbit over the fire and then ambled over to the shelves. He returned with three dusty bottles.

"Why keep a name when you belong to others?" he mused, setting the bottles on the ground. "The Watchers . . . it will be time to feed them soon. Be still, friend . . . a breath once lost seldom returns."

He removed the stoppers and tipped the bottles one by one over the cage. As each funnel of powder hit the fire, flames sizzled with red and black sparks and a jet of green smoke hissed upward.

Adriel thought the ritual unnatural. The man was extraordinarily odd—his wits probably had deserted him long ago—but his use of the powders hinted at some strange pagan worship. There were such religions, Adriel knew; Dale had told him of them before, reading accounts from tomes by another fireside: the stone fireplace in his cottage study.

Suddenly a wayward gust of wind swung the hangings behind him, and Adriel glanced over his shoulder.

"Interested in the hangings, yes?" the hermit asked.

The green vapor was mingling with the black smoke from the fire, and the sizzling flames reached higher. Shadows on the walls began changing into contorted figures: Heads, arms, horns, and shoulders appeared and vanished in the room's hazy ether. The mental whisper of Adriel's nightmare grew louder, mocking him, and he looked around in fright.

Then a true whispering began. It seemed to circle the room, flitting among the shadows.

Across the fire, the hermit's eyes shone black and yellow. "Each piece of cloth lends me its aid. They keep the draft from reaching me. My previous guests have been very generous, generous enough to give me their cloaks." His eyes narrowed. "But they have no more use for them."

Adriel scrambled backward, his knuckles tightening about his staff. His free hand fumbled for his cloak.

The hermit, all smoke and shadow, rose from the floor. He opened his mouth. Long black fangs spiked cruelly from behind his lips—impossible teeth for someone wholly human. "Where are you going, friend? No need to depart so soon. Stay for the feast! The walls are hungry, and the Watchers wait."

He moved toward Adriel, knives held high. The shadows leered from the walls, their hideous shapes solidifying.

Adriel backed up as fast as he could but tripped on a root and thudded on his back. As the hermit closed in, the whispering between the shadows grew louder and more frenzied. Invisible arms seemed to be reaching out to him from the surrounding walls. Adriel brought up his staff, hoping desperately to counter the hermit's attack.

Instead, with a sudden surge of magic, a blue light blazed forth. The glow was as pure and lucent as starfire. Shadows reared back, dissolving into the chamber's swirling smoke. The hermit dropped his knives and screeched, covering his face as if the light had scorched his skin.

Adriel jumped to his feet and raced from the chamber. He thrust aside the hanging cloaks as the hermit's screams echoed up and down the corkscrewing tunnel.

Then, heart pounding, he burst into the night.

He sprinted away from the cave, boots pounding on the path that would lead him to Bridgewater and the Seaspine Mountains. Sheets of rain flurried around him. *The Watchers he spoke of must be demons; a poor name for such a great evil. Adriel, you fool, you wandered right into their midst. If this is how your quest is to start, there's only one way it can end.*

A thunderclap boomed in the heavens, and Adriel wondered if his real-life nightmare had only just begun.

THE CLOCK TOWER

SHIVERING UNDER A scratchy cloth blanket, Kayla gazed with sleepless eyes at the ceiling of her makeshift bedroom. Above her loomed three huge iron-wrought bells—dark tongues wagging in the breeze—and above them was a dense forest of cords and gears. The wooden planks of the floor pressed against her back. She tucked her blanket under her, shifting the cloth between herself and the floor, and then lay back on her pillow, a lumpy traveling pack stuffed with dried apples, bread, a rind of cheese, and the few other items that Wren had managed to grab before he hurried them both from their home.

Despite the healing sedatives her father had given her, Kayla could not find sleep. Pain from the assassin's blow in the wine cellar had dulled to a dim throb—Wren's herbs were working quickly—but fear held her dreams at bay. This night had been by far the most terrifying of her life.

She managed to close her eyes, but she could not force away images of the assassins. Their ratlike eyes pierced her thoughts, flashing wickedly among the shutter-dark shadows in the clock tower's bell chamber. The grating of their curses still echoed in her imagination.

She thought she would never forget their faces.

Kayla lifted the blanket and peered at her arms. The herbs had numbed her senses, but purplish bruises stretched across her skin. No remedy but time would cure them. She shuddered, remembering the bite of dirty fingernails as rope curled around and around her, tightening like a coiling snake.

But she had escaped; her father had saved her. Never again would he be an oppressive menace whose stomping on the stairs signaled an end to freedom and fun. He loved her. She had known it all along. The trust and relief that passed between them as he held her in her bedroom—a tender embrace only a father could manage—had been firm and absolute. She had placed the butterfly sketch in the traveling pack, though she now felt like reading every book in Coral Castle's library.

Immediately a mental picture of the library's corpse-strewn carpet materialized above her. Her heart skipped a beat. For the briefest moment she saw the bodies of priests and scribes—robed in blood, wreathed in agony—grinding above her in the clock tower's gears.

She rubbed her eyes and turned her head until she saw the reassuring sight of her father standing at the balcony rail beyond the chamber's western archway.

He was framed between two ancient sea horse carvings. Their tails curled around each side of the arch; their trumpets blasted soundlessly into the night. Save for slight stirrings of cloak and hair, Wren looked like a third statue. Silhouetted against a star-bright sky, he peered down at their home like a guardian angel. His sword hung at his side. No longer lit by fireplace flames, the ivory hilt glimmered like quicksilver in the moonlight.

Kayla knew he was keeping watch. If any assassins returned, they would be dealt with swiftly. She had seen Lackey's corpse in their home's entry hall; she had heard Wren confront Scratch. Future intruders would fare no better. A returning Scratch would fare considerably worse.

As if sensing her eyes on his back, Wren glanced over his shoulder. Kayla rolled onto her stomach, feigning sleep. But immediately the silence was disturbed by the creaking of his footsteps on the planks.

"You were better at lying about King Lumin."

The footsteps stopped. Kayla opened her eyes, managing a weak smile. Her father could not be fooled. He stood over her, his face creased with concern, his scar a dark trench in the starlight.

"I'm fine," she said. "Those chewing roots you gave me . . . I can hardly feel a thing."

"Those chewing roots were supposed to knock you out. You should be sleeping. You'll need rest. We have a long road ahead of us tomorrow. Midrun is a day's ride from the East Gate. From there we travel north along the coast, in the shadow of the Seaspine Mountains and in sight of the sea, until we reach the cottage of a man I know, a man who can give us some answers."

A jolt of excitement shot down Kayla's spine. "We aren't going back home, are we?"

"Not until I find Damon, the so-called sorcerer those thugs were working for, and learn why he wants us dead. I must first ensure our safety. I would place you under Kendran's care, but killers of the sort you saw in the library have a time-honed knack for finding their victims. The innkeeper is proficient at breaking up bar fights, but he has no skill with weapons beyond wine jugs and beer bottles."

"I wouldn't stay behind," Kayla said, and she meant it. This was her chance at excitement and adventure. With Wren around to keep her safe—and there was no way he would leave her now, not after the incident in the house—there was nothing to be afraid of. She would get to see a world she had always dreamed about, just as her father had when he was young.

Wren grinned. "That's another reason I can't keep you here. You might land yourself in the castle dungeon by the time I returned. I've never seen a girl with a larger appetite for trouble or a bigger stomach for holding it." His grin widened. "Then again, at least the Seasong Arms doesn't provide passage to the labyrinth."

"Just how well *do* you know it? The labyrinth, I mean." *Probably more than he will ever tell me.*

"I know that it exists, and that's more knowledge than most of this city's residents can claim. The labyrinth is a relic of a time long past, a reminder of something beyond memory. There are the myths and legends, of course, collected in the pages of books I've gathered over the years, but they are no more than fairy tales and fantasies of the mind. However, I do know Kendran's inn well enough—the only secret there lies in discerning the good drink from the bad."

"And in keeping your daughter too busy to feel lonely while you're gone." Kayla felt guilty as soon as the words left her mouth.

Wren knelt at her side. "I know how that must have felt. I was a lonely child, too, Kayla. You have my regrets and my apology, but healing herbs can't help all hurts. Invisible wounds pain me every day. The tavern was my escape."

"I know, Father. I'm sorry for bringing it up. I just wish you could talk to me about your past. About you."

"Some stories bear hearing; some stories should never be told. You are the most important thing in my life, so important that I would gladly give my life to see you safe and happy." Wren moved a hand to his chest and clutched something under his shirt. A cloud seemed to pass over his face.

"I take so much joy in you," he continued as another breath of night air blew into the chamber, tousling his hair. "But worry shadows my joy, girl. Worry about your education, our relationship. Worry about your safety. Despite all my efforts to keep my past from harming you, I'm failing."

Kayla reached up and grabbed her father's free hand. "I love you. You know I do. You'll keep us safe. I know it."

A hard light flashed in Wren's eyes. "I will," he said, and Kayla was sure he spoke the truth. "Now be still. I need to examine that cut of yours. Thank Ariel, it's one that can be fixed."

He cupped her head in his hands. She felt his fingers probing the bandaging he had applied and focused her eyes on gray strands in his hair to keep from wincing. Even with their gentle exploring, his finger-tips shot a hot burning through her head wound. "Is there any pain?"

"A little," Kayla admitted. "Have any more of those . . . men . . . approached the house?"

"Several have passed by, none threatening. Two drunks stopped in the street to stare at the wreckage, but they lost interest and moved on, drinking and singing and creating a racket as if they were the only souls in the world. The clock tower's caretaker saw our house when he was walking home for the night, and it was clear that the smashed facade startled him. He hurried off, probably rushing toward the castle with a mind to report the incident. We'll have visitors from the castle in the morning, but we won't be here to greet them."

"The guards must be busy looking for the assassin I saw in the library, the one who stole the dagger."

Wren reached into the traveling pack behind her, rummaged around, and brought out a small wooden box. He opened the box's lid and removed two violet lavender-scented petals. "Lift up your tongue."

She did as he ordered and immediately felt a wave of relaxation wash over her body as the petals melted in her mouth. Suddenly exhausted, she wanted nothing more than to sleep. She tried to fight the feeling, but her eyelids seemed to close of their own accord. Sweet scents bore her from the clock tower's bell chamber into a still-water sea of dreams. She heard Wren's voice tickling faintly in her ears as a tide murmuring faintly on a far-off shore.

"These are more potent than the roots I gave you before. You might feel slightly fuzzy. If you wake up and I'm not here . . ."

Drifting quickly into slumber, Kayla did not catch another word.

*   *   *

A HARSH CLANGING erupted from nowhere, sounding in every direction.

Kayla sat up abruptly, startled and confused. *Where am I?*

She propped herself on her palms. Blinking back sleep, she tried to make sense of her surroundings. She felt fuzzy and warm, as if she had just emerged from a steaming bath. The incessant noise continued beating in her head, drumming up fresh bouts of pain.

Gingerly she ran her fingers through her blond curls, exploring the back of her scalp. They brushed against something soft and slightly sticky: a bandage. Her hand recoiled.

She glanced up. Three curved bells moved above her, swinging on thick knotted ropes. Gears rotated above the bells, but she could not hear them. The clanging of the great bells drowned out everything else in an avalanche of noise.

Then she remembered her surroundings.

Bells and gears.

She was in the Eastwatch Clock Tower, high above Nautalia, away from assassins and safe under her father's care. She rubbed her eyes, sighing in relief. She looked toward the balcony where Wren had been standing.

But Wren was not there.

The bells stopped their clanging. A new hour had come, accompanied by mounting panic. She was alone in the dark and silence.

Kayla thought of the assassins, imagined them prowling in the cold corners of the bell chamber. She quickly jumped up, kicking the blanket away. Where had her father gone? What had happened while she had been asleep? She tried to remember the last thing he had said to her before the herbs had done their work, but she could recall only a blurry image of a thumb and a forefinger slipping violet petals under her tongue. Had he left to check on the house?

She hurried through the eastern archway and made a circuit along the outer balcony. Wren had left no sign of where he had gone, but he knew what he was doing.

She had to trust him.

Kayla stopped at the spot where she had last seen Wren standing. She gripped the rail, looking west over Nautalia. Lights flickered across the city like a dragon's hoarded jewels. Constellations blazed fiercely in the heavens; night still owned the sky's stage. In the distance Kayla could see starlight rippling on the ocean. She sniffed: The briny scent of waves hung in the air. Coral Castle jutted to her left, towering above the city and the sea. She glimpsed antlike shapes of people scurrying to and fro along the parapets. They would have discovered the carnage in the library by now and begun scouring the castle for the killer.

What could her father possibly have done to deserve a death warrant? They had come for him, not her. That much had been clear. They had demanded his location, using threats and blows. Wren's past was as veiled as a shadow-draped forest. What other dangers lay there, buried among the years, lurking under sand-layered time, ready to reach out and consume them both?

She looked down at her home, but she could not see her father. Glass still littered the street; even at this height she could see the broken lamp and crystal shards spread across the cobblestones.

As she watched, two shapes crept under the eaves of the houses, moving around pools of lamplight, slithering like vipers toward her home. She held her breath and looked closer. The shapes were startlingly familiar: Scratch had returned, and the assassin she had tracked through the labyrinth was by his side.

She left the rail and went to the small opening in the wooden floor that led to a stone staircase winding down the clock tower. She took the steps two at a time and halted near the entrance at the tower's base. Standing on tiptoe, she peered through an arrow loop by the door.

Scratch and the dark-skinned assassin had reached the door to her home. They were speaking.

"This is the house. He may be inside."

"You're as stupid as you are ugly. A fighter of his caliber knows not to wait around for his opponents when he's outnumbered. It's a shame he didn't kill you and rid me of your ignorance."

"He killed Lackey."

"He would have been an unworthy opponent had the conflict gone otherwise. I have little love for Damon, but I had thought him wise enough not to trust a true assassin's work to street thugs."

"But—"

"Enough talk. You search upstairs. Wren may have left clues pinpointing his whereabouts. If we don't find him tonight, we'll find him in the morning. Damon's men are watching this city's exits both above and below ground."

Through the arrow loop, Kayla watched the men disappear into her house, anxiety roiling her stomach. What if her father was inside? He would have heard the conversation between the two men, but would he be able to defend himself from these new attackers? The dark-skinned assassin had single-handedly murdered several dozen people in the library.

With a shattering explosion, Scratch crashed headfirst through one of the upper windows. His body crunched on the cobblestones. Wren jumped through after him, landed on all fours, rolled and sprang to his feet, then rushed into the alcove of a nearby doorway.

The assassin stepped from the front door. He moved disdainfully around Scratch's motionless figure, then stopped and gazed slowly up and down the street. Candles flared in the windows of adjacent houses. The assassin cursed and disappeared into the darkness of an alley.

Wren waited a moment longer in the doorway, then dashed toward the clock tower where Kayla stood watching.

She spun around and ran up the steps as fast as she could. When she reached the bell chamber, she turned to face her father.

He clambered into the room, chest heaving, wearing the chain mail that had hung in the attic. A new pack was slung across his shoulder. "You just won't stay asleep, will you?" he asked.

"You expect me to sleep while you're dueling assassins in our house?"

Wren grimaced. "The father's blood is boiling in his daughter. Gods, I hope it doesn't burn her."

"It hasn't yet; my father's still here to protect me. But why'd you go back? You knew they'd return."

"In rushing to get you out of the house, I realized I had forgotten several things that will be important on the road." Wren tapped his vest of iron rings. "As you probably saw, I ran into Scratch. He brought one of his friends."

Kayla nodded. "I'm glad you hid. But why didn't you fight him?"

Wren unpacked a water flagon, a collapsible telescope, and a money bag that jingled when he set it on the floor. "That one appeared to have unusual talent. Had we locked swords, there is a good chance I would have died, and where would that leave you? I watched him come down the street; he moved swiftly and softly but as powerfully as a predator."

He brought out a roll of parchment, a quill, and an inkwell.

Kayla smiled.

"Don't thank me," Wren said. "We will be traveling in disguise. From now on I'll be a common laborer."

"What about me?"

"You, my daughter, will be my son."

Wren produced a large pair of scissors. Kayla groaned.

Iron Dawn

SEATED CROSS-LEGGED ON the balcony, Wren sharpened his sword, watching the dawn rise through the iron palings in the clock tower rail. Blue blushed to purple, and purple brightened to rose. Nimbus clouds scudded across the horizon, their puffy underbellies glowing pearl and crimson.

The air was refreshing, but Wren knew the day would soon turn hot and humid. He felt almost peaceful—in the cool of early morning his problems seemed to fade with the passing night—but he was under no illusions. They would have to leave Nautalia. The assassin could be anywhere, the city gates were being watched, and the labyrinth was certainly no longer a secret. The assassin knew about it; it would be guarded. Escape would be no simple game of hide-and-seek.

I have a daughter to protect. There's no room for error, he thought to himself.

Wren rubbed his whetstone along the sides of his sword. The bell chamber amplified the scraping rasp of the rock. He stopped and pressed his finger against an edge. A line of blood welled from his skin—the sword was sharp enough.

He stood and held it before him, squinting with the scrutiny of a jeweler at the thin length of tempered metal. Then he swung it, wheeling it from side to side, twirling it above his head. The sword fit his hand like a brother's grasp.

His father had given it to him long ago. Wren recalled a vivid scene of snowflakes falling through an overcast sky, wind rustling bracken and branches, smoke sifting through the trees from Lantern Watch. On the far side of a clearing Dirk crouched over the sword, scrubbing the bloodied blade with handfuls of white powder. Then he calmly walked toward Wren with the proffered sword.

Wren moved along the balcony, swinging his sword faster, harder, trying to sever the images that came next.

. . . shivering in the woods, waiting for Dirk's return . . . tracking his father through Lantern Watch, pleading, bribing, threatening when he had to, navigating alleys and streets toward the town's three wrecked ships . . . hard on the trail of whispers and rumors . . .

Sweat beaded on his brow.

. . . "sorry, boy, your father's probably dead" . . . "caught by the Torturers" . . . "Cane's gang" . . .

His muscles tightened.

. . . entering the Black Plank, sneaking to the attic where the pirate named Bulge stood over his father, using knives with ruthless precision . . . rushing the pirate with Dirk's sword . . . iron slashing his face as he threw Bulge backward through a window . . .

Wren fingered the scar on his face. It had never fully healed.

Far below, a flock of starlings burst from the branches of an olive tree. The small birds rushed over the city rooftops like a dark, swift-moving storm cloud, then angled vertically up the clock tower, careening toward Wren. They swerved by his head at the last possible instant and sped through the bell chamber, leaving by the eastern arch.

Wren strode to the other side of the tower, tracking the starlings with his sword. They grew fainter and fainter until they were no more than specks of dust floating on the wind. Wren sighed, recognizing himself in the birds, and then looked out on the land he soon would be treading.

Nautalia was splayed out before him like a reef of stone and wood. He could see the East Gate, the city's largest landward exit, set into the outer wall. After several miles of hill and field the coast widened to the north and south; then it surged eastward, rising into the Seaspine Mountains. The haggard peaks spiked from the ground like huge, misshapen daggers forged beneath the world's crust. *By noon I'll be at their feet, safe and sound in Midrun.*

Just then the sun crested the ocean, flooding the horizon with light. Wren turned from his view and lowered the sword, gazing through the bell chamber at the conflagration sweeping across the waves. . . . *you need to be working to make sure your sun will rise . . .* The words he had spoken to Kayla the night before surfaced in his mind.

His eyes strayed to where she lay curled in a blanket on the floor. Sunlight washed her face. She stirred, then sat up and stretched. Her arms strained toward the bells, brushing the ragged strands of her newly cut hair. Wren had hated shortening it, but Scratch surely had given the dark-skinned assassin Kayla's description. Now she looked as scruffy as a beggar.

"What time is it?" she asked, squinting.

Wren sheathed his sword. "Time to leave."

"When?"

"As soon as you're awake."

Kayla peeled off her blanket and clambered to her feet. The shadow of the bells fell across her face. "I'm awake."

Wren cupped her chin and gently peeled the bandage from her head. "The wound will be healed soon. It's time to go." He shouldered the two traveling packs, then lifted the trapdoor and started down the clock tower.

When they reached the street, they began threading their way to the Seashell Square Market as the city woke around them.

The Merchant Quarter was unusually crowded. Street urchins chased one another around vendors' stalls. Children squealed, and men and women haggled with traders. Guards stood here and there, glittering halberds in hand, long swords strapped at the waist, surveying the crowds with eyes shaded beneath their helms.

"Do you think we'll be noticed?" Kayla asked. She sounded either excited or nervous.

Wren hoped she was nervous; this was no time for excitement. "No one from the castle saw you in the library. The assassin and his companions on Damon's payroll are a different story, but I doubt we'll run into them before we reach a city gate. And I have a plan to pass through unnoticed."

When they arrived at Seashell Square, the ground changed to a multi-hued blend of crushed shells and sandstone that was every bit as colorful as the rainbow panorama of trader tents and merchant stalls that made up the market. Wren warned Kayla to keep her eyes open for signs of trouble as they pushed through the teeming mass of people, making their way to where his friend Flint was displaying an eclectic collection of weapons in a stall.

Flint stopped arranging stilettos on a table, straightened, and blew through his scarlet beard. "Blazes, it's Wren Tident, up early and looking for iron. How are you feeling?"

"There've been happier beasts in the Rattlechain Pens."

"You look like hell," Flint agreed. "Why the torn clothes and smudged face? After last night—"

Wren shook his head. "I came over to inquire about those." He pointed at a group of throwing daggers, searching for unwanted listeners from the corners of his eyes.

The five knives, strapped together by a leather belt, glinted side by side in the morning light, resting on an oil-slick cloth. Each was slight and sharp and weighted at both the tip and the handle—perfect for throwing. Wren picked up a knife and balanced it on his index finger. Its point held in the air as if caught in an invisible vise. "How much for the set?"

Flint paused, then smiled, catching on to the game. "I'll not part with them for less than forty silvers."

Wren grimaced. "You're a fat-fingered pickpocket. There's no set of knives worth that price."

"Insults won't help. These are the best weapons you'll find in this market."

Wren knew he was viewing some of the finest weaponry in the city. If you wanted to buy the best, you bought it in the Seashell Square Market; Nautalia had no finer collection of tradesmen. *And for what I need, there's no finer merchant than Flint.* "I could buy three times as many from another vendor at half your price."

"Then I suggest you start looking," Flint said, and began rolling up the knives in the oiled cloth.

Wren stopped him. "Twenty."

"Are you mad?"

"No, but I am a friend."

Flint bent over the stall. "And it's a good thing you are. Just what sort of trouble are you in?"

"Bad trouble."

"Is there any other sort? That business at the inn . . . fainting in the midst of a Jikari game, then rising from the floor like a man possessed. You're tied up in evil business, Wren. Otherwise we wouldn't be haggling over knives. It's all for show—they're free of charge, of course—but you need to tell me what's happening to you! I've spoken with the others, and we want to help. But we can't unless we know what you're facing. You've saved us from bruises and broken bones in many a tavern brawl and have been a good friend in other ways. This is our chance to return the favor."

"I've been sworn to secrecy in an oath I cannot break, but someone's paying men to end my life. Hired killers broke into my home last night. I think they're connected to the story I can't tell, though I don't know how."

"That was *your* home?" Flint sounded astonished.

"What are you talking about?"

"Seashell Square's been buzzing with rumors of killings—one in the castle, the other at a residence near the clock tower."

"These rumors are real. An assassin came for me, Flint."

Flint shook his head. "What happened?"

"I barely managed to escape, but the killer is still searching for me and my daughter. And he's not alone."

Just then a clarion sounded, rending the air with its trumpeting call. People hurried to the sides of the square as a retinue of mounted knights appeared from the direction of Coral Castle. Armor graven with sea horses flashed in the sun, and spear tips twinkled. The soldiers galloped through the parting crowd, their purple and silver cloaks waving behind them.

"Clear a path," called their leader. "Make way! Make way for the Royal Guard."

The knights rushed through the square and disappeared from sight, leaving clouds of dust in their wake. Soon the sound of pounding hooves was swallowed back into the noise of the crowd.

Flint swore. "The whole city's up in arms over the murders. Dragons and demons, Wren, what have you gotten yourself into?"

"Nothing I can't get out of."

"What about the assassin?"

Wren crossed his arms. "I won't endanger my friends. This is my business, and I'll be the one to deal with it. None of you are suited to this sort of thing. You're merchants and fishermen, not fighters."

"What about your daughter? Is she tougher than us? Shorn hair and dirty clothes aren't going to hide her from me. You're taking her with you."

"I have no choice. Assassins are roaming the city, yearning to carve me up in some back alley and leave me to rot. I'm not blind to her danger. But I have a better chance of keeping her safe if she stays by my side."

Flint would not budge. "The six of us have decided that we *will* help you, if only to see you safely through the city gate."

"You're a fool," Wren sighed.

"But a loyal one, I hope. I'll gather the rest. Where should we meet you?"

"Come to Caravan's Crook. I plan on having Teran smuggle us from Nautalia as soon as possible."

"Good plan." Flint stroked his beard. "Now let's finish bartering. A merchant can't let his guise of greed falter. My final offer is thirty," he shouted, feigning anger. "You'll pay the price my craft deserves."

"I'll take them." Wren shook some silver coins from a pouch onto the table. "Count yourself lucky."

Flint swept up the coins and rolled the throwing daggers into their cloth. Wren took the bundle and walked from the stall to where Kayla stood, scanning the market crowds.

"How was it?" she asked.

Wren showed her the knives.

"They look sharp."

"They're deadly." He shrugged off his traveling pack, placed three of the knives inside with the other supplies, and tied the others to his sword belt; then he tapped the coins from the cloth back into his money pouch. They dropped one by one, clinking like drops of silver rain.

"He gave the money back?"

"It pays to know the right people." Wren began pushing his way across the square. "Stay close. We're visiting Teran, a friend of mine who can smuggle us as cargo on the next caravan to leave Nautalia."

He realized he would almost be enjoying himself were he not so concerned about Kayla. Secret escapes, merciless foes, disguises and weapons . . . he was even wearing mail under his tattered tunic. It all took him back to his days as a mercenary, an adventurer questing for trouble. But he was older now, and these assassins were out for his daughter . . . he just did not know why. *When I find out, I'll have use for my sword and Flint's knives.*

They crossed Seashell Square and came to Caravan's Crook. Three metal cages hung from a wooden scaffold near the tavern entrance, holding rotting corpses. Maggots inched along half-eaten faces as flies swarmed between the bars. Rusted chains groaned and creaked as the cages turned.

Someone from the castle must have moved the horrific display from the castle dungeon to a public setting, hoping to dissuade the murderers from further crime. Kayla looked as though she might faint.

Wren knew his daughter should not have to see such a disgusting sight, but she had already seen worse, and he feared she would see still worse in the days to come. He put a hand on her shoulder, guiding her into the tavern.

Although the sun had not yet reached its zenith, Caravan's Crook was a gristmill of talk. Rumors fled from lips, took refuge in ears, and cycled back through lips again, changing in every telling. The tavern was packed so thickly with human bodies that the walls seemed to bulge with the constant chatter. Most of the tables were already full— chairs creaked, and men and women talked over food and drink, gesturing heatedly.

Wren paused in the doorway. Sunlight passed dimly through the room's dusty windows, and the scents of melting wax and burning oil mingled with tobacco smoke. He threaded between the tables, moving toward the bar. Several people shot him curious glances. Patrons seldom brought their children into places like this. He should have had Kayla wait outside, for now she was attracting unwanted attention.

A scruffy-looking boy was serving drinks at the bar. He glanced up at Wren. "What do you want?"

"I'm looking for Teran. Find him and tell him a friend needs his immediate attention." Wren passed a coin across the bar. The boy snatched it up and hurried into a back room.

Wren leaned forward on the bar and shut his eyes. He was weary from his sleepless night atop the clock tower, but he could not afford to sleep yet. *It's been a while since I've gone without sleep.* He shook his head and rubbed his eyes, then turned around to check on Kayla.

She was not there.

He scanned the room frantically. Had she been caught in a knot of people? Men and woman glanced back at him. He looked to the right and saw that a small door leading to an outside alley had been left ajar.

Blood rushed to his face. He shouldered his way toward the alley, shoving through the crowded room, slipping one of Flint's throwing knives into his hand as he drew his sword.

THE BLIGHTED VILLAGE

Adriel crouched in the cavity of the mountain pine, rubbing his arms for warmth. Tired and soaked, miserable to the bone, he listened sadly to the storm.

Storms, Adriel thought, were one of nature's darkest devices, gathering slowly, condensing in masses of frustrated energy, sending warning signs before them. Then they broke, exploding in the sky like gods and demons waging war in heaven. During his childhood Adriel had been severely frightened of storms. Dale often had told him storms were the world's way of reminding man of his considerable insignificance, his humble standing in the grand scheme of creation.

Adriel certainly felt insignificant now, insignificant and as scared as if he were still that young boy all those years ago. This storm *was* different, though. It was under this storm that Adriel's life had blown apart. The storm would pass, but it foretold something worse to come.

Wind shrieked, and rain hammered against the pine's hollow trunk, filling the cavity with the sounds of a thousand tiny collisions. Adriel's staff, dull and quiet, lay on his knees.

The light that had flashed in the hermit's cave had vanished, receded without even the faintest glimmer. Adriel had not been able to summon it again. He wished he could; with only shadows for company, the magic would have been a welcome companion.

It was dark beyond the opening in the trunk, but from time to time great bolts of lightning crackled across the sky. Each flare revealed a beleaguered landscape of storm-battered hills cowering beneath a churning mass of thunder and cloud. Although their peaks were hidden, Adriel knew he was near the Seaspine Mountains. During the last few miles of his journey the land, which had been rising sharply, began growing more uneven and coarse. The hills had been scarred with furrows and spotted with boulders. Pockets of trees had begun looming through the rain. They were twisted, stunted things clinging to the ground like barnacles on a reef.

In the morning Adriel would be able to get his bearings, and he hoped to reach Bridgewater with another hour's walk. He was near the sea. The mountains were close behind him, and the village of waterwheels could not be far.

Still rubbing his arms, he tried to make sense of his encounter in the cave. What sort of man would willingly summon the grotesque shapes that had appeared on the walls? The hermit could not have been human, not with those impossible teeth, and the shadows had clearly alluded to a demonic presence. But the monster that had called them . . .

Thunder boomed, and forked lightning whipped fiercely from sky to earth, tearing the horizon.

Adriel shuddered, remembering black fangs and tessellated knives. Rabbit corpses dripping blood; smoke and powders; frayed cloaks swaying in a narrow, root-covered tunnel—they plagued his mind, torturing him with hints of death and damnation.

The magic came once, Adriel thought. *It will come again when I need it, just like Dale said it would.*

He wished he could believe himself.

Shifting his back against the inside of the trunk, Adriel calmed his breathing. He needed sleep. He concentrated on drawing air deep into his lungs and thought back to Dale's cottage, envisioning the last meal he had shared with his master. It seemed like a lifetime ago, but the comforting memory of the older wizard sitting at the table made the interior of the pine a little less lonely.

After several more minutes, he drifted into a restless slumber . . .

* * *

. . . moving through a forest, gloom spreading through the trees . . . whorls of mist webbing the earth, grabbing at my boots, writhing around my legs like pale snakes . . . horses whickering in the underbrush . . .

. . . trees thin around a clearing . . . a stone altar, cracked and worn, rests in the center of the clearing like a tumor bulging on the forest floor . . . idols surround it, brooding in the murk . . .

. . . leaving the safety of the trees, creeping to the altar . . . drawing closer, watching ravens pick at a body, ripping at gobbets of tissue . . . when they spy me, they flap into the air, crying angrily . . .

. . . bending over the altar . . . the man's rib cage is picked clean; his limbs are shredded; his eyes have been eaten away . . . beyond the clearing, a disgusting pool festers . . . stepping to the waterside as something stirs beneath the vine-choked surface . . .

. . . a single bubble floats upward and bursts—

Adriel woke with a start, squinting in a shaft of misty sunlight that streamed through the hole in the pine.

The dream had been so vivid, but early morning now caused it to drift apart, breaking in his mind like a spiderweb in the breeze. *It was just a dream . . .*

Adriel was stiff and cramped. Flecks of bark clung to his clothing. A rotten smell pervaded the pine. Mushrooms sprouted around his boots, and fungal growths matted the walls of the trunk.

He clambered to his feet, picked his cloak from the floor, and stooped under the opening in the trunk. He emerged outside. Dew had mingled with the residual rainwater as thousands of crystal drops quivered on the grass. The world seemed groggy and gray, a soot-covered sketch of the real thing.

Adriel took a hunk of bread from his traveling pack. It was soggy, and there were blue spots of mold on one end of the loaf, but he devoured most of it, anyway. He was famished, but his mind was taken with nightmares and not the food.

It seemed to him that it was only a matter of time until his latest nightmare came true.

When he finished eating, Adriel walked around the pine. He leaned on the trunk and faced the mountains. They rose into the slate-blue sky, hulking spires of clouded stone. They were much nearer than he had expected. He shouldered his pack, took his staff in hand, and began treading through the rugged foothills as they piled one after another into the mountains.

* * *

SOMETIME LATER ADRIEL came within view of Bridgewater.

It was the first time he had seen the village in several years, but the sight was not a welcome one; there was something wrong about it, something darkly foreign. The sun was partially veiled, and in the gloom the silhouettes of two gristmills appeared on the horizon, eerily still. Waterwheels hunkered beside the mills, massive and motionless. This was strange. Each wheel rested in a river, and unless the rivers had dried up or been dammed, the wheels should have been turning. The snow-melt feeding them could not have ceased, and Bridgewater's residents would never do anything to impede their flow. Their livelihood stemmed from the currents coursing through their village.

Bridgewater snuggled between Rust and Worn, twin mountains named for their ragged contours. The village had been built on an elevated field where three rivers—two from Rust and one from Worn—meandered down from their mountain-peak holds to meet in a fertile oasis. The plateau on which the village lay stood above Adriel, high atop a granite shelf. One of the rivers spilled over the shelf in a fragmented waterfall, bursting on rocky outcroppings, splashing down each one before changing its angle in foamy chaos.

Adriel realized he would need to ask the watchman—there was

always a sentry on duty—to lower a ladder; for years the path had been blocked by a makeshift barrier of overturned wagons, splintered water-wheels, and piles of mortar-bound brick.

The watchman's post hearkened back to an earlier time when Bridge-water was in its infancy. The Seaspine Mountains and the Starlight Sea had been home to a hardy people—fishermen and farmers, weathered workers with tough, gaunt features—and the village of Bridgewater had existed as a fulcrum between the coastal folk and the inlanders who resided around Merrifield. Adriel knew there were still descendants of the coastal folk left in Bridgewater, but their numbers were dwindling, and they seldom traveled. None had ever ventured near Dale's cottage, and his master had told him that few ever would. The watchman would be on the lookout, but he would not be expecting visitors, not from this side of the mountains.

Adriel approached the base of the shelf. "Hello!" he called, cupping a hand to his mouth. "Who has the watch?"

An owl-like face popped over the ledge. "Who asks the question?"

"Adriel."

"What do you want, Adriel?" the watchman asked. His hair was short and gray; his ears were far too small for his curved bulbous cheeks, and his eyes were large and rounded.

"The road's blocked."

"I can see that."

Adriel fidgeted. "Will you throw me a ladder?"

The watchman's owl eyes narrowed. "You're the first person I've seen this side of the Seaspine for several weeks. Where are you coming from? The land behind you is wilderness."

"I live by the sea, in a cottage with my . . ." Adriel hesitated, realiz-ing that he could not reveal his magical background to someone as wary as this watchman. He shouted, "My father."

"And what brings you to Bridgewater?"

"My business is my own."

"If it involves this village, I must know it, or you must reach your destination by another route."

If this watchman has feathers, I'm flustering them, Adriel thought. He called back up to the watchman: "The only other gap is the Ivory Pass, which is east of Midrun, miles to the south. My business is in Merrifield beyond Bridgewater's borders. I won't cause any trouble, and I'll be gone within the hour."

The watchman shook his head. "You'll find few in this village keen to aid strangers and even fewer with aid to give. We're in a bad way here, and the way is worsening. Still . . ." He paused. "You look harmless enough."

A rope ladder rolled down from the shelf top above.

Adriel grabbed hold and began his ascent. The granite behind the ladder was slick with moisture. Algae clung to the shelf like tufts of green hair. Spray wetted Adriel's skin as the watchman stared down at him, holding something long and shiny. When he reached the top, the watchman disappeared into a thatched hut to stash his sword. He returned without his weapon.

Adriel leaned on his staff. "I appreciate your help."

The watchman began hauling the ladder up the shelf. "My name's Farr. I get paid for this, though these days it's a simple job."

"It's a desolate country back there," Adriel agreed.

"That's the reason I'm cautious. Sorry about the sword, but those left in Bridgewater are all on their guard. If I had sensed you to be a threat, I would have cut you loose. There's a bane on the village. Rivers are withering away, and the people wither with the waters."

Adriel examined the village as Farr brought up the ladder. His earlier disquiet proved well founded.

Bridgewater spread along the field between Rust and Worn, houses and mills deposited along riverbanks. The village consisted of some two hundred homes, an inn, a smithy, and three small stores. On the outskirts were several farms and shepherd hovels. A few dozen mills were scattered about, some used for grinding grain, some for kneading cotton, but all the mills were motionless. *Nightmares in the day have nowhere to fade,* Adriel thought to himself.

Not a single waterwheel turned. Their axles and gears had been jammed. Each was interwoven with bulky knots of thick, crimson vines that emerged serpentlike from the rivers.

Farr secured the ladder on the shelf top and stepped next to Adriel. "What a sight."

"What are those things?" Adriel asked, pulling his cloak tight about his shoulders.

"We think it's a curse, black magic, monsters crawling from the riverbeds. No one knows for sure."

Adriel looked to the roadblock. Two men stood behind it, one holding a crossbow and the other grasping a spear. "How long has it been like this?"

Farr gestured to a dilapidated building that sagged under a massive net of the creepers. "The first of the vines appeared a week ago, seizing Drysby's mill, nearly driving the old thread spinner mad with fright. Not a day's gone by when they haven't lengthened and latched on to something new. We can cut them and burn them, but they always return."

"I wish I could help."

Farr blinked in surprise. "Blazes, that staff you're carrying . . . Are you a magician?"

Adriel was startled; he had forgotten how unusual the staff must look to people unfamiliar with wizardry. "I'm afraid not," he said, surprised at how easily the lie floated to his lips. "It's a beautiful walking stick but no more magical than a branch has any right to be. My father bought it in Nautalia years ago, a trinket to remind him of the seaside city."

"Pity," said Farr, gazing at the staff's sapphire. "A magic worker might be just the thing we need. But there are so few left these days, and none would wander into the upper reaches of the Seaspine . . . not for the likes of us."

"You have my prayers," Adriel said.

Farr shook his head. "Prayers can't help the damned." He trudged toward the hut and vanished inside.

Adriel started into the village, imagining the watchman's owl-like face peering after him.

He crossed a narrow stream and entered a dirt gully of a street hemmed in by rows of gloomy houses. Few others moved about, and those who did were downtrodden and quiet, their faces boarded up with fear. Many of the homes were also boarded: Beams had been fastened on doors, and planks barred scores of cracked windows.

Adriel drew level with one of the riverside mills. A boy and a girl played near the road. The boy sat on a tree stump, blowing on a pipe. His eyes were closed, and his head dipped and rose with the instrument's swaying cadences. The tune was simple and slightly sad. Giggling, the girl ran circles around him, her hands trailing a sea-green ribbon through the air.

Behind them rose the rotting mill. The mill's waterwheel, splitting against its arrested momentum, strained to turn with the river as the current sloshed past. Crimson vines had woven through the spokes; they were slowly tearing the wood apart like a sea monster dragging down a ship.

A man was hacking at the growths. Sweat beaded on his back, and his arms flexed furiously as he moved from spoke to spoke, swinging his ax. Iron crunched on wood, notching the waterwheel, severing the vines that held it in place.

At Adriel's approach, the boy stopped his piping, and the girl seated herself beside him. Her ribbon fluttered to her lap like a wounded bird. The man lowered his ax and turned toward Adriel.

His eyes were yellowish, myopic baubles, and his hair was ocher-colored. His face, gaunt and drawn, had the texture of hardened wax, and a stubbly beard clung to his chin. "What do you want?" he asked harshly. "Come to gloat at our misfortune?" He looked like a stiff, dirty candle.

"Not at all. I . . . I wanted to see if there was anything I could do to help."

"Who the hell are you?"

"I'm a journeyman. My provisions have run out, and I need to find a place to purchase food." *Farr was right—these people aren't exactly commendable hosts.*

"Daddy," said the little girl, "why is he carrying a magician's stick?"

"Not now," the grizzled man said. He squinted at Adriel. "We don't sell anything here. Best you move on and leave me to my work." He turned back to his waterwheel and began hacking again at the vines. His two children sat quietly on the stump.

"I meant no offense," Adriel said.

The man did not respond, but his daughter smiled. "It's okay," she said softly. "I like you."

"Be quiet," said her father, "or you can go inside the house."

"It's scary in there," the girl protested.

"If you make me angry, I'll make it worse out here." He swung his ax quickly and broke a spoke.

"Leave her alone," the boy said. "This must be a magician. He can blast away the monster with his staff, can't you?" He looked imploringly at Adriel.

Adriel shook his head. "I'm no magician. I have no magic."

The boy's eyes fell, and his father continued wordlessly at his work.

Adriel began moving away down the street, feeling helpless. *If only I really were a wizard. How could Dale have named me one?* Then he smiled. *Maybe there is something I can do.*

He took his coral flute from his belt and began to play. The boy and girl watched, enchanted by Adriel's fingers as they danced on the flute. Bright notes trilled through the air. They came faster and faster, blending into a fey, joyful melody that leaped and crashed and leaped again, swirling in a musical tide.

The boy picked up his pipe and joined in. For a moment a complex harmony sighed and swelled, rich and sweet, bringing Adriel and the children into a new and better place.

Then the father dropped his ax, and the music stopped as swiftly as it had come.

Adriel lowered his instrument. The man looked at him, but his wax-like face seemed to melt, softening with his eyes. "That was beautiful," he said, "as pretty a thing as I've ever heard."

The girl jumped up and ran to Adriel, thanked him, and flung her ribbon around his neck.

"It was nothing," Adriel said.

"It was everything," said the girl's father. "You may not consider yourself a magician, but that was magic in my mind. There's a place farther on in the village where you can buy food, though you're more than welcome to remain with us and share our table for the day."

"It's a kind offer," Adriel said. "But I must move on."

"Then look for a sign reading 'Calico King.' You'll find supplies there."

Adriel nodded at the man and waved at the children—the boy and girl waved back—then turned and started walking. He unwound the ribbon from his neck and tied it about his staff.

When he reached the Calico King, he bought a slab of smoked meat, a wineskin, and a loaf of bread. The food required most of his money, but it was of good quality, and Adriel, keeping in mind the dire situation of the villagers, did not begrudge the owner's price.

Adriel followed the gully street around a smithy, a tavern, and several more houses. He crossed a bridge that spanned a rushing stream, its waters bloated with melted snow and ice, and left Bridgewater, passing by a painted sign that read "Woolthread." Suddenly the road angled sharply, cutting knifelike into the rocky shelf to zigzag down toward the fields below.

Adriel paused to gaze over the land. Before him the countryside dipped and rose in a sea of hilly waves. In the distance he could see an inn by the side of Woolthread Road. Farther along, Merrifield rose above a hilltop palisade, crowning the land in a circlet of wood and iron.

Corin was down there somewhere, a young boy with no idea that he carried the fate of the world on his shoulders. Agents of the enemy would be there as well, lurking in Merrifield, prowling the taverns and streets with sharp eyes and sharper weapons. Dale's warnings had been stark: Danger was everywhere.

And the boy was oblivious to that danger.

Adriel had to find him, had to warn him. He gripped his staff tightly, his knuckles whitening. He hoped he could save him in time. *And I'll be on the lookout for a mercenary named Wren. Burning blood, I'm an actor on a stage traversed by strangers.*

Just then the sun emerged from behind its cloud cover, drenching the land in light. *Like a fiery lance,* Adriel thought, remembering the words Dale had spoken the previous night. *And here I am, hardly more than a boy myself, looking beyond a threshold into a country I never knew existed.*

Despite the sunshine, Adriel knew shadows gathered on the horizon, shadows that would not dissipate like the storm. There were those in Merrifield who, like the demonic hermit, had little love of life—those who would gladly extinguish his. Adriel hefted his staff into his hand and began to make his way down the rock-hedged road, leaving the blighted village behind as he descended toward unknown terrors. He was frightened, but his coral flute bumped reassuringly at his side, and his staff, its sapphire sparkling, shone with the light of a navigator's star.

REFUGEES

ORIN LIMPED DOWN the path toward the Honey Barrel, a bread sack slung over his shoulder. Occasionally, he stopped here or there to scuff the ground or kick a stone. Gray clouds crawled across the sky, and the wind brushed the hills, shepherding flocks of sheep and goats.

It was the same old story: Corin the delivery boy, charged by his uncle Pyke with the valiant quest of taking rolls to Jyri and rescuing coarse travelers from the grasp of hangover-induced hunger.

He mulled over his plight, wondering if he would forever be doomed to play this role in a parody of a fairy tale. After the disturbing sights of the Ravenswood, his current task seemed about as significant as a fistful of sand flung into the cosmos.

The previous night, Corin had dreamed of Farmer Twine's pool. His return from town had been a difficult one. Dapple, burdened with the items on the shopping list, had been even more belligerent than she had been in the rain, and Corin, preoccupied with ancient idols and vines, had not been in any mood to comfort her. When he finally had snuggled up in bed, Corin had fallen asleep instantly, but he was kept from a peaceful rest by his nightmare.

In the dream he had been throwing stones into the pool until the vine-choked waters began boiling. Soon he was surrounded by the idols he had seen with Dusty in the Ravenswood; they no longer were made of crumbling stone but dripping blood and gore. Their twisted bodies were armored in black scales, and they moved toward him with claws and razor-sharp fangs.

Corin wished he had someone to confide in about what he had witnessed in the forest, but after seeing the way Farmer Twine had been treated in Rookery Rest, he and Dusty had decided to keep the discovery a secret. Despite the messenger's tidings, despite the rumor of trouble in Bridgewater, the townsfolk would never believe a story about a ghostly pool told by two boys.

At least now there was no hint of rain. Corin could see for miles in every direction. Tired, he stopped and looked around, his head swerving like the needle on a compass. He saw a line of wagons inching south on Woolthread Road, approaching the Honey Barrel. A blast of wind pushed him forward on his bad leg, causing him to stumble awkwardly.

The natural order of the world was clearly in flux, and Corin was stuck with loaves and a limp. His sack pounded his back as if sharing a joke, but he was not laughing.

Still, it had been his leg and his scars that had burned near the pool; no dull ache, the pain had lanced through his body with an intense, fiery sensation he had never felt before. Something told him that his physical deficiencies were somehow linked with the occult circumstances in the Ravenswood. But that train of thought took Corin to realms of possibilities too unsettling to contemplate.

When he reached Woolthread Road, the line of wagons was passing the Honey Barrel.

It was not a merry procession. The wagons were piled high with rickety furniture and driven by a sorrowful array of disheveled people clothed in rags and staring forward with vacant expressions. Men held rusted weaponry. Women and children huddled together in tattered blankets and cloaks.

The man driving the lead wagon slowed his horse, bringing the rest of the line to a stop. The woman next to him beckoned to Corin.

"Where is Merrifield, young man?" she asked, clutching a half-naked baby to her breast. In her hand she also held a blue rattle, which she shook over the child.

Corin pointed south. "It's on a hill near the Fairsway, impossible to miss. Where are you coming from?"

"A blighted village," muttered the man.

"We're refugees," the woman explained. "You haven't heard of the trouble in Bridgewater?"

Corin arched his eyebrows. "There are rumors in Merrifield of people fleeing down from the Seaspine, but no one's given them much thought. What's going on up there?"

The man chuckled hollowly. "Climb up and see for yourself. You won't believe the things we've seen."

"You'd be surprised." Corin gazed down the line of wagons. The refugees were a sad army of peasants. Pale garments were tied to the backs of the wagons and rippled in the wind like flags. The weaponry of the men consisted of pitchforks, scythes, and hunting bows. "Will you stop in at the Honey Barrel?" Corin pointed to Jyri's inn. "There's good food and drink."

The woman shook her head. "None of us brought much money— just our clothes and the food we could pack. We'll continue moving until we're far away from Bridgewater . . . until we've found a safe place to live."

"Nautalia would digest us in her labyrinth of streets," the man added, "and northern wastes are no place for us. Tradesmeet is harsh, and the Sea of Dreams is harsher. We head east."

"Dark stories have been spreading from there," Corin warned. He remembered every word of the conversation between Sir Giles and Sir Aaron, the two messenger knights.

The woman was about to reply, but her baby began to cry. She cradled it in her arms, rocking it back and forth, cooing softly and shaking the rattle.

The man glanced up at the overcast sky. "We've lingered long enough. I come from a village of the damned, boy. It can't get any worse." He lashed his reins, and his horse began trotting away.

Corin turned and limped toward the inn, as the wagon line of refugees lurched to life with creaks and groans.

Once again, Corin pondered the merits of delivering bread when the world's sanity appeared to be collapsing all around him.

Magic House

KAYLA STARED AT the small blue door from the middle of the alley. The translucent image of the butterfly—the same one she had seen on the side exit in Caravan's Crook—glittered and rippled, almost as if made of living light. A cage of black bars prevented its escape. The butterfly's wings strained against the bars, but it could not break free.

Kayla shivered. The wings were blue-patched and white-veined, identical to the butterfly Wren had scared from her room the night before. Why had the image appeared? Who had conjured it? It was obvious that someone wished her to follow it.

And she knew this much: Whoever it was could use magic.

Fishing nets sagged between the gables of buildings on either side of the alley. Hooks, lures, and boating tools hung limply in the warm air, dangling from strings twined about the nets. To Kayla's right the alley curved down to the Tidal Wall and the trader docks. Beyond the wharves the sea stretched into the horizon. Sunlight splashed on the swell, and seagulls drifted lazily, squawking above the waves. The alley rose to Kayla's left, moving from the Merchant Quarter to the residential streets where the clock tower stood against the mountains.

Overhead a seagull perched on the netting in a feathery ball of fluff. It faced the small blue door, cocking its head up and down. Its eyes glinted with curiosity.

Kayla examined the home into which the door had been set. With purple walls and white trim lining its bottle-glass windows, it stood out from the chain of homes like an amethyst locket on a pearl necklace. The rainbow shingles on its pointy roof glittered in every color imaginable. It looked like a dwelling from a fairy tale.

Save for the seagull, the alley was empty. Kayla ran a hand though her hair—it felt so *odd,* a chiseled mop, a frizzled mess—and decided to peek behind the door. Wren was still talking to the bartender in Caravan's Crook, so she knew she had not been missed yet. *There's time for a quick look inside,* she thought.

As soon as her fingers touched the door, the butterfly vanished. Still, she pushed the door open and was amused to see silver stars twinkle across the front of it. In the alley behind her the seagull gave a throaty warble and flapped from its roost with a flurry of wing beats.

Spellbound, Kayla entered the house.

As it turned out, the home's entryway was rather less entrancing than its carnival-colored facade.

Kayla found herself in a square, bleak room devoid of furnishings. The walls were white; the floor and ceiling were plain wood. Another door, brown and smooth and far plainer than the one through which Kayla had just passed, was set into the opposite side of the room. To her right the wall was pierced by a rough hole of a window that looked as if it had been formed by the nibblings of field mice. Through the dusty windowpane, she could see the ocean.

Wait, this can't be right, she thought, confused. *There should be a building on the other side of that wall.*

Kayla stepped to the opening and glanced through. Instead of Nautalia, a bare, rugged coastline dropped down toward a pink-sand beach. No homes, no clock tower, no tidal wall or docks, no bluestone streets, no Coral Castle—nothing but a seaside landscape. Then, as she watched, the scene blurred as if she were looking through a waterfall; the shore dissolved, melting into a swampy wasteland. The earth heaved and bucked as cesspools opened like ruined mouths. Steam vents hissed, lashing skyward like monstrous tongues, and somehow Kayla knew that this could be the future of her city.

The room dimmed, and hieroglyphics burned blue on the walls; they matched those Kayla had seen in the labyrinth, lining the aging tunnels through which she had tracked the assassin. Disorientation struck her, and she began to feel seasick even though she was on solid ground.

Behind the window the swamp faded, blending into a desert. *The Sea of Dreams,* Kayla thought, recalling the drawing room in Coral Castle, *the desert of illusion beyond the city of Tradesmeet in the Far North.* Geysers were sucked beneath the sands, and cesspools were covered with purplish dunes. A sickle moon hung in a bruised sky, washing the desert in nether light. Stars glowered overhead. Giant crumbling monoliths, statues of forgotten gods, their features eroded into obscurity by the blowing desert sands, towered here and there, half-sunken in sifting graves.

Something as black as a bottomless well shuffled across the waste. Its dark, ragged shape was draped with tattered garments, and its walk was warped, a disjointed, near stumble.

The rag creature paused.

Moonlight drenched the sands about its feet but failed to illuminate its features. It turned its head toward Kayla, yearning to fix its dark gaze on her face; its hatred burned in her soul. It took a crooked step in her direction, but then the scene whirled, smearing once again into chaos.

The sands cleared, blown away as if by an invisible wind, and Kayla stood on a veranda, overlooking a city she had never seen. She could not tell if it was day or night. Buildings rotted alongside deserted mausoleums, maintaining tenuous moorings above the streets; vultures, not seagulls, hovered in the air, and bone fountains sat in the city squares, bubbling with a black-red liquid. People clustered about the fountains like flies. Some dipped their hands and lifted them to their mouths, others splashed their faces, and still others thrust their heads deep into the fountains only to rise, their skin stained the color of blood.

A baleful membrane hung over everything, a vast sweeping wing webbed with clouds and shadows. Kayla could almost see it stretching across the ashen sky, and it seemed to be enveloping the city below.

Then, as suddenly as it had begun, the vision disappeared, and Kayla once again was staring at a patch of bare coastline through a dusty window. Her heartbeat slowed as the hieroglyphics faded from the walls.

She looked over her shoulder: The front door was ajar, just as she had left it, and its original azure tint had returned. The brown door in front of her was still shut, but the caged butterfly now wavered on its surface, blue and white wings pressing against the bars of its cage.

Wondering if all this was no more than an incredibly vivid hallucination, Kayla went to the brown door and pushed it open. At her touch, its surface glowed with the yellow-orange of an ocean sunrise.

She entered a cramped chamber. A large elderly woman clothed in a robe so subtly colored that Kayla could not decide if it was green or gray reclined behind a cluttered table. Behind her a circular window cast a halo of morning light. The old woman's brown skin accented the whiteness of her hair, and light from the window ran through it, lending her an eerie halo.

"Welcome," the woman said. Her voice was deep and resonant but as clear as the light streaming through the window. "Sit down. We have much to discuss."

"Who are you?" Kayla asked. *This had better be short. Father will have a thing or two to say if he finds out I'm missing. He was right: Staying out of trouble is not my strong point.*

The woman smiled widely. "My name is Amber, and this is my home. Don't worry; you will find this room to be far more normal than the other."

Kayla would have preferred an earlier welcome, and this room was hardly less strange. Bookshelves heaped with aged tomes leaned against the walls. Potted flowers and plants of a dozen varieties clung to the shelf tops. A carving of three interwoven icons rested above the window. Kayla recognized one of them—the sea horse for Ariel—but could not identify the dragon or the lion. Lamps, painted jars, baubles, and crystal prisms hung from the ceiling. The floor was covered in carpets that overlapped one another like waves along a beach.

Normal was not the word Kayla would have chosen to describe the room, but at least it did not look dangerous. *And this old woman is no assassin,* she thought to herself. "You know more about me than you should. How did you conjure up the butterfly I sketched last night? How did you know I was in Caravan's Crook, and why did you bring me here? Are you some sort of magician? That window . . ."

Amber closed her eyes. "I wish for your sake that I knew more about you, enough to give you some further measure of support. I'm an Aurian enchantress, though that probably means little to you.

"The window you gazed through is a bridge between the mind and the paths of the future. It shows glimpses of things to come, visions jovial and macabre, drawn from the world's reaches like shells from the sea. I have used it many times before, and it has revealed many things, including the bedroom incident with your father last evening and your harried trek through the city streets today.

"I'm sorry for what you saw when you gazed through the glass. I can see that yours will be a trying future. Still, you will need to know certain things in order to survive the times ahead. But come, you must be tired." Amber gestured to an empty chair beside her table.

Kayla considered leaving, but something about the woman told her to sit down. "Why should I believe any of this?"

"I don't need to persuade you. You already believe me. You have the intuition and the imagination. Both are already connecting these events, aligning them with the truth."

"I must be going crazy. Some of the things I saw . . . they couldn't happen. That horrible city . . ."

Amber's smile faded. "It exists. There are some other things—not of this world—which have yet to enter your darkest dream."

Kayla bit her lip. "First the assassins. Now this. What's happening to me?"

"I'll explain, but first take this talisman. It will guide you when you need it most, when your nightmares become reality." Amber reached over the table and handed Kayla a small silver amulet; the clasp bore the likeness of the carved image on the wall. Kayla fastened it around her neck and slipped it under her shirt. The metal felt reassuring on her skin.

"I don't know what to say."

"Say nothing," Amber told her, waving her hands. "But remember this: Your father will need you before the end."

Suddenly the door behind Kayla burst open, slamming against the wall. Amber crinkled her brow.

Wren stood in the doorway, his eyes cold and hard. He gripped a knife in one hand and held his sword in the other, pointing it at the enchantress. His jaw was clenched. "Kayla, get up," he commanded. "We're leaving."

Amber cleared her throat. "There's no need for the weapons, Wren. You're safe enough here. Put them away and sit next to your daughter. There are things I need to tell you, too."

Wren pocketed the knife but raised his sword a little higher. He moved cautiously toward the table. "How do you know my name?"

"You've heard of me before. I am Amber. Before you lived in Nautalia—"

"Listen, woman," Wren interrupted. "I *don't* know who you are and I don't care to find out, but if you want to walk out of this room again, you'll close your mouth and stay behind that table until my daughter and I are gone. And don't even think of using magic. Believe me: I can kill faster than you can speak." The light from the window danced on his sword.

"Kayla came here of her own free will."

Wren grimaced. "You lured her with your magic. I know all about your kind; I can smell spell craft like sun-poisoned meat. I've had dealings with a wizard before, and I trust sorcery as I trust a thief." He grabbed Kayla's shoulder and yanked her to her feet.

Amber's eyes were heavy as lodestones; she seemed to age before Kayla's eyes.

Kayla turned toward her father. "I don't think she wants to harm us. She knows about our problem. She only wants to help."

"Your daughter speaks truly," Amber said. "Save your prejudices for someone else. I know you are reluctant, Wren, but I also know what you wear about your neck. I believe in you, but your own beliefs must match the symbol you wear, for symbols are merely a representation of belief and have no inherent power. The medallion must be animated with the power of the mind but also with the will of the heart."

"What in Ariel's name are you talking about?" Wren snapped. "I don't know anything about any medallions"—he glanced quickly at Kayla—"and I want nothing to do with you or your prophecies."

Amber rose to her feet. "All the same, there is more you need to know."

"Know this," Wren said, twisting his blade. "Lure Kayla here again, and I will kill you. That's one prophecy you can count on."

A cloud must have passed over the sun, for the beam of light diminished, darkening Amber's hair to the color of shadows. She sat down, clasped her hands together, and bowed her head. "This is a mistake, but I can't stop you. I hope Dale can survive until you reach him. Perhaps Marian will be overlooked."

With his sword aimed at the enchantress, Wren backed from the room, pulling Kayla along. When he shut the door, it banged into place, returning once again to a plain, woody brown. "I hope we won't have to go through this again."

Kayla looked for the ocean-view window, but it was nowhere to be seen. "I'm sorry, Father. But Amber—"

Wren shook his head and sheathed his sword. "No more about her," he said, and ushered her from the house.

A beggar reclined on a barrel near the back door to the tavern. He was the only other person in the alley.

Kayla looked back at Amber's home, but it had somehow become colorless—the shingles on its roof were black now. *And there* is *a building attached to the right of the house, after all,* she noted with awe.

The beggar asked, "Can a father and his son spare a hapless man a coin?"

Kayla nearly jumped, picturing the rag creature sitting in place of the poor man.

Wren flipped him a coin and stormed back into Caravan's Crook. A young, firmly built man with a clean-shaven face and a mop of chestnut hair stood behind the bar, scanning the room with his hands on his hips.

"Teran," Wren called.

The man turned toward him and raised his eyebrows. "Where'd you go? The bar boy told me you'd arrived, but I couldn't find you anywhere." His eyes were as gray as the tavern's pipe smoke.

Wren glared at Kayla, who looked away. "I was delayed."

"Everyone's ready. Kendran and Flint arrived with Guzzler; Pulley and Hook got here only a minute ago."

"Glad to hear it. How are we leaving?"

"I'll show you," Teran said. "Hurry up and follow. The caravan's leaving soon."

Outside, five armed men stood near the entrance to a warehouse where a line of horse-drawn wagons swarming with traders was being loaded with supplies. Kayla recognized the group as members of her father's gang, his gambling crew from the Seasong Arms.

Then she saw the cages at the edge of Seashell Square.

She pictured butterflies inside the corpse-clogged bars and imagined a cage surrounding her as well, rattling on the end of a chain, a chain hanging on fate. It seemed she was destined to roam the shelterless paths of the world, a destiny she now regarded with anxiety and fear. But the scenes she had glimpsed through Amber's dusty windowpane could not stifle her excitement. After all, wasn't this what she had always wanted, a diversion from the boring routine of her life? Perhaps this prison was also some kind of escape.

A sea breeze swept across the waves, blowing inland with the tide. *Fate blows both ways,* she thought, rubbing the medallion at her breast.

She watched the cages turn.

Escape from Nautalia

As Kayla warily eyed the cages, Wren watched his friends and reflexively toyed with his whetstone. It slid reassuringly between his fingers. He tried calming down, tried turning his thoughts to the task at hand, but the incident with the enchantress had plunged him into a cold, dark rage. Why couldn't these spell weavers leave his family alone? Was there no safe haven from their manipulations?

I can't think about this now. Our escape comes first. Focus, Wren!

All around him Seashell Square rumbled with a thousand different noises. Men and women laughed. Children shouted. Merchants haggled and grumbled, shoving their wares at prospective buyers. Horses snickered and stomped, and caramel-skinned traders bellowed curses as they transported barrels from Teran's warehouse to their wagons, where they secured arched canvas coverings, dyed in black and yellow stripes, over their merchandise.

Wren's friends, clad in a patchwork of rusty iron vests, leather jerkins, and uneven pieces of slipshod padding, stood near the caravan, comparing makeshift weapons like boys flaunting sticks for a game of war. Kendran held a crossbow, Flint an ax. These, at least, were no sticks, but the others were not carrying much more than crude wooden and metal tools.

Guzzler leaned on an oversized mason's hammer. Where he had managed to find it, Wren had no idea; he had never seen Guzzler, who was too fat to work and too lazy to keep a legitimate job, hold anything other than beer mugs. Pulley was hefting a pitchfork into the air with the awkwardness of a sailor who had never shoveled hay. Hook, his wrinkled face as keen as if he were gambling at a Jikari table, switched a gnarled harpoon from hand to hand with a dexterity that belied his age.

Wren wondered whether the harpoon's tip could pierce armor as it parted scales.

Despite their ill-suited weapons, they had gathered in the face of obvious danger to help him escape from Nautalia with his daughter. They knew nothing of the reason behind his departure or the events connecting him to the assassins. Then again, Wren did not know why he was being hunted himself, though the price put on his head almost certainly stemmed from his involvement with Dale and that blasted boy in Merrifield. None of his friends needed to be endangering themselves, yet here they were. If it came to a fight, which was more than possible, Wren would do everything in his power to keep them from harm.

He dropped his whetstone into one of the two traveling packs he had slung about his shoulders. "Come on, Kayla. It's time to go."

She turned from the cages. "Are you sure this is going to work?"

"We don't have many options."

Teran, studying the traders as they pushed barrels up loading planks and under the striped tops of their wagons, heard Wren's remark and rubbed his chin. "I wouldn't worry. This caravan is as safe a hiding place as you two are likely to find. I'll be on board, blade in hand, until you reach the gate." He patted the hilt of his short sword, which was strapped to his waist.

Wren grimaced. "Some of the thugs who are after us are spineless alley rats, ready to scamper back to their dark hovels at the first sign of a real fight, but the assassin I saw last night . . ."

"Flint already told us. I wouldn't worry; we can scare off a rogue or two."

Teran, younger than Kendran, was the fittest member of their group, but Wren would not have given him ten seconds against the scarred killer who had broken into his home. "Let's hope so."

Just then one of the traders, a tall man with a hooked nose and a hard-lined brow, stomped up to Teran. A bone whistle hung from his neck, and his baggy clothes were the color of the wagon tops. Black hair divided in a dozen short braids spiked from his head in every direction. "We're almost ready."

"You found what you needed?" Teran asked.

The trader nodded and smiled. Gold teeth winked behind his lips. He looked back to the caravan. "Come quick, Tint!"

A shorter, brown-skinned man hurried. "What do you want, Veil?"

Veil pointed to Teran. "Give him the supply list. He's the one we pay."

As Wren watched the scene unfolding between his friend and the two men, he sensed something unsettling about the traders but could not decide what it was. *It's not as if I'm in a position to pick and choose my company.*

Tint handed Teran a roll of parchment. Teran unrolled it, looked it over, and handed it back. "You owe me five hundred silvers for the supplies. But I'll deduct fifty for taking my friends as passengers."

Veil's eyes moved to Wren. "You need to deduct more than that, I think. This man is wearing armor. He is carrying a weapon, and his friends are also bearing arms. If I'm to take them as far as the gate, and these two"—he jerked a thumb at Wren and Kayla—"all the way to Midrun, we owe you less than the sum you've named."

"That town isn't far up the Fairsway," Teran protested. "It won't take much time."

"What good is that time if I'm not alive to see it pass?"

"Deduct another fifty, then, but that's my final offer."

Veil smiled slyly, tonguing a golden tooth. "I'll agree to that." He lifted his whistle to his lips and blew. "We're leaving," he yelled, starting back toward the caravan. "Get the last of the barrels aboard the wagons and make sure everything is doubly secure. We've a rough ride ahead."

"Traders," Wren muttered, shrugging his packs higher on his back. "How much do I owe?"

Teran stuck out his chin. "Not a thing."

"You're being as stubborn as Flint was when he gave me his five knives."

"I try," Teran said, and walked over to the rest of the gamblers from the Seasong Arms.

When Flint caught sight of Wren and Kayla, his smile was as sharp as the blade of his ax. "It's about time you got here."

Kendran held his crossbow at his side. "Blazes, Wren, where were you? You're never late for a Jikari game."

"This is no game," Wren said, wiping sweat from his brow.

"What kept you?" Hook asked. He scrunched up his wrinkled face and shifted his grip on the harpoon. "You didn't get a chance to drink last night. A headache can't be the excuse."

"Wren's always had trouble holding his beer," Pulley joked.

Guzzler slung his hammer over a shoulder. "Can't drink me under the table."

"That's impossible for anyone," said Teran, and Pulley touched his pitchfork to his temple knowingly.

Wren chuckled. "What's on the caravan?"

Kendran glanced darkly at the caramel-skinned traders. "They're the bastards who sold me the bad beer yesterday, that yellow-hornet ale from the Ravenswood. I don't envy you, Wren. Unless you brought water, you're going thirsty until you reach Midrun."

"Who's the boy?" Guzzler asked, pointing at Kayla.

Flint cuffed him on the back of his head with the butt of his ax. "That's Kayla, you drunken bastard. Wren's disguises shouldn't be able to fool any of us. They're the worst I've ever seen."

Wren groaned, and Kayla stifled a laugh just long enough to glower at him.

Guzzler rubbed the back of his head. "Sorry, Kayla. My eyes aren't used to natural sunlight. The hearth and the lamps in the Seasong Arms are the only moon and stars I can recall."

Veil strode over. "Is everyone ready?" When Teran nodded, Veil turned from the group and sounded his whistle again.

"That noisemaker hurts my ears," Guzzler said. He gripped his hammer. "I think I want to break it."

Wren rolled his shoulders. His chain mail was stiff, but at least it was not cumbersome; he would be able to maneuver as easily as he had in his home the previous night when he had tossed Scratch from the window. "If there's trouble, keep your heads square on your shoulders, but until trouble finds us, keep your heads down. It will be safer if we can avoid the men who are after me."

Guzzler snorted. "I think I want to break them, too."

"They would break you first," said Wren. He looked from friend to friend. He could tell by their faces that despite their jokes, they understood the gravity of the situation.

Kendran adjusted the quiver of crossbow bolts on his back. "We're with you, Wren, and don't forget it."

"When will you come back to Nautalia?" Hook asked.

Wren swung his packs into the second wagon in the line and climbed in, suddenly realizing how much he was going to miss his friends. "I don't know. But I will return. That's a promise."

"Find a good home for my knives," Flint said, tightening his grip on his ax.

Wren helped Kayla up beside him as his friends scrambled under the black and yellow coverings of other wagons, Kendran and Flint to the rear of Wren's wagon and the other four to the front. "I hope I won't have to use them," he said, but his voice was lost among the shouts of the traders.

Wren examined the wagon's interior. It was filled with barrels marked for Merrifield, boxes bound for Lantern Watch, and piles of parchment and scrollwork. Two black-haired, brown-skinned traders sat at the reins. Veil's whistle sounded another blast, and Wren heard whips crack. Kayla pulled her knees to her chest. Axles groaned, wagon wheels churned, and the caravan rumbled through Seashell Square Market, the barrels sloshing with yellow-hornet ale.

* * *

NAUTALIA'S OUTER FORTIFICATION, encircling the city until it joined the Tidal Wall to the southwest and the pearly spires of Coral Castle to the southeast, was tall and strong. Wide enough for three horses to gallop abreast, it was as old and blue as the Merchant Quarter's bluestone streets. A hundred purple and silver flags bearing Nautalia's trumpeting sea horse fluttered from the battlements, and guard towers stood here and there, many-windowed sentinels gazing down the Fairsway toward Midrun and the mountains.

The caravan rolled across a cobblestone plaza, approaching the East Gate, an arched tunnel bordered by two towers that had been bored into the outer wall. Wren peered over the driver's seat of his wagon, holding the hilt of his sword. Soldiers paced the parapet, their armor glinting in the sun. Two guardsmen stood before the gate, surveying the traffic that passed under the iron-tipped spikes of the tunnel's portcullis. *Hopefully alert for the men who want me dead,* Wren thought, loosening his blade in its sheath.

A soldier on the parapet spotted the caravan and called out an order. The caravan ground to a halt.

"What's happening?" Kayla asked.

"Quiet," Wren said. "I think we're going to be searched."

He watched anxiously as Veil, with spiked hair and glittering gold teeth, jumped from the lead wagon and walked toward the two gate guardsmen, who were striding up to meet him.

"Your name and your destination," demanded one of the guards.

"I'm Veil, captain of this caravan. We're moving goods from Nautalia to Lantern Watch."

The guard nodded to his companion, who started for Veil's lead wagon, where Teran, Guzzler, Pulley, and Hook were busy hiding their weapons as best they could.

Veil frowned. "What are you doing?"

"I'm under orders to inspect everything leaving the city," the guard said as his companion prodded the wagon's canvas with the tip of his weapon. "People were murdered last night, and the High King is outraged by the bloodshed. He is intent on unearthing the culprits."

"These wagons carry beer, not killers."

"All the same," said the guard, and his companion moved to the back of the wagon.

Then six soldiers, armored like those pacing the parapet but bearing staves and cudgels, approached Veil and the guardsman. They were led by a seventh, a man in chain mail who looked as coldly cruel as his naked sword. A latticework of scars marred his finely shaped features; his irises burned black in his eyes, and he wore no helmet. Thick hair curled around his face like crow feathers.

Wren had never seen the man in the sunlight, but he knew him at once: It was the assassin.

One of the guards turned and asked, "Who are you?"

The assassin stepped toward the guardsman. "I've been sent from the castle. The king wants additional forces posted at this entrance."

The guardsman inclined his head. "You can start by helping us with this caravan."

"My pleasure," said the assassin.

Both guardsmen walked toward the lead wagon, accompanied by one of the assassin's disguised mercenaries. The assassin strode to the next wagon in line—toward Wren and Kayla—gesturing to his men; they spread out among the remaining wagons.

Wren crept back from the driver's seat toward the spot where Kayla was waiting deeper in the wagon. "There's going to be trouble," he whispered to her.

She bit her lip, nodded, and wrapped her arms around her knees. Then she started and pointed to the back of the wagon.

The assassin was peering in at them. One of his mercenaries stood at his side. The assassin smiled, the scars twitching on his face. "They're in the wagons!" he cried.

Kendran leaned between the traders at the front of his wagon and sighted down his crossbow. He jerked a finger, and a black bolt twanged. The mercenary standing nearest the assassin looked down, dumbstruck by the iron point protruding from his chest.

"That's one for Wren," Kendran yelled as the traders looked on in shock.

Wren shoved Kayla behind a barrel and leaped from his wagon, drawing his sword as he flew through the air. He crashed into the assassin, knocking him over. Instantly, he sprang away and cut down, but the assassin rolled aside. As Wren's sword clanged into the ground, the plaza burst into chaos.

Flint ripped through his wagon's black and yellow cloth with his ax. He began fending off attackers as Kendran reloaded his crossbow. Teran, Guzzler, and Hook battled a mercenary and the two guardsmen. Veil, twin daggers at his side, and Tint, holding a nail-studded club, rushed with Pulley to the end of the caravan. People fled the melee as the plaza erupted in a maelstrom of clashes and shouts.

"Not good enough," the assassin shouted at Wren, and sprang to his feet.

Wren's heart hammered in his chest. "Why are you after me? How have I wronged you?"

"Business is business—and you, Wren, are the best business I've had in years."

"Tell me your name!"

The assassin smirked. "What good are names to dead men?"

Chain mail tinkled as Wren raised his sword. "You're right," he said. "Dead men have no need for names."

Suddenly a trader's body toppled between them. One of the assassin's mercenaries charged Wren, screaming, but Flint's ax circled through the air and thudded into his back, spattering Wren with blood.

Wren pushed the dead man aside and searched for the assassin, but the fighting had driven them apart.

A bloody trader advanced on Wren with a two-pronged dagger. His eyes were wild with madness, and his body shook and shuddered as a scarlet fountain pulsed from his chest.

The battle's taken hold of his sense, Wren thought. He caught the dagger stroke on his sword, reached out and grabbed the trader's arm, and bent it until the man cried out and dropped his weapon. Then he rapped the flat of his blade against the trader's head. The wounded man collapsed.

Wren darted to his wagon and looked inside. Kayla was still hiding.

"There's blood on your shirt," she screamed.

"Not mine."

He jumped on the back of the wagon and scanned the plaza for the assassin. The scarred killer was approaching the front of the caravan, where Teran, Guzzler, and Hook were brawling with the two guardsmen and one of the disguised mercenaries.

Guzzler struck one of the guards on the head with his hammer, sending him crashing to the ground. Teran batted away a swing of the mercenary's cudgel and shoved his sword into his side.

The assassin reached them, and with one clean stroke decapitated the remaining guardsman. He turned toward Wren's friends.

Wren jumped from the wagon and began running toward them, but two of the assassin's men blocked his path. They attacked from either side, one holding a spear, the other an ax.

The spearman snarled and thrust at him, but Wren knocked down the spear with his sword and stepped on its tip, snapping the pole. The spearman cursed, his balance upset by his wasted momentum. Wren raised his sword and slashed down, angling the cut at the man's shoulder. He screamed as Wren's blade split through armor, skin, and bone, but his scream changed to a hollow gurgle when the blade pierced his lung.

Wren let go of his sword and pulled the two knives from his belt, instinctively ducking a stroke from the axman. He whipped around with a knife in each hand and buried them to their hilts in the axman's neck, then reached behind him and wrenched his sword from the spearman's chest. Both assailants, gushing blood, toppled lifeless to the ground.

Wren charged toward his friends, but he had come too late.

Hook jabbed his harpoon and Teran swung his sword, but the assassin slid between the weapons and raised his own, neatly severing one of Hook's hands. The old fisherman cried out and fell to his knees, clutching at his wrist. Methodical as the clock tower gears, the assassin pivoted, spinning away from Guzzler's hurtling hammer, and brought a fist against Teran's face, knocking him to the ground.

Guzzler lifted his hammer again, but the assassin plunged his sword into the fat man before he could swing, pushing the blade through his bulging stomach until it stuck through his back. He heaved upward, lifting Guzzler from the ground. Guzzler flailed in the air and dropped his hammer; then his body ripped from the sword and crashed to the square in a burst of blood, beer, and gore.

Wren rushed the assassin, screaming curse after curse, nearly blinded by rage and horror.

The assassin, framed by the city fortifications, turned toward him and flicked up a sword dripping with the blood of Wren's friends. "Come to me," he roared.

Crossbow bolts began whistling through the air and clattering on the cobblestones between them. The soldiers on the parapet had begun firing into the fray. A black-fletched bolt buried itself in the assassin's shoulder. He roared a curse and rushed down the line of wagons, gripping the shaft as he knocked aside traders and guardsmen.

Wren dropped to the ground beside Guzzler's body, his eyes burning with tears, and watched as the assassin, dodging flailing limbs and flashing weapons, escaped from the plaza. He cupped his hands under Guzzler's head, oblivious to the crossbow bolts flying past him. At the edge of his vision he saw Teran crawling toward Hook, whose moans were terribly clear against the din of battle.

Then whips cracked, Veil's whistle blasted furiously, and the caravan charged the East Gate.

A crossbow bolt zipped past Wren's left ear. Leaving his friend's body, he gazed wrathfully skyward and ran to his wagon, which was rattling crazily over the cobblestones. He hurled himself inside just before it escaped his reach. Kayla scrambled out from behind the barrel. Wren caught her in his arms, holding her close as the wagons raced between the guard towers, speeding through the tunnel in Nautalia's outer wall.

The iron portcullis thundered shut behind them.

MIDRUN

ADRENALINE SURGED THROUGH Kayla's body as the caravan raced away from Nautalia, a black and yellow cavalcade stamping along the Fairsway.

She bounced along at the back of the wagon, holding tight to a wooden crate, biting her lip and breathing quickly. Vineyards and olive groves, shepherd huts and hilltop houses, sped in and out of her vision before she could focus on any of them. Wind ripped through the wagon, tossing parchment with invisible fingers, and the barrels shuddered as iron-spoked wheels bounced over the stony road. The drivers cursed and lashed their whips against the horses.

Wren sat against a barrel. Blood matted his tunic and smeared his face and hands. His head was bowed, but every few seconds Kayla saw a dark red drop fall to his chest like a tear.

"Father . . ."

Wren looked up, but his storm-blue eyes, haunted and cold, seemed to gaze inward.

Kayla wanted to cringe. "We escaped. The assassin didn't catch us."

Blood and sweat gathered in Wren's scar and trickled down his cheek, but it was not his own blood. "I wasn't fast enough," he said as a thick bead slid to his chin.

"You did all you could. You protected me."

"Guzzler was killed with a blade that was meant for me. I watched the assassin lop off Hook's hand. I wasn't fast enough to save them."

Kayla crossed the wagon and sat by his side, putting an arm around him.

"I'm alive because of you." She took a piece of parchment from the floor and began wiping blood from his face.

Wren shut his eyes. "You're in *danger* because of me . . ." He paused and pushed her hand away. "I think it's time you knew the truth of our situation."

But before he could tell her anything else, Veil's whistle sounded and the caravan changed course, veering from the Fairsway to a pebble path that wound up around a steep green hill.

Wren scrambled to the rear of the wagon. "First that enchantress bewitches you, then the battle at the gate, and now this."

"What's happening?"

"Veil must be avoiding Midrun, circling wide of the town and making directly for the Ivory Pass. That's no wonder—if the Nautalian soldiers catch us on the Fairsway, we'll be butchered in these wagons. I had hoped to get closer to town first. The traders are a dangerous lot."

The wagon jolted over a rut in the path, then stopped suddenly. Wren took Kayla's wrist and jumped with her to the ground.

The caravan had drawn up in a crescent along the far side of the hill, near a cracked stone wall that ran beside the path. Sheep moved like clouds on the hillside. Two orange trees grew nearby; their fruit-laden branches cast twisted shadows on the path. It seemed an idyllic spot, though the threat of conflict hung in the air.

Kayla hurried after Wren toward the trees, her boots crunching on pebbles, then pounding on dirt and grass. "Stand against a trunk," he said, and turned toward the caravan.

Veil and Tint were striding toward them. Nine men followed, holding a shoddy array of weaponry: notched short swords, daggers, long knives, and clubs. Their clothes were torn and bloody, and their eyes raged with anger.

Kayla backed up against the trunk.

Wren moved a hand to his sword hilt and brushed aside his cloak; three knives dangled from his belt. "Don't come any closer," he said. "There's been enough fighting today."

Veil's forehead bore a wicked gash below his black-spiked hair. "That sword of yours is too pretty for a corpse." Gold teeth sparked as he raised his upper lip and lifted his twin daggers.

"If you fight me, I won't be the only corpse under these trees."

Tint chuckled grimly and unhooked a nail-studded club from his belt. "Your son will join you."

Veil scraped his daggers together. "I've lost three good men, men who will never again work with me. And it's because of you and your damned friends. Pity none of them stayed on the wagons. I would have enjoyed slitting their throats and watching their lives bubble from their necks." The traders advanced in a half circle of weaponry.

Wren let his cloak fall over his knives but kept his hand by his sword. "My son had nothing to do with any of this, and I didn't harm your men."

One of the traders lifted a hatchet. "I saw you knock one of ours to the cobblestones."

Wren shook his head. "The battle had shaken his mind. He was nearly senseless. I stopped him before he could harm one of us."

Kayla's throat constricted. The orange tree's bark dug into her back, but she pushed hard against it, looking about the grass at her feet for something she could use in a fight. There were only sticks, dead leaves, and a few rotten oranges on the root-choked ground.

"Our man is still back there," Tint spit. "Dead, just like the rest of us if we're caught by the city guard." At that, something in him snapped and he lunged at Wren, swinging his nail-studded club.

Wren reached out and twisted his arm until Kayla heard a sickening crack. Tint screamed and dropped the club. Wren smashed a fist into his jaw, sending him sprawling on his back, then moved his hand to his sword hilt. The traders cursed, but no one else charged him.

Veil snarled. "He's only one man."

"I won't die on his blade," said the one with the hatchet. "Kill him yourself."

Veil thrust his daggers under his belt. "I'll remember this," he said to Wren. He hauled Tint up as the traders slouched away.

Whips snapped, horses broke into a canter, and the black and yellow wagons rolled past the orange trees, skirting the hill, rumbling south along the pebble path. Wren sank to his knees, burying his face in his hands.

As her fear faded, Kayla looked down in confusion, watching his shoulders rise and fall with silent sobs. She was transported once more to his bedroom door, where years earlier she had listened through the keyhole as he cried for his long-dead wife. Kayla awkwardly patted his back, then picked up one of the oranges that had fallen from the tree and plopped it on his head.

Wren glanced up at her, eyes red.

Kayla winked at him. "Hungry?"

"Not for that orange."

He stood up and glowered down at her. She made a face back at him, and their exaggerated expressions dissolved into uneasy laughter.

Wren turned and shook the tree; oranges tumbled from its branches. He caught one and handed it to Kayla. He dropped his packs and removed a bag of dried apples from one of them, replacing the dry fruit with fresh oranges from the tree.

"So what do we do now?" Kayla mumbled through her orange.

Wren brought out the rind of cheese, the brown bread, and the water flagon he had brought to the clock tower the night before. "We go first to Midrun and then to Dale's cottage." He sat down with his back to the trunk, tore a piece of bread with his teeth, and tossed the rest to Kayla.

She broke off a hunk. "You mentioned him last night in the clock tower. You said you knew him."

"I wish it were otherwise. He's a wizard."

Kayla was astonished. "But you hate magic."

"My relationship with Dale is slightly . . . complicated. He's calling in a debt I've owed since you were a child."

"When did you talk to him?"

Wren opened the flagon, drank deeply, and passed it to Kayla. She took a gulp and handed it back. "Last evening he brought me to him through some sort of spell. I think my connection to him explains the assassin's interest in us. Years ago a village near Merrifield came under attack. I was there with you and your mother. Dale saved your mother's life." He took another drink, then ran a sleeve across his mouth and screwed on the top of the flagon. "If we want to figure out why men have been hired to kill us, if we are to have any chance of stopping them, we're going to have to sit Dale down and force him to give us some answers."

"And some solutions," Kayla added.

"Let's hope he has some."

Wren repacked their food and smeared dirt over the blood on his tunic. He and Kayla started for the Fairsway. She peeled another orange and walked at his side.

The Fairsway cut through green hills, intersected by smaller roads and paths. Aside from the occasional orchard, the land was open and largely treeless. Few others were traveling abroad. Those who did steered wagons or rode horses, casting suspicious glances up and down the road. They gave Wren and Kayla a wide berth when they passed.

At some point hoofbeats sounded behind them. Wren moved Kayla to the roadside as a double column of mounted knights appeared over a rise in the Fairsway behind them, riding fast from Nautalia. They were armored and carried lances and shields. Their captain, clad in full plate mail, led them on a gray warhorse, grasping an unfurled Nautalian banner in a gauntleted fist.

Wren pulled his cloak over his sword and rested his hand on Kayla's shoulder. "Leave the talking to me."

Kayla winced and studied the ground as the knights galloped toward them. But the captain and his men passed them by without a sideways glance.

* * *

MIDRUN WAS NAMED for its equidistant location between Nautalia and the Ivory Pass, a narrow white-cliff valley that centered on the disreputable mining village of Spire.

A wide blue river spanned by the Kingsbridge split Midrun in two. The West Bank—the larger half facing Nautalia and the Starlight Sea— was well manicured, home to shingle-roof houses, wealthy merchants, civilized people, and expensive shops. There the air was clean, though it held a musky scent, and the streets were solid, though pocked with the wear of passing years. Most of the locals wore fancy, brightly colored clothes, but men had poniards strapped at their belts and women seldom moved alone, aware of the dangers posed by their close proximity to the wild mountains, dangers that often crept into the rougher sections of their town.

The East Bank was a decrepit basin of narrow streets and tall brick-and-mortar houses, and it lay on the riverside closer to the mountains. Each building had been constructed with only two or three windows; none were equipped with chimneys, and most roofs, whether on homes, taverns, or craftsmen's shops, were wooden and rotting and full of moldering holes that let water in when it rained.

Midrun was protected by a thirty-foot-high wall of stone that gradually transformed around the East Bank into an ugly, imposing composition of sharp wooden stakes, packed mud, bricks, and iron fastenings. Twice as many guardsmen patrolled this barrier as did the West Bank's wall, for it faced the harsh wilderness of the Ivory Pass.

When Kayla entered the town, she was surprised at her attraction to a place where the rich brushed shoulders with rascals and vagabonds. Wren had brought her to the town once before, wishing to show her a place that, at least in its well-kept areas, was an exciting change from Nautalia. Kayla remembered hating the experience: After he had taken her shopping, Wren had guided her to the Kingsbridge, a bluestone arch lined with jewel shops, but he had forbidden her to explore the East Bank across the river. She had been only eleven, but she vividly remembered standing there amid the rainbow glitter of precious stones, gazing across the river, pleading with Wren to take her to the murky streets of the East Bank where haphazard houses, framed by the Seaspine Mountains, looked like ogres, trolls, and goblins that had wandered from a bedtime story, pitched camp, and begun telling tales of their own.

Now travelers in all manner of dress were treading on the Fairsway, which ran through the center of town, but nonetheless Kayla felt conspicuous in her dirty clothes. They seemed strangely out of place amid the channels of well-dressed people milling in front of stores and shops, chatting, gossiping, and gesturing as they went about their daily errands.

"I hope we're finding an inn," she said, giving Wren a hopeful look. "I could use a hot bath."

Wren scratched his chin. "I wouldn't say no to a warm meal and a soft bed."

"The Reveler's Crown? The place where we stayed on our last visit?"

"Midrun has only two inns, and that's the only one I'd consider. The other is called the Rogue's Cloak, but it's on the East Bank. Before you were born I never used to spend time on this side of the river, but I've come to realize it's much better than the other. Still . . ." He trailed off, eyeing the finely dressed people with a look bordering on disdain.

They continued in silence until they reached the Reveler's Crown, a spacious building with elongated blue-glass windows and a semicircular portico of lacquered wood. People were jammed together on the portico, struggling to get inside. Kayla and Wren pushed up to two middle-aged ladies wearing bright hats, one pink and the other green, who were talking at the edge of the throng.

"I doubt we'll be able to enter, dear," said the woman in the pink hat.

"But I simply *must* see Master Quillan. His sketches and paintings . . . Why, one of his landscapes has been hanging in my kitchen for years and years, and I've never had the chance to thank him for it."

"He isn't heading back to Nautalia until tomorrow morning."

"I won't be up early enough to see him off . . ."

Kayla listened with interest; she had never seen a real artist at work. Nautalia had street painters, but they were not the real thing. For a moment she envisioned herself as an artist, surrounded by easels, paints, and pictures, sketching in an open-air workroom high in a city tower, but then Wren was tugging the sleeve of her tunic, pulling her away from the Reveler's Crown.

"Are we heading for the other inn?" she asked, her eyes turning reluctantly from the crowded portico.

Wren shook his head. "The Rogue's Cloak is a den of cutthroats and thieves."

"That doesn't matter; I've seen worse since last night. Besides, the assassin wouldn't search for us there."

Wren considered her for a moment. "I know the owner."

"Not surprising."

He's owed me a gambling debt for years. I'm not letting you sleep there, but I might be able to wring some help from Mace."

Just before they reached the Kingsbridge, a young knight on a great white horse approached them. He was as tall and thin as a scarecrow. A broadsword hung at his side, a shield was clasped to his arm, and he held a lance twined with a pennant that was checkered blue and white. He was girt in sparkling armor, and he wore a helm surmounted by blue and white plumes. His eyes were the color of sea foam. *Those are the eyes of a madman,* Kayla thought, *or the eyes of a dreamer.*

Wren swept back his cloak. "Who are you?"

"Sir Lancet Rhymewind," the knight said. His voice was strong and piercing yet cool as evening shadows.

"I've no business with men-at-arms today."

Sir Lancet smiled. "No argument, friend. This is my first foray into the Seaspine Coast. I'm searching for an inn where I can feed and water my horse. Last night I slept in Spire under the white-walled cliffs of the Ivory Pass. Shortly after waking, my breakfast was interrupted by a royal messenger galloping down the Fairsway, shouting news of murders in Nautalia. Since I'm sworn to combat evil, I travel to the city to find and dispose of the killers."

"How noble," Wren said dryly.

"I've even heard rumors of a dragon."

Wren paused, considering. "There's an inn behind me bordering the Fairsway. It's stuffed with people—an artist is using the common room as a stage to showcase his paintings—but there may be room in the stable."

Sir Lancet inclined his head. "You have my thanks. May Lira smile on your travels." He nudged the flanks of his mount, and the horse trotted through the crowd, making for the Reveler's Crown.

"Did you hear that?" Kayla asked. "He's after the assassins. Why didn't you tell him about us? He might be able to help."

Wren snorted. "That knight's no more than a featherheaded fool, probably out for a reward. We don't know anything about him. He's more likely to turn us in than help us. Don't forget, I must have been seen fighting at the East Gate." He started for the Kingsbridge before Kayla could reply.

On both sides of the bluestone arch were garishly painted shops with window displays that flashed with gems hauled from the mines around Spire, giving it the appearance of a dazzling royal walkway. Kayla hurried to keep up with Wren. He kept his head down, aware of the Midrun guardsmen standing in shadowed doorways, alert for thieves and pickpockets.

Frivolous people moved to and fro, clutching bags filled with newly purchased necklaces, earrings, or bracelets, laughing and smiling in the heat of the sun. From the spectacle of the Kingsbridge, Kayla observed the houses on the East Bank. They looked less monstrous, bearing a closer resemblance to beggars' houses.

Wren slowed until Kayla caught up. "When we reach the East Bank, lower your eyes if someone stares at you. You're safe as long as you're with me, but there's no need to provoke attention, and there are many men on that side of the river who don't need much provocation. The Rogue's Cloak is far from the main road; soldiers only travel there in infrequent patrols."

Kayla nodded, suddenly unsure if she should have suggested leaving the West Bank.

They left the Kingsbridge and the Fairsway, crossed a smaller dirt street, and entered an area of crooked alleys. The change was instant and palpable. The men and women around them wore blank expressions and rough-spun clothes. Most were common laborers, but Kayla spotted ruffians among them: strong, sinister men who carried brutish weapons. Several stared at her, but she did not stare back.

By the time they reached the Rogue's Cloak, Kayla regretted her suggestion in full. The inn's black-timbered facade, windowless save for a small transom above the door, stood shoulder to shoulder with smaller, disheveled houses. A sign bearing the likeness of a thug, slant-eyed and robed in a crimson cloak, hung over the door from above the transom.

As the sign swung slowly, a skinny woman with ropy hair pushed through the door, retched, and then sauntered back inside.

Kayla grinned nervously. "Is she a friend of yours?"

Wren flashed her a dark look and headed for the door.

The inn's interior was packed with people sitting at round iron tables. Red lanterns hung from the low ceiling, casting the dark, windowless room in a ruddy light. Wisps of steam rolled up the descending half of a stairway and into the room through an opening beside the bar.

Kayla trailed Wren, avoiding contact with anything. When they reached the bar, a toothless man greeted them with a frown.

"That you, Wren?" he asked, corking a wine bottle with cracked hands. "Where've you been?"

"I didn't know I meant that much to you, Skiver."

"You don't. But your purse is something else, something we'd kill to have around here. Our ale's still sweeter than any woman. Why'd you disappear? You used to be good business."

"I've been business for several people today. Pity I'm in such short supply. Where's Mace?"

Skiver rubbed a finger along his gums. "Downstairs in his steam room, but you won't want to see him. He's still upset about that Jikari game you won. Good thing you didn't take the money. You wouldn't have made it to the Fairsway."

As she followed Wren to the opening beside the bar, Kayla glanced over her shoulder. Skiver was staring at them with an undecipherable expression. "Your friends seem nice," she said brightly.

Wren ignored the quip and started down the steps.

At the base of the stairs, a door flanked by two red lanterns had been left halfway open. The lanterns lent a bloody hue to the steam streaming through the door.

A short, muscular guard sat on a stool, armored in boiled leather and an iron cap. When he saw Wren, he snapped erect, unhitching an ax from his belt. "Who're you?"

"Let me through," Wren said. "I'm here to see Mace."

"He's busy."

Throwing knives appeared in Wren's hands. "I've asked you to move. I won't ask again."

Then, from beyond the door, a voice said, "Get out of his way."

Wren made his knives vanish under his cloak as the guard lowered his ax and moved aside.

Kayla entered a steamy room with a ceiling of sagging wood. Mace sat at a desk of overlapping iron plates; they looked as if they had been hammered together by a drunkard. A coal fire burned in an alcove on the left-hand wall. The coals spit and hissed as water from a hidden source hit them, clouding the air and pouring steam into the room.

Mace had a fat, porous face. Five scars ran from his bald head to a ragged stump where there should have been an ear. A stained tunic was plastered to his skin, and his eyes were a sickly yellow. "It's been a long time, Wren Tident."

"I hope the years haven't dulled your memory."

"You're here for the money, then?"

Despite the room's substantial heat, Kayla noticed Mace shivering with what appeared to be a feverish chill.

Wren folded his arms. "Only a horse and riding gear. If you give me that, I'll consider your debt paid."

Mace lifted a mug from the iron desk and drank it dry. "Why should I square up with you?"

"I'm giving you a way out. You owe me more than a mount."

"Come with me," Mace said, narrowing his eyes. "I'll get your horse."

Upstairs, Mace went behind the bar and muttered something to Skiver, who nodded and left the inn. Then he began gulping wine from the bottle that Skiver had been decorking.

"Where's he going?" Wren asked.

"To fetch your horse." Mace fixed his yellowish eyes on Kayla. "Who's this, then? That's no boy."

"She's no concern of yours."

Mace tossed the bottle behind him; it shattered on a rounded keg. "You've just made her my concern. Her hair's too short and her face is dirty, but everything's dirty around here. And she's such a pretty little thing." He reached a fat, blue-veined hand toward her, and she shuddered.

Wren clenched his hands. "Stay away from her."

Mace's laughter sounded like the water sizzling on the coals. "Don't get angry. We can share. I've got a room upstairs—"

Before he could go any further, Wren grabbed him by the neck of his tunic.

Just then Kayla saw two men enter the inn. Their faces bore no scars, but she recognized one of them from the battle at Nautalia's North Gate. "Wait!" she shouted, tugging Wren's arm from the innkeeper.

Mace rubbed his neck. "Skiver must have misheard me, Wren. It looks like you won't be riding away anytime soon."

Wren seized Mace by the hair, slammed his face on the bar, yanked him up, and threw him into a shelf of bottles as the thugs ran toward them, shoving people aside. As Wren spun around, the common room erupted in a brawl. Kayla followed him along the right side of the room, ducking fists and beer mugs.

The rope-haired woman jumped in front of Wren, screaming curses, spittle running down her chin. A chair flew into her back and knocked her to the floor. Kayla picked up a glass bottle with the vague idea that it might protect her.

Someone kicked over a table. Wren dodged it and jumped over the rope-haired woman, hitting a man with a pierced nose who had lurched toward Kayla. While Wren shoved him away, Skiver emerged from the middle of the melee, rushing him with a dagger. Kayla ducked around her father and hit him with the bottle. Clutching his head, Skiver toppled back into the fight.

Then Wren was shouldering his way through the exit.

Kayla started after him, but something thudded into her back, forcing her to the ground just outside the inn. Spitting dirt, she pushed herself up and watched as one of the assassin's mercenaries materialized in the doorway. He stepped under the Rogue's Cloak's transom, swinging a spiked ball and chain in circles around his head.

Wren's sword appeared in his hand. "That's the perfect weapon for a crowded fight."

"Shut your—"

Wren charged him, thrusting with his blade. The mercenary frantically swung his weapon, but it wrapped around Wren's sword. Wren jerked up, ripping the ball and chain from the other man's grasp, then slashed an x stroke on his chest. The thug's eyes rolled up in his head.

"Give my regards to Mace," Wren said, and pushed the corpse back into the inn. He turned to Kayla, sheathing his sword. "Let's go."

They raced through alleyways until they reached the Fairsway; then they crossed the Kingsbridge—drawing angry looks from people they bumped aside—and kept running until they reached the crowded portico of the Reveler's Crown. Kayla and Wren skirted the mass of people until they reached a flat wooden building conjoined to the inn. It was a stable, but its doors were shut.

"They're locked!" Wren shouted, pulling on them. He looked down the street past Kayla. The scarred assassin, newly disguised in common clothes and with a bandaged shoulder, strode toward them, flanked by two more men. They were still some way off, but they had spotted Wren.

Her father sprinted toward the portico and dived into the crowd of clustered people. Kayla moved in his wake as they shoved their way left and right, ignoring the shouts and yells. She stumbled into the inn after Wren and found herself rushing through a series of small, crowded rooms filled with art displays. Easels were banged aside, splashing garishly dressed patrons with paint. Wren pushed between the two ladies who had been standing outside the inn, knocking their bright hats from their heads. More shouts began sounding behind her.

Then she was in the stable, shutting a door behind her. Wren hurried under a hayloft and entered a stall that sheltered a white horse that looked strangely familiar. Kayla glimpsed a lance twined with a blue and white pennant propped in a corner, half-buried in hay. "What are you doing?"

Wren finished tacking up the horse, swung onto the saddle, and slipped his feet into the stirrups. "You said you wanted Sir Lancet's help. Now you have it. I'll give the horse back when we're not being chased by men who want to kill us."

As Kayla climbed up beside him, the stable door burst open, and the assassin rushed through and planted himself in front of the exit. Wren snapped the horse's reins. As it bolted through the stall, he hurled one of his throwing knives at the assassin.

Slicing his sword at the last possible instant, the assassin swatted the knife away, jumping aside as the horse swept past, and charged onto the Fairsway.

Kayla held Wren's waist as they raced through town and out through the gate in the West Bank's wall, veering onto a western road where meadows turned to farms, then fallow fields, then barren hills. To her right mountains stretched into the distance. *Like a rocky spine bordering the sea,* she thought. She looked behind her: Nautalia was hardly more than a silver glimmer by the ocean.

THE LIGHTHOUSE

A SWORD OF orange fire streaked the western horizon, the last light of the dying sun, and Wren, riding the knight's horse, imagined flames dancing across the sea. An ocean wind blew landward, stinging his face and whipping the horse's mane.

Kayla shifted behind him. "How much farther will we ride tonight?"

"Until we find shelter," Wren said, squinting in the wind.

"Where does your friend live?"

"Dale is no friend of mine. His cottage lies all alone, near the ocean, with only waves and gulls for company."

"Tell me how you met him."

Wren looked out to sea: The orange fire was sinking. Stars brightened above the ember glow, pale in the fading light. "That story should not be told at dusk," he said, and Kayla was silent for a time.

* * *

AFTER SEVERAL MORE miles Wren spotted a solitary stone tower rising in the twilight. It was a lighthouse.

He reined in his horse, opened a saddlebag, and took out a collapsible telescope, which he extended and lifted to his eye, peering back along the way he had come. At first he could see nothing. But then, among the blue and purple hills, he glimpsed three horsemen, riding fast.

"What is it?" Kayla asked.

Wren snapped the telescope shut. "They've followed us."

He kicked the horse into a gallop, guiding it toward the tower.

*   *   *

NIGHT HAD FALLEN by the time they reached the lighthouse.

Towering above the dunes, it rose from the rocky shore like a petrified trunk, a once-living thing that had died ages earlier. Mist drifted around the tower's base, settling between the dunes and wandering out to sea in slow, aimless currents, floating like a river of lost ghosts who had wandered from their graves. The lantern chamber, its glass shattered long ago, was a ruined shell embracing the tide of night. Only the faintest traces of starlight reached the chamber's core, causing a dull glow where once a bright flame had burned.

Wren was spellbound, caught up in the dark enchantment of the place. He had never seen the lighthouse, but he knew it had stood there, spiking above the sand and the sea, since long before his birth. There was a story to this place. It whispered to Wren, yearning for him to explore the tower's dark past, to discover its darker secrets. It lay in the mist, and it rested between the stones.

It brooded in the lantern chamber.

Kayla hugged his waist. "Where are we?"

Wren steered the horse to the lighthouse. "I don't know. I've never been here before."

Waves broke on the boulder-strewn beach, and wind rustled the sea grass as the horse walked warily forward. Saddlebags jangled; hooves clipped on the overgrown path.

"Can we move any faster?" Kayla asked.

"Quiet," Wren warned, resting a hand on his sword.

"What is it?"

Wren tightened his grip. "There's something wrong here, something that should be left undisturbed."

"And we're going inside?"

"Either that or face the assassins. I'll take my chances with the tower. But we should be as silent as the dead. If we trouble the spirits of this place, they may return to trouble us."

The door, a grate of iron, waited in the side of the lighthouse like the entrance to a dungeon. Fog swirled through its rusted spikes.

Wren dismounted and pushed the door open. It creaked as it moved inward, vanishing into blackness. Kayla swung from the horse. She stepped to the doorway and peered inside, but Wren pulled her back. He unwound the lantern from the saddle, flicked open one of its panes, and used a flint to light the wick—an orange flame sprang to life. Holding the lantern before him, he stepped into the lighthouse.

The interior was circular and hollow, bare except for a wooden stairway that wound its way upward. Lichen covered a floor so cracked that it could have been mistaken for a shattered mirror had it not been made of stone. Shadows slid up the walls and coiled snakelike on the stairway.

We shouldn't be here, he thought, but he knew this was the best chance they had of evading the assassins. If they were discovered, they would be as dead as that which haunted the tower.

He turned to Kayla. "I think it's empty."

She nodded, leading the horse inside. A gust of wind followed her, eddied about the interior of the lighthouse, and passed back into the night, closing the door as it left. Iron creaked into place, and fog poured through the grated spikes once more.

Wren tied the horse to the stairway rail, then took Kayla's hand and started up the stairs. Rotten boards groaned under his boots. Every so often Wren skipped a step, judging it too unstable to hold his weight.

Kayla squeezed his hand. "Do you think they will find us here?"

"That depends on who you mean by 'they,'" Wren said, lifting his lantern above his head.

Every so often they passed tiny windows, hardly bigger than arrow slits. Through them, Wren caught glimpses of the night outside: surf breaking on the shore, rolling dunes, fog-shrouded ground about the tower. As he passed the windows, he swept his cloak over the lantern and pictured the way the lighthouse would look were he not careful to hide the light: a spear of darkness, deeply shadowed, with one small light winking from window to window, drifting upward like a firefly.

Finally they could go no farther. The stairway ran through a trap-door in a stone ceiling, the floor to the lantern chamber. A hole had been eaten in the trapdoor, but Wren could not see through it.

He glanced down. The tower floor was lost in a well of ink.

Handing the lantern to Kayla, Wren pressed on the trapdoor. It opened slowly and then fell with a bang. Echoes burst up and down the tower. Wren froze. He listened for sounds not made by the trapdoor, but the echoes subsided and were replaced by silence.

"So much for staying quiet," Kayla muttered.

Wren glared at her, holding a finger to his lips.

He climbed into the lantern chamber, put out his light, and helped Kayla into the room. *I can't let the assassins know we're up here. The moon and stars are enough to see by.*

Five stone pillars supported the edges of the roof, which peaked above his head. A stone-walled fire pit dominated the center of the chamber, and a brazier hung from chains above the pit. Had the light-house been in use, the brazier would have held coals and a fire, but Wren could tell it had not flared for many years.

A chilly wind blew through the chamber, tousling his hair. He wrapped himself in his cloak and walked around the pit, stopping at the brink of the lantern chamber to gaze over the coast. He could not see the assassins, but the shoreline was too murky for him to see much of anything.

"Father, look at this."

Wren turned.

Kayla was crouched on the floor by the pit, holding a book in her hands, her shorn blond locks twisting in the wind.

"This is the first time I've seen you interested in reading," he said. She did not look up. "It's a journal."

Wren squatted at her side. The pages were covered in line after line of spidery text, and in many places the ink was smudged. He skipped the illegible sections, reading in the starlight.

After a quick breakfast of gull eggs, Lynn and I took Melody to the shore. We watched our baby girl with delight as she played on the beach, building castles in the sand. Lynn, who traveled to Nautalia in her youth, said they reminded her of the High King's castle. Having never been to that pearly city, I could only nod in agreement.

Come noon, Lynn gathered Melody in her arms, and we sat together and shared a meal of bread and cheese. While we ate, the tide washed away Melody's sand castle. She cried a little but then immediately began on another, her tears bubbling into giggles as it quickly took shape.

Wren flipped several more pages.

There was a storm tonight, and Melody was terrified. . . . hurried to ignite the brazier . . . barely in time to save a ship . . . steered clear at the last second as our warning signal flared through the black rain.

A chilly gust of wind ripped through the lantern chamber, folding over a large section of the journal.

Wren held the binding tighter, scanning the new page with growing dread.

I curse the gods, all of them. Melody ran to hug Lynn during another storm, knocked her off balance and through the open trapdoor . . . lies dead, lifeless eyes locked in fear.

Damn Ariel, damn Lira, damn them to where the demons lie. Damn my daughter, the one who took my love from me.

Wren turned the page, but it was unwritten. He moved to the next.

. . . can't stand the sight of her . . . despise her, the ugly thing. How could I ever have loved . . . I watch her from a distance . . . She has grown cold and silent. Tears have left her, and that is . . . Her sobbing curdles my blood.

The Watchers tell me to do terrible things, and I cannot make them stop. I don't bother with the lighthouse anymore. Let the ships crash. An hour ago, my arm caught in the tower door, and I laughed like a madman.

Wren felt Kayla gazing at him. He looked at her, pausing, his thumb on the edge of the page.

She nodded.

He pushed it over.

I strangled Melody an hour ago, crushed her vile white throat, and I threw her body below the brazier.

My hands decay as they lengthen and widen.

The Watchers curse me as flesh sloughs from my nai . . .

The handwriting melted into a scrawl, and the rest of the pages were blank.

Kayla stood up and backed away from the stone-wall pit, blue eyes wide with horror.

Wren rose, placed the journal on the floor, and hugged her, feeling the pounding of her heart.

"Father," she began, but then she closed her mouth. The sounds of horses had broken the silence.

Wren shoved her down and dropped to the floor. Staying low, he crept to his previous vantage point.

The three horsemen he had seen through the telescope were approaching the foot of the lighthouse. Mist curled about their black mounts. One gestured toward the tower; the others shook their heads. Cloaks flapping in the wind, they halted, discussing something among themselves, though Wren could not hear what they said. The horseman who had gestured snapped his reins and kicked his horse closer to the tower. His hooded face strained upward. His features were hidden, but Wren could feel his eyes searching among shadows in the lantern chamber.

Then the others moved back, the closest wheeled around, and all three galloped away, rushing toward Bridgewater and the mountains.

Wren was about to rise when a dark, crooked form hobbled from behind a dune, staggering toward the lighthouse in the mist. It looked up at the lantern chamber just as the horseman had, and Wren, pressing himself to the floor, knew that it could see him. The crooked creature raised a misshapen hand, pointed at him with a claw, then staggered into the lighthouse.

Wren swore and pushed himself up.

Kayla hugged herself, managing to keep between the pit, the stairs, and the outer edge of the lantern chamber as uneven footsteps echoed up the stairway. "Did one of them find us?"

"Something did," Wren said. He began sparking his whetstone in his lantern. *Damn you, wick. Burn!*

The candle did not catch, but the thudding on the stairs grew louder.

Wren pointed at Kayla. "Stand away from the trapdoor."

"What is it?"

"I wish I knew."

He knelt by the trapdoor and looked through the hole. Without a light, he could not see farther than a dozen wooden steps. Uneven footfalls continued sounding up the stairs.

Then the creature staggered into view, disturbing the darkness. It was barely human.

Clothed in rags and strips of algae, the creature would have been tall, but it walked hunched over as if its back were broken in several places. Its limbs, long and thin, were bent at grotesque angles. Eyes as slim as Flint's knives squinted in its shriveled face, their irises black as unlit coals.

When he saw the creature's hands, Wren's heart skipped a beat; they were as large as its head and longer than its forearms. Claws jutted from cuticles of bone where skin bunched like poisoned growths. *Is this the man who killed Melody?* he found himself thinking. In answer, the creature reached toward him.

Wren stepped from the trapdoor and drew his sword. It glittered in the starlight as it slid from its sheath.

As claws poked through the trapdoor hole, Kayla stifled a scream.

"Stay back," Wren shouted.

The trapdoor rose.

Wren shifted his grip and swung his sword in a sparkling arc. The blade cut clean through one of the creature's arms, but the sword's flight, slowed by skin and bone, was caught halfway in the other arm.

The creature thrust up its head and bit the sword, jaws tugging it from its wounded arm as it hoisted itself into the lantern chamber.

Wren moved back and delivered a two-handed cut against its side, tugged the sword free, and thrust it through the creature's chest.

With a silent snarl, the creature gripped the blade with its remaining hand. Black blood spurted from the stump on its arm, the gash in its side, the hole in its chest, and it began dragging itself through the blade toward Wren, who pulled frantically on the hilt—but his weapon had stuck fast in the creature's ribs.

Kayla shouted and hurled the journal through the air, hitting the creature in its face.

Wren pulled a throwing knife from his belt, sawed through the creature's other hand, and kicked it backward through the trapdoor. Then he planted his feet firmly on either side of the fissure and grasped his sword as the weight of the creature's body pulled from the blade.

When it wrenched free, it crashed on the stairs and smashed through the railing, tumbling into darkness.

There was utter silence . . . then a thud.

Far below the knight's horse whinnied, stamped, and then grew quiet.

Wren listened, breathless, but the silence remained.

Kayla came to his side and looked down into the black well that was the tower. "Is it dead?"

Wren put an arm around her shoulder. "It was already dead, I think. Perhaps we just killed it again."

* * *

BUT WHEN THEY reached the bottom of the lighthouse, the broken floor held only the frightened horse, a splattering of blood, and two huge, misshapen hands.

ONE-EYE

ADRIEL SAT ON the side of his bed at the inn, staring through the room's west window as the sun set over Merrifield, shading the hills beyond the palisade. People holding trinkets and packages moved from the Spinribbon Fair up the town's winding streets. Four stories below, storekeepers bustled around the edges of the square, closing windows and locking doors.

Basking in the warm evening air and feeling his weariness ebbing into the blankets beneath him, Adriel listened sleepily to the music of laughter and clinking glassware rising from the inn's common room. He wished he were home with Dale, practicing magic or reading in the study. He wished he were hearing waves on the shore.

Carpeted with animal skins and walled with pine logs, the room was cramped, holding only a dresser and a rocking chair. A small painting of a black-winged rook hung above a tiny brick hearth. His staff and traveling pack rested near the door, which he had shut to maintain some semblance of privacy, but there was another window in his room that had neither curtain nor shade. Open to one of the inn's hallways, it peered at him like a glass eye.

The sky darkened to violet. Windows began glowing with candles; doorways brightened with lantern light. Adriel considered kindling a fire in the hearth, but it was ashen and woodless, so he stayed on the bed, watching the scurrying townsfolk as shadows lengthened in the room.

The remainder of his journey to Merrifield, aside from a run-in with a troupe of intoxicated musicians, had been largely uneventful, though his staff had drawn plenty of stares. *It's almost as if I have an aura,* he thought. *People seem to know I've been touched by magic.*

He had been picking his way down the foothills from Bridgewater when the road split near a lion carved from stone, partially hidden by weeds and brambles. A sign had pointed east to Merrifield. Led by an elderly fife player, four gaudily dressed people had appeared over the crest of the hill, heading toward him: two young men with violins, a middle-aged woman strumming a harp, and a boy beating a squirrel-hide drum.

They had been a buoyant group, but with the exception of the boy, they had reeked of alcohol. The fife player and the woman had whispered, pointing to Adriel's staff. Then they had asked him if he was a magician, if he was putting on a magic show at the fair. He had told them it was just a walking stick, but he could tell they did not believe him.

Since then he had passed through the fair and into Merrifield, drawing looks wherever he went. Meanwhile, there had been no sign of Corin. Not that Adriel had asked anyone. He had hardly any idea where to start searching.

As he reflected moodily on his situation, a cloaked horseman entered the square. Two black rapiers were strapped to his back; their hilts jerked up and down as he rode toward the inn, and a weird horse-limbed shadow stretched behind him, dragging over the cobblestones.

Standing to gain a better view, Adriel watched the man dismount and lead his horse into the inn's stable.

"That one's up to no good," he said aloud, but then a knock pulled him from his thoughts. He hurried to open the door.

Oswald stepped into the room, holding a platter of food. "I trust everything is to your liking," he said, setting the meal on the dresser. He spotted the dark hearth and put his hands on his apron-tied waist. "You should have told me you were out of wood."

"I'm fine, Oswald. All I need is sleep."

Adriel had met the innkeeper an hour earlier when he had entered Rookery Rest looking for a place to stay. Oswald had seemed pleasant enough, but he also had seemed overly concerned with Adriel's welfare. *It's probably because of my staff,* he'd thought at the time.

Oswald set the tray down on a small wooden table. "The road leaves most men tired. Still, I hope you'll join us downstairs, at least for a short time." He wiped his hands on his apron and left the room, closing the door behind him.

Adriel started on the platter the innkeeper had brought. The food was good, but there was nothing to drink. *He must really want me to entertain the drunkards in the common room,* he mused.

As he finished the food, Adriel decided to do as Oswald had asked, though he decided to leave his staff in his room. Perhaps someone at the inn knew Corin. In any event, he might be able to get a closer look at that horseman. Then again, Adriel was not sure whether the horseman would stay long. He had not looked like the type who enjoyed company.

* * *

WHEN HE ENTERED the common room, Adriel spotted the horseman sitting alone in a corner, nursing a drink. The man had only one eye; a clear crystal had been set into the other socket. He stole furtive glances at the one-eyed man until the man glanced back. Then Adriel looked down quickly.

A freckled, brown-haired boy approached Adriel, holding a foaming mug. "Here you are," he said, "a fresh pint of our best beer." He set it on the table and stood back, shifting his feet.

Adriel took a drink. It was bitter, but it left a pleasant warmth in his chest. "What's your name?"

"Dusty."

"And are you Oswald's son?"

The boy nodded and did not move.

Adriel took another swallow. "What do you want?"

"You're a magician. The one everyone's been talking about . . ." Dusty looked at him hopefully.

Adriel sighed and shook his head but then had an idea. "I've come a long way. I need rest. But in the morning I'm putting on a show at the fair."

Dusty grinned. "I won't tell anyone until you're safely out the door."

He started to leave, but Adriel reached out and grabbed him by the sleeve. "Wait a moment. I have a question of my own. Who is that grim man with the rapiers over there in the corner?"

"He calls himself One-Eye," Dusty said quietly. "He showed up yesterday with a couple of rough-looking companions, demanding room and board. My father didn't like their looks, but he never turns away patrons. Ask someone about the rooks in the watchtower."

Adriel began observing One-Eye again as Dusty left to bring him another mug of beer.

He had drunk it and started on a third when two men in leather jerkins—one short and portly, the other tall and gaunt—entered the inn from the stable door and made their way surreptitiously to the one-eyed man's table. Adriel took a deep drink, watching over the rim of his mug as they seated themselves. Oswald hurried over to the table, but One-Eye waved him away.

When the innkeeper had retreated behind the bar, the two leather-clad men began talking, though the common room's racket was so loud that Adriel could not hear what they said. One-Eye slid a coin pouch across the table, and the shorter of the newcomers snatched it, plunged it into a purse, and left the common room with the taller man at his heels.

Unsettled by the men's behavior, Adriel went back to his room, undressed, and climbed under the covers. He wondered if they were connected to the assassins Dale had warned him about.

His eyes grew heavy, and soon he fell asleep.

* * *

ONCE DURING THE night he woke from a fitful dream, sure One-Eye was peering at him through the room's hallway window. But when he sat up, blinked, and looked again, there was nothing to see.

* * *

ADRIEL WOKE EARLY with a pounding headache. Outside, dawn was creeping slowly into the sky.

His temples throbbed, his mouth was dry, and his throat felt as if it had been stuffed with sand. He sat up unsteadily, reorienting himself to a room that teetered as though perched on a cliff. Squinting, he rolled out of bed and started toward the washbasin, but he tripped on a leg of the rocking chair and crashed on the floor. He lay with his back against the carpet of animal skins, feeling like a furry pelt himself: stiff, stretched, and coarse.

I'm never . . . drinking . . . again.

He spent several minutes recovering and then went downstairs, where Dusty served him a breakfast of bread, mushrooms, and bacon. When Adriel finished, he left Rookery Rest, Dusty close on his heels.

"So you're really putting on a show at the fair?" the freckled boy asked.

Adriel turned. "Are you coming?"

"I wouldn't miss it for the world. But don't start without me! I have to pick up my friend who lives down Woolthread Road."

"I'll wait as long as I can." Adriel paused. "Find me afterward. I'll want to know if you enjoyed the magic."

"I'll be there," Dusty said, and ran for the inn's stable.

Adriel started down the street, heading for the fair. *This had better work. I'm almost certain One-Eye is connected to the assassins. If I don't find Corin soon, those thugs will find him first.*

Wherever Adriel walked, townsfolk pointed at him and nudged one another. Boys and girls trailed him as if irresistibly drawn to the sapphire on his staff. At first he smiled—his new plan seemed to be working— but soon his smile faded. None of the children were limping; Corin was nowhere to be found.

WRECK AND RUIN

WREN RODE THROUGH the night and into the morning as stars paled like a thousand fading torches. Dunes sped past, an endless line of dark sand-shrouded barrows. Kayla breathed deeply, trying to expel the horrors of the lighthouse, but thoughts of the huge hands strangled her mind.

By the time they halted, the sky was dull and gray. Wren swung from the saddle and helped her dismount.

She looked seaward, shorn hair tossing in the wind. Clouds curled clawlike over the leaden waves, reminding her of the creature's broken back and bone-white skin. Amber's words swam before her eyes. *There are some things—not of this world—which have yet to enter your darkest dream.* The enchantress had been right: Kayla had since seen several sights beyond any nightmare.

Wren guided the horse to one of the few twisted trees that grew near the shore. "Dale's cottage is nearby," he said, looping the reins around the trunk. "We'll travel on foot from here."

Kayla nodded. Would Dale talk as Amber had, speaking in cryptic riddles? The wizard might be able to tell her more about the medallion, but that would depend largely on Wren. *You have a habit of shortening unwanted conversations with your sword, don't you, Father?*

She waited until he finished knotting the reins, then asked, "Do you remember what Amber told us, the very last thing she said?"

"She mentioned Dale, but her words meant nothing to me. These magic workers are all in league with one another." Wren patted the horse's neck. "That's one group I won't be sorry to leave."

"Amber thinks he's in some kind of trouble."

"Dragons and demons, Kayla. You had better pray she's wrong. If the wizard isn't here after all we've gone through to find him . . ." Wren sighed and rubbed his forehead, then started for the sea.

They reached the dunes and turned west. The wind rolled Wren's cloak like a black wave. Seagulls glided overhead.

When the first board appeared half-buried in a dune, Wren seemed unconcerned, but his expression blackened when he saw the next. They multiplied, warped splinters embedded in the shore, shards of broken glass and bits of crockery, then bricks and chunks of mortar. Shingles curled everywhere like sea creatures plucked from their shells.

As Kayla struggled up a particularly steep dune, her foot hit something solid. She tripped, pitching forward on the sand.

Wren helped her up, and she looked back where she had fallen. A film of sand covered a strange silver shape. Wren wiped away the sand, revealing a medal of a dragon, a lion, and a sea horse. It was identical to the one Kayla had seen in Amber's home, a near mirror image of the medallion she wore at her breast.

A shadow flitted across her father's face. "It can't be . . ." He threw back his cloak and raced to the top of the dune.

Kayla hurried after him, her feet sliding in the sand. She reached his side and looked down the slope.

The ruined corpse of a cottage smoked at the edge of the dune, as desolate as the charred ground surrounding its skeletal foundation. The stone foundation smoldered, enclosing room-size cavities. Broken glass sparkled angrily. At the center was a carcass—an animal of some sort—impaled on a stake.

Wren's face confirmed Kayla's fears. Dale's cottage had been destroyed.

He clutched his chest as he had in the clock tower. "By the gods, how could this have happened?" He gazed at the wreckage a moment longer, then started drunkenly down the dune.

Kayla followed with hestitation. Wind pirouetted as she picked her way through the debris, covering her mouth against the cindery air. Glass crunched under her boots. Rubble lay everywhere in singed piles; nothing had been left intact. Kayla neared the stake, thinking the animal might have been a fox, but she could not be sure. Hardly any traces of its pearl-colored fur remained.

Wren turned in a slow circle. "Damn you, Dale!" he yelled. "What do I do now?" He staggered to a wall that faced the sea and slumped against its blasted surface, covering his face with his hands.

Kayla wrenched her eyes from the stake and walked to the wall. Rough stones dug into her back as she sat next to her father. What was there to say? The only person who could have explained their situation fully was probably dead. Now it would only be a matter of time until the assassins caught and killed them.

She thought back to the events of the last several days: her fight with Wren in her bedroom, the battle at the city gate and their frenzied race through Midrun, the sight of her father slicing his sword across a man's chest, the lighthouse creature's coal-black eyes. She realized that she had memories most people could gain only from the pages of books.

Books . . .

How long had it been since she had sat in her bedroom window, ignoring her father's history book, sketching a butterfly at sunset? Only the night before last, but she felt as if it had happened long ago and to someone else entirely. Tears welled in her eyes. She tried to stop them, but they slid down her cheeks insistently.

"Perhaps we could go away," Wren said softly, "far, far away across the sea where no one could find us." He put an arm around her shoulder. "We could return to Nautalia. Buy passage on a small silver ship and search for a new home."

Kayla thought of spiderwebbed rigging and billowing sails, salt-stained sailors laboring on a wave-swept deck. A prow glistened in her imagination, a carved bowsprit plowing sun-flecked foam.

She laid her head on her father's shoulder. "We'd spend weeks at sea, weathering storms and helping the crew."

Wren stroked her hair. "That sounds like an adventure I could handle. Dawns would wax. Moons would wane. And we would sail on, guided by the sun and stars, navigating the deepest currents of the world."

"I'd finish your history book," Kayla said, wiping her eyes, "and you could use your sword to prepare the ship's food."

"There's nothing I'd like better." Wren rested his head on hers, and Kayla did her best to smile through her tears.

The tide surged along the beach, and a fresh wind rose, blowing away the scent of ruin. Exhaustion overcame them. In the bones of the cottage they closed their eyes and slept.

* * *

KAYLA OPENED HER eyes to a room she had never seen before. A window shone dimly in a ceiling of dark crisscrossing beams. Outside, white cliffs climbed into the sky. A ladder led to the window. She threw the bed's blankets from her body, sleep dissipating instantly.

She rolled to the edge of the bed, experiencing the same sensations that had beset her in the clock tower when she had awakened under the bell chamber to find Wren missing. On the verge of panic, she rose off the bed. The wooden floor of the room cooled her bare feet. She padded to the ladder, climbed it, and pushed open the window. A surge of chilly air slapped her face as she clambered onto a balcony that perched on the roof like a crow's next.

The planks of a driftwood roof sloped down to a granite promontory that jutted over the sea. Waves rushed forward in perpetual bombardment, hurling themselves against the embattled rocks, bursting and booming beneath the house. Above her, caves and crevices perforated the white cliffs. Seabirds flew along the cliffs, gliding through the spray-drenched air as they flitted into and out of the dank fissures. The claw-like clouds had lengthened in the sky.

Kayla couldn't comprehend her surroundings. *Didn't I fall asleep in the remains of Dale's cottage?*

She climbed back in from the crow's nest and tugged on her boots, then tried the room's only door. It opened to a narrow hallway. Over-cast light seeped through round seaward windows. Muffled voices sounded through the door at the end of the hall.

Kayla went to the door, pushed it open, and found herself in a kitchen thick with smoke. Wren was speaking with an old woman at a table. His cloak was draped over the back of his chair and gathered in a dark puddle on the floor. Cupboards lined the walls, interspersed with more of the round windows Kayla had seen in the passage. A fire burned in a stone hearth, licking the sides of an iron cauldron.

Wren turned. "You're finally awake! Kayla, this is Marian. She's an enchantress, one of Dale's friends."

"I'm happy to meet you," Marian said huskily, peering at Kayla with red-rimmed eyes. She pushed herself from the table and gestured to an empty chair, saying, "Sit down, dear, and I'll get you something to eat." She might have been younger than Amber or several decades older. Deep lines creased her face. Her hair was long and as white as the cliffs that rose above her home.

Kayla sat next to her father, unable to decide which was stranger, that she had been transported to this house without waking or that he was talking to an enchantress with his sword sheathed.

"How'd you sleep?" he asked.

Kayla crossed her arms. "How did we get here?"

Marian paused in front of a cupboard. "Dale told me too much about your father for me to risk waking him first. When I arrived at the remains of . . . of his cottage . . . I found you slumped against a wall . . ."

"She's close to Dale," Wren whispered, and Kayla nodded curtly.

"After recovering from the sight of his home . . ." Marian bowed her head. "I put the two of you under a sleeping spell. Then I found your horse, put you in my small wagon, and brought you here to rest."

Wren snorted. "I probably would have agreed to come if you had wakened me and asked."

Marian took a bowl from the cupboard and filled it with stew from the cauldron. "I've had enough trouble calming you down already. Dale told me about your bias against magic, and I was able to catch a glimpse of your conversation with Amber, such as it was."

"You know her?" Kayla asked, feeling slightly queasy. No one had used magic on her before; the idea that someone could was a bit unsettling.

Marian returned to the table, eased herself back in her chair, and slid the bowl to Kayla. "She's the only spell weaver with whom Dale and I still had contact, aside from Adriel, of course. There are only four of us left. Many years ago Blaze and Lorelei set out for the Summerset Isles to search for others, but they never returned."

Kayla lifted her bowl and took a sip. The stew sent a warm shiver through her stomach. "Aurians," she said, wiping her mouth. "Amber mentioned that word, but I don't know what it means."

Wren shook his head. "I've stunted your education in more ways than one. I wanted to keep you oblivious to all this, but I think our circumstances warrant an explanation. Sometimes there's just no hiding from the truth."

"What are you talking about?" Kayla put down her bowl. "What haven't you told me? And *what* happened to Dale?"

Marian reached beneath her chair and brought up a thin white staff sparkling with a sapphire, which she tapped on the table. The kitchen's smoky air darkened as the table began radiating blue light.

Kayla pushed her bowl aside. Curiosity stifled her hunger as the light swirled on the tabletop. It was just like the magic window in Amber's house.

"Dale was attacked by a sorcerer named Damon," said Marian, "a man twisted and consumed by black magic. I wish I had been at his side when the sorcerer came. I would have stood with him, though it probably wouldn't have done much good. Time is weighing heavily on me . . ." She trailed off, and the swirling light gave way to an image of a man with a crystal eye.

"Who is he?" Wren asked.

Marian's features hardened. "One-Eye, one of the two assassins charged with your death."

"So there's another," Wren began, but the image on the table changed to a view of the scarred assassin riding through a village with the thugs who had traveled with him to the lighthouse. Their horses were passing a giant motionless waterwheel shackled with crimson vines.

"That bastard's been tracking us for two days now," Wren snarled. "How much do you know about him?"

"He's called Sarin."

"That's all you have to say? He murdered one of my best friends, and he'll gladly murder me!"

Marian silenced Wren with a raised hand.

"Wizards and enchantresses channel magic. It's a tool the gods gave us to watch over their creation, and we do not use it whimsically. To do so would be to subvert the essence of our power. The line between good and evil is often slimmer than a spinner's thread, and for those who wield magic, it may occasionally be crossed with the slightest act of pride or ambition. Those who use the tools of heaven do well to use them properly. Magic reveals certain things, but only what it deems necessary. I share the skill with Amber, though I'm sure Kayla has discovered that Amber's is greater than mine. I do know that Damon found the assassins and sent them to Cade, who pressed them into his service and ordered your death. But that was an error. When his men endangered your daughter, Wren, Cade lighted a firebrand he will find hard to extinguish. It would have been better for him to let you reach the boy unmolested."

Kayla was overwhelmed. Sorcerers and assassins and wizards . . . What was this, some sort of fairy tale masquerade? "Will someone *please* tell me what's going on."

Marian lowered her staff. The blue light faded from the table; the surrounding darkness receded, and gray light seeped through the windows once more. "I'll start at the beginning . . ."

Kayla listened with growing astonishment as Marian spoke of the three gods in heaven and the demons under the earth. She spoke of Cade and his brother, Corin, and of Cade's attempt to raise a demon from the earth by using a magical dagger on his brother, thereby reversing its magic and subverting it to wicked ends.

When Marian finished, Kayla leaned back unsteadily. "I should have told you sooner," said Wren, and she nodded numbly.

Marian turned toward Kayla's father. "Find and guard Corin. It's the only way to stop the assassins, and it's the only way to save our world. Has Dale described the boy for you?"

Wren grumbled out a "yes," and then paused. "You're sure Kayla will be safer with me than with you?"

"I hope Dale is still alive, drawing Damon away from Merrifield as he had intended, but if the sorcerer catches him, he may learn where I live, and I can't hope to defeat him. I'm old, Wren . . . too old for fighting. You must avoid Damon at all costs, even after meeting with Adriel. The young wizard isn't nearly ready for such a confrontation. And I would only slow you down. Adriel will need you all the more since neither Dale nor I will be with him. Your horse can only carry two, and you must reach Corin as soon as possible."

Wren stood. "Then we are indeed bound to our fate."

"So are we all," said Marian, "but the important choices are ours to make." She hobbled slowly from the kitchen.

Wren and Kayla exchanged a glance and followed her outside.

The promontory surrounding the house fed a narrow path that jackknifed up the cliffs. Several yards from the house, the knight's horse tossed its head irritably, shaking the tethers binding it to a henhouse. Chickens scuttled about the horse's legs, picking at the ground around its hooves.

Marian shook her staff at the hens, sending them clucking frantically in all directions, then turned to Wren. "I wish you all my luck."

"I'll need it," Wren said dryly, mounting the horse. "Mine seems to have run out long ago."

Kayla jumped up behind him, and he flicked the reins, starting on the path. Scree flew out from beneath the hooves of the horse, tumbling to the jagged rocks below. Seabirds' calls echoed around them. Holding tightly to her father's waist, Kayla looked behind her one last time.

Marian was still standing near her house, her face as bleak as the cliffs.

* * *

THEY RODE INLAND on an overgrown path that cut directly through the foothills and into the mountains. Clouds rolled away, leaving behind a sinking sun. When they reached Bridgewater, eventide was darkening the mountains in sheets of purple shadow.

The road leading to the village curled around a waterfall. A barrier blocked the road, but it was unguarded.

At first it seemed they were alone, but just beyond the roadblock Kayla spotted a pair of men digging a hole by an oak. Above the hole a skull had been nailed into the trunk. One man held a pickax, the other a spade. Candlelit lanterns dangled from the lowest branches. Two dirt mounds lay to the right of the hole; a coarse, threadbare cloth covered an object to the left.

"Who are they?" Kayla asked.

"Grave diggers," Wren said, kicking the horse toward the tree. "Don't worry—they have no business with the living."

"Then why bother them?"

"They know secrets only the dead can tell. Open your eyes, Kayla. Where do you think we are?"

Past the grave diggers, the village spread between mountains like a vast, dark cocoon. Coveys of houses clung to the banks of the winding rivers. Waterwheels dipped into the waters, but grappling cords of blood-red vines—those Marian's magic had revealed—blocked them from turning. "The assassins were here," Kayla said, and Wren nodded grimly.

The pickax paused at their approach. The man who held it straightened, squinting at them. Dirty sweat soaked through his tunic, and grime matted his hair. "Are you here to mourn Farr or one of the guards?"

"All three," Wren said. "How did they die?"

"You're not from around here," the other man muttered. Humpbacked and wrinkled, he dug into the grave's lantern-lit loam. "You'd best be on your way. I've come to learn that strangers mean death— strangers meant death to these men today." He threw a load of dirt over his shoulder and hefted his spade.

"Use your head," said the man with the pickax. "Does the young one look deadly to you?" He tossed his tool by the side of the hole and turned to Wren. "They were killed early in the afternoon after challenging three men who sought to cross the roadblock."

Wren shifted his weight in the saddle. "Can you tell me what the murderers looked like?"

"We didn't see them; we only heard shouts and screams. But they rode black horses. I can only speak of those who have died. None have had a funeral. Most of the townsfolk are dead or gone or locked up in their homes. We have only the rhythms of our hearts to keep us company now."

"And those are sure to fail," added the man with the spade. "The candles in these lamps will burn, and their wicks will melt into nothing. Just like the lives of the men we bury beneath this oak."

A candle fizzled and sputtered like a will-o'-the-wisp. Kayla shivered.

The man with the pickax grinned cynically. "I've churned the earth for a hundred souls and buried a hundred corpses, and I'll churn it for many more until dirt fills my mouth and nose and packs my unseeing eyes. Dying is a business, and I work on the moneymaking end of things."

"The worms we feed will turn on us when it's our turn to be buried," said the other man, and dug his spade into the grave soil. "No doubt they are eager to taste the hands that have fed them."

"Thank you," Wren said. "You have been most . . . helpful." He clicked his heels, and the knight's horse trotted away.

Kayla looked over her shoulder, eyes moving from the grave diggers to the skull mounted on the tree trunk; two dark sockets stared at her, cold, pitiless windows that gazed into the end of all things.

In a voice so low she could barely hear it, Wren muttered, "The game may only have one ending, but my turn's not up yet."

* * *

BRIDGEWATER WAS NEARLY desolate. Dead fish rotted on the river-banks. Vines clawed from the waters. People clothed in patchwork garments scampered from them like frightened rats. Bloodless faces pressed against dusty windows, then disappeared into shadow.

Wren and Kayla crossed through the town and started down Wool-thread Road, riding into the twilight.

THE MAGIC SHOW

CORIN TOSSED AND turned in his bed, desperately trying to remember his dream. He was wrapped in warm fox furs and cotton-stuffed quilts, but he was far from comfortable. The beautiful tapestry his sleeping mind had woven was unraveling quickly into meaningless fragments. Brief glimpses of shape and color were all that remained, and even they were slipping from his conscious loom faster than he could weave them back together.

He had been at a lakeside watching dragonflies flit above the water, listening to the hum of their wings, his finger marking with lazy jabs their careless skimming and darting. The sun had glimmered on the lake with shards of rainbow crystal. A girl had come toward him, walking barefoot in the soft green grass, and her eyes had danced with laughter. He had risen with a smile and outstretched arms to greet her, but the scene had blurred and vanished, leaving him alone in his room. His heart ached with the memory of her laughing eyes.

Talk about a rude awakening, he thought unhappily.

Climbing out of bed was one of the hardest tasks Corin faced each day. Pushing off the cozy, soft covers, dragging his head away from his pillow, blinking back the shreds of a sleep too short by half . . . He had to force his way along each step toward wakefulness. And the dream made the process that much harder to bear. But try as he might, he could not fall asleep again. Glimpses of the girl and the lake shimmered behind his eyelids.

He sighed, pushed off the covers, and stretched, looking around his sparsely furnished room with resignation, wondering if the dream would visit him again some other night. He could only hope.

Restless, he padded across the floor to the room's north window and put his hands on the stone sill. A gray thread laced the horizon; the dark and somber sky had begun to shift toward morning.

He pushed open the windowpanes and gazed out over the slumbering countryside. Down to the left snaked Woolthread Road. The Honey Barrel squatted like a mushroom by the roadside. Jyri was probably deep in the thralls of a drunken sleep, and his workers and guests would not rise for at least another hour.

A light breeze blew Corin's sandy hair across his eyes. He indulged the playful teasing of the tangled locks, goose bumps prickling on his arms. He reached for the windowpanes but stopped when a faint sound caught his ear. Near the edge of his house the delicate frames of his uncle Pyke's beehives stood like sentinels awaiting the break of day. A barely audible buzz drifted up from the hives to his room, and he was reminded with a regretful pang of dragonflies drifting over a clear blue lake.

Corin watched the sky pale, his thoughts lost in their wanderings, his bare arms and chest tingling in the chilly air. *I need to get out of here and get my mind off that dream. I'll go take a walk before Pyke wakes up.* Shivering, he closed the window.

He opened his closet, pulled on a blue tunic and a pair of brown trousers, turned to the washbasin, and splashed his face with a numbing handful of water. Then he remembered the magician.

Suddenly he had no more need for a walk. Barely resisting the urge to jump and shout, he almost kicked himself for forgetting.

The previous night he had been down in Jyri's common room when a small troupe of musicians came inside asking for room and board. They seemed friendly and talkative, engaging the dozen or so patrons who were already there in idle conversation. When asked about their destination, they said they were making their way to the Spinribbon Fair to set up a stage where they would be playing the next day. Someone then asked for a sample from their repertoire. Easily enticed by the snare of attention, they quickly agreed and spent the next hour striking up tunes. Their songs were wild and whimsical, their rhythms were fast, and the whole inn was soon drenched in a flood of music and ale.

During the excitement, one of the musicians—the fife player, Corin thought—downed a foaming mug of beer and banged it on a table, bellowing, "Has anyone seen a magician pass through?"

No one had, but those few who could still see straight focused their attention on the man. He was obviously pleased with his sudden audience and made a long, drawn-out affair of telling them how his group had met a magician along the road. Corin was still too young to be allowed by either Jyri or his uncle to drink very much, so he had a reasonably sound recollection of the conversation, one that was probably more intact than anyone else's.

"The magician," said the fife player, "was headed for Spinribbon Fair. He carried a white staff with a sapphire at its end, and he seemed to be in a hurry. Curse me for a fool, but he couldn't have been much more than twenty."

Jyri gave a deep-throated chuckle. "The whole world must be heading that way, and they're all passing through my inn! Just think of it, the whole world right under my roof." He laughed again, somewhat self-consciously this time. "I must be bigger than I thought."

Jyri was very fat and was in a perpetual state of discontent about it.

"Oh, you've had too much to drink again, Jyri," one of his regulars remarked. "The only newcomers here are these musicians. No magician has stopped by yet."

"If that is so, he's not likely to, either," the fife player interjected. "He passed by us quickly enough on the road, stopping only to make sure he was headed in the right direction. He must have been a foreigner. All the roads running through this country lead to the Spinribbon, and that's a fact. He was probably seeking lodging in Merrifield."

Jyri grumbled something about how his inn was better than any two-bit establishment down the road, but Corin could tell he was interested. As for himself, he was brimming with excitement. Magicians were a rarity in the lands surrounding the Seaspine Mountains, but rarer still were those who granted simple farmers and craftsmen the pleasure of a magic show.

He must be planning a performance if he really is headed for the fair, Corin told himself happily. *And that's one show I'll be sure not to miss.*

After several more questions concerning the magic worker, the music resumed. By then it had gotten late, and Corin knew his uncle would have begun to worry. He left the inn tired but hopeful, promising himself that he would seek out the magician the following day.

Corin washed his face, brushed the knots from his hair, and tied his boots, remembering his promise to see the magician's performance and renewing it with vigor.

As he began cleaning his teeth, he heard a steady thumping through his floor from below. The thumping stopped and was replaced by a burst of laugher. His uncle was awake and at work in the kitchen.

Pyke worked for Jyri as the Honey Barrel's resident baker; he prepared the breads and assorted other foodstuffs with which Jyri lined his larders. From an early age Corin had found himself running errands involving the transportation of food or the conveyance of instructions along the path between the inn and his home. The work was mostly tedious. His body, though strong and lean, always ached by the time he had finished the day's labors.

He placed the brush down, already considering the best way to ask permission to visit the fair. Optimism was far better than pessimism in most situations, and he was optimistic now, but the chores Pyke undoubtedly had in store for him probably would keep him from the fair until it had shut down for the evening. *I've got to hurry. There's no way*

I'm letting this magic worker move to new territory beyond Merrifield before I get a chance to see him.

Corin flung open the door and started down the stairs. In his hurry he stumbled and made a desperate attempt to grab for the railing with a flailing arm. He missed by a mile and tumbled down the staircase, landing on the floor in an embarrassing heap. Throbbing in a dozen places, he clambered to his feet, cursing his clumsiness. This was not a dignified way to begin an important conversation.

Rubbing his shoulder, he entered the kitchen.

The floor was built of sandstone; the walls were painted robin-egg blue. Across the room a brick and clay kiln was baking bread. Pyke's medal of the three gods hung above the kiln, shining faintly. Round windows, their shutters thrown back, looked out on the hills. Flower boxes lined each sill, blooming with snapdragons and violets. Morning air drifted over the flowers to mingle with the scent of rising bread.

Pyke, working as busily as one of Jyri's honeybees, grinned at Corin from behind the cutting table. "I didn't know my nephew was an acrobat," he said. His large hazel eyes twinkled with amusement as his hands flattened a sticky glob of dough with the rolling pin Corin had bought for him two days earlier. "You'll bring fortune to the Starcross name if you put those talents to work at the fair."

"Maybe," Corin said. "But fame would arrive with the fortune. You wouldn't enjoy that. Sometimes I wonder if your whole world revolves around Jyri's inn."

"Why shouldn't it? We live a good life here. The country is beautiful, and the work isn't too difficult. We live in a good home, and we never lack food. My nephew, it seems, is as restless as ever. Quite a striking contrast from his peace-loving uncle, wouldn't you say?"

Corin laughed. "I prefer to think of myself as adventurous. I wouldn't mind traveling from time to time to see what else the world has to offer. As for you, I'd ask that lump of dough you just murdered before describing yourself as peace-loving."

"If I weren't this forceful with the food around here," Pyke said, shaping the dough with his calloused hands, "your breakfasts wouldn't be nearly as good as they are. And that's one luxury you couldn't bear to part with. Take a seat at the table. I'll give you something to eat in a moment."

Corin did as he was told. His uncle was absolutely correct: Breakfast at the Starcross house was not something to be missed. He watched Pyke work in happy silence as dawn brightened the kitchen.

His uncle, light-skinned and heavyset, looked as if he spent all his time toiling in a mountain cave. Burns and lesions crossed his fingers. His chest was as burly as any barrel; his forearms, their skin visible up to the elbow where the sleeves of his white cooking tunic were gathered in tidy rolls, were knotted with muscle; and his face was as smooth as a newborn's.

Pyke set a heaping plate of eggs, bread, and cheese in front of his nephew and went back to his baking, humming a cheerful tune. Corin set into the food hungrily, thanking the gods for his uncle's benevolent mood. When he cleaned the plate, he pushed it aside and got to his feet, facing the man who held the fate of his day—and a rolling pin—in his hands.

"Uncle," Corin began, "I have a favor to ask."

"Don't waste your time asking me anything."

"But—"

"Don't waste your time with that, either."

"But, Uncle—"

"Did you hear what I just said? If you're going to get to the fair in time to see that worthless magician, you had better bring Jyri his morning loaves on your way down to the road. It would be unfair of me to leave you unrewarded for the rain-ridden trip you took the other day."

Corin was astonished. "How did you know about him? I didn't see you at the inn last night!"

Pyke smiled shrewdly. "Here, take this." He picked up a bulging sack from beside the kiln and tossed it to Corin. "I woke up early and made these ahead of time so you could be on your way as soon as possible."

"Thanks," Corin stammered. "You're the best!"

With the sack over his shoulder and a grin on his face, he tossed his uncle a mock salute, raced out the kitchen door, and found himself on his way to the Spinribbon Fair.

His uncle's bread sack rubbed his shoulder raw, and his left leg throbbed as though under attack by a horde of Jyri's honeybees, but he did not care: His mind was on magic and magicians. He moved as quickly as he could, climbing over fences, crossing streams on old stone bridges, shouting at groups of sheep that had wandered across his path. The huddled clusters blew apart like bits of dandelion fluff, scattered by the wind.

He reached Jyri's inn flushed and breathless and glanced down Woolthread Road. Hills veiled Merrifield and the Spinribbon Fair, but Corin imagined fireworks leaping above them, streaking skyward from a magician's staff, where they exploded in wheels of color and smoke.

He passed through the stable yard and entered the inn, impatient to be on his way. It was cool and dark inside.

The common room was a mess. Spent candles stood on tables, piles of melted wax and burned wick. Unlit lamps hung crookedly from the ceiling. The fireplace held only a few cinders, and even they seemed lifeless, glowing dully in the light that sifted through the tavern windows. A golden harp slouched in a corner of the room, a neglected testament to the previous night's revelry. Overturned mugs lay on tables and chairs. Broken plates were strewn across the floor. Flies buzzed lazily, landing on crumbs or on the sticky stains where ale had been spilled.

Footsteps began stomping down the stairs, too loud and heavy to belong to anyone other than the innkeeper. *Not good. Jyri will want me to help him clean, and that would take a week . . .*

Corin dropped the bread sack on a table and fled the tavern, slamming the door behind him.

He made relatively good time, but his leg prevented the escape from being as fast as he would have liked; he did not lose sight of the inn for some time. Still, this day's trip, compared to the trip he had made to Merrifield the day before yesterday, put him in a wonderful mood. This time there was no rain or fog, no belligerent donkey to coax through the mud, and a magic show to watch instead of a shopping list.

The sky was like a vast blue sea. Puffy white galleons plied the air, cloud-spindled masts pearling in the dawn. Westward, the Seaspine Mountains cut across the sky. Corin's leg began to tire, but he pressed on, spirits sailing with the clouds.

Then a horse-drawn cart appeared around a bend. The horse and cart were unfamiliar, but he knew the driver at once: *Dusty.*

Corin moved to the roadside and waved. Dusty waved back. Corin was glad to see his friend, but he wondered where he was going and what he was doing on the road at daybreak.

Dusty brought the cart to a halt and propped an arm on the driver's seat. "I wake up early, take one of my father's wagons to pick you up, and find you already halfway to Merrifield."

"I'm glad to see you, too. Why'd you come?"

"You won't believe what I'm going to tell you."

"Something about a magician at the Spinribbon Fair?"

Dusty looked astonished. "How did you know?"

Corin climbed up next to him. "Yesterday a troupe of musicians staying in the Honey Barrel saw a young man with a staff at the Bridgewater Fork. The man told them he was heading for Merrifield."

Dusty grinned. "I served him drinks last night. His name is Adriel. He told me to find him after his show."

Now Corin was astonished. "I've got to come with you!"

"He said I could bring a friend."

"You must be better at waiting tables than I thought." Corin leaned back, elated. "The things that happen in your father's inn . . . This is going to be amazing. My uncle met a magician back when I was still a child, but I never dreamed I would meet one myself."

"I saw one once, but it was so long ago, I can hardly remember the details . . . just some smoke and a colored scarf."

Corin shook his head. "I was probably caught in some chore around the house."

"We're both worked way too hard," Dusty agreed, then paused. "I was thinking we could tell him about Farmer Twine's pool. After all, he *is* a magician. I'm sure he'd believe us."

"Good thinking." *A magic worker wouldn't have laughed at Twine, and he won't laugh at us, either,* Corin thought.

When they reached the fair, they tied the horse to a feeding trough and started searching for the magician. All about was color and excitement. Children chased one another around tents draped with flags and banners. Actors played out tragedies on gaudy stages; acrobats flipped and cartwheeled; wrinkled alchemists hawked bottles of magical, bone-soothing brine; and girls in summer dresses swayed to the music of lutes and lyres. They passed pavilions where journeymen regaled teenagers with harrowing tales of valor and bravado. Far-traveled merchants manned stalls of exotic wares: jars of rainbow sand from the Sea of Dreams, cages of jabbering parrots captured in the Summerset Isles, a painting of a fiery-haired mermaid rising from the Starlight Sea. One booth featured an armillary sphere that revolved with hidden clockwork, its celestial spheres circling a golden sun on silver orbits. The clever device held no charm for the boys. They pressed on, moving through the marvels, searching for the magician.

Soon Corin and Dusty found themselves joining an excited crowd in front of an empty stage, hardly more than a platform of barrels and wooden planks. A blue sign stood nearby; on it were the words "Evening Stars," and below that, in smaller print, "The Magic of Twilight Dreams."

As Corin watched, a young man climbed onto the stage. In his hand he held a gnarled white staff twined with a green ribbon.

Dusty nudged him. "That's him."

The magician's hair shone like spun silver, but his cloak was plain and brown. Corin held his breath; the crowd quieted. Several children squealed. Then there was silence.

"Welcome," said the magician, looking rather nervous. "I am Adriel, a magic worker who has journeyed from the coast." He stretched out his arms. "Watch closely but do not be afraid. Whatever appears cannot harm you as long as I am here, standing on this stage."

He bowed his head and wove a hand over his staff as if spinning at a loom. Sweat beaded on his forehead, a vein stood out on his neck, but nothing happened.

People began muttering. Dusty cast a sidelong look at Corin, who shrugged, eyes riveted on Adriel.

Suddenly there was a bang and a blinding flash of light. A large translucent egg levitated in the air before Adriel, rotating wildly in ever-changing directions. With a crack it split in two. A dragon sprang forth, identical to the one Corin had seen on the fountain in the square and on his uncle's medal. Its varicolored wings shimmered in the sunlight.

The dragon curled around Adriel, who looked more surprised than anything else, and then imploded into an orb of rainbow light that hovered several inches above the sapphire on his staff. He spoke a single word, and the orb burst apart into a dozen dragonflies: purple, blue, and orange. They hummed from the stage over the audience, leaving colorful spirals behind them, vanishing one by one in showers of blazing sparks.

For a moment there was utter silence, and then the audience broke into applause, with Corin and Dusty clapping loudest of all.

Adriel looked flabbergasted, but he gathered himself and bowed, smiling widely. Then he stepped to the edge of the stage and scanned the crowd. His eyes found Dusty, moved to Corin, and widened.

"Incredible!" Dusty said, shaking Corin's shoulders. "I've never seen anything like this!"

Corin shrugged off his grip. "I think the magician recognized me."

"What are you talking about?"

"He gave me a look. I swear it!"

Dusty regarded Corin slyly. "Adriel *did* tell me to meet him after the show . . . We should ask him if he knows you."

Suddenly gasps and murmurs rippled along the crowd. Corin's gaze snapped to the stage, but it was empty. He blinked and rubbed his eyes, but as if by some final trick, Adriel was gone.

FLIGHT

Adriel jumped from the stage and plunged into the audience, shoving through the press of bodies. Bellows and curses battered his ears. People elbowed one another, jarring their neighbors.

Shouts erupted as two of the assassin's men struggled toward Dusty and Corin.

The crowd parted, and Adriel stumbled into the boys. They stared at him, excited and confused.

"Follow me," Adriel said, raising his voice over angry shouts. "You're both in danger, and there's no time to explain."

Dusty nodded at Corin, who took a quick look around and said, "I thought I saw you looking at me. Just don't move too fast"—he glanced down at his leg—"I have trouble running."

Adriel hurried away from the stage with the boys in tow. He circled around a striped pavilion, where he paused near a heap of painted crates and looked back for the assassin's men. They were forcing their way through the crowd.

"Your name is Corin," he said, turning to Dusty's friend.

"How did you—"

"There's time for that later. Two men are coming to bring you to their master, and he will likely kill you. Once you're safe, I'll tell you what I can, but now I need you to do exactly as I say."

Dusty crossed his arms. "Is this some kind of joke?"

"What do you think?" Adriel asked, and glared at him. The boy's freckled face suddenly showed signs of fright. "Is there a place where you can hide until I come for you?"

"The watchtower on my father's inn."

Adriel rubbed his staff. "What if you're seen? One-Eye is part of this, and he's staying there. *Blazes,* here they come." The thugs had shouldered through the crowd's fringe and started in his direction. He motioned Corin and Dusty into the pavilion. "Crawl under the back of the tent and head for Rookery Rest. I'll meet you in the watchtower as soon as it's safe."

The boys let down the pavilion's entrance flap, and Adriel turned to face the men, holding his staff before him.

* * *

THE TENT WAS empty. A Jikari board sat in the center, ringed with vacant chairs. Indigo carpets covered the ground. Corin moved to the back of the tent and started lifting the cloth, but Dusty waved him back. "Come here and listen," his friend hissed. "We need to figure out what's going on."

"Why don't you start by telling me everything you know," Corin whispered angrily.

"What do you mean?"

"Adriel said these men are staying at your inn!"

Dusty looked defensive. "I had no idea they were after you. You're just a baker's son, Corin. Sorry to be blunt, but kidnappers are usually concerned with interesting people."

Outside, a voice demanded, "Who are you?"

"No games, magician," another man growled. "Where've you hidden the boy?"

Corin held a finger to his lips and tapped Dusty on the shoulder. He pointed to the opposite side of the pavilion, skirted the Jikari board, and wriggled under the fabric, emerging in a copse of tents. When Dusty joined him, they scrambled to the cart and hurried from the fair.

Dusty guided the cart under Merrifield's palisade, starting on a street that curved to the right, winding toward the top of the hill. Turning to Corin, he described the thugs at Rookery Rest: One-Eye, the man with twin rapiers, and the pair of mismatched ruffians, one as short and fat as a candle stub and the other as tall and thin as a wick.

Corin's anxiety threatened to choke him. *What could they want from me? What harm have I ever done?*

Dusty stopped talking and pulled back on the reins, halting the cart at the edge of Merrifield's central square. They looked around for signs of trouble, but everything seemed normal.

The watchtower loomed above the inn's shingle roof, a teetering battlement peppered with arrow loops. A screech sounded inside, and four rooks burst from a hidden nook, streaking across the sky like a flight of black-feathered arrows.

Dusty narrowed his eyes. "The birds are restless. Oswald must have forgotten to feed them."

"I hope they make good company," Corin grumbled. "We don't know how long it will be until Adriel joins us."

Dusty urged the horse across the square and down an alley that bent around the stable to the back of the inn. He knotted the reins on an iron ring, then opened a door and peeked into the kitchen. "Mother is serving drinks with Oswald in the tavern," he said, and beckoned Corin inside.

Low wooden beams arched across the ceiling, roped with bundled herbs and salted meats. Food was heaped on counters and shelves. Coils of smoke snaked from a fire pit to sting Corin's eyes. A side of venison rotated on a spit above the flames, glistening with rivulets of juice.

Dusty opened a door at the back of the pantry and entered a small brick wine cellar crammed with bottle-filled racks. A ladder rose through a hole in the ceiling. He grabbed the ladder and looked over his shoulder.

"I can manage," Corin said.

Dusty started up.

Slivers of light pierced the arrow loops, lancing through the tower. Dusty stopped to open a trapdoor. Corin bumped his head against his friend's boots and cursed, then followed him into Oswald's rookery.

The room was a madman's attic turned aviary. Rooks hopped along the rafters; black feathers and rusted tools littered the floor. Hunks of broken furniture leaned against the walls. Dust sifted through air, smothering everything in layers of age. Another ladder led toward a ceiling that was all but hidden by ropes, chains, and moldering roof joists.

"That one leads to the lookout platform," Dusty explained, "but we won't be going up there if we hope to stay hidden." From some dark corner a rook croaked in agreement.

A rotten hole of a window had been bored into the decayed wood of the western wall. Corin limped toward it and looked out on the town, the hills, and the Seaspine Mountains. To the north, roofs layered Merrifield in terraces of shingle and thatch. Beyond the palisade, Woolthread Road snaked through pasturelands until it reached the Honey Barrel. Corin could barely see the inn: a lonely speck near the dun-colored road.

"So what's this all about?" he asked, turning from the window. "Why did you want to hide in here?" He often had played with Dusty in the watchtower as a young boy and had many fond memories of the rookery, but the danger of his situation had changed the boyhood fort into a fugitive's prison.

"No one comes up besides my father," Dusty explained. "And we can avoid him easily enough." He scratched the back of his head. "This was the best place I could think of."

"We should have told him. Oswald could speak with those men. Then they would realize their mistake. It *is* a misunderstanding, don't you think?"

"My father would laugh himself to death. This whole situation still seems mad, and I've *seen* the men who are after you. It's hard to believe, but we heard them ask for us outside the tent."

"Adriel might be a magician," Corin said, "but trusting someone we hardly know doesn't seem right."

Dusty reached down, picked up the shaft of a hammer, its head rusted away, and danced around, thrusting dagger strokes at imaginary enemies. "I'd rather have him on my side than a dozen bodyguards. When he comes for us, we'll figure out what's going on, then deal with it." Dusty dropped the shaft and walked back to the ladder hole. "Are you hungry? I hope the kitchen's still empty. I'm going back downstairs to get some food. We might be up here for a while."

He went down the ladder and returned several minutes later with a large gray sack. Inside were a loaf of sourdough bread, two mugs, and a small cask of beer.

Hours lagged in long, slow silence. Whenever someone spoke, it was largely to disrupt the incessant skitter-scrabble backdrop of bird claws. Dusty made several more trips down the ladder to pilfer food from the kitchen. The afternoon came and went, but Adriel did not appear.

The chamber darkened as the sun slid behind the Seaspine Mountains through the toothed window. Orange light splashed on the walls and trickled to the floor, leaving the rafters dim.

Corin was just about to suggest going downstairs to find Dusty's parents when croaks issued from a dozen black throats. Four rooks flew through the window, gripping an ungainly burden. They landed in the carcass of a broken beer barrel that curled like a rib cage in a murky corner of the watchtower. Other rooks descended with frenzied wing beats.

Dusty chuckled. "Idiot birds. What are they doing?"

"Feeding," Corin said, heading for the barrel.

The rooks churned together like maggots. Beaks stabbed up and down, pecking, jabbing, gulping tiny gobs of flesh.

Dusty appeared at his side and covered his mouth. "Blazes, Corin, that's disgusting."

Dread stiffened Corin's spine. He fought an impulse to gag, then kicked the barrel uncertainly. It rocked back and forth, and a whirlwind of black feathers exploded upward, sprinkling his hair and shoulders with blood, leaving behind a pulp of mauled tissue speckled with bone. Five stumps, the fingers on what had been a human hand, clutched a crimson vine.

Corin's stomach lurched. He stumbled to the window and vomited. Dusty stared at the barrel, cursing under his breath.

Corin spit out bile. "It's from the Ravenswood," he said, cringing at the sour taste in his mouth. "Look at the vine. The birds must have taken it from . . ." The connection was too strange, too impossible.

"Farmer Twine's pool," Dusty said. He opened his mouth to speak again, but a rook swooped down from the rafters, battering its wings against his face. Dusty flung up his arms. The rook retreated, but others took its place. More assaulted Corin as he rushed to help his friend, raking him with their talons.

Dusty shouted and swung down the ladder hole in the floor. The rooks dived after him.

Corin went after his friend as quickly as he could, swatting aside the birds. They ripped at his neck and hands. Blood dribbled from a dozen cuts. He shook his head wildly, jerking his eyes away from their beaks. One bit an eyebrow and cocked back its neck, tearing skin and hair.

He reached the bottom of the tower, jumped off the ladder, and stumbled from the wine room, through the kitchen, and out into the alley. Dusty slammed the door behind him, locking the rooks inside.

The boys wiped their wounds, breathing heavily. "Gods," said Dusty, "the world's gone crazy."

Corin would have agreed, but his heart was racing too fast for speech. Then two men ambled around the stable, one short and fat and the other tall and angular. Corin's heart beat faster.

"It's them," Dusty whispered, "the men who are after you." He hastily untied the cart and jumped up on the driver's seat.

Corin clambered up beside him. The cart pitched forward, wheels chattering on the cobblestone alley. He looked back in time to see the men start sprinting. "They've spotted us!"

Dusty hunched forward, madly whipping the reins. "We don't know where Adriel is. We can't get back to Rookery Rest. We have nowhere to go, Corin!"

"Make for the Honey Barrel." Corin sucked in his breath as the cart careered around a corner, scattering a group of young children. "Jyri should be able to help us. And Adriel *is* a magician. I'm sure he can find out where we've gone."

"I wish I were as sure as you," Dusty said, swerving the cart onto a street that would take them out of town.

* * *

ADRIEL'S CONFRONTATION WITH the assassin's men escalated rapidly. Threats piled up fast, and it would have taken a turn toward physical violence, but several members of Adriel's audience approached the pavilion, demanding to know the reason for this strange behavior. Avoiding the crowd, the ruffians shouldered their way into the pavilion, calling for Corin and Dusty to no avail. Adriel hurried away, leaving them to their futile search.

When he reached the inn, he caught a glimpse of One-Eye through the door to the common room. Not wishing to be seen, he chose an alcove on the side of a tailor's shop and waited for an opportune time to cross the square and enter the watchtower. The tower almost mocked him, a spiral of dark stones and jagged timbers. Corin and Dusty were inside, nearly within his reach, but he could not go to them.

Adriel's attention oscillated between the watchtower and the common room. He hoped One-Eye would leave, but as minutes turned into hours, his body stiffened and his head began lolling with fatigue.

The sun dipped below Merrifield's western roofs. Shadows swallowed the fountain of the three gods as sunbeams slanted over the notched line of roofs and chimneys, splashing the eastern shops in shades of burnished gold.

As quiet as the spreading shadows, the two thugs approached the inn from the direction of the Spinribbon Fair. Adriel jerked up his head.

Suddenly a yell burst from the watchtower, and several rooks flew from the window, gibbering. People milling about the square looked up as a cluster of men spewed from the tavern, One-Eye in their midst. The assassin saw his companions and hurried toward them, then stopped and pointed to an alley beside the stables. The two thugs circled around the back of the inn. One-Eye stayed in the square, staring at the doors to the tavern and stables, waiting.

Adriel jumped up and sprang away from the tailor shop, running down a street that he hoped would take him unexposed to the other side of Rookery Rest. The street forked, and he stopped, wondering which direction to take.

As he stood there, Dusty and Corin raced past on a cart, the two thugs hard on their heels.

Adriel doubled back on a parallel alley, putting on a burst of speed, hoping to cut off the two men before they overtook the boys.

* * *

THE HORSE LUNGED forward.

Corin knew they were moving as fast as they could, but they could not shake the assassin's men. Merrifield was shutting down for the evening, but here and there tenacious merchants still flaunted their wares, nettling those returning home with irksome shouts and bids. Dusty cracked the reins, shouting and cursing at people to clear their path.

The alley evolved into a house-lined avenue packed with merchant stalls. Most of the stalls displayed rows of colored gourds and wind chimes. At the sight of the fleeing horse and cart, the few people in the alley scrambled for cover.

The cart juddered wildly, passing beneath the watchful eyes of the windows on either side, while the men hurried after it.

* * *

WATCHING FROM A side alley, Adriel waited until Corin and Dusty had veered out of his vision, then stepped into the street and raised his staff, planting himself in front of the mercenaries. They skidded to a stop and drew their swords.

"We have no quarrel with you," said the taller of the two, but he sounded hesitant, almost fearful.

The short one snarled. "I knew you were helping those boys."

Adriel stood his ground. "I won't let you touch Corin." A breeze whispered down the alley, rattling the wind chimes, and the gourds clinked together in a mockery of applause.

"Get out of our way, magician," the short one said. "We've money to make, and not for fighting you."

Adriel did not move.

"I'm going to split you in two," said the shorter man. He gritted his teeth and looked at his companion. "Help me gut this bastard."

The taller thug spit. "What about his staff?"

Adriel stepped forward. "You saw my magic at the show. I'll use it on you if you don't leave. Go back to your one-eyed friend and tell him to give up the hunt. Corin and Dusty are under my protection."

After a moment of indecision, the two men leaped into action, rushing toward Adriel and swinging their swords.

Adriel closed his eyes. He concentrated, feeling the strands of power he had wielded on the stage as they pulsed from the earth into his staff, flowing up the oak into his hands, his arms, his chest, and then his mind. When he opened his eyes, the sapphire on his staff radiated a blue glow. Trusting in the magic as he had at the fair, Adriel lifted the staff and pointed it at the charging men.

Rips sounded up and down the alley, and dozens of trinkets flew from their stalls, snapping the threads and ropes that bound them in place, shooting toward Adriel from every direction. The mercenaries stopped in midstride and gaped at the phantasmagoric sphere of wind chimes and gourds that swirled through the air, spinning around the magician, jingling nonsensically. One by one the trinkets shot at them. They batted aside the first few, but the stream of animated objects intensified. A chime hit the taller man, cutting his cheek and leaving a red gash. Several gourds got past his companion's sword and barreled into his stomach, winding him. The barrage continued until the thugs dropped their weapons and ran from the alley, yelping like a pair of chastened dogs.

Then the sphere of trinkets surrounding Adriel collapsed, falling like lead balls to the ground.

Adriel slowly lowered his staff, gazing at the sapphire in wonder. *I did it,* he thought, *though I have no idea how. The flare in the hermit's cave and the magic show weren't accidents. I must be a wizard now.*

He clenched a fist in triumph, then raced after Corin and Dusty.

When he reached the palisade, he paused by Merrifield's north gate, where he caught a glimpse of a cart on Woolthread Road, disappearing into the hills. He started after the cart, wondering where Dale was and what he was doing, knowing his master would be proud.

* * *

INEXPLICABLY, THE ASSASSIN'S men seemed to have given up their pursuit.

Corin looked behind him again and again, searching in vain for a glimpse of the men as Merrifield diminished behind him. Hilltop houses darkened and blended into shadow as color bled from the sky. Lanterns and candles were set in windows; smoke curled from chimneys. Aside from the traffic trickling between the town and the fair, the road was empty.

"Any sign of them?" Dusty asked.

"Not yet," Corin said, shaking his head. "I don't understand it. They were *right* behind us."

"How did we lose them? We cut a path wide enough for all of Merrifield to follow."

Corin groaned. "I hope no one recognized us."

"Our escape from town will be the talk of Rookery Rest for days," Dusty said gleefully.

"And we'll be despised by all the people we nearly flattened," Corin added.

Dusty lapsed into silence.

Corin's thoughts turned to the watchtower, to the unnatural behavior of the rooks and the bloodied hand they had brought. When they reached the Honey Barrel, Dusty turned the cart into the stable yard, unhitched the horse, and led it to a feeding trough near the door of Jyri's private stable. A team of starved-looking mules stood in one of the stalls, a spotted gelding in another, and in a far corner, three black horses were nibbling hay.

Corin limped back to the roadside and looked toward Merrifield. A man, cloaked and hooded, was making his way toward the inn. Stomach twisting, Corin turned north. A white horse bearing two hooded riders trotted around a hill. The taller of the two flicked his reins, urging the horse to greater speed.

Swearing, Corin retreated into the stable yard, told Dusty what he had seen, then quickly led him into the inn.

Jyri was nowhere to be seen, so Corin and Dusty made their way across the common room, which was sparsely populated but noisy, and through a side door, which they locked behind them. They ran down a short flight of steps and into a small brick stable.

Three lamps hung from the ceiling. While Dapple dozed in her stall, Jyri's packhorse, recently recovered from his fever, nickered and pawed at his bedding of trampled dirt and straw. In a corner, above a mound of hay bales, a dirty slit of a window looked into the common room.

Dusty went to the stable doors and shook them: They were latched and barred. "Do we have a plan?"

Corin reached inside one of the lamps and pinched his fingers together, snuffing out its flame. "Not really."

"Then what are we doing?"

Dapple stirred as Corin put out another lamp. "This is Jyri's private stable. There's no better place to hide. Climb up to the window before it gets too dark." He put out the third lamp, plunging the room into shadow, felt his way over to the hay bales, and climbed them. Then he crouched at the window with Dusty, waiting to see if any of the men he had seen on the road would enter the inn.

Somewhere behind them in the darkness, Dapple woke and began grumbling.

* * *

WHEN WREN REACHED the inn, the sky was black. He walked the knight's horse into the stable yard.

Scattered torches illuminated the stalls. Opposite the roadside entrance, the inn's facade welcomed Wren with brightly lit windows, a painted signpost, and snatches of conversation and laughter that drifted into the night. Wren dismounted stiffly and helped Kayla down, then led the horse to an empty stall.

Kayla stretched. "I can't remember the last time I slept in an inn."

"Mine was last month in the Seasong Arms, after a particularly enjoyable night. I remember a few lucky rolls of the Jikari dice."

"And a few too many pints of ale?"

"That, too," Wren agreed, and started for the inn.

Kayla rubbed the small of her back. "My whole body aches. I wouldn't mind a pint myself."

Wren chuckled. "You wouldn't enjoy what I drink."

"I've had it before."

His grin fled. "Where?"

Kayla put a hand on his arm. "Your wine cellar, Father."

"But you can't have enjoyed it."

"Loved it."

He glared at her. "Beer is for grizzled old men, Kayla, not you."

"I like to drink what Father drinks," she said innocently.

Wren paused at the tavern door. "Your father is a fool. Remember, keep your head hooded. We don't know who's inside."

He entered the Honey Barrel, seating himself in a corner table opposite Kayla. Patrons laughed and drank around them. Nearby, two men were griping about the innkeeper; they had finished their drinks long before, but no one had come downstairs to refill them.

Wren looked closely at his daughter from under his hood. "Kayla?"

"Yes?" she said sweetly.

"I am *not* your role model. You shouldn't be drinking so young. It's horrible for you. I can't believe you actually enjoyed it."

She grinned. "I hated it."

"Are you lying?"

"I've seen you many times after you've come back from Kendran's, and it's never been a pleasant sight."

Wren scowled. "Blazes, Kayla, you had me worried."

One of the two griping men swore loudly. "Where the hell is Jyri? I need another drink, and I need it now. This has something to do with those three grim fellows. I'd stake my life on it."

"Bastards," his companion muttered. "They barge in and march upstairs like they own the place, and that's the last we see of the innkeeper. I'm not waiting any longer; it's time to take matters into my own mug."

As he walked to the bar with his friend, the inn's door opened and a cloaked man stepped through, holding a long, strangely shaped stick.

Wren gripped the edge of the table. *Curse me for my stupidity. I should have checked the stable yard. That's no common traveler.* He rose from his seat, keeping his sword hidden under his cloak.

"What is it?" Kayla asked.

"We're leaving," he said. "Don't take off your hood."

* * *

ADRIEL ENTERED THE stable yard, caught sight of the cart, and sighed heavily. *The boys are here.* He pushed through the inn's door and entered the common room, looking over the tables.

Only half the chairs were filled, but that was no surprise; the Honey Barrel was far removed from town. Two hooded figures in dark travel-stained cloaks were seated in a corner. A sword was belted to the tall one's waist. His companion, shorter and smaller, was weaponless.

Adriel went to a vacant table, pulling his hood farther down his face. He was confident he could deal with the cloaked men if they turned out to be enemies, but he could not risk exposure yet, not until he found Corin and Dusty.

As he surveyed the room, the taller man got up, swept his cloak over his sword, and headed for the door, his companion at his side. *Those two are after Corin or I'm a wizard's fool.* Adriel steeled himself, rose, and followed them from the inn.

* * *

"QUIT SHOVING ME."

"I'm not."

"Dusty, your elbow's gouging out my eye."

"Oh. Sorry."

In the darkness of the stable, Corin peered through the window, jostling with Dusty for space. His hands itched from the hay, and his friend kept prodding him in the eye. There was also a good chance that the three men who had just entered the common room wanted him dead. And Dapple would not shut up. It was not a good situation.

"Your elbow is in my eye again."

"That's my hand."

Dapple snorted and kicked the side of her stall, then grumbled again. Corin remembered leading her to town in the pouring rain, rubbing her flank, coaxing her through the mud, and scratching her behind the ears. *How could I ever have sympathized with the beast?*

"Look through the window," Dusty whispered.

Corin looked and smacked into Dusty's shoulder. "Will you stop taking up all the room?"

"No time for that; they're leaving."

Sure enough, the two riders Corin had seen were making for the inn's front door, the man with the walking stick following cautiously. Directly beneath the stable window the two men filling their drinks from kegs behind the bar turned and watched them go.

Corin cleared his throat. "What do you think?"

"They all looked like assassins to me," Dusty said.

"But they didn't sit together, and they approached the inn from opposite directions."

A knee shoved into Corin's stomach as Dusty shifted to get a better view. "I'm sure one of them is after you. They weren't customers. None of them ordered anything to eat or drink."

Corin whacked him back.

Suddenly a man clad in black descended the steps that led to the bedrooms at the top of the inn, his dark face marred by scars. Behind him marched two cloaked rogues, holding Jyri, who was bound and gagged. Laughter and talk subsided as everyone in the common room turned to the men.

Dusty sucked in his breath. "We're dead."

Corin's hands tightened on the windowsill.

The scarred man stepped forward. "Sorry for disturbing your revelry. You can go back to your drinks and this pig of an innkeeper can go back to serving them so long as we get what we want."

"The two boys," said one of the scarred man's companions. "We saw them cross the stable yard from a bedroom window. Blood will be spilled unless we find them."

One of the men behind the bar motioned toward Jyri's private stable. "I saw them go through that door."

His friend pointed to the place where Corin and Dusty were hiding behind dirty glass. "This window was lit before. They might still be inside. Do what you want with them but leave us in peace."

"I will leave when the boys are found," the scarred man said. One of his companions snatched an iron key ring from Jyri's belt and began crossing the room. Several people stood, but the scarred man turned toward them, sword in hand, and they eased back into their seats.

"Let's go," Corin whispered. "I'll ride Jyri's packhorse; you take the one tied to your wagon."

He scrambled down the hay bales and put a bridle on Jyri's horse while Dusty fumbled with the stable doors. When they opened, Dusty hurried to his cart, untied his horse, and swung onto its back as Corin rode out.

A sickle moon washed the stable yard with pale lunar light. In the glow of the moon and the torches, Corin could see that they were not alone: The staff bearer faced the tall and short companions, who were seated on their great white horse. The swordsman's weapon was drawn.

"All of you keep back," Corin said.

"The boys are under my protection," said the staff bearer to the horsemen. "Leave us or I'll deal with you myself."

Dusty started. "Adriel? Is that you?"

The swordsman cocked his head and lowered his blade "Dale's apprentice?"

Adriel nodded. "Who are you?"

The swordsman ignored him. "Then you must be Corin. I haven't seen you since you were an infant."

Corin crossed his arms. "Answer the wizard's question."

"I've been sent here to guard you," the swordsman said.

"You mean stick him with your sword?" Dusty asked.

"I'm no assassin, though I've shed men's blood before." The swordsman eyed Adriel up and down. "I'm Wren Tident. I was sent here by your master."

Adriel lowered his staff. "Gods . . . he told me you would come. But who is that behind you?"

"His daughter," said the girl, and pulled her hood from her head. A shorn tangle of dirty-blond curls tumbled to her neck. "My name is Kayla."

Dusty coughed. "I thought you were a man."

"We don't have time for this," Corin said. "They are coming for us."

"Then we must leave *now*," Wren said. "Tell me quickly: Did one have a scarred face?"

Before Corin could reply, a sharp, cold laugh pierced the chilly night air, and the scarred man stepped from the shadows. "He does. And now this hunt comes to an end." The assassin's men flanked him, long swords in their hands.

Adriel swept back his cloak. "I am a wizard, one of the last living Aurians, and I don't make enemies lightly."

Save for the breathing of the horses, silence descended on the stable yard; the two men behind the assassin eyed Adriel uneasily.

Sarin narrowed his eyes. "Interesting . . . I've heard the legends, of course, but I've never met an Aurian. Once I saw a grave in the Summerset Isles . . . The stone marker was dedicated to one of their order, but it was ancient. None are still alive."

"I'll teach you otherwise," Adriel said.

Sarin tapped a finger on the pommel of his sword. "Teach me, then. I'm ready for your lesson."

Adriel lifted his staff, its jewel a dark crystal, and bowed his head. A breeze brushed the grass in the stable yard; the sapphire flickered to life with a flame of magical puissance, sending shadows scurrying from its glow. But then the light faded, leaving the jewel a dark crystal once more. Adriel's eyes opened and he shook his staff, but nothing happened, not even a spark. "I don't understand . . . The magic is gone!"

Sarin's laughter was harsh and cruel. "A cheap conjurer, that's what you are. Nothing more than tricks for fools and children. But I'm no child—even less a fool—and pretty lights don't scare me."

Then all their eyes turned to the entrance to the stable yard.

A drum, a harp, and a fife were heard as the troupe of musicians ambled into the stable yard, laughing and singing on their way back from the Spinribbon Fair. Then the front door of the Honey Barrel burst open, and Jyri charged out with several men who were gripping chairs.

When Sarin and his two men turned, Adriel swung up behind Corin on his mount. The horse sprang forward at Corin's kick, parting the musicians as the stable yard erupted in a chaotic melee.

Three horses burst from the stable and pounded madly down Woolthread Road under the ghostly light of the sickle moon. Dusty rode on Corin's right, Wren and Kayla on his left. Adriel gripped Corin tightly as their horse lunged forward. Hills whirred by, nearly formless in the night.

After a minute of reckless galloping, Wren slowed and asked Kayla for his telescope. She reached into a saddlebag and handed Wren a bronze cylinder. He put it to his eye and twisted his neck, peering over his shoulder. "Blazes, the three of them are coming. They're gaining fast."

"Follow me," Corin shouted. "We'll lose them in the Ravenswood."

THE RAVENSWOOD

KAYLA BURIED HER face in Wren's cloak as they galloped after
Corin. The Ravenswood sprawled before them, as imposing as a
citadel. Dark, tangled branches and scraggy trunks came into view as
they neared the hills. Sarin's shouts sounded behind her.

Dusty looked back every few seconds, relaying the positions of the
assassins. Adriel clenched his staff as a drowning man grips driftwood,
shaking it and muttering. Kayla silently pleaded for his staff to work; if
the wizard could regain control of his magic, they might stop their pur-
suers without bloodshed.

They plunged into the forest, and Corin began leading them on a
winding path. Dusty kept his horse close behind, and Wren brought up
the rear. Hooves pounded, throwing up chunks of dirt. Kayla felt the
eyes of the assassins on her cloak. Any second, one of them might get
close enough to snatch her from her horse, and her back tingled every
time she heard a curse or shout.

As they rounded a corner, she saw a fallen log blocking the path.
Corin yelled out a warning as his horse leaped over it, hooves grazing

rotten bark. Kayla clutched tighter to Wren's waist as their mount cleared the log.

With an arm around Corin's waist, Adriel swiveled in the saddle, brought up his staff, and pointed it back at the assassins. The ground beneath the assassins' horses exploded. Dirt sprayed everywhere, obscuring the path and flying between the trees like a sandstorm.

For a moment Kayla dared to hope, but then the three riders broke from the billow of dust, their cloaks flapping like vulture wings.

The dark path narrowed to a tunnel of wild, thorny trunks. The moon flickered through gaps in the leafy canopy. Trees rushed by, looming above them like warped, hulking beasts.

Wren spurred his horse faster, hugging the path, a madman navigating an even madder trail, hurtling recklessly over toppled logs and overgrown stumps that were as dangerous in the darkness as any blade.

His cloak flipped up in Kayla's face. As she threw up her arm to thrust it aside, a blue incandescence bloomed around her. Kayla heard another explosion. She grappled with Wren's cloak and pushed it down, then looked back. A cloud of earth swirled over the pathway, larger and denser than before. Again the horsemen broke free, continuing their charge.

Dusty lashed his reins madly; Wren swore under his breath. Corin pressed ahead, keeping his head low.

They came to a thin stream flowing down a gully, and Adriel shouted something to Corin. Shallow water gurgled over pebbles, sluicing through the trees, as their horses splashed through the stream and bounded up the embankment.

Corin pulled on his reins, coming to an immediate stop, forcing Dusty and Wren to veer aside to keep from crashing into him. Adriel raised his staff a third time and leveled it at the stream.

Like a long-dormant fountain that had been given new life, the water began to froth. As the assassins plunged into it, swinging their swords, the stream erupted. Pebbles flew skyward. The three black horses screamed and reared back, flinging their riders from their backs.

A triumphant yell burst from Kayla's lungs. Dusty whooped and clenched his fists as Adriel grimly lowered his staff.

"Ride!" Wren shouted, driving his heels against the flanks of his horse.

The others wheeled and followed, leaving the assassins scrambling in the mud, cursing and lunging after their frightened mounts.

* * *

BY THE TIME they stopped, the sounds of pursuit had long vanished. They dismounted at the edge of a clearing, and Corin stumbled when his left leg touched the ground. Weirdly shaped rocks were scattered amid the tall grass of the clearing.

"That was exciting," Dusty grumbled. He began massaging his thighs.

Wren turned to Adriel, who was leaning heavily on his staff. "That was almost too late. Why wouldn't your magic work sooner?"

"My magic comes and goes," he said. "I'm a wizard but no master of wizardry."

"What about your show?" Corin asked.

Adriel shook his head. "I had no idea it would go so well. Everything you saw was a matter of luck."

"Luck?" Wren scoffed.

Kayla looked at her father reproachfully. "Remember, without Adriel, the assassins could have caught us."

Moonbeams streamed between the trees, dancing with a silver glow on Adriel's spiky hair, delineating the sharp contours of his face. Kayla was surprised at how young he looked; his features were hardening toward adulthood, but they retained a younger boy's innocence.

"Luck or not," Corin said, "if he hadn't found me at the fair, I might be tied to the back of an assassin's horse."

Kayla wondered how Corin, a boy no older than herself, could possibly be the catalyst for the world's undoing. His hair was nearly as blond as hers, though streaked with brown, and his face was strong and defined. Kayla had noticed his limp as soon as he had dismounted—his left leg was more a crutch than a limb. But his eyes, deep green and flecked with gold, sparkled like emeralds.

Wren grunted. "We'll see who saves whom when it comes to fighting. I'll take my sword over a piece of painted wood any day."

Kayla squinted at the stones in the clearing and suddenly realized what they were. "Look," she whispered.

The stones were cracked and crumbling. They were carved in the shapes of arcane monsters, idols to spirits of the void. A corrugated obelisk rose in their midst; it was an altar, and on the altar was the body of a man, lashed down with ropes and chains. Crows, ravens, and rooks hopped up and down on the body, ripping clothing, pecking at flesh. Trees arched over the clearing, bending toward the birds like worshippers in an occult sanctuary. Beyond the grass, mist churned across a sickly reddish-gray pool.

Adriel took a step back. "Where have you brought us, Corin?"

"I don't know," Corin stammered, blood draining from his face. "I didn't mean to lead us *here.*"

Dusty whistled softly. "It's Farmer Twine's pool . . . ," he said, trailing off.

Adriel turned to Dusty. "You've been here before?" he asked. When Corin and Dusty nodded, he took another step back. "I had a nightmare about this place. I saw that man's face in my dreams."

Wren cursed, took a deep breath, and put a hand on Kayla's shoulder. "It's a sacrifice—don't go near it," he said. "Whoever did this is probably long gone by now. I'll make sure it's safe, but we've got to keep moving."

The others nodded, and he crept into the clearing, hand on his sword hilt, his cloak rustling darkly. The stone idols rested quietly, their silence pierced only by the scavenging birds.

When he reached the altar, Wren paused and examined the body. "Dragons and demons, indeed." At the sound of his voice, the jet-black birds looked up, fastening their hungry eyes on his cloak.

The rest of the group slowly entered the clearing, creeping up behind

Wren. As they did, the birds flapped away, a dark spiral of wings. Their screeches echoed among the trees, fading into the vastness of the forest.

The man's corpse was mutilated: His arms and legs were bloody ribbons, ribs poked through his tunic, and his eyes had been picked clean. Only sockets stared up at the night sky. Black feathers clung to the bloody altar.

Corin's eyes widened. "It's Farmer Twine," he whispered.

Dusty thought he might retch. "And he's missing a hand . . ."

Wren looked up. "You know him?"

Corin nodded numbly and limped to the other side of the clearing. The others drew next to him as he gazed down at the pool. Vines threaded through the water and snaked into the surrounding forest.

Wren put an arm around Kayla. "They're the same as in Bridgewater."

Adriel nodded. "I was there."

"They've spread," Dusty said. "There weren't this many before."

Corin leaned against a tree. "What in Ariel's name is happening?" he asked aloud. The group just stared at him in silence.

Then Adriel moved closer to Corin and began telling him of the hermit he had seen in the cave on his way to Bridgewater. When he finished, Wren and Kayla described their experience with the creature in the lighthouse. They explained how they had met Marian and passed along what the enchantress had told them. Finally, Adriel recounted his conversation with Dale in the observatory.

Corin could not believe what he was hearing. "But why does he need me to free the demon?" he asked at length. "I can't be any use to him."

Adriel paused as if deep in thought, looked at Corin, and then looked away. "He needs your blood for dark magic that I do not understand."

Corin pounded his fist against the tree. "How is this happening? I didn't ask for any of this."

"The question," Dusty said to his friend, "is, What do we do now?"

"We hide," said Wren.

In the end, they decided to head south for Lantern Watch—the nearest port, aside from Nautalia—where they would board a ship and sail away to a safer place, fleeing the sorcerers and their assassins across the waves. They agreed that Nautalia was out of the question, as guards probably were still searching for Wren and his daughter.

As they talked, a single bubble broke on the surface of the pool, bursting in a crimson splash.

Wren eyed the water. "It's time to go," he said. "We shouldn't remain here any longer."

He led the others back to the horses. They mounted as they had before, Adriel with Corin and Dusty riding alone. When Kayla climbed up after Wren, he snapped his reins and began trailing Corin on the path once more, winding south through the Ravenswood.

Behind them more mist gathered above the pool, and another bubble floated slowly to the surface.

BLACK RIB TRIDENT

WHEN THEY REACHED the end of the forest, Wren took the lead, following the path south and then southwest, skirting Merrifield by orienting himself to the twinkling lights on the town's dark hill. The path he chose joined with Woolthread Road, which angled south along the Seaspine Mountains. This they rode for another half hour, putting as many miles between themselves and Merrifield as possible before looking for a place to spend the night.

Dusty spotted a dense thicket on the side of a hill. Adriel led them into the bushes and brambles, his staff glowing faintly.

Once they had secured the horses, they ate some of the meager stores from Wren's baggage. Adriel had left his provisions in Rookery Rest, and neither Corin nor Dusty had brought any food; they had left everything, including their cloaks, behind. Then they bedded down on a carpet of grass and leaves. Overcome by fatigue, the two boys and Kayla soon fell asleep.

Wren spread his cloak over the boys, and Corin's eyelids twitched open. He looked up blearily, then closed his eyes and rolled onto his side.

Surrounded by the darkness of the thicket, Wren remembered how he had helped save Corin all those years ago . . . how he had galloped away from the village of Ember with Dale and Lori . . . how he had fled the monstrous creatures and the haunting crackling of flames . . .

He sighed and glanced at Adriel. The wizard was huddled in his cloak, staring at the ground.

"You should sleep," Wren said.

"So should you."

"I don't sleep well anymore. What's bothering you?"

Adriel's face was haggard. "I have nightmares . . . visions of shadows . . . shadows and death."

"Dreams can't harm us."

"Mine have been coming true."

"The corpse on the altar? What else have you seen?"

"A dark tower and a darker sea . . ."

Wren told him, "It will turn out well in the end."

Adriel smiled weakly, then lay down and curled up beside his staff.

Wren stayed awake for a time, gazing up through the thicket at the stars as Kayla slumbered beside him, snuggled under her cloak.

* * *

IN THE MORNING Wren shared a light breakfast from his supplies. He led the others south on the road.

The hill country gradually flattened, giving way to meadows and farms. People worked in the fields, weeding crops and repairing fences. Merchants trundled wares along the road, and a constant stream of villagers moved between hamlets. A few waved, but most stared straight ahead, their faces drawn and grim.

As the afternoon turned to dusk, the road wound around a copse of trees, crossed a stony riverbed, then curved around a tumbledown farm.

Wren regarded the buildings skeptically. A barn sagged against a ruined stable; the farmhouse was a rickety heap, and broken fences divided thorn-strangled crops. He stopped his horse at the roadside. "We could spend the night here," he said. "It looks uninhabited."

Dusty objected. "It looks like a madman's refuge."

Wren glanced back down the curve of the path they had just trodden; an alpenglow lined the mountains above the twisty tree line. "I don't like the looks of it, either, but we need to leave the road soon. I don't want to spend another night running from assassins."

Kayla spotted someone moving toward them from the fields. She pointed, and everyone turned.

Sure enough, a man was picking his way toward them through the tangled crops. He was garbed in a rough-spun tunic and held a pipe between his teeth.

"There's the madman," Dusty muttered.

Corin turned to Wren. "How much farther is Lantern Watch?"

"We're near the Black Rib Trident. From there it's an hour's ride to the Shale Throat and then another hour until we reach the town." Wren readjusted his packs, considering. "There's no choice. We have to talk to this man. He's already seen us. I'll ask if he has room and board, but we'll need to pay him to keep quiet about our passage on this road."

The man drew near, eyeing them carefully. "I've crops to tend before nightfall," he said, "and a wife who needs tending, too. I've no time to bandy words. Who are you, and what do you want?"

"Journeymen," said Wren, "in need of a roof for the night. We thought your farm was deserted." He jangled a pouch of coins. "I have silver."

"I won't be swayed by money. My wife is with child, and she expects to give birth near midnight."

"We only need cots—and stalls for the horses."

The farmer's eyes lingered on Wren's sword. "Will you be passing through the trident?"

Wren nodded.

"Then perhaps my friends can help you. They live in a patch of woods near the ribs. Their house is cramped, but it'll be better than nothing . . . for a price. They're known to spare paying travelers."

"I thought no one lived near the ribs. It's more a wasteland than anything else," Wren said.

The farmer sparked a flint over his pipe. "My friends make a good living. They're usually glad to help weary wayfarers with their burdens." He puffed and exhaled smoke.

"How will we find them?"

"When you reach the ribs, call out 'Roper' and someone will come. You won't have to wait long."

"My thanks," Wren said, slipping the farmer a coin. He told him to keep their group a secret, then turned and kicked his mount, leading the other horses down the road.

The sun burned into the west, leaving swaths of russet and orange in its wake. Wren began thinking the corrosion of the farmer's home stranger and stranger. A palpable unease settled on his shoulders, and he found himself peering between the trees growing in intermittent patches near the road. It seemed as if skulking creatures were peering back.

He had passed through the ribs before on his journeys to and from Lantern Watch: first, after his mother had died, Dirk had taken him from the town and embarked on an adventurer's life; then, years later, they had returned on a matter of business between Dirk and his brother, Cane, a pirate more attached to gold than blood. These journeys had left Wren with only a sword and a scar that ran from his temple to his chin.

He glanced down at his blade. Was it a remnant of Dirk's presence, guarding him from the horrors of the world, or was it a curse, dooming him to repeat the past? Perhaps he would die as Dirk had, and Kayla would return through these ribs alone, bearing her father's sword.

The wizard Adriel might be of some help. It seemed he had little control over his magic, but his staff had kept Corin alive and saved them all in the Ravenswood. Wren had difficulty acknowledging this—

he had no wish to be indebted to magic of any sort—but Adriel's power was undeniable.

Kayla leaned forward. "What's wrong?"

Wren shook his head. "Men can be broken by the burden of their past."

"The past only has the power we give it, Father."

"Perhaps. But that doesn't make it easier to bear."

Several minutes later Woolthread Road diverged in three directions: east, south, and west. The huge stones of the Black Rib Trident, each curved and pointed, arched like the skeleton of some colossal beast over the hub where the roadways met. The surrounding land was as battered as an old shield. Little cyclones of grit and dirt spun in and out of existence, twirling around scattered trees.

The left-hand road ran east toward the villages of Stardell and Turncross. At the start of the middle road, blackbirds circled over a small grove of oaks. The westernmost road followed the cliffs of the Shale Throat to Lantern Watch. Nearby, the cliffs broadened into a cauldron of black, cragged slopes, encircling the forested valley in which the coastal town lay.

Wren kicked his horse forward, cupped his hands to his mouth, and called out for Roper. There was no reply.

He had always thought the Black Rib Trident a place to stir volatile ruminations; indeed, now his musings were dark and troubled. As the blackbirds cawed and croaked, he looked suspiciously down each of the roadways.

Then he saw the corpses and stiffened.

A harridan swung from a tree beside the mouth of the eastern road; a younger, blond-haired man hung beside her. The man's eyes bulged, and his neck had been purpled and chafed by a noose. A fox chewed one of his low-hanging legs, wolfing down bits of flesh. Flies buzzed around the tree as the blackbirds circled closer.

Before Wren could react, a gangly red-haired man stepped out from behind a boulder, carrying a length of noosed hemp. He stared at them with pale blue eyes.

Wren drew his sword. "Who are you?"

"You called for Roper," said the man. "He's come."

Adriel pointed his staff at him. "You hung those two people."

"They struggled mightily. Don't make the same mistake."

"What do you want from us?" Wren demanded.

"Hand over your horses, coin, and other valuables. Banditry's a hard trade, and it's been growing harder. People are avoiding the roads these days."

"That cursed farmer set us up," growled Wren.

Roper chuckled. "He's no farmer."

Wren nudged his horse forward. "If you challenge us, I'll ride you down."

"No, you won't. Put down your weapons or I'll string you up with the old woman and her son." Roper clapped his hands, and figures in dirty furs and patched cloaks began emerging from behind the stone ribs: two bowmen, an axman, and four others with notched spears, swords, and daggers.

Corin and Dusty edged their horses closer to Wren's. Adriel remained poised in his saddle, staff at the ready.

"Drag them from their horses and bring me the swordsman," Roper said. "He'll be the first to hang."

Kayla leaned forward. "They're on foot," she whispered. "Ride for it, Father!"

Wren backed up his horse. "We can't risk breaking away. They might mark us with their arrows."

As the bandits advanced, a loud whinny pierced the air, and hooves sounded on the road behind Wren. One of the bandits pointed and shouted. Wren turned his horse just as a gray horse thundered past, nostrils flared, mouth frothing. An armored knight sat in its saddle.

"Sir Lancet!" Kayla shouted, and Wren instantly recognized the slim young man from whom he had stolen a mount in Midrun.

Lancet raised his lance as he galloped toward the bandits. The two bowmen released their arrows at him, but he caught the shafts on his shield and plunged his weapon through one of the archers. Releasing the lance, he cut at the other with his sword. The bandit's bow cracked, and he fled; the rest of the marauders scurried into the trees, Roper running fastest of all.

Corin and Dusty cheered, and Adriel smiled broadly. Wren's relief did not last long. He turned and looked at Kayla, pursing his lips; her eyes reflected his concern. Sir Lancet had no reason to treat them any differently than he had treated the bandits—after all, they had stolen his horse.

The knight sheathed his sword, dismounted, and removed his plumed helm, revealing matted blond hair that curled down his neck. He walked his horse toward Wren, staring at him with blue-green eyes. "Thank the gods of land and sea I arrived in time to avert disaster. Now one less rogue walks Ellynrie."

"Your aid is most welcome," said Adriel.

Sir Lancet lifted a hand to brush away the praise but then caught sight of Wren's horse. "What devilry is this?" he asked, narrowing his eyes. "Have I saved thieves from thieves?"

Corin raised an eyebrow. "What are you talking about?"

Wren held up his hands. "Let me explain."

Lancet redrew his sword and spread his feet. "You're the soulless cowards who stole my mount."

"Wait," Kayla pleaded. "Just listen."

The knight lowered his sword a little.

"We were being chased through Midrun by assassins," Wren said, "the same men you were pursuing. If we hadn't taken your horse, we would have been caught and killed."

"You have an affinity for mortal peril," said Lancet. "Why are you involved with such murderous scum?"

Wren hesitated, considering his next words. If he told tell Lancet the whole story, he might avoid a confrontation and perhaps even enlist his aid. Quickly, Wren decided it was necessary. If he could not adequately explain why he had stolen the knight's mount, he would have to risk a fight. As the wind rose, he pulled his cloak closer and began to tell his story from the beginning.

When he finished, there was silence. Then Sir Lancet sheathed his sword. "This tale sounds like a desperate, foolish lie, but against all odds I believe your words. They seem mad enough to hold the truth."

"How did you get a new horse?" Wren asked. "And why are you here? We left you behind in Midrun."

"My adventure started once I followed your directions to the Reveler's Crown and stabled my mount," Lancet began. He told them how he had scoured Midrun for the assassins, returned to the inn, found his horse missing, and sought a new mount, listening all the while to tales of people who had seen a great winged beast. He bought a new horse and resolved to track what he knew to be a dragon. The sightings led him through the Seaspine Mountains, then south toward the Black Rib Trident.

"Now I face a choice," Lancet said. "Do I continue following the dragon or help you on your quest?"

"Why would you risk yourself for me?" Corin asked.

"Fate has brought me to this juncture and placed these paths before me. This is no chance meeting. The man who rides my horse is facing murderers I sought to slay. Your fate, Corin, appears to have bound us together." Lancet turned toward Wren. "If what you have told me is true, I cannot let this boy fall into his brother's hands."

"Your help would be a great asset," Adriel said.

The knight bowed. "I'm honored to ride with a magician."

Dusty looked up at the sky. "This is all very heroic, but we need to start looking for shelter."

Wren nodded. "Roper didn't turn out to be as hospitable as the farmer promised."

"Wait," said Lancet. "Before we start, there's one thing I need."

"And what's that?" asked Wren.

"My horse."

Evening deepened as they set out on the southern road, Wren guiding them on the new gray mount that Lancet had brought. They passed between the cliffs of the Shale Throat, which rose higher all around them, sheer walls of dark, sharp rock. As they rode toward Lantern

Watch and the sea, they grew tired and hungry but did not halt. The path was deserted, and they had little food. Corin spied a distant firelight atop a jagged cliff, and after some deliberation Adriel volunteered to investigate and began to climb the crag, staff in hand, as the others led the horses into a thicket above the road.

* * *

IN A SHADOWY bedroom at Rookery Rest, Sarin and One-Eye sat at a table, poring over a map.

"This would never have happened if you had finished your end of the job," said Sarin. "Why did it take you so long to find the boy?"

"I was told he lived in town," One-Eye muttered. "How was I to know he lived out in the hills?"

"Did you ask around for him?"

One-Eye tapped his crystal eye. "I'm not someone in whom people confide."

Sarin frowned. "I stole the dagger and sent it east with Damon. He's taking it to his master in the Tower of Shadows. If you had found the boy, we could have washed our hands of this whole affair."

"And pocketed our pay," One-Eye agreed. "But it wasn't my fault."

"Aye, I'm sure that your hirelings are as incompetent as mine."

Four other men sat in chairs around the room, nursing bruises. The tallest put a hand on the shoulder of the shortest. "It was that bastard magician," he said. "There's no use in trying to fight magic."

Sarin turned toward him. "Keep your tongue behind your teeth or I'll cut it from your mouth and throw it to the rooks atop this cursed inn."

The man who had spoken closed his mouth and did not speak again.

One-Eye shook his head. "But how do we find the boy? No one knows where he's gone."

"Seems it's turned into a guessing game, and we must outguess our prey. I'm sure they'll keep moving."

One-Eye chuckled, and his glass orb flashed. "Games can be cheated."

"They won't journey back to Nautalia."

"Nor east," said One-Eye. "They'd be fools to travel toward the Tower of Shadows."

"And they won't stay here."

"That leaves north . . ."

"And south."

One-Eye took a coin from a pouch tied to his waist, flipped it, and watched as it spun through the air. When it landed, he snorted and snatched it up.

"We go south," he said.

Sarin nodded. "Lantern Watch."

"I have an associate there who can help us find them, the leader of a pirate gang called the Torturers." One-Eye placed the coin back in his pouch. "It makes sense. Other than Nautalia, that town is the nearest port. I've known men who've used it to escape unwanted attention."

The assassins divided their men, sending two northward and bidding the rest to stay in Merrifield to watch for Corin and his companions. Then One-Eye and Sarin left the inn and rode south on Woolthread Road. They passed a small farm and spoke briefly with a farmer. Between puffs on his pipe, the farmer confirmed that he had seen two men, two boys, and a girl with curly blond hair ride down the road only a short time before, followed by a knight on horseback.

When the assassins reached the Black Rib Trident, they spotted two people hanging in a tree, dismounted, and strode over to the corpse of the bandit that lay on the southern road.

One-Eye bent over the body, chuckling. "A thief robbed of life. Death is a master of irony."

"It's fresh," said Sarin.

"Could our quarry have done this?"

Sarin dipped his fingers in the bloody hole near the corpse's chest and shook his head. "None of them had a lance."

Just then a man with fiery hair stalked from the trees, carrying a length of rope that had been tied into a noose. A rabble of bloodied, beaten men followed him onto the road. "Put down your weapons and hand over your horses," said the man. He swung the rope from his fingers.

Sarin roared with laughter, and the attackers stepped back, visibly unnerved. One-Eye began walking toward them, smiling, both of his rapiers drawn.

* * *

THE BANDIT WAITED at the abandoned farm for several more minutes, then followed the scarred man and his one-eyed friend down Woolthread Road, congratulating himself on the success of his ruse. As he trotted along, he sucked eagerly on his pipe and contemplated his share in the spoils.

At the trident he cried out, confronted by the sight of his lifeless companions: They lay under the shadow of the ribs, their throats cut, their gutted entrails strewn on the ground. Birds swooped down from the sky, flocking atop their bodies.

Near the fringe of a stand of trees, three people hung from a gnarled oak. One of them was Roper. Gallows rope had been wound about his neck.

* * *

ADRIEL REACHED THE top of the crag and crept near the edge of the basin.

Three women wrapped in threadbare cloaks huddled around a fire, eyes fixed on the burning logs. Two were brown and bald, with young, supple bodies. The third, old and pale as smoke, clutched her wispy hair with grubby, soot-stained fingers. Shadows writhed on the ground.

The pale woman stood and raised her arms, chortling, "Sear us, you torrid tongues, and blaze away our sight . . . when eyes cease, the Watchers will give us clairvoyance . . . serve and toil, and they will caress the faithful, drawing them through the folds of the earth and into their eternity."

She began dancing about the flames. For an instant Adriel saw her haglike face; it bore puckered holes instead of eyes.

"Now gouge," the pale woman hissed, facing the flames once more. "The Watchers, our lovers, are coming." Her two companions drew burning stakes from the fire and raised them to their eyes, chanting tonelessly.

Adriel turned away with a reeling stomach and crept back down the crag. Swaths of indigo and violet bled around the world's rim. A gibbous moon hung over the cliffs of the Shale Throat, and a smattering of stars glowed weakly above the gloaming. Adriel tensed for the women's screams, but he heard only their incantations until even they had faded and were gone.

When he reached the thicket where his friends were waiting, they looked up with expectant faces. They had hoped to finally find refuge from the twilight's chilly pall, but Adriel could only shake his head.

The firelight above them wavered and winked out. Hooves pounded on the road below. Adriel looked down. Two horsemen were galloping toward Lantern Watch. He waited until they disappeared from view, then climbed onto his horse and started toward the road.

One by one the others followed, wending their way into the Shale Throat.

LANTERN WATCH

WREN HAD NOT been to Lantern Watch since the murder of his father.

The town had been a dark stain on his maps, an unapproachable co-ordinate. The memories had been too horrifying to confront. Long ago, he had tracked down his father's killers, a gang of pirates who called themselves the Torturers, but since then Wren had been marked a wanted man. *I won't stay here long enough to be found,* he thought as they wound their way along the road. *As soon as we find a ship, we sail into the west.* If they were not able to escape across the sea, chances were that he would face a final confrontation with the assassins in Lantern Watch. With the help of the knight and the wizard, Wren stood a better chance against Sarin and One-Eye, but the assassins seemed to have endless supplies of sword fodder. And then there were Cade and Damon, the sorcerers who, according to Adriel, were powerful beyond measure and unlikely to give up their hunt.

"Are we getting close?" Corin asked, jolting Wren from his thoughts.

"The town lies through those trees," Wren said, pointing to the small wood before them.

Sir Lancet rested his lance on his shoulder. "I've heard tales of this place, rumors sired by the pirate gangs."

"I can't wait to meet the locals," said Dusty, trying to force a joke.

"Lantern Watch was born from a shipwreck," said Wren.

The riders listened intently.

"Legend has it that two pirate ships sighted a merchant vessel traveling toward Nautalia from the city of Meridian in the Summerset Isles, the very place we are trying to reach. Hoping to evade the pirates, the merchant ship sailed into a storm, but it crashed on a rocky stretch of shoreline near a fishing village. The pirates, too, were forced aground, and the three crews banded together with the villagers for survival. Most of the people in Lantern Watch are descendants of the pirates and the merchants, a treacherous breed."

"Conceived in the womb of a stormy sea," Sir Lancet murmured.

At the edge of the wood, a crude sign lettered "Lantern Watch" pointed into the trees. They rode in single file on the forest path. Red glass lanterns burned from boughs arching above them. Fireflies flashed here and there, glittering between the trees.

The group passed the clearing where Dirk once had handed Wren his sword. Wren remembered the scene as clearly as he had atop the clock tower. *Snowflakes sifting from an overcast sky, wind rustling bracken and branches, smoke sifting through the trees from Lantern Watch. Dirk crouching on the far side of a clearing, scrubbing the bloodied blade with handfuls of white powder, then coming toward him with the proffered sword . . .* He pushed the memory aside—it was not winter, and Dirk was long dead—but his hand strayed to the pommel of his sword as if to grasp his father's hand.

Dusty tried to strike up a conversation, but no one felt like talking. Kayla wrapped her arms tightly around Wren, glancing fearfully into the trees, but he told her there was nothing to worry about. And there wasn't. Not yet. The pirate gangs of Lantern Watch seldom strayed this far from the sea.

Wren heard a rattling of axles and wheels as a cart creaked around a bend in the road. Lancet's hand moved to his sword, but Wren stopped him. "Put your weapon away. It's only the lantern lighter. He's no trouble to us."

The wagon rumbled forward, piloted by a wizened man who carried a long pole tied with a candle.

"What are the lanterns for?" Lancet asked.

"Lantern Watch is named for them. The townsfolk believe they ward off evil spirits, though I wonder at their philosophy. How can they believe in such things and continue living their wicked lives? Once they die, many of them will join the spirits they fear."

"It seems like folly to me," said Lancet. "These folk are too superstitious for their own good."

They reached the end of the wood and found themselves on a grassy slope, overlooking over the town and its crowded harbor.

A sunless warren of dilapidated houses and foggy twist-knot streets stretched toward three hulking ships that were wrecked and rotting. Their keels glowed with a dark patina under the stars. Hundreds of red lanterns flickered in the mist, mesmeric and infernal, like feral spirits on a darkened plain.

For a moment no one spoke, but then Kayla broke the silence. "The three ships from the story."

"The very same," said Wren. "*Siren*'s to the left, the home of . . . evil women. *Gorge*, the largest, is reputed to have been the merchant vessel, and it's riddled with shops, but the shopkeepers are more like thieves than traders. Then there's *Umbra*, off to the right. That's the ship of the pirate gangs."

Sir Lancet dropped his lance from his shoulder, moving it into a more ready position. "Who would live in such a place?"

"We should find passage to Meridian as soon as possible," Adriel said, and everyone quickly agreed.

Wren urged his horse down the slope toward town. "There's an inn near the shore, a hive of scum and riffraff but a gathering place for sailors, too. We can learn what's available there." He readjusted his traveling packs and kicked his horse toward Lantern Watch.

They stuck together in a huddled group, winding through the streets until they reached the inn. The skeleton of an albatross had been nailed cruciform above the inn's door. A lantern dangled from the transom on rusted chains, turning in slow circles, casting the facade in sullen, crimson light.

"Is this the cursed place where your father was killed?" Sir Lancet asked, turning toward Wren.

Wren nodded. "The Black Plank."

Across the alley, the ships loomed over the inn. Their brine-stained bones, gnawed by wind and scavenging water, arched sharply above them. Lights pulsed from openings in the rib-cage hulls and swayed from masthead crossbones. The sea had spit them onto the shore, but now it licked them like a dark, greedy tongue, whispering "murder" along their rusted bulwarks.

Wren felt as if he were still a boy, standing before this very inn, wondering if he had reentered a world from his past. Fear insinuated itself into his mind. *The sea is hungry,* he thought. *Perhaps it desires to swallow me, too.* He looked at Kayla; her eyes were riveted on the ships.

Corin brushed hair from his eyes, looking at the bleached bones of the albatross. "Isn't there a safer place?"

"It reminds me of the Rogue's Cloak," said Kayla.

"I'm afraid it's a bit worse than that place," Wren said. "Some in Lantern Watch kill easier than they breathe."

"A breathtaking talent," Dusty said, but no one laughed.

Wren led them into the stable and dismounted, then pushed open a side door and entered the inn, coughing in the rank, smoke-sullied air.

A fool in motley was chained to the bar at the far side of the room, dancing and singing nonsensically. People flung empty mugs and bits of food at him. He lithely dodged the missiles. A dog crouched in a corner, wrestling with a bone. Kayla reached for Wren's hand, threading her fingers through his. Panicked shadows slid up and down the walls.

Rough-faced men and women sat at tables, eating and drinking, cursing and laughing. A hole brooded in the center of the floor, ringed with a wrought-iron railing; a dark beam of wood lay over the pit.

Kayla tightened her grip on Wren's fingers. "What's down there?" she asked.

"Better if you don't know."

He picked a corner table and started toward it, then saw Veil and Tint across the room, seated at a Jikari board with three colorfully clothed men who could only be pirates. Veil started at the sight of Wren. He whispered something to Tint, who turned and spoke to the pirates. The two traders left the inn without giving them even a second glance.

Wren did not mention the traders to the others. They had not seen Veil and Tint, and it would only have discouraged them further if they had. Besides, the remnants of the caravan had been thoroughly licked and beaten. *No one will trouble us,* he tried to reassure himself.

Suddenly one of the pirates rose drunkenly from the table. He swaggered over to Adriel, cursed at him, and gave him a shove. He sneered and made as if to shove him again, but Adriel moved quickly aside. The pirate blundered in the air, fumbling for a handhold. He tripped and crashed to the ground as his two companions jumped to their feet, rapiers in their hands.

"Gut the bastards," cried the drunken pirate, rolling onto his hands and knees and whisking a dagger from his belt.

Adriel backed away. "I don't want any trouble." Wren and Sir Lancet drew their swords, flanking him.

Corin pulled Kayla behind him. Dusty balled his hands into fists. Shouts and laughter died away, and the tavern grew silent save for the grumbling in the pit and the mad singing of the fettered fool.

At the sight of blades, the pirates lost heart and lowered their rapiers. They dragged their man to his feet and slunk from the inn, cursing under their breath.

Wren turned to Sir Lancet. "Check on the horses. Those pirates will gut them if we give them a chance."

The knight nodded and disappeared into the stable.

When he had shut the door behind him, the entrance to the inn burst open. Three powerful-looking men and a lithe, wild-haired woman barged inside, Veil and Tint at their heels. Other men filed behind them and into the tavern, holding loaded crossbows. Someone handed Veil a fat bag of coins, and he left the inn with Tint.

"What is this?" Corin asked. "Who are these people, Wren?"

Wren knew each of the pirates; their faces had seared his memory like blisters of the mind.

Cane, the leader of the gang, limped to the center of the room with his obsidian staff, tugging on a lock of blue-black hair. "Can this be the same craven boy I chased from town all those years ago?" he asked, fixing his single eye on Wren. "I'm surprised you've lived this long."

Wren gritted his teeth. "Let these others go, Cane. They have nothing to do with our quarrel."

An orb of clear glass shone in Cane's other socket, reflecting the room's light like a rubicund prism. "The Torturers have been without clients for several weeks. There has been naught but shadows in *Umbra's* iron cells." He rapped his cane once against the floor.

Bulge, a hulking mute corded with muscle, stepped behind Wren and knocked him to his knees. One of his ears had been ripped halfway off. He wore no shirt, but an iron plate studded with spikes and rivets was sutured to his torso. A huge spiked hammer hung from his belt.

"Jezebel," Cane shouted. "Attend to the wizard. Kleaver, you can have Wren."

The woman kicked away Adriel's staff and began binding him with rigging. Her limber body was as thin as her sword, which was said to keep time to her honeyed voice while she sweet-talked her victims. The man named Kleaver took Wren's traveling pack, threw it onto a table, and began rummaging inside, ripping the leather with his claw-gloved hands. Warts covered his face, the manifestation of a disease that Wren knew was gradually taking his life. *It's been sixteen years . . . How is he still alive?*

Cane switched his staff to his other hand and smiled. "Bulge has been eager to get his hands on you, Wren. He didn't enjoy it when you threw him from the attic window above this inn."

Bulge, the mute, said nothing, but tightened his grip.

Cane laughed. "Your attempt at revenge was a failure. Your father died just the same."

"Dirk was your *brother*," Wren said.

"He was a thief. I gave him long enough to pay his debts. When the two of you left town, I sent my men to collect. Dirk had no gold, so he paid his debt in blood." Cane leaned heavily on his staff. "It seems your reputation as a wanted corpse followed you here. I've been hired to turn you in to Sarin and One-Eye, assassins who will surely do their work on you."

The strength fled from Wren's limbs.

Cane looked pleased. "I have no idea why they've concerned themselves with you," he continued. "One-Eye and I go back a long time, and I know his skill with blades." He tapped a finger against his glass eye. "The assassins are paying me for something I'd have gladly done for free. They may get to kill you, but they didn't say anything against torturing you first."

Kleaver grabbed something inside Wren's traveling pack and withdrew the box containing the petals Wren had given Kayla in the clock tower. He forced them into the mouths of Corin, Dusty, and Adriel.

Kayla struggled as he pried her lips apart, but she was held in place by two other pirates. Wren strained against Bulge's grip and cursed until his daughter's body went slack from the sleeping herbs.

Cane limped in front of him. "Welcome back," he said, and brought his obsidian staff down on Wren's head.

There was a blinding flash of pain, then darkness.

TORTURERS

"WAKE UP," a girl whispered. "Wake up!"

Wren tried to open his eyes, vaguely aware of a throbbing near the base of his skull, but his lids would not budge. Confusion muddled his senses; pain mangled his thoughts.

"What's wrong with him?" a boy asked.

Another boy stammered, "He might be dead."

"Don't say that!" the girl hissed.

Wren heard a slap.

"Why'd you hit me?"

"You deserved it, Dusty," said a fourth voice. "Take a closer look. He's still breathing."

This all felt strangely familiar. Wren was certain he had been in a similar situation before, nearly unconscious, struggling against a void, listening to a morass of faceless voices.

"Father . . ." the girl begged.

The pain in Wren's head intensified.

"Father, wake up!"

His eyes fluttered open.

Kayla stared down at him, pleading with her eyes. Then she flung her arms around him and buried her face in his tunic.

Wren cracked his lips open but could only grunt. He lifted his arms toward her, but they felt sluggish, leaden, and their movement seemed to send a rasp grating across the floor. He looked around wearily, surprised by the iron manacles clamped to his wrists.

He heaved himself up. Nearby sat Corin, Dusty, and Adriel, bound in interlocking ropes and chains.

"Where are we?" Wren croaked.

Kayla winced. "I don't know."

"We were hoping you could tell us," Dusty muttered, rubbing his cheek.

Curved wooden walls, dank and covered in lichen, surrounded them. Moss grew on the ceiling; the stones of the floor were rough, uneven, and cold to the touch. A door of rusted iron, inset with an arrow slit, had been shut against them. Red light trickled through the slit and seeped under the door.

As Wren's pain subsided, he remembered the details of their capture. "We're in a cell," he said, "probably carved from *Umbra*'s hull. We've been taken prisoner by one of the pirate gangs."

Dusty swore. "How did you know the man with the cane? Have you been inside this place before?"

Wren fought down panic. "None of that matters. We've got to escape."

Adriel stared helplessly at the floor. "The door's locked, and they've taken our weapons. The only window is barred."

Wren began to rise unsteadily. Stars dotted the patch of night sky visible through a barred porthole in the wall opposite the door. He stood and tottered toward the porthole, chains dragging across the floor.

"Who are those men?" Corin demanded.

Wren grabbed the bars. "Torturers," he said. "The pirates who killed my father."

As he finished speaking, footsteps sounded outside the door. The red light filtering into their cell was blotted out. A lock turned, and the door swung open. Cane hobbled into their cell, blue-black hair glowing weirdly in the red light that spilled into the room from the corridor beyond. The pirate paused and leaned on his cane, eyeing them each in turn.

In the silence Wren heard waves; they moved far below the porthole, beating against the ship.

Cane's smirk widened into a smile. "All awake, I see, and looking as hale as a pen of suckled pigs ready for the butcher."

"Don't do this," Wren said, staring at his captor's single eye. "We've done you no harm."

"You're Dirk's son." Cane hobbled forward, obsidian cane ringing on stone. "I'm being paid well to hold you, but the torture will be free." He stopped several feet in front of Wren. "Sarin and One-Eye had better take their time. I don't want to deprive my colleagues of their fun."

From the corner of his eye Wren saw Dusty creeping toward Cane; the boy was slightly behind the pirate, moving in the blind spot to the right of his glass eye.

"I'll give you silver," Wren lied, trying to buy Dusty time, "more than they've got to give."

"I've taken your money already," Cane snapped. "And I doubt you've got any more. It doesn't matter: I'm not in the habit of going back on pacts sealed with assassins."

"What are you doing here, then? Have you come to taunt us? Please, Cane, let the others go!"

"They're part of the package, Wren."

As the pirate took another step forward, Dusty yelled and sprang from the floor. Cane whirled around and cracked his staff across the side of Dusty's head as Wren leaped at him, plowing into his back. They fell in a tangle of limbs, ropes, and chains. Wren struck at Cane's face once, twice. Then a fist crunched into his mouth.

He spit out blood as men shouted and rushed into the cell. Rough hands gripped his shoulders and hauled him to his feet. A knee plunged into his stomach. He saw a snarling bearded face just before it drove forward and connected with his forehead. Fresh pain jolted his skull.

Someone kicked his legs out from under him. Wren collapsed as the men grabbed Kayla and the others. Hands ripped his tunic, pummeled his chest, rammed into his face.

Wren tried to kick out, but a pirate caught his leg and bent it back until he screamed and went limp.

Several pirates hauled him up, set him on his feet, and struck him in the back with the hilt of a sword, shoving him from the cell. He stumbled into the corridor, which was nothing but a blur of crimson light and cursing men, frantic movements and weapons, ropes and chains.

Cane appeared before him and cracked a hand across his face. "You'll be put on the rack for that."

The men behind Wren spun him around, poking and prodding him, beating him down the corridor. Briefly, he saw Adriel, Corin, and Dusty as they were herded in the opposite direction.

Kayla appeared at his side, blood running down her face. "Father!" she called, and tried to look at him, but one of the men behind her forced her head down.

Wren lurched against a wall, momentarily breaking free from one of the men who held him. A lantern crashed to the floor. Someone slipped on the broken glass and swore, but Wren was already spinning, using his momentum to wrench himself away from his other captor.

"Put out the flames!"

"Grab him!"

Suddenly a huge vest of nailed iron materialized before his eyes, glinting in the glare. Giant hands clutched the back of his head and slammed his face into the armor. There was a bright flare of pain, and he was pulled back, leaving a red smear on Bulge's iron vest.

Blood poured from Wren's nose. Sweat stung his eyes. He heard Kayla shouting but could only see Bulge with his distorted vision. The huge man was grinning brutishly and grinding his teeth.

The strength drained from Wren's limbs again, and he was half shoved, half dragged along the corridor. They went through a series of rooms filled with hordes of men and women, pierced and covered in tattoos, drinking and laughing and taunting him and his daughter. They went down several flights of stairs, finally ending in a small chamber with a single trapdoor.

One pirate bent down and opened it. Another shoved Kayla forward, lifted her, and carried her down into darkness.

Cane hobbled into view, his face blotched with fresh bruises. "The rack will stretch you slowly," he said. He grabbed Wren by the throat and pushed him through the hole in the trapdoor. "The Torturers are thorough."

Wren crashed head over heels down a set of wooden stairs and sprawled onto the floor. It was nearly pitch-black; only a single torch burned with a faint light. There were no windows in the cell. Corroded walls of wood and crumbling brick surrounded him, dank and grim.

The floor rolled, and he was lashed by waves of pain. Kayla wept as he was shoved against a wall and fastened with chains. He turned toward her voice and tried to speak but only managed to cough up blood and bile.

* * *

CORIN SAT WITH Dusty, cradling his friend's head, wiping away the blood that oozed near his right temple. It dripped down his cheek as if fleeing the spot where Cane's staff had bludgeoned him. Dusty moaned softly, calling for his father and mother, calling for Corin, his words nearly incoherent. His eyes showed only slivers of his pupils.

Corin had no idea what to do. He ripped a strip of cloth from his tunic and dabbed it against Dusty's cut. Scrapes and purple bruises covered both of them.

A stack of dirty boards had been piled in a corner of the room. Two lightless lanterns hung from the ceiling. A spiderweb stretched between the warped frames of the lanterns.

Corin gingerly laid Dusty on the floor and crawled over to the boards, shivering. He began sifting numbly through the objects, his mind nearly blank, fingers snagging on splinters, but found nothing that would help him break from the room. *This must be what hell is like . . . Dusty will die for his loyalty, and I will die because of my brother's madness.*

Corin crawled back to Dusty and lifted his head from the floor once more. The walls of the cell seemed to constrict around the two of them. He looked up at the dark stone ceiling and watched a spider spinning on the web. *The assassins will take me to Cane. He will kill me to raise a demon but die fighting it and fail in his revenge. We will all be pawns in the world's ending.*

Dusty's faced twisted in agony, then relaxed. His eyes flickered open, and he smiled bravely. "We're still alive?"

Corin nodded.

Dusty tried to sit up, but his arms gave out, and he collapsed to the floor. He pursed his lips, narrowed his eyes, and tried again. This time he managed to sit up. "That pirate's quicker than he looks," he said with a hint of his old chuckle, but his mirth dissolved in a coughing fit.

Corin grabbed his shoulders, steadying him. "Slow down, Dusty. You've got to relax. We're not going anywhere anytime soon."

Dusty wiped his mouth and looked around. "These walls won't hold us, Corin. I wouldn't worry yet. We'll get out of here." He winced and touched a finger to the welt near his temple. "You should really consider getting a staff. It makes a damn good weapon."

As Corin handed him the cloth he had torn from his tunic, the iron door screeched and groaned inward.

Two men entered: the giant mute with the iron vest, the one whom Wren had called Bulge, and Kleaver, the shriveled, warty dwarf with the clawed gloves. Bulge's vest was stained with blood. He wore a black chain around his waist from which dangled dozens of mismatched knives.

"Stay away," Corin stammered. He scrambled with Dusty to the pile of boards, pushing his friend behind him.

"That freckled boy looks hurt," Kleaver rasped. "Move aside and let me tend his wounds."

Bulge laughed, clacking his stump of a tongue to the roof of his mouth as the dwarfish man drew a rusty saw-toothed blade from the chain and turned toward Corin, licking the knife.

* * *

WREN MOVED HIS fingers across the torn skin of his face and into his hair, then around to the back of his head. He felt a lump.

Kayla cried softly beside him, holding her knees to her stomach, rocking slowly back and forth.

Wren shook his head to clear his senses. The torch sizzled and spit from its sconce. He examined the cuffs on his wrists and ankles, pulling on the ropes knotted between his chains, pulling the chains themselves, tugging them against their wall-mounted brackets, but he was tightly bound.

Wiping his face, he found that his left eye, already puffy, was swelling even further. He bowed his head and thought of Lori.

"What was she like?" Kayla asked, wiping her eyes.

Realizing he had spoken his wife's name aloud, Wren turned to Kayla and smiled sadly. "She was as beautiful as the first flower of spring, as wild as wind on the sea, and she was as loving a mother as I've ever seen . . . If only you had seen the way she used to gaze at you . . ."

Kayla looked at the ceiling. "I wish I could remember her."

Wren dropped his head. "I wish I could hold her." He paused, remembering. "But she's in a better place now."

"Do you think heaven exists?"

Wren was not sure. The gods were a fable manifested in stone, a carved piece of history given life only in the imagination, and he had seen such darkness in his life, had experienced so much loss and pain. First Dirk had died, then Lori. And now his only daughter suffered beside him, damned because of his past.

Wren knew of the spirits festering under the earth and had fought their blighted followers, and knew there must be a higher light to counteract these specters; but that light, selective in its grace, had never shone on him, and remained a veiled star. Where were the signs of heaven in a world that harbored such evil? Wren had seldom seen them along his shadowed road. The skies over his path had been ever-clouded, and now that path was ending in a place where clouds and shadows merged. All his hopes were unraveling, unmasked as the false dreams of a foolish man, a haunted wanderer and failed father who could not imagine heaven as his home, and would not honor the gods. Yet even as his soul swooned, he realized that Kayla might see a different truth; that she, untainted, need not share in his despair. In her innocence, she might be able to imagine something better. *Sometimes dreams were better than the truth.* Perhaps her dreams, if kept alive, would forge new truths in time.

He looked at his daughter. "I think it does."

She bit her lip. "I think so, too."

Even in the shadows of the cell, her eyes shone with such hope that Wren, wracked by pain and despair, could almost believe.

But any hope of an afterlife had to come mostly from trust, and Wren, trusting in nothing but his sword, suspected that he was not a likely candidate for entry into any celestial sphere. *Even if there is a heaven, I won't be joining Lori when I die.*

The trapdoor rose and shut, and the two assassins descended the dungeon steps.

One-Eye waited by the stairs, while Sarin swaggered over to Wren. Kayla gasped as the scarred assassin set the edge of his blade against Wren's throat. "You're in a predicament," he said.

Wren chuckled grimly. "Once I'm free, you're a dead man. I know your name now, Sarin."

The assassin smiled. "On that, I believe you're mistaken—not about my name but about our fates. I think my partner and I are entitled to a little recreation before we kill you. It's only fair, considering all the trouble you've caused us."

One-Eye drew one of his rapiers, severed Kayla's bonds, and grabbed her arms. Wren lurched forward as his daughter struggled against him.

Sarin slapped her. "Be quiet or I'll kill you in front of your father."

"Let her go!" Wren screamed, straining against his shackles.

"I think not," said One-Eye. He shifted his grip on Kayla and traced a finger down her neck.

Sarin shoved a rag in her mouth. "We're wasting time. Bring her upstairs and we'll have our fun."

One-Eye hoisted Kayla over his shoulder and started up the stairs. Her shouts came out as muffled moans. Wren met her eyes; then One-Eye climbed through the trapdoor, carrying her from view.

"I'll be back for you soon," Sarin said. He sheathed his sword and followed his partner, slamming the trapdoor behind him.

Wren slumped to the ground and bowed his head, bound by his chains in the darkness of the dungeon.

* * *

ADRIEL LOOKED AROUND the cell, shuddering as he dangled over the brick floor. The weight of his body pulled on his arms; each arm was drawn taut by a chain, and each chain was fastened high above his head.

Rot had eaten away at the wall on which Adriel had been trussed up and hung. His chains were locked to iron bars that held together the peeling boards. More bars dug into his back like cold, hard fingers. He turned his head and looked through the shattered wall of his prison.

The pirates had thrown him into a chamber near the top of the ruined ship's hull. A red glass lantern swarming with moths and crawling with insects glowed outside, just beyond his reach. Ocean air whined between the chinks.

Several hundred yards away another dismembered ship scarred the beach, a dark, hulking phantasm enshrouded in mist. Broken masts skewered the moon and stars. Adriel shivered, remembering its name, *Gorge,* and watching the crimson-eyed lanterns peer back at him through the night.

To the right of Adriel's cell a bridge spanned the sea between the two ships.

Below the bridge, the ocean assaulted the rocky shore, each wave as violent as a hatchet stroke. It seemed a battle as old as the earth, one that would end only when the shingles of the world had eroded into dust, swept back to a watery grave.

The door to his cell opened, and the woman who had bound him in the Black Plank sauntered inside. Her dark eyes swept over his face; her slim, supple body moved lithely, a vessel of poise and deadly grace.

Standing before him, she reached out to cup his chin. "What a pretty face," she said with a dark smile.

"Who are you?" Adriel asked, sick with the cloying scent of perfume.

Her hand moved to his throat. "Call me Jezebel. Most men do." A key hung by a thread from her waist.

Adriel calmed the beating of his heart. He had been stripped of his staff, but he knew he could master this small act of magic. Desperate, he concentrated on the key. "Have you come to kill me?"

"No," she said sweetly, drawing a dagger with her other hand. "I'm here to torture you."

Adriel forced out a sob, trying to buy time. "What do you want? I'll do anything . . ."

Jezebel's smile brightened; the thread began to sway. "Try not to squirm. I don't want to slip." She pressed the dagger to the nape of Adriel's neck and began drawing it down, shearing his tunic.

Suddenly the thread snapped, and the key flew to the manacle on Adriel's right wrist. He kicked away from the wall and slammed his boots into Jezebel. The key turned, unlocking his arm, but before he could use it to loosen the other chain, Cane burst into the room.

"Curse you, woman," he roared. "What are you doing?" He cursed again and whacked his cane across Jezebel's leg. She cried out and turned on him with the dagger, stabbing his arm.

Cane leaped away, jerking the weapon with him, but landed on his bad leg. He went down, then rolled to his feet and leaped at Jezebel. She backed away, hands upheld.

"Forgive me," she stammered. "I didn't let him go. I didn't mean to wound you. It was an accident, Cane!"

He grabbed her hair and forced her down. "Taste your own iron," he said, unable to control his surging fury. She screamed as he began stabbing her, the spittle of his rage frothing from his mouth.

Cane plunged the knife several times until, quite suddenly, he twitched and dropped the dagger. Adriel watched in horror as he gurgled up a thick black liquid that also began bubbling around his glass eye. Cane's arms and legs juddered against the bricks of the floor, then cracked and hardened into grotesque angles. The back of his tunic ripped open, and a pair of dark, stunted wings pushed up and unfolded.

Adriel retched, remembering the hermit in the cave and recalling Wren's story of the lighthouse creature.

The monster Cane had become bent over Jezebel, using hooked talons to pin her to the floor. She shrieked and convulsed. His wings twitched and fluttered, dripping slime. Blood wet the floor.

Adriel forced the key into the shackle on his other wrist. When he turned it, the iron bond sprang open, and he fell in a heap.

As he pushed himself up, the sound of bones crunching was replaced by a menacing silence. Slowly, he stood and faced the monster Cane. Cane was staring at him, slack jaws dripping gore. Adriel backed up against the wall of the prison, holding up his hands defensively.

Cane groaned wretchedly, a hideous, protracted wail of misery and hate. He picked up Jezebel's corpse and spread his wings, then sprang at Adriel, gnashing his crooked teeth.

Adriel dived, pain exploding in his shoulder as one of the monster's claws tore through skin and muscle. There was a crash. Boards snapped, and iron bars were wrenched from their sockets.

Clutching his shoulder, Adriel rose and staggered over to the wall. It had opened like a wound.

He looked down as Cane plummeted to the beach, a broken figure of twisted limbs and blotched flightless wings. A nearby shout replaced the monster's guttural cries. Adriel scrambled across the room and hid behind the open door of the cell.

A pirate holding a crossbow barged inside, then skidded to a stop and lowered his weapon, stupefied by the carnage strewn across the floor. "Dragons and demons, what happened here?"

Adriel answered by shoving the door into his face.

The pirate yelped and collapsed, triggering his crossbow. A bolt thudded into a wall.

Adriel jumped on him and pried the weapon from his fingers. He tugged the bolt free and reloaded as his shoulder pumped out blood. The pirate was unconscious. He yanked a black sash from the pirate's garb and bandaged his shoulder, and then he left the room, supporting the crossbow with his right arm.

He entered a short, low-ceilinged corridor that curved slightly, running parallel to the side of the ship. Frantic, he debated his next action. He was alone and painfully wounded. His staff had been taken. He did not know the route to his cell and was unaware of where Corin and the others were being held. Pirates infested the ship.

"Gods," he whispered, curling his left hand around the medallion on his chest. "What do I do now?"

✳ ✳ ✳

WREN WHISPERED HIS daughter's name, delirious with grief and despair. He tore at the fetters on his ankles, chafing the skin, then reached under his shirt and closed his fingers around Dale's medallion.

He held it before his eyes, stared numbly at the dragon, the sea horse, and the lion, wondering if the gods were real, if his doom was a punishment for the sins of his past, and he cursed them silently. Then he cursed Cane and the assassins, Corin and his brother, Dale, Amber and Marian—all of whom had played a role in bringing his life to ruin. He railed against the demons, those who served them, and the wretched world of Ellynrie from which they strove to rise.

As he huddled in utter despair, sounds filtered through the ceiling.

Wren heard a yell, the clashing of metal, and then a crash. He stuffed the medallion under his tunic. The trapdoor swung open, and a pirate tumbled down the stairs, where he sprawled on the floor below the torch, his throat cut. A thin cloaked man with a bloody sword ran down after him.

The man approached Wren and threw back his hood, revealing blue-green eyes and shaggy blond hair. It was Sir Lancet.

"How did you find me?" Wren breathed.

"It wasn't easy," said the knight. He began unlocking Wren's chains. "I could not aid you in the Black Plank's common room, not with so many of those base bowmen at the ready, so I followed the pirates back to their ship, donned a cloak, and sneaked inside as subtly as a wraith. I overheard where you had been taken and came here straightaway."

"Hurry," Wren commanded. "The assassins have taken my daughter. I have to catch them in time!"

Lancet swiftly cut his ropes. "I briefly glimpsed two men on the stairs. They were struggling with a small figure, but I couldn't see who it was."

Wren stood unsteadily. "That must have been Kayla. Where were they taking her?"

"The stairs are at the end of the first corridor from this cell. They probably wind to the top of the ship."

Wren cleared his head and calmed his stomach. "I'm going after them."

Lancet followed. "The halls are filled with chaos. I've stung several hornets and stirred up the nest. Pirate gangs are fighting one another, brawling in the passages, hurling each other into cells. It's a hellish scene." He took out a small blade. "This belongs to you. It's your throwing knife. I found it in the armory where they're keeping your sword, our supplies, and the wizard's staff."

Wren took the last of Flint's weapons, thrust it into his belt, then hurried to the dead pirate and picked up a rapier from the corpse. "What will you do?"

"Find Corin and set him free. I know where he is held." The knight shrugged off his cloak: His scarecrow body was clad in armor. "I have no more need for disguise. Are you ready to fight?"

Wren nodded. "Let's go sting some more."

* * *

CORIN GRABBED A beam from the pile of old boards. Dusty grasped the broken end of a stave. Bulge scratched his mauled ear and his bald scalp as Kleaver inched closer with the knife.

Then boots sounded on the planks of the passageway, shouts drifted into the cell, and a group of men ran past the doorway, holding axes and spears. An arrow sped after them and buried itself in the back of one of the men.

Bulge growled, unhitched his hammer from his belt, and lumbered from the room.

Kleaver pocketed the knife, mashing the claws on his gloves together. "It seems there's trouble to settle before I finish with you." He bounded from the cell and slammed the door shut.

Corin darted to the door, shook it, beat against it helplessly, then stood back and began cudgeling it with his board. The wood snapped, and he turned to Dusty. "What do we do now?"

As he spoke, the door began opening. Dusty tossed Corin his stave. He caught it and wheeled around to face the intruder.

Sir Lancet stepped into the cell, breathing heavily. His face was streaked with sweat, and his armor was dented.

"It's you!" Corin shouted.

"I'm afraid so," said the knight. He helped Dusty to his feet. "Can you walk?"

"Yes."

"Then follow me quickly. We have to get you out of here. Several fires are burning in the lower levels of the ship."

"Where are the others?" Corin asked.

Lancet peered from the doorway. "The two assassins captured Kayla, and Wren is chasing them toward *Umbra*'s deck. The three of us are going to the armory to regain our weapons and supplies. Keep your heads low and your ears open for any word of Adriel. I haven't found the wizard yet."

Outside the cell, Dusty stepped over the body of the arrow-slain pirate and picked up his ax. They started down the empty passageway as the scent of smoke filled the air.

*   *   *

WREN RACED UP the stairs and entered a large room filled with tables, chairs, and brawling men. He was confused for a moment by the assault on his senses: the bright, gaudy clothing of the pirates, their curses and shouts. Bulge swung his massive hammer in their midst. Rapiers flashed in the murky red light of the room, where several lanterns had dropped and burst into flames. Wren glimpsed One-Eye shoving Kayla up a narrow stairway. Sarin was guarding his partner's back, his sword bloodied.

As Wren charged into the carnage, a pirate dived at him with a spear. With a mighty swing of the rapier, Wren lopped off the tip of the weapon, following through to take off the pirate's head. Instantly, he spun to block a sword stroke. An ax glanced off his shoulder. He kicked a nearby chair at the swordsman and turned to slash blindly with his rapier, catching the ax wielder in the face. Wren jerked the rapier free and continued forcing his way through the melee, thrusting and cutting in all directions.

As he drew near the stairway where Kayla had disappeared, Bulge crossed his path. The giant opened his mouth in a silent scream and charged him with his hammer.

Wren threw his rapier. It cartwheeled in the air—a silver blur—then thudded into the mute's chest, just above the iron plating. Wren ran forward and yanked it free. A torrent of crimson droplets sprayed his face. Bulge groaned and teetered, then crashed to the floor.

"That's for my scar," said Wren. He kicked the body of the Torturer and rushed up the stairs.

THE ARMORY

S IR LANCET PAUSED by the door to the pirates' armory. "Wait here. I'll go in first to make sure it's safe."

Corin and Dusty did as they were told. The knight opened the door and slipped inside, shutting the door behind him. Almost immediately they heard curses and the drawing of weapons.

Dusty reached for the door.

Corin grabbed his friend's wrist. "Lancet can handle himself. He's not nearly as wounded as you."

Dusty shook him off. "I won't let him fight alone."

"You heard what he said," Corin hissed as the sounds of fighting issued from the armory. "He told us to stay here. He's a knight, and so far he's managed to do fine on his own."

"He's risking himself for us, Corin!"

"But you're in no shape to help him!"

"Maybe not," Dusty said, "but I plan to try." He flung open the door and rushed into the room.

Corin swore and ran after his friend.

Inside, giant torture devices towered above the men. Sir Lancet, beset by three pirates, backpedaled slowly, retreating toward the far wall, which was dominated by three elongated windows.

Dusty hurled himself at one of the pirates and knocked him in the head with the flat of his ax. Lancet blocked a blow and jumped at another man, knocking him down as the pirate whom Dusty had bludgeoned staggered and fell. Corin threw his stave at the third pirate, but the man spun away, jumped over Lancet—who was still grappling with his companion on the floor—and rushed toward Corin with his sword held above his head.

Dusty barreled into the pirate, causing him to drop his weapon.

Corin dived for the sword and snatched it up, then slashed at the pirate's spine. The man fell away from Dusty. Corin looked to his friend, but Dusty just stood there, eyes glazing, blood trickling from the corner of his mouth.

Only then did Corin see the tip of a knife jutting through his stomach.

The knife turned, and Kleaver stepped around Dusty, grinning wickedly. "Now it's your turn, boy."

All emotion fled from Corin as his friend toppled to the floor. He cried out and charged Kleaver. The stunted man raised his arms, caught the sword in clawed gloves, and tore it from Corin's hands. He turned the sword back at Corin and rushed forward, aiming a killing blow.

Suddenly a wounded Lancet staggered between them. Kleaver's claws struck out, the sword pierced a weak spot in Lancet's armor, and the knight exhaled sharply. With the last of his strength Lancet reached out with his sword and hacked at the Torturer's neck. Both men crashed down together and did not rise. The other three pirates were dead.

Corin knelt beside Dusty. His friend stared up at him, struggling not to cry.

"Corin?"

"I'm here."

"We're far from home . . ."

Corin nodded numbly. "I'll take you back."

Dusty shivered. "I don't think you will." After a deep pause he said, "I wonder how Rookery Rest will get along without me. The rooks will probably try to take over the inn." He grinned weakly and then looked hard at Corin. "Make sure that doesn't happen."

Corin struggled to smile.

Dusty hacked up a gob of bloody bile. As Corin wiped it away, Dusty's eyes began to shut.

"I'm scared," Dusty said softly, "but I'm glad you're with me."

"Please," Corin whispered. "We'll get you help."

Dusty smiled one last time, then shuddered and closed his eyes.

*　*　*

AFTERWARD, CORIN COULD not remember how long he lay beside his friend, crying, thinking of their adventures, of all the times they had shared. When finally he stopped, he knew what had to be done.

"I'm coming to find you, Cade," he said.

Then he stood and left the armory, searching through the fire and carnage for a way to leave the ship.

*　*　*

WHEN WREN REACHED the top of the stairs, he rushed down a corridor lined with closed doors. The assassins might be taking refuge behind any one of them, waiting for the violence to pass. But something told Wren they were still moving toward the top of the ship.

He heard Adriel shouting and followed the wizard's voice around a corner and through an opening in the ship's keel, stumbling outside onto a bridge that connected the wrecks of *Umbra* and *Gorge*.

Crimson light spilled onto the bridge from the entries into the ships.

Adriel was standing in the middle of the bridge with a loaded crossbow trained on Sarin and One-Eye. Kayla was near the other end of the bridge, kneeling in front of the assassins. One-Eye clutched her hair, which shone silver-blond in the starlight. Sarin's cloak whipped in the wind like a living shadow.

"Father!" Kayla cried.

Wren started across the bridge, rage and panic dueling for control of his senses. "I'm coming!"

Adriel tried to keep his crossbow steady. "I have only one bolt."

Wren stopped beside Adriel. He drew the rapier and held it before him. "Release my daughter."

Sarin was impassive. "And if we don't?"

"You die."

One-Eye crossed his rapiers over Kayla's neck. "You gamble like a madman!"

Sarin growled, "The wizard won't fire while my partner holds your precious daughter."

"He's right," Adriel whispered. "My arm's hurt, and I've never used a bow before. What if I hit Kayla?"

Wren clenched his teeth. "Aim high."

Sarin tore his cloak from his shoulders and ripped his blade from its sheath. "This game ends now," he said, "and I'm wagering on us." A scarred smirk spread over his face as he strode forward.

"I'm never a man to miss a bet," Wren said. He started across the bridge as black waves reeled and crashed a hundred feet below.

They met at the center and began circling each other slowly. Their swords remained just a hairbreadth apart. Then Sarin darted forward. His blade locked against Wren's, and they began moving in a dance of whistling iron.

Back and forth they fought, reeling in defense, pressing the attack, always seeking for an opening, some weakness in the other's guard. The night was alive with the song of their swords.

Sarin's technique was superior, honed from a lifetime of ruthless combat. Wren barely had time to think or react as the assassin's sword slashed at him in cool, deadly patterns. He fought back desperately, chaotically. Sarin cut at his right, his left, and then his right side again. Wren barely parried the blows.

But then the assassin swung at his left once more.

Anticipating the move, Wren ducked the stroke, lunged forward, and drove his sword through Sarin's chest.

The world slowed. Inch by inch Sarin began to fall, scrabbling wide-eyed at the embedded blade.

Adriel gave a shout and triggered his crossbow. The bolt streaked toward One-Eye, but the assassin ducked and lifted his rapiers, and the bolt whizzed over his head. In a single smooth motion Wren released his sword and drew his last throwing knife, hurling it toward One-Eye as Sarin's limp body thudded at his feet.

One-Eye hacked down at the ropes holding the bridge to *Gorge,* severing them, but as his rapiers continued their downward arcs toward Kayla, Wren's knife sped straight and true and buried itself in his single eye. He staggered and dropped his rapiers, took two awkward steps, and toppled from the bridge, clutching the hilt of the knife and falling like a dark star into the sea. The black waves swallowed him, and he was gone.

As the bridge groaned and creaked, Kayla tried to stand; still bound, she swayed unsteadily.

Wren wrenched his sword from Sarin's chest and darted toward her. She threw herself at him, and he caught her in his arms.

"Run for it!" Adriel yelled.

Wren sawed through his daughter's bonds, setting her free as the bridge teetered and groaned; then he charged with her back across the bridge. As they ran, the rest of the ropes snapped, and the bridge gave out behind them, falling into the depths of the ocean. Wren threw Kayla toward Adriel. As the wizard caught her, he jumped for the scarlet-lit opening in *Umbra's* keel.

He grabbed the edge, hauled himself up, and darted into the ship with Adriel and Kayla, gagging in the smoke.

* * *

THEY THREADED UNCONTESTED through the smoky organs of the burning ship; in the confusion sown by their escape and the sparking of the fires, the pirates were unable to distinguish friend from foe. After several frenzied minutes, they reached the back of the ship, where a huge iron door had been left ajar. They rushed inside.

The room was nearly silent. Sounds of death and dying came as if they were echoes from far away.

Sir Lancet sat against a wall, his face streaked with blood, sweat, and soot, one hand curled around the hilt of his sword and the other resting on Dusty's chest. The corpses of the three pirates were scattered across the floorboards.

Wren rushed forward, stooped down, and looked at Dusty. "Blazes, what happened here?"

He examined the wounds in Lancet's sides, then took Dusty's wrist and felt for a pulse. Kayla and Adriel approached slowly, staring in horror at the boy's blood-soaked stomach.

The knight shook his head. "He is dead, Wren. We . . . came here, and . . . the pirates . . . they fought . . ." He paused, his breathing uneven. "I killed the bastard who slew him."

Adriel swore under his breath. Kayla stepped back, eyes wide.

Wren spotted their cloaks and traveling packs. "Bring everything here," he said. They gathered their supplies—Adriel's staff and Wren's sword had been stowed with everything else—and brought them over.

Wren began tearing a ribbon of cloth from one of the cloaks, but Lancet shook his head again.

"Please," he said. "I am . . . dying . . . and you do not have much time. Corin is still alive."

"Where has he gone?" Adriel asked.

"He vowed to travel to the Tower of Shadows to find . . . find his brother. You must follow . . . help him."

Wren leaned over the dying knight, who coughed and continued speaking. "Wren, take my sword. I die with one task unfinished. The dragon I was pursuing . . . is still abroad . . . and was rumored to be flying toward Stardell. My home, Castle Star, lies in your path. Carry my weapons, and if . . . if you encounter the dragon, slay it in my name."

"What about you?" Wren gripped Lancet's shoulder. "We can't just leave you here."

"Do not weep . . . for me. I have sustained a mortal wound defending my honor and have . . . nothing more to fear."

Kayla looked away.

Sir Lancet smiled up at her. "Have courage," he said. "Death . . . is only the next great quest."

With that, the light faded from his blue-green eyes. He closed them gently and rode into another world.

As they stood over the bodies of the boy and the knight, mourning them in silence, the wall behind them began to shudder, sending the weapons that had hung there crashing to the floor. Smoke billowed into the room; flames licked across the floor. In the outside corridor, a group of weaponless men ran past, screaming and cursing the pursuing fire.

Wren nodded to Kayla and Adriel, who quickly slung packs over their shoulders. They sidestepped the crackling flames and hurried to the windows.

The timbers of the ceiling began to give way, and the flames sped toward them. Wren fastened his cloak about his neck, shoved Lancet's sword in his belt, and buckled on his own sword and sheath. He grabbed a chair and hurled it through the central window. Glass exploded into the night.

He ran to the hole he had made. A skinny ladder climbed up the side of the ship. He crawled out onto a small wooden sill but quickly threw himself against the ship as ocean winds buffeted him, threatening to cast him into the waters below.

He waited until the gusts subsided before turning to help Kayla and Adriel climb through after him. Kayla paused at the window and looked behind her: Dusty and Lancet had been obscured by the churning vapors. Wren squeezed her shoulder and started up the ladder.

They climbed slowly, stopping when the wind was at its worst. Fighting vertigo, they hauled themselves over a railing and onto the quarterdeck.

Umbra's topside was an eerie, corpse-strewn landscape, silent save for intermittent screams that echoed from the fire-swept passages and chambers below. Smoke issued from stairwells and doorways, rushing onto the deck and curling up the ship's three masts, filling her ancient skeletal sails with a ragged wind that bore the scent of death.

Wren pointed toward the bow of the ship, where a wooden ramp ran from the prow to the beach, and led the others around the navigator's wheel and across the deck, watching the smoking openings into the ship with wary eyes.

They reached the mainmast and started down the ramp; it was wrapped with huge rusted chains that dropped to the beach, ending in barnacle-covered anchors that were embedded in the sand. When they reached the shore, they started toward the town. Slushy sand slurped at their boots, and frigid winds stung their faces.

Suddenly Adriel stopped and looked around, searching for something.

"What is it?" Kayla asked.

Adriel ran a hand through his hair. "I saw a man who turned into some . . . some sort of monster, like the hermit I saw in the cave and the creature that attacked you two in the lighthouse. He fell from the ship and landed somewhere near here, but I can't find his body."

"No use worrying about that now," Wren said, starting forward. "We have to keep moving."

At the edge of Lantern Watch, a crowd had gathered to watch the ship burn; men and women eyed Wren skeptically. Wren pulled his cloak tighter and quickened his step. If the onlookers were curious, something in his eyes told them he would answer no questions, and they held their tongues. If they meant harm, the sight of his weapons and bloody clothes kept their knives and daggers away, and he led Kayla and Adriel into Lantern Watch unmolested.

The town was in an uproar. People streamed down the streets toward the shore, shouting and talking excitedly. Wren, Kayla, and Adriel made their way to the Black Plank. They entered the stable, and each one swung onto a horse; any pirates who had been stationed to guard their mounts were long gone.

Kayla turned her horse toward Wren, who had taken the knight's horse, slinging the lance across his back. "Corin's horse is missing."

Wren nodded. "We might be able to catch him before he leaves town."

They rode from the stable and continued at a gallop through fire-lit streets, scattering pockets of villagers, but no matter where they turned, they could find no trace of Corin. They emerged from the pall of smoke that was spreading through the town. When they reached the edge of the forest, they paused and looked back at Lantern Watch. The red gleam of the fire backlit the houses and taverns, a final dark image of the evil place that had cost them their friends.

Pushing back their grief, they sought solace by charting a course of action.

Wren wiped a soot-blackened hand across his face and spoke softly to Kayla. "So much pain and bloodshed . . . Perhaps we should just return to Nautalia. Corin is gone and did not leave a trail."

Adriel stared hard at Wren. "I won't be going home. I have no home. There's only one road that I will take: the path Corin has chosen."

"We could go back to Nautalia," Kayla said, eyes flashing. "That would be the safe thing to do. But when I was in my bedroom, avoiding your lessons, I longed for something important, something that would give meaning to my life. I searched for it in the labyrinth, I searched for it in the streets; once we got caught up in this adventure, I thought I had finally found what I was looking for. Now I know different. Not all adventures make for songs or sunny stories. Dusty and Lancet are dead, but we still have a chance. We can go home, Father, or we can listen to our hearts and follow the dark road ahead."

Wren's eyes were filled with pain. "Kayla, please, you don't know what you're asking. I have to keep you safe."

"I admit that I'm frightened, Father; terrified would be closer to the truth. But isn't this what honor is all about? Doing what seems right without counting the cost? We must stay with Corin."

"She's asking you to do the right thing," Adriel said, "and there will be no safety once Cade uses Corin to summon up the demon. If you think Nautalia's walls can keep out that darkness . . ."

Kayla nudged her horse closer to Wren's. "Would you go home if you were on your own without me to worry about? Well, I am your daughter; your blood flows in my veins, and I'm going east!"

Wren turned toward the ocean and watched the wreckage of the pirate ship as it burned next to its two beached sisters, a massive pyre flaming above the shore and the sea. He turned back to Kayla.

"And I'm coming with you," he said.

* * *

CORIN PAUSED AT the entrance to the Shale Throat. Behind him lay the wood, beyond the wood a nimbus of red lights, and beyond the lights the sea. Tears welled in his eyes. He offered up a silent prayer and brushed the tears away with the back of his hand, then guided his horse eastward, toward his brother.

THE DRAGON OF STARDELL

FOR DAYS AFTER she left Lantern Watch with Adriel and her father, the loss of Dusty and Lancet hung over Kayla. The knight's wistful romance, the playful mischief of the freckled boy—both were gone from this world forever. Kayla had not known them very long, but she missed them sorely, and that, she knew, was a mark that could have been left only by loyal friends. In her spare time, she tried sketching but found that her mind soon wandered.

Wren and Adriel were feeling no better. At night, her father stared moodily into the flames of the cooking fire while the wizard played slow, sad melodies on his coral flute, his eyes shut tight against the world.

The sad absence of Dusty and Lancet was not their only burden; the three companions also shouldered a grim sense of foreboding. It chipped at their resolve and coaxed forth their fear.

Kayla did not know what evils lay ahead. The impending dangers taunted her by day; by night, they haunted her dreams. Wren kept mostly silent, always alert for the slightest sign of peril. Adriel slept in sporadic bouts. Once, as the wizard rode ahead with her father, Kayla heard him whispering of occult images, of visions that revealed the Tower of Shadows.

They tracked Corin, asking villagers, travelers—anyone who would stop and listen—if they had seen a blond-haired boy who walked with a limp. Every so often someone would point the way, expressing concern about why a lone boy would wander so far from his home, but more common were those who replied with bleak indifference, grown used to the sight of wayward souls.

The kingdom was in upheaval. Refugees from this town or that roamed the thoroughfares, moving listlessly from one bleak destination to the next, seeking a place that knew no fear or pain.

But such safe harbors were hard to find.

Following the roads on which her father led her, Kayla caught sight of more crimson vines and saw other unsettling sights.

Each was a cosmic sign, Adriel guessed, that the natural order of the world was in flux. All signs pointed to the awakening of demons under the earth.

* * *

LEAVING LANTERN WATCH by way of the Shale Throat, they made their way through the Black Rib Trident. The dead bandits had vanished, their strung-up prey cut down. Instead, five grimy knights sat by a row of freshly dug graves. Wren asked after Corin, and their captain pointed down the eastern road, which led to the Midland Plains.

Two days later they came within view of the Midland Spires, mountains stretching from west to east, dividing the eastern half of the kingdom, the southern plains from the northern forests. To Kayla, each snow-capped peak seemed a wintry castle of stone, part of an ageless, sweeping rampart that bridged earth and sky. Fields reached away from the slopes, tended by sun-baked farmers and sweaty young farmhands, hoeing, raking, writing on the land with horse-drawn quills.

They woke on the fourth day and continued again on the coarse road they had been riding until, with the mountains looming on their left, they came upon a mule's carcass sprawled near the hooves of their horses. The outline of its ribs was clearly visible through its spotted, dirt-caked flank. Its bones seemed to press outward in a desperate attempt to escape, while the once living beast that had caged them stared into the east with lifeless eyes. Flies buzzed about its slit throat.

Kayla caught her father glancing uneasily at Adriel and looked eastward with growing dread.

An hour later, they came across an entirely different horror: the charred remains of a group of wagons smoldering at the roadside. Kayla stared numbly at the blackened corpses that littered the ground. At the forefront of the destruction were the burned bodies of a man, a woman, and her baby.

Wren dismounted and remained in a crouch for a time. When he got to his feet, he looked at the sky with narrowed eyes, grasping a singed blue rattle.

* * *

THAT NIGHT THEY entered a hamlet, stabled their mounts, and purchased lodging in a half-timber inn. No one in the tavern knew of an attack on any wagons, but several men told tales of missing sheep and cattle, and one ugly crone, rocking in a rickety chair by the hearth, spoke in a creaking voice of her grandson, a strapping boy who had been devoured at dusk by a shadow that had swept down from the sky.

* * *

A FIFTH DAY passed. On the morning of the sixth they drew near Stardell, the town where Sir Lancet Rhymewind had lived and the first they had approached since leaving Lantern Watch.

Kayla and Adriel beheld Lancet's tower, the spike of white stone he had called Castle Star. Wren, who had journeyed these ways before, led them on without a second glance, though Kayla knew he felt the same regret that stung her heart, knowing the brave knight would never see his home again.

She pulled her cloak close and looked down the road. Blue clouds striped the violet sky; the world was hushed and still. Stardell's skyline cradled the horizon, a dusky, uneven line of rooftops and chimneys nestling like a gem in the croplands. Wildflowers shivered in the cool air, and sparrows chirped overhead. Castle Star blushed in the dawn, its merloned towers and walls purpling.

As the two horses cantered along, clip-clopping on the worn dirt road, Kayla grew calmer. The beauty of their surroundings was a welcome respite from the terrors she had seen on her journey. She followed Wren into Stardell, riding slowly along the cobblestone streets. At first her peaceful mood seemed to harmonize with their quiet surroundings, but soon a chilly wind began to pick up. Shortly, the air began to tingle and the sky slowly darkened; a thunderstorm was building on the horizon. The townsfolk whispered and pointed as the riders passed. To the east, shadowy clouds spread across the sky. By the time they had crossed the town and started out across the fields, the first drops of rain had begun to fall.

Amid the fat drops they could see a line of farmers moving back to Stardell, pushing wagons or driving teams of oxen. Shepherds, too, were moving, ushering their flocks to whatever shelter they could find. There were hardly any trees; the landscape stretched out in front of them, marked only by the mountains on the left and the town they had left behind.

"Look!" Kayla cried, pointing to what seemed like a section of dark cloud that was flying against the wind, far above their heads. The cloud whirled and dived, spreading, and then broke away from the stormy sky, materializing as a sight that struck them all dumb with shock.

"The winged shape," Wren whispered. "The rumors Kendran heard were not unfounded, after all."

"I've seen this beast before," Adriel said. "Several days ago, when I was walking along the beach, I . . ." He lapsed into silence, watching the dark shape circle closer, framed by the thunderheads.

The creature looked as though it had been born of a diseased mind: Its four leathery wings, which swept the air with an unearthly ferocity, were torn and scabrous; its scaly hide was splotched with black and violet patches that rose to bare spikes of bone; its eyes were obsidian coals, burning with rage. From its reptilian snout shot clouds of smoke and darts of flame.

"Father, this can't be real." Kayla looked at him imploringly. "A creature like this must be a nightmare."

Wren gritted his teeth. "I think we've found Sir Lancet's dragon. I've seen one before, long ago in the Summerset Isles—" He broke off, for the dragon had begun to fly to the earth.

It dived toward a group of farmers who were loading a wagon; its tail, sharp as a razor whip, curled through the air, ending in spearlike serrations. The farmers began screaming, and Kayla watched in horror as they started to run. The dragon swept down, grazing the earth with its clawed legs, and opened its mouth: A plume of fire shot forth and consumed the farmers. The dragon rushed through the inferno it had created and rose up, a flaming body in its jaws. It wheeled in the air, swallowing the body in a greedy gulp, and then turned toward Kayla, Wren, and Adriel, who were mounted in the middle of the country road. The dragon roared once, and the cry ululated, echoing and re-echoing as men and women shouted in the fields and broke for cover, burrowing into haystacks and diving under wagons.

"Dragons and demons, indeed," Wren said under his breath.

Adriel grasped his staff. "It's coming our way. We can't outrun it."

Wren lifted the knight's lance, its blue and white checkered pennant hanging limply in the rain. "We have to fight. Kayla, find shelter!"

"There's no place to hide," she said.

As she backed her horse away, the dragon screamed out again and began speeding toward them, jaws opened wide.

Adriel raised his staff, but the crystal would not light. Wren cried out a challenge and kicked his horse forward, leveling his lance at the dragon. The beast swerved aside, inches from the tip of the lance, and climbed skyward, beating a wall of wind against rider and mount.

Wren turned his horse as the dragon dropped toward him again, gnashing its teeth. He drove his heels into the sides of his mount, but at the last second, his horse reared up in fright and threw him from the saddle. He hurled the lance as he fell, but the dragon caught the weapon in its teeth, snapping its shaft in two as if it were no more than a matchstick. It swept past with a crash of heat and stench, buffeting them with its ragged wings. Adriel just managed to stay in his saddle.

Wren stood up from the muddy ground and drew both his swords. "Use your staff, Adriel!"

"I can't summon my magic!"

"Then stay with Kayla. I'll do what I can."

Its rage heightened by its failure, the dragon curled around with dizzying speed, screaming and lashing its tail.

Wren stood his ground. Sensing a new sort of resistance to its wrath, the dragon slowed and came to a halt, alighting on the ground and stretching out its hideous wings. Summoning all his courage, Wren sprang forward. The dragon lunged at him with a flurry of snapping jaws and sweeping claws. Wren threw himself to the ground and rolled beneath its outstretched neck, ending in a crouch below its stomach. He thrust the sword upward, but the dragon lifted just out of reach.

Immediately, it swung its tail, slamming Wren in the side, knocking him to the earth. As its tail wrapped around Wren's legs, the dragon settled on the ground, folding its wings into a smoking cocoon. It lowered its head to feed.

Kayla froze in terror as Adriel cursed, struggling with his staff.

Suddenly a blade tore through one of the dragon's wings and ripped downward. Wren leaped through the wound and spun around. Thick black blood smoked on his swords. The dragon screamed, lifting its tail. From her mount, Kayla could see that the end of the beast's tail had been severed.

Kayla cried out as the dragon turned toward her father and opened its jaws, vomiting fire.

Though everything in him wanted to run, Adriel stood his ground and lifted high his staff, and there, under the lightning-flecked clouds, his crystal flared; strength left his body and flowed through the white oak. Blue fire burst toward the dragon, setting its back aflame.

The dragon roared and swiveled its head, focusing fathomless eyes on the wizard. Darting its head forward like a snake, it struck, snapping its fangs inches from Adriel's face. Adriel leaped back, gritting his teeth, but kept his staff leveled at the dragon. It reared up, shying away from the flames.

Choosing that moment, when the dragon's attention was diverted, Wren darted forward under the wings and with all his might drove his rune-covered sword into the soft indentation where wing attached to the scaly chest. Bellowing in agony, the dragon lurched to the side, landing with a thunderous crash amid the wreckage of a farmer's hay wain.

Kayla watched as Wren picked himself up and staggered over to the dying monster.

"This is for Sir Lancet Rhymewind," he said, and drove the knight's sword through the dragon's head, into the damp earth.

In a final paroxysm of pain, the dragon lashed out with its tail, driving it deep into the ground. Fire flickered in its mouth, and then the decayed body shuddered—wings jerking, tail thrashing—and fell still. The grass in front of its fangs smoldered in the wind and rain.

In that instant an eerie peace settled over the landscape. Farmers and villagers peeked out from their hiding places, unsure, blinking their eyes in disbelief at the great evil Wren had just extinguished.

Kayla swung to the ground and settled her horse. Her father was standing dumbstruck as she slowly led her mount toward him.

Adriel arrived on his horse, leading Wren's mount by its reins. He jumped to the ground, walking uneasily toward the slain beast.

"That was—" But Adriel could not find the words as Wren stepped toward the dragon and pulled his sword from its massively muscled breast.

"Corin," was all Kayla could muster. Slowly, she pulled herself back onto her horse.

As the drops of water fell fast and hard, Adriel and Wren remounted. Kayla turned to her father and asked, "What about Lancet's sword?"

Wren sheathed his own blade. "I will leave it here in honor of the knight."

Duel at Turncross

As Corin rode eastward into the end of summer, the days passed like flashes of feverish fire, and he moved like a shadow under the sun. But when the moth-white moon shone down from the sky, time warped into a nightmarish eternity chronicled in the feral tongues of his evil dreams.

He thought often of Dusty and wished his friend were with him still. At night, if he could not sleep, Corin wondered how different his life would have been had the tides of fate chosen another course and swept him to some far-off shore. Even now he might be riding toward his home, a small house at the edge of a quiet town, his father and mother on the porch, sharing laughter over glasses of wine, trying to hide their anxiety as they looked into the distance for a sign of his return. When he imagined those things, Corin wondered if his brother Cade imagined them, too, and his heart, aching, threatened to tear itself apart and scatter among the cold, uncaring stars.

He passed through lands he had never seen before, rode well-traveled roads, and begged in the shadow of the Midland Spires until at last he passed through Stardell, following the path to Turncross. For two days, as he neared the kingdom's eastern edge, the country grew wild and coarse around him.

On the evening of the third day, he caught sight of a lonely dwelling atop a barren hill. He kicked his horse up the dusty track and stopped near the door, listening to the grass rustling in the evening breeze; it sounded like the creaking of old wooden boards.

A girl sat by the door to the dwelling, working at her spinning wheel in the twilight. The color of her thread matched her chestnut hair. She looked at him and did not speak, then turned her eyes back to her work.

From his saddle, Corin glanced doubtfully down to where the houses of a dour village huddled together beneath the deepening sky. "Is that Turncross?" he asked, rubbing his mare's neck.

The girl's hands guided the thread around a whirling spindle. "Yes," she said, and the grass around her whispered, *"I would go back if I were you."*

On the horizon beyond the village, the sky was the color of a clotting wound. Corin, watching the colors fall from heaven, knew he had reached the last crossroad of his journey, had arrived at some point of final choosing. He turned in the saddle and saw that the sky behind him was clearer, and he was tempted to leave this cursed realm. But the more he looked back the way he had come, the more he realized that the sky there was darkening, too. Forward or back, it made no difference; night was spreading over the world, and the darkness would come no matter what choice he made.

Corin decided on his path then—he would not take the other. To do so would be to abandon that for which Dusty had died and to forsake his brother utterly. He knew he would probably fail in the end, but his dreams, even if they came crashing down around him, would not have been dreamed in vain.

He gave his mare a kick, and she began to trot. As she started in the direction of the village, the sound of the girl's threadwork faded. The image of her spinning remained with Corin for a time.

He entered Turncross and continued down the main street of the village. People watched him pass from candlelit windows, astonished, perhaps, that this strange boy was riding into the east. The street was almost empty; the few people still abroad were hurrying for their homes.

After several minutes the main street curved, and Corin caught sight of a three-story tavern. He made his way to the door. Someone inside would know the way to the Tower of Shadows. As he tied his horse to a rail, he looked up; an overhead sign read "The Black Candle Inn."

Corin took a deep breath and raised a hand to the door, but a laugh rang out, sharp and cold. Slowly, he turned around.

A hunchbacked man stood some way down the street, garbed and hooded in a common black robe. He held a crooked staff that ended in a violet jewel. As Corin watched, the man vanished in a swirl of dust; after a moment, he reappeared closer on the other side of the street, accompanied by an eddy of grit from the road. The last of the townsfolk scurried away, leaving Corin alone in front of the inn.

"Who are you?" he asked, trying to sound braver than he felt.

"Damon," the man said. His voice had a harsh accent. "I am here to bring you to your brother."

"How do you know him?"

"He is my teacher. Our home is on the eastern horizon, where the moor rises up over the sea."

"The Tower of Shadows," Corin said.

Damon nodded. "My master was surprised when he discovered you had come. He did not think you had the courage to make this journey alone. We are undertaking a great task, Corin. Soon you will have vengeance for your parents."

"I did not come for revenge," Corin said. "I'm here to stop Cade before he kills us all."

"Is that so?" Damon asked, and laughed. "You will stop nothing, boy. Your brother is summoning Apollyon the demon in order to extinguish its presence from our world. Like it or not, you are to play a vital part in the destruction of the spirit."

He lifted his staff. Corin's limbs froze, pinioned together, and he fell like a deadweight. Tentacles of nether light pushed through the road and wrapped around him, binding him to the earth. He gasped and tried to cry out, despairing, but as his voice caught in his throat, hope came in the sound of thundering hooves.

Wren, Adriel, and Kayla galloped down the street. The mercenary and the wizard dismounted and strode toward the sorcerer.

Damon turned toward them. "So your friends tagged along," he said.

"I know that voice," Kayla whispered to herself, staring fearfully at Corin. "I heard him on the night the assassins broke into our house."

Adriel held his staff before him. "Leave this place. Let the boy go."

"Who are you to threaten me?" Damon asked. "Are you Dale's apprentice?"

Adriel's staff appeared to shimmer in his hands. "How do you know him?"

"I went to his home, captured him, and brought him to my master."

Adriel swore. "Is he still alive?"

Damon chuckled. "Barely."

"I'll kill you for what you've done!"

"Dale could not defeat me," Damon said, "and you are a fool to try. Your callow powers are nothing."

The wind picked up, tussling Adriel's cloak and tugging his hair. Pebbles grated across the road; bits of paper cavorted through the air, but Damon's clothing remained untouched.

"A failed apprentice, that's what you are—a mere boy whose courage exceeds his stripling magic."

Crackling arcs of violet light wreathed the sorcerer, rippling up and down his limbs. Dark halos gyrated from his feet and spread outward, colorless rainbows enveloping the earth.

Adriel plunged his staff into the ground, and a blue shield of undulating light surrounded him.

Damon pointed his staff at Adriel. Black flames shot forth, curled and flexed around Adriel's shield, then bounced off and thrashed through the air. The skeins of magic slammed into buildings, writhed up walls, and skimmed along rooftops, setting them ablaze and sending cinders skyward.

Sweat soaked through Adriel's tunic as the sorcerer pressed his attack, releasing a relentless discharge of wicked spell craft. Adriel's heart hammered as his use of magic taxed his mind and body. His defenses weakened, and the blue barrier issuing from his staff began to shrink, cowering under the flaming whips.

Turncross shook and buckled: Timbers snapped, windows burst, and chimneys crumbled like sand castles buffeted by a seaside storm. The Black Candle Inn burst into soaring flames.

As gouts of fire leaped into the night, Adriel's shield faltered. The flaming black whips constricted about him, searing his skin and hurling him down to the road.

Damon hobbled over to Adriel's smoldering body. He lifted his robed hand and twitched a finger.

Adriel's staff skidded away from his grasp, coming to rest near Corin.

Damon looked down. "So ends the last of the Aurians," he said, and raised his staff for a final blow.

With a shout, Wren rushed forward, dodging burning debris that fluttered down from the sky. He cried out a curse and raised his sword, but Damon only sneered and stretched out his staff.

Wren was knocked from his feet as if he had been struck in the chest. His sword fell through the air and stuck in the middle of the road. Kayla cried out and darted to his side, leaving the dubious safety of a smoking house. Damon twitched a hand in her direction, and a rush of heated air slammed into her, knocking her down beside Wren.

But in his triumph, the sorcerer had forgotten the magical cage he had placed over Corin. The bars of nether light dissipated and seeped back into the road. Free, Corin crawled on his hands and knees toward the staff and picked it up; at his touch, the sapphire sparkled.

Damon looked down at Adriel in disgust. "Die, fool, in despair."

Adriel smiled faintly. "Not today."

Corin brought up the staff and pointed it at the sorcerer. A lance of blue light shot from the sapphire and burst through Damon's torso. The sorcerer screamed once, then collapsed and lay still.

Adriel breathed a sigh of relief, then closed his eyes as darkness stole over his vision.

Corin dropped the staff, went to Adriel, and shook him, but the wizard did not respond. Wren and Kayla were also unconscious, their eyes closed, their chests rising and falling slowly.

A voice inside Corin told him that the dark magic eventually would fade and they would regain consciousness. But he would not wait.

"When you wake up, please don't follow me," Corin murmured. "You've done enough already." He tracked down his horse, swung into the saddle, and left Turncross, starting across the moor.

* * *

AFTER A TIME Kayla awoke, went to her father, and shook him. She rose from his side and found a water trough, cupped some water in her hands, and splashed it on his face. He sputtered and sat up, then hugged her tight.

They revived Adriel and began searching for their mounts. When they found them among the smoking buildings, they swung into their saddles and urged them at a gallop into the east.

THE TOWER OF SHADOWS

CORIN GAZED ACROSS the moor and knew in his heart's core that he had come to the end of all things.

In mile after mile of ruinous progression, the badlands stretched toward a line of jagged cliffs, lying on the world's rim like a broken sword. A cataract of shadow marred the sky's dark lens. Far above, the moon was a dab of iridescent blood, and stars flickered like sallow beads of candlelight. Corin's soul swooned, his heartbeat as faint as the wavering stars.

He turned his horse and looked westward, back the way he had come, yearning to leave this place, to return to his home in the hills near Merrifield.

Right now, Uncle Pyke might be baking the morning bread or sitting in the Honey Barrel, sharing jokes over a mug of ale. Corin brushed tears from the corners of his eyes, imagining the Seaspine in place of the dark cliffs. He struggled to remember how the mountains looked on a sunny day, the way they soared skyward like the turrets of a fantastic castle, and for a moment he thought he heard a peal of laughter drifting from the Spinribbon Fair.

Then his thoughts turned to Dusty, and a flood of memories slid wrenchingly through his mind.

Farmer Twine, riling the townsfolk in Rookery Rest. The mischievous light in Dusty's eyes, the way that light had glittered as Aaron and Giles had argued over rumors, his determination to investigate the truth of Twine's story. Their adventure in the watchtower, escape from Merrifield, and spectral descent into the red-lit underworld of Lantern Watch.

Dusty coughing up globs of blood and bile, hands pressed against the gash in his stomach.

His shivers as he died.

Corin turned his mount east and faced the cliffs once more. "Your death won't be for nothing," he said, holding back his tears. He looked back one last time, then flicked the reins and started toward the cliffs.

* * *

WREN PULLED UP his horse and pointed to a distant white speck. "It's Corin," he said, "riding for the tower."

Adriel was grim. "This place is damned, but we must go after him."

"I'm ready," Kayla said.

"Are you sure you're coming?" Wren turned toward her. "No one will fault you for staying behind." He hesitated. "I don't want to lose you. I don't want to lose you the way I lost your mother."

In response, she kicked her horse forward.

Wren nodded, the ghost of a melancholy smile flitting across his face, and followed his daughter.

* * *

CORIN KICKED HIS heels against the sides of his mount, spurring his horse across the moor. Her hooves unearthed clods of dirt. Her mane whipped behind her, and a trail of grit and dust billowed in her wake. Corin looked up, wondering if the stars saw the two of them as a comet of white fire, speeding toward some final doom.

Lifeless and barren, the moor was a charred lesion on the earth, a remnant of some searing destruction. It looked like a distorted mirror, a broken reflection of the firmament.

As his horse galloped across the waste, Corin's thoughts descended into a hazy, muddled void. He blinked and shook his head. Illusions and mirages were confusing his senses. His horse sweated, flanks heaving. Her eyes bulged, though whether from fear or from exertion, Corin did not know. He hugged her neck, steering her eastward, trusting in her strength.

* * *

ACROSS THE MOOR, above the cliffs, in the highest recesses of the Tower of Shadows, a pair of eyes stared from a window into the night, watching Corin's approach. The eyes widened in recognition.

"Come," a voice hissed. The single word resonated in the chamber.

a pause, then

"Come to me, my brother."
The voice ceased, and the eyes withdrew from the window, disappearing into darkness.

* * *

WHEN CORIN REACHED the cliffs, he reined in and dismounted, the trail of dust settling behind him. Wind tore at the precipice, dislodging scree and hurling it down in tiny avalanches.

"We made it," Corin said, patting the mare's neck.

He guided her in among the few withered trees and uneven rocks that littered the ground, looking for a way up. There were no stairs, ropes, or ladders. The cliffs mocked him, an impenetrable battlement.

Corin caught the trace of a rotten scent. His horse picked her way through detritus until they reached a cave. Red vines hung over the opening, swaying in the wind. Corin spoke soothingly to the horse, took a lamp from a saddlebag and lit its wick, and then tied her to a nearby tree. She whickered and pawed the ground but did not struggle. A fly buzzed by Corin's ear and landed on a leafless branch.

He gazed up at the crimson moon and then entered the cave, shuddering as the red vines brushed his skin.

Inside, a tunnel wound upward like a nautilus shell. Corin's light threw back the darkness. Mold clung to the walls and ceiling; skeletons were heaped across the tunnel floor. Flies flew among the bones, buzzing angrily. The flies disturbed Corin more than anything else. They had nothing to eat but mold that looked too poisonous to sustain life.

Suddenly a hiss echoed in the tunnel. "Come, little boy . . ."

At the fringes of the lamplight, twisted limbs gestured to him.

"Come to the top of the cliffs . . . We won't harm you, *cursed* boy . . . not our key to the door . . ."

Corin took off at a limping run, forcing his legs to move faster.

"Faster . . . faster . . ." hissed the voice, and then it was joined by others, ebbing and flowing like shadows of sound. "Cade is in the tower . . . Go to your brother and save him if you can . . . Our key . . ." The voices were garbled, echoing in the tunnel, growing louder, turning into screams.

"Damn you, *boy!*"

"Wretched fool!"

"Unlock the door!"

As Corin barreled up the tunnel, the pandemonium swallowed the sound of his foot beats snapping bones and exploding fungi. The blood in his ears pounded. Sweat streamed down his face, soaking his clothing. His lamp swung wildly. Contorted limbs wormed in and out of view. The stench worsened, thickening into a spore-laden fume. Corin held his mouth to keep from gagging.

The winding tunnel leveled, and Corin spotted an opening that led into the night. He put on a final burst of speed, screams and hisses surrounding him like shapeless curses. He scrambled forward, stumbling on fragmented bones. Then he reached the exit and hurled himself through. Instantly, the demonic shrieks vanished.

"What were they?" Corin whispered, catching his breath. His leg ached with a subdued yet steady pain. "Blazes, what were those things?"

A plateau carved with fissures ran north and south along the top of the escarpment; at its edge the Tower of Shadows loomed over the sea, its windows dark save for one at its peak, which pulsed with a sickly purple light. Red vines clawed up the tower, throbbing like veins. The moon and stars were gone. A vortex of clouds circled overhead; shapes lurched in and out of the miasma, corruptions of the human form.

Corin took a deep breath, then limped to the tower door. He raised a hand to push it open, but it swung inward before his fingertips. He stepped inside.

A stairway spiraled upward, stone steps worn and riddled with holes. Clusters of flies buzzed up and down the steps.

As Corin limped up the mangled stones of the tower stairway, a sense of impending tragedy weighed on his shoulders. The end of all his hopes waited for him in the dark chamber above. The journey across the moor, the struggle through the fetid tunnel, and now the last stage of the climb in the ruined tower seemed to have sapped all life and light from his mind. Yet even as he felt this crushing burden of despair, a vague but compelling vision entered his mind, a recollection of his life with his uncle, scenes of the small town that had been his world when he was younger, the sounds of laughter at the Honey Barrel. The land of Ellynrie, with its green hills, sparkling seas, and ever-changing vault of sky above, seemed far away but infinitely precious.

Suddenly the image coalesced into a vision of the three gods on the fountain near Rookery Rest, the gods of Ellynrie, who were part of the very fabric of this land and who, Corin was sure, would not sit idly by as the demons rose from their depths to devour the earth. As he climbed the last few steps, the vision of the fountain sparkled in his mind, bathed in light. In a moment it crystallized into a single image of power and love from which flowed the land, sea, sky, and above all the people of Ellynrie; in that instant he knew that no price was too high to champion this image against the rising tide of evil.

When he reached the top of the stairs, Corin stood before a rugged stone wall inset with a door of splintered wood. A purple glow filtered through the frame of wrecked boards. Corin reached for the door, but it opened before he could touch it, as soundless as a final breath.

"For you, Dusty," he whispered.

Then he entered the chamber.

* * *

WHEN THEY REACHED the end of the moor, Wren, Kayla, and Adriel searched along the cliffs until they found Corin's horse, which was tied to a withered tree. They dismounted and secured their mounts.

As they entered the cave, Adriel raised his staff, and a clear blue light dispelled the gloom.

* * *

CORIN'S HEART THUMPED as he looked around the tower room, but his brother was nowhere to be seen.

The chamber, washed in wine-colored light, was circular, with a conical ceiling that ended in a vault of rafters. Shelves protruded from the walls, stuffed with scrolls and tomes. A ring of webs stretched from shelf to shelf like a net. Three spaces broke up the webbing: a westward window, the chamber door, and a looking glass resting on the eastern wall.

A table sat in the middle of the room. On it a single wax candle glared with an impossibly bright violet flame. Flies crawled on the table and the candle. The mawkish glow threw their shadows against the walls, shades that seemed to wriggle in the spiderwebs.

Corin went to the window, his footsteps echoing in the shadows. The rock-ribbed plateau fell away, dropping down to the moor. Corin made out the entrance to the tunnel and peered into its depths, his mind racing. *Where are you, Cade?*

Suddenly three figures charged from the cave toward the tower. A blue light shone around them. It almost seemed that they carried a star. Corin was shocked; he had hoped to lose them in Turncross. For a moment a demented choir of screams and curses chased after them, and then there was only the buzzing of the flies.

Corin was about to shout down to them when he felt eyes on the back of his neck. His voice caught in his throat, and he turned slowly. The looking glass glimmered darkly on the far side of the chamber. Corin circled around the table and stared into the mirror. It was not his reflection that stared back.

Instead, he saw someone who bore only a vague resemblance to himself. The reflected man had a disheveled appearance; he was older by several years, garbed in a patchwork robe, and his piercing eyes were different, too, shaded a strange kind of violet. But his hair was the same dirty blond. Corin knew the image in the mirror. *My brother.*

The candle flame sputtered. Whispers arose, similar to the hisses that had sounded in the tunnel, only these croaked and bubbled as if the throats that uttered them had been slit with knives. Corin looked around the room, but nothing seemed out of place. When he looked into the mirror again, the image of his brother was not alone.

The shadows of the flies mutated into grotesque shapes that began creeping toward him. Corin's lamp fell from his numb fingers and shattered on the floor. He swung a fist, hoping to destroy the surface on which the monstrous shadows crawled, but his hand passed *through* the looking glass. Knowing that he had found his destination, he braced himself and willed his body to follow his hand . . .

. . . and the next thing Corin knew, he was clambering to his feet in a dank subterranean corridor. He turned around and looked through the mirror, back into the Tower of Shadows. Beneath him was a damp cave floor; the walls around him glistened with moisture. Flies swarmed in the warm, heavy air.

Corin limped down the corridor. Scattered torches burned in iron clasps, weaving shadows along the walls. As the passage narrowed, sloping slightly downward, the air grew warmer. Beads of sweat gathered on Corin's face, and he was forced to take longer, deeper breaths.

At length the passage curved left, then right, finally feeding into a cavernous chamber.

Four torches flickered here and there, but their lambent light was dim. Knives and daggers pinned a black-haired man to a wall, driven through his body at weird, sharp angles. The man's head lolled; his limbs sagged. A huge iron-wrought door carved with evil shapes— many identical to the idols in the Ravenswood near Farmer Twine's pool—was set into the stone wall at the back of the chamber. Hundreds of flies churned across its surface.

Corin's brother stood behind a rough-hewn altar that rose like a cracked headsman's block from the center of the chamber. He grasped a sapphire dagger in one hand, its jeweled blade glowing with prismatic light, a shifting blend of cerulean and darker, submarine hues.

"Welcome, Brother," he said, fixing his violet eyes on Corin. "You've grown since last I saw you." In his other hand he held a gnarled staff of black wood topped by an amethyst. A corona of distorted air wavered around the crystal.

Corin shivered. "Cade."

There was a pause during which only the flies and the flames could be heard; then Cade set his staff into a socket somewhere in the floor. One of the torches sizzled and winked out, reappearing as a tongue of purple light that, like the amethyst, blurred the air around it.

Cade smiled thinly. His face looked gaunt and thin in the murk of the chamber. "The creatures in the tunnel didn't trouble you, I trust. Sarin and One-Eye made it to the tower unmolested, and you are far more vital than the assassins to the plans of those abominations."

"The plans?" Corin asked guardedly. "There was something about a key."

Another torch flared into purple flame, and Cade chuckled quietly. "You are that key, Brother. Those wretches want this door open as much as I do, though they have a different purpose."

"Who . . . *what* are they?"

Cade narrowed his eyes, drawing his slim eyebrows together. "The Coven, a dark congregation of nearly mindless slaves. They were men and women once, but through their own sin and vice they have been claimed by the demons. Now they are no longer human."

A third torch sputtered.

Corin fought to calm his breathing, striving to make sense of his brother's words. "Then how are you still free after all the evil you've done? The assassins you've hired, the sorcery you've learned . . . How are you not like them?"

"I know many secrets and am my own master." Cade rested his free hand on the altar. "Do you know of my plan? Of the work I am doing to avenge the murder of our parents?"

"I know that you will fail."

"Will I?"

The fourth and final torch flickered in magical rebirth, and the stone walls of the chamber refracted the purple light cast by the flames, but brighter still was the Exilon dagger, swirling with its fathomless colors.

Cade half turned and pointed at the door. "There lies Apollyon, imprisoned, the master of the demons. Long has he lain, and long has he slept, waiting for a time to awaken, to rise and devour all the lands of Ellynrie. I know this, Brother, and need no wizard's warning."

Corin stepped toward him. "What makes you think you can defeat him? You're only human, Cade."

"I am more powerful than you know. It was hard to reach this cavern, but I learned the necessary spell craft, and I discovered how to open this door. I can summon Apollyon. He has no power over me. I will kill him, Corin. *This* is the hour to avenge our murdered parents."

"The demon will destroy you!" Corin shouted. "Will you place so many lives in danger?"

"For justice, yes."

Corin ground his teeth together. How could his brother be so blind, so lost to the truth? "You're no better than the monsters in the tunnel. They *want* you to open that door. They know you'll be overpowered. And who is that man skewered on the wall? Some cog in your sick plan?"

"A wrench in the gears, more like," Cade said icily, "but one that I've removed. The fool was once a wizard. Now he awaits his death. But time waits for no man, Brother. Lie down on the altar."

"You truly mean to kill me?"

"*Kill* you?" Cade let out a bark of laughter. "Is that what your companions have been saying? I just need a small amount of blood, a drop on the dagger. Only then will my preparations be complete. No pain, I promise. And it will be well worth our vindication."

"This . . . this can't be right . . ." Corin took a deep breath, hoping desperately to turn his brother aside from his course. "Come back to Merrifield with me. We could be a family again. Don't throw away your future because of the past."

Cade drew himself up, wrapping his ragged clothing closer, tightening his grip on the dagger.

"You know nothing. The slaughter of our parents might be meaningless to you, but I was old enough to see it, to remember it. The images from that night have haunted me ever since in all their bloody clarity. I was there, in the village of Ember, when the Coven attempted to bring a demon up from the folds of the earth. They put the village to the torch, and I watched from the window of a burning house as monsters mauled our parents. I couldn't save them then. But I have spent my life in search of power—true power—and now is the time for action."

He looked down at the altar, staring into the past. "Don't you understand? If I vanquish this demon, the others will fall, and the Coven will be no more. Everything I do is done for the sake of our mother and father. Aid me, Brother. Help me summon Apollyon, and I will vanquish him forever."

Corin hesitated, torn with indecision. Cade had not planned to kill him, after all; he only needed a drop of his blood. There would be a slight prick, then the demon would come through those doors and his brother would fight it. Perhaps he actually *was* powerful enough to win.

Corin did not remember his parents, but Cade surely did. His brother's rage was valid, and his enemy was an enemy of all men.

But then Corin looked at the body of the black-haired man sagging on the wall. He remembered Sarin and One-Eye, the men they had killed, and the sorcerer Damon, destroying the town of Turncross. Most of all, Corin remembered Dusty's death. He steeled himself, knowing that his brother truly had fallen into darkness. *I must stop you, Cade, before you damn us all.*

"My best friend died because of you," Corin said fiercely. "His name was Dusty. He was killed while we were fleeing your assassins. I won't help you. Why do you think I came here, Cade? I know nothing about sorcery or demons. I was raised by a simple baker in a fair green country and I live a simple life, but that life has been good. I'd share it with you. Please don't turn against me . . . not today."

Cade's voice hardened. "I've not had your luxury of a kind home, and I won't be persuaded to turn aside now."

Corin took a deep breath. "If you're determined to walk into darkness, I will stop you if I can."

"Then you are a fool," Cade hissed, and slowly raised his arm.

Footsteps echoed in the chamber. Startled, Cade looked down the corridor as Corin spun around. Wren and Adriel burst into the cavern, panting, one's sword drawn and the other's staff held high. Kayla followed hard on their heels. Corin's eyes widened: A silvery light sparkled on each of their chests, though they seemed not to notice it.

"Just in time," Adriel gasped, the sapphire on his staff shining with the same blues of the dagger.

"How did you get here?" Cade cried. "The mirror was supposed to let only my brother through!" He noticed the silvery glow at their chests and took a step back. "Damn your Aurian magic."

Following his gaze, their eyes widened in wonder. Kayla pulled out her medallion, and the others did the same. Each flared brightly with vivid light, but even as they watched, the lights around the icons weakened and faded.

Then Adriel saw the man dying on the side of the chamber, high above their heads, saw the trails of blood that had run down the rocks beneath him—twisting, forking, merging—where they had dried, frozen like some diabolical scripture. "Dale," he whispered, sinking to his knees.

Wren leveled his sword. "Drop the dagger, sorcerer, or deal with me."

Cade laughed grimly, violet eyes flashing. He flicked a finger, and

Wren jerked once before dropping his sword, which flew to the wall opposite the one on which Dale hung. Kayla and Adriel were ripped from the cavern floor and hurled alongside him, bound by invisible cords.

Cade turned his attention back to Corin. "At first, I thought I was the unlucky one. Fate decided that I would not be rescued from Ember and given a father to love, a father who would love me back, who would raise and cherish me. But over the years I have come to realize that perhaps I wasn't so unlucky, after all."

He twitched another finger, and the knives twisted in Dale's body. Blood trickled from the wizard's mouth. He groaned, eyes fluttering in pain. Adriel shouted and wept. Cade paid him no heed.

"I was given the chance to make my own way in the world. No meddling wizard decided my path. I wandered all of Ellynrie in search of the means to gain my revenge and came across bottomless wells of power—dark, yes, but capable of destroying all those responsible for taking my parents from me."

He stretched out a finger on his other hand and pointed it at his brother. A force tugged Corin down, and he began sliding along the floor toward the altar.

"I sailed to the Summerset Isles in search of stronger powers. There I came upon a friend of Dale's, an Aurian wizard named Blaze who made me his apprentice. But Blaze had begun to delve into witchery and other arcane arts of darkness. From him I learned many things. When I knew what was needed, I killed him and returned to the northern fringes of the Nautalian Kingdom. There I wandered the Sea of Dreams, pursuing one illusion after another, until I discovered where Apollyon had fallen from heaven. And it was there that I found Damon and bade him join my cause."

Cade jerked his hand. Corin rose from the ground and tumbled onto the altar. He strained against his brother's sorcery, but the magic binding him to the slab of black stone was too strong to escape.

"Now Damon is dead, curse him; the blasted fool couldn't even dispatch a wizard's apprentice." Cade smiled thinly at Corin. "I came to the Tower of Shadows years ago and since then have been working to raise the demon. Now I am ready. The pieces are set, and the time of my vengeance has come."

He jerked another finger, and the knives and daggers holding Dale to the wall twisted one final time.

The wizard let out a choking gasp. His eyes opened in agony and then closed as his body went limp.

From the altar, Corin heard Adriel begin to scream.

Cade ignored him and lifted the dagger above his head, but as he concentrated on Corin, his hold on the others loosened, and Kayla broke away. She dropped to the floor and rushed to help Corin, but Cade turned and flung out an arm, binding her once more with his magic.

In that moment, however, Corin felt movement in his limbs. He lunged up from the altar and grabbed the hand with which Cade held the dagger, bending it backward.

Cade shifted forward, but he moved too abruptly. Corin pulled him onto the altar, wrenched the dagger away, and held it to his brother's throat.

As Cade looked up with disbelief flashing in his eyes, Corin experienced a moment of transparency. Through his brother's eyes he saw a vision of darkness spreading from the Tower of Shadows toward a pearly city. There, wind-whipped banners lined the walls and white towers, and ships glided to and from wharves under a great bluestone wall adorned with carved sea horses that blasted trumpets toward the sea. A great castle shone at the edge of the city, and a clock tower rose from the houses, its pinnacle glinting, its hands turning. As Corin watched, the darkness overtook the city, and the white towers began to fall, crumbling into the streets below. The castle shattered, and the hands on the clock tower stopped. The clock face exploded outward, raining down stone, marble, and glass.

Then Corin beheld a vision of a pure white light spreading over all the lands he had traveled, and the colors of the earth, sea, and air swirled together, creating one moving image that merged with the light.

Corin again regarded his brother and thought of what might have been: Cade had taken a dark road, while he had traveled a better path, a path away from the shackles of hatred. He knew he could not kill Cade. If he cut his brother's throat, he would be no better and would have turned in despair toward the darkness he had seen devouring the shining city by the sea.

"I can't . . ." he whispered. "Damn you, Cade, I—"

Cade snarled and batted away Corin's arm, then grabbed him by the throat. He wrenched the dagger from Corin's grasp, cried out, and stabbed him in the side. Corin gasped as iron slid into his flesh.

Cade pulled out the dagger, eyes wide, and reeled back in shock.

The great iron door at the back of the chamber began opening inch by inch. Screams exploded through the widening crack, reverberating through the chamber, insidious and legion. Flies imploded in a great mass and swarmed through the door. The knives and daggers jerked out of Dale's body. As the dead wizard fell to the cavern's stones, the weapons were sucked through the door. Dale's limp corpse slid after them and disappeared. A black wind roared through the door and whirled around the chamber, extinguishing the torches.

Cade's shock turned to triumph. He stepped down from the altar, grabbed his staff, and faced the door, his wounded brother forgotten. His body pulsed with power. The amethyst on his staff glittered, its light fusing with the dagger's light, creating a brilliant sphere of violet and blue above the altar.

"Come to me, Apollyon," he shouted. "Come and face your doom!"

The black wind did not touch Corin. As strength ebbed from his body with each pulse of blood from his side, he watched Wren and Adriel drop down from the wall and Kayla rise from the floor. They clutched their medallions, which sparked with a silver light that kept them from being pulled through the door.

Cade stood his ground, facing the screams and the horrible wind, made bold by his triumph, quivering with anticipation and fury as the gap into the abyss widened.

But then, without warning, the door began to close.

"What is this?" he screamed. "What's happening?"

Adriel called out, "Your sacrifice, Corin! It has undone the spell!"

Suddenly hydras with huge, vaporous claws reached into the cavern. The claws darted toward Kayla and Adriel but could not touch them. They changed course and tried for Wren and at first began to grab him, but they could not close their grip and changed course yet again.

Cade held out his staff. Magical flames of violet and blue flew toward the monstrous claws but were swallowed in their darkness. The claws encircled him, and he cried out in fear.

Faint as he was, Corin reached out and grabbed his brother's hand. Cade dropped the dagger and his staff, terrified, and latched on to Corin. They struggled to hold on to each other, but Cade's fingers slipped and the claws dragged him through the door and into the abyss. The dagger and the staff followed him through, and the iron door clanged shut, banishing the screams and the hellish wind.

For a moment there was utter silence. Tears streamed down Corin's face as he stared at the door, his brother lost to him forever.

Then Wren was at his side, helping him up. Adriel approached to examine his wound. The wizard's face was creased with worry. He shouted and pointed at Corin's side. As Corin looked down, a gasp escaped his lips; his wound had healed fully. He swung down from the altar, but when his feet touched the cavern floor, his leg no longer pained him.

Eyes widening, he stood straight and tall, sensing that all traces of his limp were gone forever.

"Thank the gods," Adriel said. His staff lent the chamber its only light. "You are no longer crippled."

Wren shook his head slowly, amazed. He looked around the cavern. "Let's leave this place," he said. "It's time to go home." Flooded with exhilaration, the others nodded. They followed him as he led them back through the gloom of the corridor, which had grown cool and dark.

They found the mirror as they had left it. With Wren leading the way, they stepped through it one by one.

* * *

WHEN AT LAST they came to the base of the tower's sheath, Wren shouldered the door open, and they ran from the stairway, blinking with disbelief as they stumbled out into the open air.

"Look!" Adriel shouted, and pointed to the sky. "The night has ended, and morning has come. All things are made new."

The dark clouds above them scudded and began to thin, and beams of dawn light shot down like spears from heaven. As their glittering shafts smote the earth, they streaked across the ruined plateau, surging over the cliffs and dancing away across the moor, moving toward the west. Then the mantle of darkness that hung over the sea was swept from the waves and blown in curtains of wretched mist to vanish before the rising sun.

Kayla smiled, and Corin's tearstained eyes shone for a moment with wonder—but then the tower groaned behind them, and flurries of grit dashed down on their heads.

"Run!" Wren shouted, covering his nose and mouth. Coughing, he led the others in a dash for the tunnel.

With a roar, the top of the Tower of Shadows collapsed inward, bringing the rest of the tower down with it. As the dark stones splintered, breaking apart like a world of shadows caught between two suns, the vines that bound them dried and crumbled to cindery ash. Even as the ashes scattered on the wind of the morning and were swept into the sky or flung into the sea, the shadows of the plateau—of boulders and fissures, of valleys and seams of cragged stone—seemed to retreat and hide, but finding no refuge in the sudden brilliance, they faded like nightmares banished at daybreak.

As the tower crashed into the ground, a tide of sand and blasted rock rose from the earth and sped outward, tumbling into the ocean or down onto the moor. The four companions flung themselves inside the tunnel just as they were about to be overtaken. Breathing heavily, they began to navigate the spiraling cave, watching warily for the creatures that had lurked there; of the monsters there was no sign.

Along the way, the moldering growths that clung to the walls withered like the vines. The wind, fresh with the scent of the sea, swirled through the tunnel, passing through its crevices, whistling where once there had been whisperers, trilling through the bones of skeletons and through the sockets of skulls, bearing away the odor of death.

When they emerged from the cave, Kayla spotted a single butterfly flying across the moor, its blue and white wings flashing, and she grinned at Wren.

The four companions saddled their horses, and Adriel held aloft his sparkling staff. "Now this story has ended," he said, "but a new one is about to begin, for the tides of fate are ever-flowing." He turned to Wren and Kayla and asked, "Where will the two of you go now?"

"Back home, I hope," Kayla said, and looked longingly toward Nautalia. "But we're not parting yet."

Wren nodded. "The road ahead is long and will be merrier if we travel it together, if only for a little while."

"And you?" Adriel asked, turning to Corin. "Will you go back to your uncle?"

"I don't know," Corin said. He paused, seeing in Adriel's eyes the pain of Dale's passing, a pain he knew would never heal fully. "I'm not sure if I can be happy in Merrifield now that Dusty's gone."

"Then I could use your help. My work is far from done." When Corin looked at him questioningly, Adriel gave him a sad smile. "The Coven has suffered a great defeat, but they haven't been destroyed. Nor will they be until the ending of the world." As he spoke, the wind unfurled the green ribbon tied about his staff.

He brightened then and clapped Corin on the shoulder. "I'd consider a career in magic if I were you."

Wren sat silently in his saddle, watching with his stormy blue eyes as sunbeams glided on the horizon.

Beside him, Adriel lowered his staff, no longer the bumbling apprentice he had met at a wayward inn. Shades of Dale's spirit crossed his harrowed face. Wren remembered arguing with Dale on the beach, blinded by anger. He lowered his head, regretting the harsh words he could never take back.

Corin glanced over his shoulder, back the way they had come, as the last rumbling echoes died away.

Wren saw him as a baby, clutched to his mother's breast, crying in front of a burning house. The baby had become a boy, the boy a young man sitting straight in his saddle with his head held high. Right now his green eyes were lingering on a point atop the cliffs. There, a screen of dust was spreading, obscuring the place where he had lost his brother.

Kayla shifted on her horse, her shorn blond hair stirring in the new wind.

Wren looked at her and was suddenly back home in Nautalia, entering her room to find her on her bed, pretending to read a history book as the sun set on the world outside her window. He had been angry at her for dreaming the wistful dreams of a fiery young girl, but those dreams had taught them both things that could not be found in books. He pictured her in Lantern Watch, speaking of courage and honor, determined to stand by Corin. Instead of conforming, she had become her true self and, in doing so, had helped him to regain what he had lost on the day his wife had died.

He considered the bitter shell he had formed against the world. Perhaps his ability to connect with others was being restored, and he couldn't deny that Kayla had played her part. Now that he had committed to a higher cause, he could begin to commit to her; he could see beyond his fears and allow her to live her dreams. The link with his past renewed, Wren saw his wife in his daughter and renewed his link with her. A burden lifted from his heart as his shell of bitterness broke.

He murmured the names of his wife and his father, looked to Kayla, nodded to himself, and sat a little taller. With a shout and a snap of his reins, his horse bolted forward, and he began leading the others toward their homes.

As they rode into the west, Adriel slipped his staff into his belt and raised his flute to his lips. His melody drifted before them on a pathway lit by the dawning of the sun.

SciFi
BOW

Bowling, Drew C.

The tower of
shadows.

5477

$19.95

DATE			

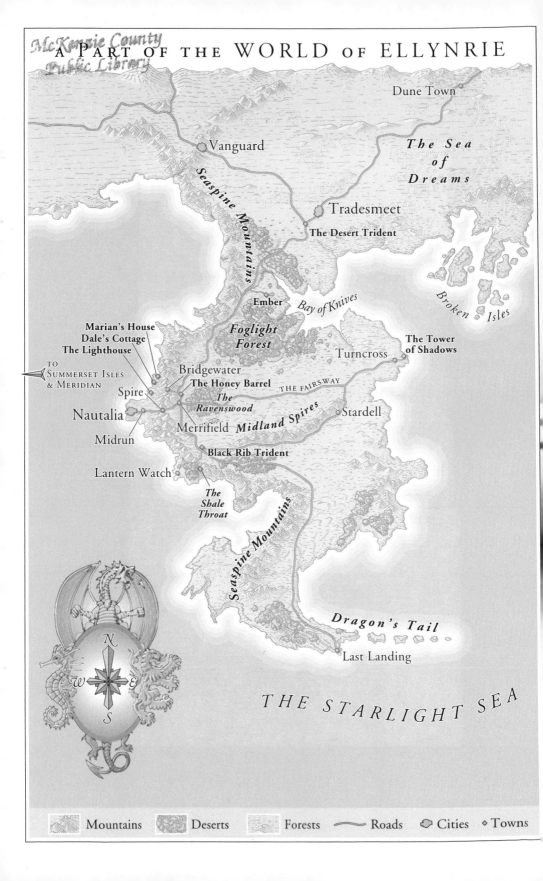